Down and Out in the River City

Wm Stage

Also by Wm. Stage

Ghost Signs: Brick Wall Signs in America

Mound City Chronicles

Litchfield: A Strange and Twisted Saga of Murder
in the Midwest

Have A Weird Day: Reflections & Ruminations
on the St. Louis Experience

Pictures Of People   Portraits 1982 – 1993

The Practical Guide to Process Serving

Fool For Life – A Memoir

The Painted Ad: A Postcard Book of
Vintage Brick Wall Signs with Margaret Stage

Not Waving, Drowning [Stories]

The Fading Ads of St. Louis

Creatures On Display – A Novel

No Big Thing – A Novel

St. Francis Of Dogtown – A Novel

A Friend Of King Neptune – A Novel

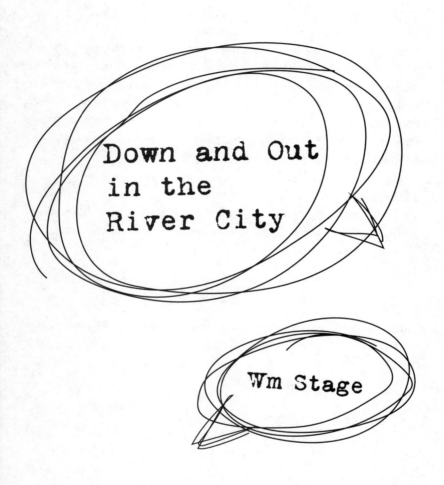

Down and Out in the River City

Wm Stage

Floppinfish Publishing Company Ltd.

St. Louis, Missouri

This book is a work of fiction. References to real people, events, establishments, organizations or locales are intended only to provide a sense of authenticity, and are used fictitiously. All other characters, and all incidents and dialogue, are drawn from the author's imagination and are not to be construed as real.

Stage, William – Wm. [1951 –]
— fiction, contemporary
1. United States—the Midwest—Irish-American neighborhoods
2. St. Louis, MO—murder / homeless encampments—vigilantism—tavern culture

ISBN 979-8-21853259-8

Cover Photo: Wm. Stage 2003
www.wmstage.com
Cover and Interior Design:
Michael Kilfoy, Studio X
www.studiox.us
Printed in the United States of America
Set in Adobe Jenson Pro

floppinfish

For the good Sisters of
St. Agnes Foundling Home,
Kalamazoo, Michigan 1951

How many times I've wondered
It still comes out the same
No matter how you look at it or think of it
It's life, and you just got to play the game

— Brook Benton
"Rainy Night In Georgia"

"They of the Towne had servid process upon him."

— William Henry Turner, 1577
Selections from the Records
of the City of Oxford, England

He walked out of the Civil Courts building and saw pandemonium. Folks milling about the blocked-off street and Poelker Park in small groups, shouting epithets, raising fists in anger, haranguing the knots of police in riot gear who stood vigilant around the perimeter of the gathering. It wasn't like this before he entered the hallowed halls of justice some ninety minutes previous. The pot had yet to boil, but Francis and nearly everyone else in St. Louis knew it likely would reach the boiling point if, as expected, the judge gave an acquittal in the murder trial of former police officer Jason Stockley. That verdict must have come down while Francis was in the courthouse, waiting outside Division 9, show cause order in hand, hoping to ambush a deadbeat dad who was supposed to appear on another beef. The order never got served because the defendant was a no show and Francis, unwilling to give up even after an hour of waiting, passed the time by reading *Maximum Bob* by the great Elmore Leonard.

And what was happening now, this throng, mostly black with a scattering of young white faces, could have been a scene in one of Elmore's crime novels. The natives were restless all right, whipped up in righteous indignation, eager to raise hell with white society, ready for battle with command authority. The courtroom itself had been standing room only and the much-anticipated verdict, announced by the Honorable Timothy Wilson, first fell on the spectators' ears and quickly passed on to the waiting crowd outside the courtroom, which included news teams from Channels 4, 5, and 2 as well as CNN and NBC BLK. Before you could say Come on down and join the protest, TVs in homes and bars across the city were spreading the news: White cop acquitted in the death of Anthony Lamar Smith, age twenty-four, a black man. This incident happened in 2011, six years before, Stockley shot Smith in his car five times after a high-speed chase through city streets. Stockley said he acted in self-defense and believed Smith was reaching for a gun, but prosecutors accused Stockley of planting a weapon to justify the shooting. Stockley pleaded not guilty to the charge of first degree murder and waived his right to jury trial, which meant the judge decides issues of fact. Judge Wilson said he agonizingly reviewed the evidence and found the facts established that Stockley's use of force was an act of self-defense. As for the theory that the weapon found in Smith's car was put there by Stockley to cover his ass, Wilson said, "An urban heroin dealer not in possession of a firearm would be an anomaly."

That Stockley was now a free man—he had left the force soon after the incident and was living the life in Florida or some other sunny clime—and Smith's "murder" going unpunished was salt in the wounds of activists, militants, and opportunists, some of whom were involved in the riots three years earlier, in the suburb of Ferguson where another unarmed black man was shot and killed by a white officer, and who were still chafing at the thought of White Privilege lording it over them.

Francis took in the scene and realized he was in the midst of a powder keg about to ignite. There were hundreds of protesters and maybe fifty cops. He saw a water bottle sail through the air and hit a cop on the shoulder. A bus bringing more cops to the scene was hit with rocks, its windows broken, the dignified statue of Ulysses Grant on the lawn of City Hall looking on. Protesters brandished Black Lives Matter signs like weapons and some carried enlarged pictures of Anthony Lamar Smith, the dead drug dealer hosting this event. A chant rose over the din, "If we can't get no justice y'all can't get no peace!" Others had a more succinct cry: "Fuck The Police!" The cops stood by, sentinels poised for action.

In the ranks of blue, he spotted George Dolan, a guy from Dogtown sometimes seen in Francis' neighborhood bar, Murphy's. He walked over, said, "Hey." George had a shield in one hand and a baton in the other; his helmet had a Plexiglas visor to cover his face, made him look like a welder. George moved his gaze from the protesters to Francis.

He nodded recognition, gave Francis a tired smile. He lifted the visor, raised an eyebrow, said, emphatically, "You don't wanna be here, man. It's gonna get hairy any minute now."

"I'm leaving, you can bet on it," said Francis. "Just wanted to let you know I'm with you. Whatever shit's going down here, I hope like hell you come through it unscathed."

"I can take a little scathing," said George, philosophically, a What're Ya Gonna Do look on his Irish mug. "The disrespect is harder to take, but I can deal with that too. I just hope I can resist the temptation to seriously crack some skulls." He chin-pointed to an obese black woman looking like Medusa with long serpentine dreadlocks waddling by, carrying an upside-down, tattered American flag. "Case in point," he said.

Francis imagined George wailing on this woman—whack! whack!—the baton coming down on her head over and over. Imagined her friends rushing over to help and George's fellow officers coming to his aid and voilà! a full-blown melee.

More cops were arriving in patrol cars and buses, police HQ only six blocks away, joining the ranks already present, filling in gaps. What had been a loose semi-circle of police bodies around the protesters was now becoming a rather tight circle. Francis said so long to his friend and started to head for a gap in the cordon. He was almost there, almost through, when he heard his name called.

He turned and saw Rashid Arthur, the 12th Ward Alderman whom he'd once done some work for, namely serving a protection order to a malevolent constituent who threatened to "fix that nigger's wagon." Rashid was dressed in a leisure outfit and looked like he'd just stepped off the tennis court except the dangle of gold chains around his neck would get in the way of his game. He sported a three-inch 'fro; all it needed was a hair pick with a clenched-fist handle sticking out. "Great to see you here," he said, giving Francis a fist bump. "You answered the call, huh?"

"Oh yeah, you got to. Solidarity an' all that."

"Damn straight," said Rashid, nostrils flaring. "We can't let this stand. You let them roll over you now with this bullshit verdict, what's next? Lynchings in the public square?"

What set him apart, aside from his flashy attire, Rashid stood uncommonly erect like he had a steel rod up his ass.

Francis nodded agreement. "You have no choice but to speak out, justice demands it."

Rashid leaned into Francis, said somewhat conspiratorially, "I've already spoken with Harmon Waldron, head of the N-double A-CP here. He's going to ask President Trump and the Justice Department to review the acquittal."

Francis let that sink in. "You know how to get things done, it's obvious. Those guys will see the folly in this, yeah?"

"They'd have to be blind not to," said Rashid. Through his ivory tortoise-frame specs he looked Francis over, frowned. "You need a prop, man. You can't come to the party without a prop. Here, take this, I'll get another." He'd been toting a sign, but it was turned around so Francis couldn't read it. He handed it over, the sign on white poster board attached to a stick. It had a black circle with a message within: My Skin Color Is Not A Crime."

Francis held it up, waved it around. He felt silly holding such a sign. "Nice," he said. "Thanks, pal, mighty white of you." He regarded Rashid deadpan for a few seconds, waiting for a reaction that didn't come. "Kidding!" he said.

Rashid grinned a bit, showed some teeth including the dazzling double gold crown he was known for. "Kid about that all you want," he said, gravely, "but take this thing seriously. Miscarriage of justice is serious as a…uh, a constricted bowel."

"You bet, I'm with you all the way."

"Okay, good. I got to move on, I see my peeps over there, we're planning on marching to the mayor's house later. Come join us."

Francis moved on, happy that he didn't have to hurt the guy's feelings by letting on what he really thought of this assembly, that it was dumb and futile and only served to bolster and yes, validate the defiant spirit of those present. It didn't even amount to civil disobedience, the sort that Thoreau practiced, just a bunch of up-in-arms citizens itching for a fight. But he had to admit it was entertaining in the way street theater is entertaining.

But the gap in the police line was now closed. In fact, egress was blocked everywhere he looked. The police were standing shoulder to shoulder and had formed a sort of enclosure and the folks within that enclosure were as fish to be netted. While Francis was still in the courthouse, a captain had gotten on the bullhorn and announced that those present were part of an unlawful assembly and must disperse immediately. Nobody acted on that suggestion. City Hall and two courthouses were right there within rock-throwing distance. The police waited until their numbers were sufficient. The upper echelon discussed various strategies—tear gas, rubber bullets, and finally settled on kettling. Also known as trap and detain, kettling is a crowd-control technique used by police which involves officers surrounding protesters to corral them in a limited area. Protesters either leave through an exit controlled by the police or are contained, prevented from leaving, and arrested.

The tactic had been used in Europe during mass demonstrations with what law enforcement would call success and what demonstrators would call bullying. Kettling has proved controversial because it can result in the detention of innocent bystanders as well as agitated protesters.

Francis with his silly sign was not seen as an innocent bystander.

The cops advanced on the crowd within the perimeter; step by step they closed the circle, tightened the net. Francis watched dumbfounded. He'd waited too long and now he couldn't get out. The cry went out, "This is it, we're in the shit now!"

Instead of withdrawing, folks were pushing back against the cordon, but they were no match for the overall brawny men in blue. One jackass with a pile of hair beneath a scarf the colors of a Jamaican flag tried to jab one of the cops with the stick of his sign. The cop snatched the sign away and broke the stick over his knee. People were screaming at the cops how they weren't doing anything wrong and they, the pigs, needn't be such assholes. They would pay for this, their lawyers would see to that. They would be lucky to keep their jobs! Hundreds of cell phones were held aloft, set on video mode. This atrocity would be recorded in perpetuity.

If the police were at all bothered by this vitriol they weren't letting on. Their faces, somewhat obscured by the glare on their visors, were devoid of any noticeable expression except possibly grim. And they pressed on, stepping mechanically like robots in a scary dream, closing in until the protesters were contained like, well, fish caught in a net. There were big fish, little fish, chubby fish, hungry fish, fish with valid media credentials, fish with spurious media credentials, fish with backpacks, fish with peasant dresses and ponytails, fish with bench warrants out on them, fish with yoga pants, fish with gonorrhea who should have been at the STD clinic instead of here, fish with canes, fish with halitosis, fish with mismatched socks, fish smoking joints, fish with pierced tongues, fish who had to use the restroom, fish with hives and other skin conditions.

As a process server, Francis sometimes worked with police, and he liked the city police as a whole. He picked one cop, broad-shouldered, and appealed to him. "Look, officer, I'm a special process server, licensed by the sheriff's office. I just came out of the civil courts building there and walked into this. I'm not part of this group." He was walking backwards as he spoke because the cop was stepping forward. Francis pulled the show cause order from his back pocket. "See?" he said, thrusting it in his face, "this was the paper I tried to serve, but the guy never showed and I got to read five chapters of Elmore." The cop seemed to look right through him and kept on coming. Francis backed up some more and backed right into a knot of protesters who were backing up themselves. He was suddenly aware that he still had the sign that Rashid had given him. He let it fall to the asphalt, stepped on it, grinding it this way and that. He made a show of spitting on it contemptuously. "You see?" he said to the same cop. "That's not my sign, it's a prop and it doesn't speak for me. This isn't my thing. I'm with you, man. Now let me through, will ya?"

And then the circular cordon reached its desired degree of contraction, motion ceased. The protesters were crowded together, nowhere to go. An announcement was made that they should all calm down, they would not be harmed. They would be released in an orderly fashion and they should have their IDs ready. The obstreperous protesters would have none of it. They began shoving and pushing against their oppressor, shoving and pushing among themselves. And then Francis was manhandled, a woman pushing a stroller with a dog inside was manhandled, a videographer was manhandled and his camera knocked to the asphalt, the lens cracked. Some ten yards away Francis saw that Rashid Arthur was being set upon, fighting back and punching away.

Among their numbers in the net or kettle was one fellow who definitely would not go gentle into that good night. A hulk of a man, maybe thirty, in a black tank top showing off massive biceps, heavily tattooed, and khaki Carhartt work pants, his ample belly lopped over the belt. With his open, bearded face and muscular neck he looked like a stand-in for that WWE rassler from the 80s, The Junkyard Dog. Like Rashid Arthur, he had a gold tooth, not one but two side by side which had some design etched in, and showed themselves when he bared his teeth. And with such a fierce expression he attacked the police, getting around their shields, grabbing them by the shirt and knocking them off balance, throttling one poor cop. The police had to break rank to try to subdue him and the batons rained down on the man's head and torso. At one point, they knocked the black Kangol bucket hat off his head, exposing a set of thick, matted locs or "wicks" about five inches long. Very stylish. One cop went to grab the dreads, maybe pull some out— dumb move—and he snatched the cop's fingers and bent them back so that a crack was heard. More blows. Bloodied, he let out a roar and continued his assault with even more fervor. People around the clash stopped with their own scuffling and looked on. What sort of devils were inside the man was anyone's guess, but it was quite a spectacle.

Before long, a chant went up from the penned-in crowd, CLEE-OH! CLEE-OH! They were egging him on, Francis saw, he was their champion. It wasn't a far leap to imagine this bruiser with his colossal determination as a gladiator in a Roman coliseum, a juggernaut to be sure.

He kept it up for another minute, showing no sign of fatigue, but then out came the pepper spray, the tasers. The lethal one-two law enforcement punch, a shot of mace followed by a taser strike to the torso. The man went down, writhing on the pavement, cursing, wiping at his eyes. But then, before the cops could keep him down, he was up again and though temporarily blinded he went back on the attack and this time he was able to get to the closest cop, get his sinewy arm around the officer's neck in a chokehold. He bellowed and squeezed with all his might, hoping to kill the man. The cop quickly lost consciousness and slumped to the pavement. At the same time five uniforms were on the man like magnets on steel. They weren't going to give him a third chance. They tased him again and then again and beat him unmercifully until he saw stars and his eyes rolled back in his head. So much for that.

Francis couldn't believe he'd been rounded up with these troublemakers and misfits. The indignation was staggering. How would he explain it to his wife, his kids, the guys at the bar. Oh, those palookas would give him the ribbing of his life. What's the matter, Francis, your white pals in Dogtown ain't good enough for you? After the protest had fizzled out and the participants had resigned themselves to being ushered out of the net and into buses where they were ferried to police HQ over on Olive Street and processed, they all had time to consider their situation. Most of them were going to be released and given a citation for unlawful assembly or disturbing the peace or being a public nuisance, some shit like that. A few, maybe less than a dozen, who had been particularly troublesome, who had been witnessed throwing things, vandalizing patrol cars or buses, inciting others to violence, resisting arrest—a badge of honor among activists—those folks were in the lock-up. The champion Cleo chief among them.

However, the mood among the detainees here in the police station was not cowed or penitent. If anything, they were even more turbulent, more discontent, feeling that their well-deserved demonstration had been cut short. They were covered under free speech and the authorities had taken that away from them, treated them like criminals. Was this America or Communist China? What the fuck, man!

Meanwhile their brothers at arms, fellow provocateurs not captured in the big net, were making their voices heard throughout downtown, calling for the resignation of the mayor and police chief and anyone else in power. Harassing startled shopkeepers on Washington Avenue, spray-painting dire slogans on windows. Another contingent, seeing their chance at utter mayhem, busied themselves by flipping cars and setting fires. It appeared that the City of St. Louis was in for a siege.

Francis *et al* were penned in a large open holding area somewhere in the bowels of police headquarters. It may have been an assembly room for awards ceremonies, something like that, and all freestanding tables and chairs had been removed so no one would get bashed in the head. There were vending machines, but all their contents had been taken, including change. If someone had to use the restroom, tough, they had to hold it. Francis, in a corner, leaning against the wall, passed the time watching and eavesdropping on casual dialogue all around him.

"I once marched with Jesse Jackson in Chicago, you know?"

"Yeah? What was the cause?"

"I forget, but it was righteous."

"Probably something to do with social injustice."

"Fuckin' A."

"That's cool. I smoked a number with Spike Lee, you know?"

"Who's that sister in the combat boots and tank top? Damn, she lookin' fine."

"Healthy to be sure. I can introduce you."

"You know her?"

"Hell no."

And over there by the soda machine: "Look here, those cocksuckers busted my finger."

"Yeah but you saw Cleo, didn't he give them hell? Oh, that was a sight, a glorious sight, him and those cops."

"Yeah, you know who he is?"

"Cleo, Man of the Hour. Isn't he in a band?"

"Yeah, that, an' he's also Anthony's cousin."

In the midst of his being a fly on the wall, a chimp masquerading as a man sidled up, spoke from the side of his mouth: "Say, man, you in the market for a flat screen TV?" The guy had a bad tooth or something that was fouling the space between them. "Sixty-five inches, direct lit, voice-assist, top of the line. Got a few I need to move, give you a great deal."

* * *

The line was getting shorter, the protesters being released one by one. Each person had to sign some forms, and wait until their belongings were returned to them—weapons and contraband removed. Confiscated were sixteen knives, folding and otherwise; two 9mm handguns, fully loaded; a squirt gun filled with ammonia; numerous razor blades, various baggies and containers holding weed, meth, crack cocaine; a couple of needles and a spoon; and a pack of Black Cat firecrackers. Then it was Francis' turn to taste freedom once again. The guy ahead of him had uttered these parting words to the cops in charge, "You think you're done with us? No, man, you ain't done, not at all, we just getting started."

Francis was handed his keys, wallet, pocket change, cell phone, his lucky buckeye that he always carried, process server ID on a lanyard, and the unserved show cause order which was crumpled and smeared with goo.

"Did you have to mess up my court order?" he asked.

"No talk. On your way, go."

"I'm an officer of the court."

The cop glared at him. "No, you're a shit stain on the City's nice clean linen."

He walked out of the police station. It was night now. He was usually home by six, after a few pops at Murphy's. Martha would wonder where he was. His car was only a few blocks away, across from City Hall. With all the rampant vandalism would it be okay? City Hall, he mused, as he began walking. This episode begins and ends with City Hall, the mayor's office where some four years prior he had walked in and served the mayor, as representative of the City of St. Louis, with a wrongful death suit brought by Anthony Lamar Smith's survivors that ultimately netted the family $900,000 before lawyer's fees were extracted. Francis rounded a corner and the thirteen-story Civil Courts building with its green pyramid-shaped roof came into sight. The National Guard, vigilant and armed, now stationed around the perimeter of both the Civil Courts and the Carnahan Courts across Market Street; the governor had mobilized them, anticipating a race riot. City Hall was on the same corner, the three buildings comprising the stalwarts of downtown architecture.

The streetlights led him to his Ford Escape, which appeared as he'd left it. He turned the ignition and it started without hesitation. He sat there a minute before leaving, mulling things over. His life had very much been impacted by the killing of this drug dealer. Rounded up like a common reprobate, having missed happy hour, put in a bad mood. On the flip side, he'd made some dough from this, having served the lawsuit that left the deceased drug dealer's kin flush with money for the rest of their lives. And what did he, the instrument of largesse to the family of Anthony Lamar Smith, get for his role? Fifty bucks.

— 2 —

"What, they didn't give you your one phone call?"

"They did and I called Imo's for a deluxe, extra large."

"Funny."

They were standing in the kitchen, he and Martha, talking about their day. The street lights had been on for two hours. He'd popped a can of Busch, and she had a glass of Merlot. Her day pretty much the same as always at Pastori's On The Hill, her family's restaurant where she was maitre d' except on this day a soccer team from Kansas City came in, twenty-two of them, no advance warning, just When can we eat? They were doing an exhibition game at The Dome, she explained. "Some of the servers asked for autographs although they hadn't heard of any of them. And they weren't what you'd call big tippers."

His day, he told her, started out great having served four papers before noon and then lunch at O' Connell's with a friend. That was followed by a leisurely walk around Francis Park, and then hightail it to the courthouse to ambush the deadbeat dad in the hallway only he never showed. "And then," he said, "then I walked into a circus, a freaking demonstration with every agitator in St. Louis. Never saw so many people in one place with an ax to grind. With all the cops in riot gear, I should have moved out immediately but I saw a couple people I knew, including George Dolan in uniform, and I stuck around to talk to them and, before you know it, too late, I can't leave."

"Always the social butterfly even in the face of danger," she said, but not in a reproachful way. She was not one to chide and he loved that about her mainly because he was an easy target for chiding.

"It was a real eye-opener, I'll tell you that. I found myself conflicted. On the one hand I couldn't relate to the protesters, they seemed so grubby and self-serving. But on the flipside I could see their point, sort of, that here was another example of mistreatment by the white man and they weren't going to put up with it. Except it wasn't mistreatment, more like 'he said, she said.' The cop claimed the drug dealer was going for his gun and he acted in self-defense. The prosecutors say the cop planted the gun to cover his butt, although their proof of that is sketchy. Yet, the black community is eager to believe that. I mean, that's expected, right? A cop lying to save his ass." He shook his head. "It's a hell of a situation, and with the mob I ran into down there I'm afraid it's going to last for a while."

"Grudgingly." He looked at her, puzzled. "I could see their point *grudgingly*. I mean if that lowlife didn't have a gun when the cop stopped him, he could have had one, right?"

"Well, yeah, maybe…"

"You better be even more careful when you're up North," she cautioned. She knew he was often in the poor, run-down neighborhoods in North St. Louis, knocking on strange doors, serving summonses and subpoenas. He would be the only white guy around, ripe for mugging or worse, but in twenty-eight years nothing bad had ever happened, not even being called a derogatory name like cracker or ofay or whitey— honky was too silly to be offensive. He figured they took him for a social worker or building inspector.

"I will, babe," he said. "But you know it's not easy to think that, because of this unrest, things are going to get nasty between the races."

"Ferguson and now this," she remarked. The 2014 riots in Ferguson, about ten miles from where they now stood, brought unwanted national attention to St. Louis. In that situation, an unarmed black man believed to have just shoplifted at a market was stopped not far away, walking in the middle of the road. A struggle between Officer Darren Wilson and the suspect ensued and eighteen-year-old Michael Brown was shot and killed. It was August in St. Louis which means blazing hot and Brown's body lay under a blood-soaked shroud in the street for hours while crime scene techs gathered forensics. Meanwhile occupants of the low-income housing in that area poured out of their dwellings to congregate at the site and lash out at the police. Michael Brown was known and maybe liked by many. The upshot? Weeks of painful rioting, looting and violence that left the entire city on edge. A second wave of rioting happened three months later when a Grand Jury declined to indict Officer Wilson.

"What I'm saying is, I remember when you'd be walking along, say, and you pass a black person and he says 'hello' to you and you say 'hello' back. Might be a smile in there too. Could be in a park or the grocery store or the gas station, there was a friendly nod. And this wasn't years ago, this was last month."

"Things change," she said, "and not always for the better."

He took a pull on his beer, burped. "I got a citation," he told her. "Court date of October 4. Forty-five dollar fine is what I heard. I'll just pay it and move on, forget about this nonsense."

She set her glass on the counter, moved into him, put her arms around him, tilted her head upwards. He caught her scent, redolent of oregano and any other spices and herbs common to the kitchen at the restaurant. It aroused him. He kissed her deeply, and in a reverie he relived their courtship, when he would sit behind her and her grandmother in church. How he followed them to the coffee shop after church and sat close by, searching for a chance to begin a conversation. How this scenario was repeated for several weeks until one time *nonna* went to use the restroom. He saw his chance, cleared his throat, looked her way so that she knew he was talking to her. Then he delivered perhaps the lamest opening line ever uttered by a potential suitor. He asked, "How did you like the sermon?" It took off from there, but it wasn't without roadblocks, he being Irish and of solid working-class stock, she being Italian and ten years younger. It wasn't a problem for them, no, but for her family, very traditional and old world. The word was they were connected and that had him on his best behavior for the longest, displaying politeness and chivalry of a courtier. It was only talk, Francis decided, for there was no evidence of any mob connection. Besides, anyone who knew anything about St. Louis knew that, historically, at least in the 20th century, organized crime was dominated by Lebanese names. Still, he kept his courteous conduct with the Pastoris, it was easy.

Two years after that encounter in the coffee shop, they were married in St. Ambrose on The Hill. It was the most splendid affair he had ever attended, his father-in-law, Peppino, made sure of that. It was also the happiest day of his life until Isabella was born in 1995, followed by Vittorio in 1997. They bought a house in Dogtown, only a half-mile from The Hill where she'd lived her whole life. He certainly felt divided—but not conflicted—culturally, between the two well-known neighborhoods, Irish-American and Italian-American, his and hers. Fact, he loved them both. Fact, he had stickers on his car for Dogtown *and* The Hill. The years passed and Francis was slowly assimilated into the Pastori *famiglia* with their many elaborate *festas*—the baptisms, first communions, confirmations and of course the weddings with their manic renditions of *Funiculi Funicula* and the funerals with the plaintive wailing and rending of clothing, well, *some* of them. Bella and Vito grew into fine young persons, and he and Martha were constantly reminded how lucky they were. But now the nest was empty with Bella married and a nurse in Indianapolis, and Vito a junior at Mizzou with his sights on becoming a sports commentator.

The kiss lingered and he found himself adrift in warm, pleasant sensation. She came up for breath, took in his consuming blue eyes, whispered, "I love you."

— 3 —

"Don't forget to take the trash out when you leave," she said.

"How could I forget, it's my favorite chore." he answered.

"It's beginning to smell," she added.

"That attracts flies," he said, "before long there'll be maggots."

"Good, I can add them to the polenta. They'll blend right in, add protein too."

In twenty-four years of marriage they'd never had maggots in their garbage. Their home was well-kept on the order of a realtor's model home. She also made a fabulous breakfast each morning and he wouldn't miss it for the world. Right now he was tucking into a plate of polenta and salsiccia. Coffee and OJ to wash it down. She sat across from him, the window to the backyard behind her. A squirrel was upside-down on the bird feeder, scarfing black oil sunflower seed. It was 6:45 and soon they would be out of doors and into the day, typically gorgeous for September in St. Louis.

"What's on your plate today?" she asked.

He looked at his plate. "Not literally, silly."

"Me and Cale are doing a stakeout in South City. Summons for paternity. The guy knows it's coming and once he's served he's on the hook for child support. Three times I've tried and three times no response, although I'm pretty sure he's in there. I told the lawyer we need to put the full press on the guy and that it would take two people."

"Right, one for the front and one for the back."

"You got it. My feeling, no more than two hours. I'll be bored out of my skull by then."

"You don't have the temperament for a stakeout. Too antsy."

"I'll say a rosary to pass the time." She knew he wasn't kidding.

* * *

He pulled up in front of the two-story wood frame on Tamm Avenue and honked twice. There were two doors on the porch, one for the bottom unit and one for the upper. A man south of forty, six-one, clean-shaven, short brown hair and glasses, dressed in black T-shirt and jeans came out of the door to the bottom unit. He waved with a smile and strode with a noticeable limp to the waiting car. Cale Twohey threw his backpack in the back seat and took the passenger seat.

"Onward, Jeeves," he said. Francis gave a smile and asked if he'd peed recently.

"That's a bit personal, isn't it? Do I ask you questions about your personal habits? Did you brush your teeth today, Francis? Put on deodorant? Screw your wife this morning?"

"We're doing a stakeout, knucklehead. No toilet available."

"I can hold it."

"It's your bladder."

They got to the location, a two-story red brick just like every other house in the City. They parked a few doors down. Francis said, "Not sure what car he drives or where he keeps it, out front or in the back. There's a garage at the alley and there's a door to the backyard so he can go from the house to his car and we'd never see him from the front. So, I'll take the front, you take the back."

Cale nodded, made no remark. "Questions?"

"Yeah, what am I doing in the alley while I'm waiting for him to maybe come out?"

"You could twiddle your thumbs. You could reminisce about your lost loves. I don't know, what would you like to do?" He looked at his watch. "Seven-thirty, let's give it ninety minutes. I'll take you around."

Francis found the house in the trash-strewn alley. He stopped. "Shame there's no windows on that garage or we'd know if his car's there."

"And whether he's even here at all."

"Well, we got to try to say we tried, and look at it this way, we're getting paid thirty-five an hour for sitting on our asses."

"Yeah, I like that. Let's give it two hours."

Cale grabbed his backpack and got out. Francis gave him a copy of the summons to be served. He went to the backseat and took out a folding chair. "See, I'm thinking of you, your comfort."

Cale grinned. "Thanks boss." There was a dumpster near the garage, big blue thing with bags of refuse poking out the open lid. He went over, stood there, looked down. He nudged a desiccated possum carcass with his boot. "Well, at least I'll have some company."

"Anything happens you call my cell. I'll do the same for you. All right, I'm away. Let's serve this guy."

Francis settled in position, two doors down, opposite side of the street, facing the front of the house. He looked for any sign of activity in the house, saw none, the blinds drawn. He contemplated just walking up to the door and knocking, maybe the guy would be curious and answer. No, that would tip him off. Besides, he'd likely caught sight of Francis during one of his three trips here already. He knows he's the target of a lawsuit, but he doesn't know to what lengths the process server will go to complete the job.

He had the radio on barely audible. 550 AM. McGraw Milhaven and Kelly Jackson were interviewing the Lieutenant Governor about the gambling machines that were popping up in bars and restaurants in Missouri. The LG was saying they were technically legal because, when you put your dollar in, the machine told you whether you were going to win or lose and knowing that took away the element of chance. It wasn't strictly gambling. The LG didn't like these unregulated machines, he was going to lobby the politicians to create legislation to close the loophole. Francis liked talk radio, he was always learning something. He looked at the time, seventeen minutes had passed. He thought of Cale, sitting near a smelly dumpster back there, waiting to pounce like a cat on a mouse. Once again, he thought how grateful he was to have found such a partner.

Francis had been a self-employed process server since 1988, twenty-nine years now. He had built up a clientele over the years, mostly word of mouth, and he was making a good living doing something he enjoyed. He gave no thought to retiring, not as long as he could drive a car and knock on doors. He was fifty-six now with ailments plaguing him, most grievously arthritis in both knees. Some days every step he took was painful, stairs seemed daunting at times, especially stairs without railings. Halfheartedly, he began to think about taking on a partner. He was making enough that he could afford to pay for help. This partner wouldn't be easy to find because certain abilities were a must—to be able to think on your feet, to know when to be assertive, even forceful, and when to be felicitous, to be able to stand up to hotheads and scathing verbal abuse. Then one day, he came upon Cale Twohey, whom he believed had the instincts needed to be a process server on the mean streets of St. Louis.

They met at Cochran VA Hospital on Grand Avenue. Both were in the pharmacy lobby waiting on their meds. Cale was on a city forestry crew, bored with trees and shrubs, looking for a change. He had been in the army, had joined up like Francis but long after Francis, and he'd done two tours in Iraq. He was infantry, 9th Division, 36th Brigade, and had seen action in Fallujah, Haditha, and close fighting in the streets of Baghdad. It was during the battle of Basra, however, spring 2008, that he and three fellow grunts had the misfortune to drive their Humvee over an IED planted in the road only an hour before. Two of the four were killed outright, a third sustained only a broken arm and Cale had to be extricated from the wreckage to learn that his left leg and foot were horribly mangled. He was twenty-six at the time. His military adventures cut short and, upon discharge, he returned home to St. Louis where he embarked on a long-term regimen of physical therapy at Cochran. But no amount of physical therapy was going to fix that limp. Sure, custom orthotics in his footwear helped, but he'd never walk straight again. He could live with it.

That day in the pharmacy Francis laid out a proposition that intrigued. Cale would accompany Francis on his rounds, learning the trade firsthand from the Master. At first he would get a meager salary, that is, coffee and donuts, beer after they were through, usually around two o' clock. He would bring his own lunch. He would get to pick the radio station for one hour a day. He would smoke his Marlboros only with the window open and never blow smoke in his direction. Did he smoke pot? Yeah, sometimes. He would do that elsewhere, not in my car. After he got to the point where Francis could trust him to not fuck up too badly, he would start getting his own papers to serve. He would be tooling around the City, tracking down defendants and respondents, giving them papers that may change their lives for the worse. Francis would create the return of service and submit the bill. Cale would get 80 percent.

"I can do this," he said. "I want to do this."

"It may not be quite as exciting as a firefight in Fallujah, but I guarantee you'll never be bored."

Now he was lounging in the folding chair in the alley, munching on an apple. Cale's backpack held other goodies, an oatmeal chocolate Nutri-bar, Planter's Peanuts, and a can of Coke. He was thinking about later taking his Triumph Thunderbird out on some farm roads across the river, cornfields and soybeans rushing by, after he got done with whatever Francis had for him. Then, a noise. Someone in the garage. He heard a car start. He got up, got the summons ready to hand off. The garage door opened, a car began backing out. It had to be one of those remote garage door openers because the guy was already in the car. This was the sort of situation Francis was always talking about, one where you had to think on your feet. Cale stepped into the moving Honda Civic, the rear-end nudging out, shouted "Hey!" The Civic kept on coming. He slapped the trunk, and the car stopped. A diminutive guy in a striped sports shirt, bald pate smooth as an eggshell, jumped out, shaking with rage. The car was half-in, half-out of the garage.

"What's your problem, man?"

Cale approached and the guy shrank back a little. "I see you're irate," he said, "and that's understandable because you've been avoiding service and now you're caught. Here you go." He handed over the summons. There's something about the act of handing something to someone else. Even if it's something the person really doesn't want, the urge to take it is strong. Haltingly, the man took the papers, glanced at the face of the summons, gave a derisive snort and dropped it at his feet.

"Fuck you," he spat. "You're not serving me here in the alley. You've got to do it at my home."

"Wrong! Where did you hear that?"

"My lawyer said. You can take these papers back."

"Your lawyer is an idiot. Look, I'm not arguing with you, you're served, simple as that."

The guy muttered some imprecation which sounded like "fucking pissant" and got his feisty little self back behind the wheel. He continued backing out and Cale had to get out of the way. When he got the car straight, he peeled out, spraying gravel in Cale's direction. The garage door closed and the process lay there, forlorn, in the alley.

* * *

"It's called service by refusal," said Francis, stirring his coffee which was black. "He knew you're a process server with papers for him and he chose not to accept. You don't have to actually take the papers to be served. It's good service, the circumstance just needs to be notated on the return affidavit."

Cale nodded understanding. "But say it's windy. He drives off, leaves the papers behind, they blow away, he never reads them."

"That's on him," said Francis.

"He probably thinks he's not served since he didn't take the papers." He forked a mound of goop into his mouth.

"Then he'll find out soon enough, don't you think? He ignores the counts on the petition, the next step is a show cause order. He ignores that, the sheriff deputies come after, haul him before the judge."

Cale finished chewing. "The wheels of justice, huh?"

"I've always thought of it as a conveyor belt."

They were in the Courtesy Diner on Kingshighway. It was 9:20. Cale was having a slinger, a St. Louis specialty sometimes described as a culinary car crash. Francis, having had a hearty breakfast, was happy with coffee. Across the street was a bar they sometimes went to, The Royale. Beyond that, to the north, the southwest corner of Tower Grove Park, two-hundred ninety acres of greenery and cultural attractions in the heart of the City.

"So what else is on for today?"

"First you're going to finish eating that slop. Then, you're going to the law office of Mary Pat Rinker to pick up two subpoenas, which need to be served by tomorrow. Then, I want you to stop by Catholic Legal downtown where there's a guardianship summons waiting. You drop that off at my place and I'll do that after I'm done with these other jobs."

"The subpoenas, businesses or homes?"

"Not sure," said Francis. Of all papers to be served business subpoenas were the easiest, like being a glorified courier. Banks, schools, hospitals, places of employment, you simply leave it with a receptionist, a manager, supervisor, practically anyone who works there, get their name and title and you're done.

"Okay, yeah, I'll do that. Anything else?"

Francis looked him in his brown expressive eyes. "Just enjoy the rest of your day."

His phone was on the table in front of him. A ringtone from the opening bars of "Eight Miles High" by The Byrds sounded. "Hello? Yes this is me, what's up? Okay." He listened, his brow furrowing, a concerned expression came over him. "All right. Please say your name again. Elliot Lambert, Dr. Elliot Lambert. You don't mind I'd like to discuss this in person. Yes, please. St. Mary's on Bellevue, Medical Building A. Sure, I know it. I'll be there, say, an hour."

He clicked off, looked at Cale. "You won't believe this…or maybe you will."

— 4 —

"No appointment," he told the receptionist in her swivel chair with pictures of her grandkids all around. "I'm not a patient, but Dr. Lambert wants to see me."

"Hm," she said, skeptically. "Have a seat."

It wasn't long before a distinguished looking gent in a blue dress shirt and red and gold bowtie under a white lab coat came out and made straight for him. He had gray hair combed back with a widow's peak at the fore and crow's feet around his blue eyes. Handsome guy, he looked a bit like the older Pierce Brosnan. He held out a hand. "Mr. Lenihan, I presume." A stab at humor. Francis wondered how he should play it, the guy didn't seem to be grieving. He was here working, after all. Maybe it had been a while since the son's death. "Please, come back to my office."

The gold plate on the door said Elliot Lambert MD Internal Medicine. It was a nice office that overlooked the parking lot of St. Mary's Hospital across the street, the place where both Bella and Vito had come into the world. Francis had always felt good about St. Mary's. He took a seat, Lambert paced or shuffled as he spoke. "Thanks for coming and taking an interest, I'll get right to it. My son, Austin, was a good kid with notable accomplishments—when he was younger, that is. For instance, he excelled at tennis and actually placed first in the Arthur Ashe Invitational Tournament in Forest Park. He was sixteen at the time. He attended John Burroughs all four years and was in the chess club and the wrestling team. He was a sizable kid and agile, he could pin an opponent in under a minute."

Lambert paused, wrung his hands together. "And then a change came over him, possibly drugs, possibly some sort of mental breakdown or aberration. He became sullen and moody. He'd leave the house on Friday morning and we wouldn't see him until Sunday evening, wouldn't call even though we asked him, *pleaded* with him. Oh, I know that can be chalked up to typical teenage behavior, but nonetheless it was very concerning to his mother and me.

"Well, he graduated from Burroughs—barely—and had been accepted at Northwestern in the fall. Looking toward a major in psychology, with my blessing, I might add. This was two years ago. Then, one day at the end of June he comes to us, says matter-of-factly, 'Mom dad, I've joined the marines. I leave tomorrow.' Well, you could've knocked Adelaide and me over with a feather! Talk about a sidetrack. So he went off to boot camp, Parris Island, and we didn't hear from him, only a rare phone call, but he seemed like he was okay, fitting in, you know."

"I can relate," said Francis. "I joined the army right out of high school to get out of probation for some regrettable, um, indiscretion. Enlisted on a whim more or less, but it worked out for me. I take it, not so much for Austin."

"Quite the case," said Lambert. "One day he shows up at the house and tells us he's been 'kicked out' of the military. The marine corps gave him a general discharge and sent him packing, he didn't make it past boot camp. Behavioral problems is what I gathered, he was vague about it and the marine corps certainly wasn't going to tell us. Whatever it was, it was still there. I mean his mental state was rock bottom. We got him counseling, but he went once and then never again. I must tell you, Mr. Lenihan, it is very disconcerting for a parent to not able to help their child, to watch helplessly as he deteriorates into a mental wreck, someone incapable of helping himself.

"At any rate, he struck out on his own. No car, little or no money, no plan, just a backpack and his cell phone and good luck keeping that charged. What wheels were turning in his head, I don't know but he ended up in various homeless shelters and finally in these camps you hear about in the news, the ones where the health department is always trying to get them to move on. The biggest one is down by the river, just north of the Arch. Tents and makeshift hovels, a haven for bums." He frowned sadly. "It's like a Hooverville from the Great Depression, a sprawling shantytown, filthy, squalid, and all sorts of other unsavory adjectives. I know because I went there looking for him. This was back in May, well before Austin died. It took a couple trips because, you know, they tend to wander off during the day, begging on street corners, sleeping in libraries, whatever they do. I showed a picture of him and some said he looked familiar, others claimed they could point me to him for a fee. Oh, I paid the fee, a five here, a ten there, but of course nothing came of it. Finally I found a man, Charlie Spinner, said he was once a professor at Washington University, and this man claimed to be friends with Austin, said that Austin was loaded into an ambulance only a week before, probably recovering in some hospital. His condition? I asked. Probably an overdose, according to Charlie, 'there's been some bad meth going around.'"

"Jesus," said Francis. "And it gets worse?"

"Oh yes, I searched several hospitals and no sign of him. And it turned out it wasn't a legitimate ambulance that took him away but someone with a vehicle and no one at the camp could say who it was. Meanwhile, he must have come upon a situation where he could exist away from the homeless camp because it appears he didn't go back there. Then one day in August he called out of the blue. It was a Sunday morning and, fortunately, I was home to get the call. He sounded dreamy and distant and, when he asked if Whiskers was all right, I knew he had lost his mind. Whiskers was a Persian cat that he'd had as a little boy, and he loved that animal. I said that Whiskers was fine but she misses him. Won't he come home and take care of her? I offered to pick him up immediately. He said all right and that he was on North Grand near the Guest Host Motel. He would wait for me. I looked up the address of this motel then jumped in the car. I got there—what a fleabag, people passed out in doorways in their own vomit, drugs being sold openly. I was aggressively propositioned by a slattern in an ill-fitting bikini who wouldn't take no for an answer. That's all I need, my picture in the tabloids for some vice-related charge. Secret Life of Doctor Revealed!"

Francis smiled as did Lambert. "So, I asked at the desk, I searched the area all around this motel, no sign of Austin. He'd vanished once again. You can imagine how despondent I was. It was just a few weeks later, August 31 to be exact, that I got a call from the coroner's office. 'Mr. Lambert, we have a body here that we believe is your son. So sorry for you if it is, but would you please come here as soon as possible to make an identification.' It was him, of course, and they had found him in that camp along the river that I mentioned. Cause of death, an overdose of fentanyl."

"A bad one, I hear," offered Francis.

"You better believe it," said Lambert, "a synthetic opioid that's up to fifty times stronger than heroin. Pharmaceutical fentanyl is prescribed by doctors to treat severe pain—*I've* prescribed it—but right now in this country there's an epidemic of ODs from illicit fentanyl which, of course, is unregulated and those who sell it don't give a damn how potent their product is or who it kills." He looked at the floor, searching for the next pronouncement. "The latest stats," he continued, "indicate that over one-hundred fifty people in America die every day from overdoses related to synthetic opioid, fentanyl chief among them. Imagine that. So much sorrow and wasted lives over an urge to get high, achieve some sort of warped nirvana. It saddens me beyond belief.

"So, wrapping up here, we received his belongings, Adelaide and me, and there wasn't much. He was wearing his dogtags, but his wallet gone along with the Fossil Chronograph watch that I'd bought him. It was just his clothes, grubby as you can imagine for having only one set. Your card was in a pocket of his pants. Why? Did you meet with him? I'm hoping you can clear up that mystery."

"Show me a picture, I might recognize him."

"Of course." Lambert went to a credenza and brought him a framed photo of Austin in a Marine Corps uniform, cap included. His intense blue eyes staring straight into the camera. Francis shook his head in the negative, handed the picture back.

"There's a reason, we just don't know what it is," said Lambert.

"Maybe…maybe he was being harassed and bullied by someone at the camp and he wanted to slap an OP on that person. He asked around and someone who happened to have my card—I give them out freely—said, 'Here, call this guy, he'll help you with that.'"

"OP?"

"Sorry, order of protection. You go to the adult abuse office at the courthouse and apply for one at no charge, but then you have to pay either the sheriff or a guy like me to get it served. But no one would think to have the sheriff serve someone at a homeless camp. It just wouldn't happen. That's what specials are for, we're process servers who investigate as well. We go the extra mile for our clients. Do you have the card in question?"

"Sure," said Lambert, reaching into a drawer on his desk. "Here."

The card, blue, green, and white, was creased and smeared with what looked like molasses. It read FRANCIS X. LENIHAN LICENSED PROCESS SERVER ST. LOUIS CITY AND COUNTY SOLID EXPERIENCE and gave a phone number and P.O. Box as means of contact. He turned it over. It read 2ND ATTEMPT PLEASE CALL WITH AVAILABILITY. No name, no clue as to whom it had been addressed. "Hmm," he pondered. "I probably wouldn't have left such a note if the address was here in the City. Generally, I leave a note when the address is a bit of a drive, and I'm hoping to cut down on mileage. Hoping, also, that by tipping off this person they don't make themselves scarce and avoid service altogether."

"But you can't recall writing that on the back?"

"No, sir, I can't. Maybe it'll come to me later. Maybe when I'm washing dishes at home. Lots of things come to me when I'm doing that. I don't know why."

"That's interesting," said Lambert, finally taking a seat behind his desk. Then, addressing Francis quite earnestly, "Listen, I'd like to hire you to look into what happened with Austin from May to August of this year, from the time he left the homeless camp supposedly in an ambulance but more likely a private car to the time when he returned. Where did he go? Who was he with? I think there's more to this than a simple overdose."

"You want a private investigator for that."

"You said yourself 'we're process servers who investigate.' I'll make it worth your while. Please."

"I don't know, I'm pretty busy with my regular clients."

He already had his checkbook out and scribbled a figure on the top check. He showed it to Francis. One thousand dollars. "To get you started," he said.

"If I do this, I don't act alone. There's another, my partner Cale Twohey."

Lambert tore off the top check and wrote another figure on the next one. He signed it. "How's this work?" The figure had grown to $2500.

Francis was now embracing the thought of unlimited drinks and chicken wings at Murphy's Bar in Dogtown. "Well, okay, we'll give it a shot. But no guarantees. All we can do is try."

"That's all I'm asking." Now Lambert saw him looking at the art on the walls for the first time.

"It's a hobby of mine or should I say indulgence?" he explained. "I collect what's been called edgy art or provocative art, much of it conceptual, like blow your mind conceptual. Dramatic imagery, and some of it quite dark. Think *Piss Christ* by Serrano or Robert Mapplethorpe's *Black Book* photographs. I have a modest collection of Mapplethorpes. I have a long list of pieces I'd love to acquire, but they're so pricey. I'm afraid I have to be content with either limited editions or original pieces by up-and-comers."

Francis fixed on a stark black-and-white graphic featuring a grotesque, morose-looking man, eyes downcast, shoulders slumped, arms between his legs, sitting on a bench in a prison cell or some facility, crude graffiti on the wall behind him. "Yeah, I see what you mean."

"That's the twisted work of Stéphane Mandelbaum, a Belgian artist who I collect. Young, lavishly talented, he was an artist *and* an art thief. In fact, he was murdered for having stolen the wrong piece. He took a forgery instead of the real painting, whether intentional or not, we'll never know. What do you think?"

"It's definitely not your Norman Rockwell." Lambert laughed. He indicated a stack of *ARTnews* magazines on his desk. He said, "Art is no longer about warm sentimental cliches à la Rockwell. Art today is about ideas—macabre, titillating, in-your-face, even self-destructive. That's what's selling now in galleries, but the future is always in flux."

— 5 —

"WELL, IF IT ISN'T THE STAR OF THE 5 O' CLOCK NEWS," said Rory Denigan as Francis walked through the door, a big goofy smile on his mug. "Here, I saved a seat for ya." Rory patted the empty stool next to him at the bar. Francis took the seat and Tommy the barkeep brought him a pint of Busch that he'd poured as soon as he saw Francis get out of his car. Francis raised the glass, saluted Rory and Tommy and anyone else within range, and drained practically the whole thing in one long gulp. "Ahh," he said, wiping his mouth with the back of his hand, "first one always tastes the best."

"So tell us about it," urged Rory, "what was it like to be in the middle of all that…all that, what do you call it? Commotion? Frenzy? Mayhem?"

"How about an old-fashioned riot?" said Ed Gannon down the bar. "We seen you on the news, getting rounded up along with all them spooks." Ed was the head of Local 68, the pipefitters union. Rory was a rehabber who started early so he could occupy this barstool and drink himself silly. The regulars all knew this was Rory's seat.

Francis knew this was coming and he had given some thought as to how to handle it, the barbs and reproaches of this bibulous delegation. He gave a snort, said, "It sure wasn't me you saw. Are we talking yesterday? I was down in Jeff Co all day serving subpoenas to witnesses in a rape case." Jeff Co was Jefferson County, the adjacent county to the south of St. Louis.

"Haw!" said Mickey Queenan, the high school teacher with his coffee and Bailey's Cream. Mickey was also known as Mickey One as there were three drunks named Mick or Mickey in Dogtown. "As good a bullshitter you may think you are, that one isn't gonna fly 'cause we seen you on the news big as life an' unless you got an identical twin it was none other than Francis Lenihan, friend of the oppressed, eh?" Mickey and a few others had come over to hear what Francis had to say and to add to the dialogue where they might.

"Yeah," said Ed Gannon, "you looked like you were saying something to the camera, like 'Get me a lawyer.'"

Several guffaws at this, then a character named Ted Pollack said, "Or how 'bout 'I may not be a nigger but here I am in the thick of it, stirring up trouble with 'em, going to jail with 'em.'"

Francis was never chummy with Pollack. Now he shot him a look. "Was that really necessary?" He shook his head disgustedly. "Geez."

In fact, a pall had fallen over the gathered for they all liked Francis, the glue if not the lynchpin that held this bar together over the years, and only wanted to give him some good-natured ribbing. Hell, it was expected, but Pollack's comment was over the top. As for Francis, he was gathering steam over the remark and all the attention in general because this was his bar, his home away from home.

"Tommy," he called, holding up his empty pint glass.

Rory addressed Ted Pollack. "It's a good thing there aren't any, you know, niggers in here to hear you say that."

Francis understood that whether these guys knew it or not they didn't have a hard-on for blacks as a whole. Not since Ferguson had he heard any disparaging remarks about race. To a lot of whites, and maybe himself but probably not, there were blacks and there were niggers. To Rory and Ted and the others the niggers are what they see on *Cops* and other police shows. Or demonstrating quite vocally near the courthouse. The ones with their pants hanging halfway down their ass, annoying everyone at stop lights with their hyperactive sub-woofers, and the ones killing, dealing drugs and bringing down their race. They are not, conversely the hip black guy who works alongside you on the assembly line or the friend's friend. Those people are cool, they just happen to be black. These jokers have made a very tidy moral judgment, Francis thought. They can flip on the nigger switch when the black person does not fit into their definition of what is comfortable. It also gives them an outlet to put someone down who is perceived weaker or less worthy than they are.

"There were two in here last month," offered Mickey. "They had one drink and then walked right back out the door."

Tommy brought Francis a fresh pint. "That's on me," said Ted Pollack. "Sorry if I upset you."

Francis turned on his stool, looked them all over. There were six now, sitting or standing in a half-circle around him, drinks in hand. "Look, it's a simple explanation. I was in the Civil Courts building on assignment and while I was in there the verdict came down and those protesters were ready in the event that verdict wasn't to their liking. The cops were ready too. The stage was set and that not guilty verdict was the bell that called all the actors out on stage. I walked out of the Civil Courts and the protest was in full swing. I should have got the hell out while I still could, but I saw a couple guys I knew and stopped to talk. Then it was too late, the cops decided to use the big net and kettle us fish."

"Yeah," said old James McNeary, nodding, "that's what they call it, 'kettling,' a police tactic for controlling unruly crowds. Don't know if it's been used here before, but they do use it in Europe."

"It's just something that happened," said Francis. "I don't begrudge the police for how they handled it. They had to do something. Things were definitely getting out of control."

James McNeary said, "Did you hear about the mayor's house? The protesters decided they'd march on the mayor's home, rattle her cage. Well, they didn't have the address quite right and when they got to her street, one of those hoity-toity private streets off Kingshighway, they threw rocks and stones and bricks at the wrong house!"

"Can you imagine?" said Phil Connor, another wag, "the homeowner in there freaking out."

"The mayor lived next door or nearby," said McNeary. "She's probably looking out her window, watching, thinking, Jesus wept, that could be my house." In a falsetto McNeary had done a comic impersonation of Mayor Lyda Krewson's plight, and they all chuckled.

"You want a bump of Jamie, Francis?" Rory Denigan patting him on the shoulder. "How about shots all around? Tommy, bring us all a healthy shot of Jameson, will ya?"

Things had gone from somewhat tense back to normal, the conversation had shifted away from racial tension which was still happening with invasions of angry blacks into hitherto "safe" venues such as the Galleria, shouting at shoppers, demanding this or that—had gone from talk of turbulent current events to more prosaic talk of baseball scores, some fantastic sale at Home Depot, when Lorenzo Crespi walked in. Lorenzo was the only regular in Murphy's of Italian descent, and he thought himself quite the wit. He made straight for Francis, stood before him. "My man! My man! You looked fantastic on TV. We were cheering you on, hoping you'd take a poke at one of those mean men in uniform."

They all supposed he was being sarcastic. His brother was a city cop. Then Lorenzo saw something on Francis' shirt, and, theatrically, he plucked this imaginary something from the fabric and held it up to the light. "Why, this looks like a nig-nig-nig, uh, African-American hair, all kinky and nappy like a coiled spring. What, you didn't get your clothes cleaned after your stay in the pokey, all those other jailbirds rubbing up on you? You know there's a One Hour Martinizing over on Macklind. They'll get all those little unwanted souvenirs, wash them right out, man, down the drain."

"Oh, Jesus," said Rory Denigan. A few others rolled their eyes. Someone said, "Not cool."

Crespi smirked at Francis, waiting for a response. Nothing. He broke into a wide grin. "Kidding!" and went to pat him on the shoulder. Buddy buddy. Francis grabbed his hand and bit him on the thumb.

"Goddamnit, Francis!" swore Crespi, sucking his poor thumb.

"My father used to call me that."

— 6 —

IN THE OLD DAYS, BACK BEFORE HE MET MARTHA, he would stay at the bar until nearly bedtime, then stumble home and get his car the next morning. But now that he was married he would drink for an hour or so and then make it home in time for dinner, and that was certainly something to look forward to. Many times she would bring home from the restaurant some wonderful pasta or chicken spiedini or steamed mussels with fennel and tarragon, just to name a few. He was not a Foodie, not by a long shot, but he liked whatever she brought home and he made sure they had a nice selection of vino to accompany the dish. Tonight it was eggplant Parmesan. She had carefully scooped it from the styrofoam container to a beautifully decorated platter, still warm, the aroma filling the kitchen.

"How do you like it?" she asked.

"Beats warmed-over corned beef and cabbage," he said.

"What was the best part of your day?" she asked. "Besides this wonderful meal."

"Hm. I got all green lights on Grand from Chippewa to Martin Luther King. On my way to serve a trial subpoena."

"Did you get it done?"

"Oh, yeah."

"But that's the second best thing? Wow, it doesn't take much to make you happy."

He nodded. "It's the little things, babe."

They ate some more and neither felt any need to talk. He put his fork down, took a drink of Merlot. "Well, I took a very nice payment for an investigation into the death of a young man." He cocked his eyebrow the way he did when he felt that she should be impressed. And he explained, starting with the surprise phone call to the visit to Lambert's office concluding with a rundown on Austin Lambert's mental health. "Twenty-five hundred," he said, "just to look into it."

"And you're not even a private investigator."

"Oh, but I am. I just don't have a license."

"So what's your plan, Stan?"

"I'll have seconds on the eggplant, thank you. I could become a vegetarian on this stuff." He spooned a healthy portion on his plate. "Well, I'll team up with Cale. We'll hit some homeless camps, mainly the big one down by the river, the one that's in the news from time to time, the city trying to get them to move on—to another city."

"Or some outbreak of disease."

"Yeah, that too. We'll have a picture, show it around, find someone who knew him. That's a start."

"Everyone you speak with is going to be thinking 'What's in it for me?'"

"Understood," he said. "And there may well be something in it for them."

"Foul play not suspected?"

He stopped midway to a forkful of eggplant Parmesan down the hatch. "Official cause, fentanyl OD, but that doesn't mean it was self-administered. Somebody may have wanted him gone, it's possible."

She brushed away a strand of auburn hair that threatened to touch her plate. "That he had your card in his pocket, a mystery right there, huh?"

"Yeah, a real head-scratcher and a testament to my popularity. Pass the wine, please."

"Naples, Corfu, Palermo, Valencia, Genoa. To name a few," she said, looking at him quizzically. "Those are stops on the Mediterranean ten-day cruise, which twenty-five hundred would pretty much cover."

"I love how you've already spent my dream paycheck. But yeah, you know I could go for that, get you back to your roots."

"My family has roots in Northern Italy, the Lombard region, but there's no sea nearby. We'd have to travel by motor scooter."

"Burro, maybe. It would add to the romance of the trip."

— 7 —

"YOU GONNA MAKE ME WORK TO GET AN ANSWER, HUH?" The man before him was a sorry specimen, ragged, gaunt, withered, matted beard and hair. Ready for a job interview he was not. He said his name Dee and that he'd lived in this woebegone place for more than a year. Said he lived off the charity of others, mostly church groups who brought them food and toiletries out of pity. They found him wandering around in a sort of daze. Francis had chatted him up, explained their purpose here, showed him the picture of Austin Lambert as a jarhead. Dee merely stared at it, perplexed.

"He's thinking," said Cale. "I can see the gears turning." Cale had a pocket notebook and pen ready to jot down anything of value.

"No, he's off on a daydream. Wherever he is, it's not here."

Finally the cobwebs began to clear. "That guy, that guy!" Dee exclaimed, pointing at the picture. "He liked the Clementines, those oranges they give us."

"Okay, good," urged Francis. "Can you recall who he hung out with? Any of his pals?"

"Or maybe it was that other guy liked the oranges," said Dee. "What time is it? Soup today at eleven. Every day at eleven. Today it might be, um, might be, mm, you know, that stuff looks like snot, tastes like seaweed."

Francis thought he saw something crawl down the man's cheek and go into his beard. "Yeah, sure. But back to this guy in the picture. Austin, his name. Who else did you see him with? Anyone you can point out?"

"Jesus Christ," said Dee, "I already told you three times. He was here and now he's not."

The camp was along the North Riverfront Trail, began at the north end of what used to be called Wharf Street and now was named after some politician that no one remembered. The old Union Electric Light & Power building, long shuttered, the starting point. The scenic trail along the river had been built for walkers, bicyclists, rollerbladers, and was never intended to support a community, but here was a big sign as you entered: WELCOME TO HOPEVILLE USA. It was a tent city peppered here and there with slightly more permanent makeshift structures, like backyard forts that kids would build. To their right, eastward, maybe thirty yards, a steep, rutted bank went down to the river, a flood wall flanking the trail, extending some two-hundred yards from the trail's beginning. It was early morning and even though it was warm and would get to the low eighties today, there were fires, wisps of dark smoke curling up from piles of busted furniture and barely flammable construction materials, foraged from nearby abandoned buildings. Port-a-potties dotted various locations, compliments of City Hall, and, yes, a soup kitchen which opened at eleven. A blackboard informed that Vichyssoise would be in the pot for today.

"That's a joke, right?" said Cale, chuckling. "Vichyssoise, my ass. More like Mulligan stew."

"Someone's got a sense of humor," said Francis.

"What's the population here, you figure?" asked Cale.

"Less than a hundred permanent or semi-permanent."

Cale sniffed. "It's a goddamn sad place, don't you think? Open garbage always depresses me."

They came upon a bedraggled group gathered around a fire contained in a metal trash bin, inmates in this gulag on the Mississippi. "Say fellas," began Francis, "we're trying to locate this guy, Austin. Was a resident here earlier this year." The picture was passed around, eliciting variations of "Nah." One fellow stood apart from the others. He was missing a couple of important teeth and he wore a long purple scarf that draped over his bare torso like a gypsy. "Look, man, you ever hear that saying 'You catch more flies with honey than vinegar?'"

"Sure, we heard it."

The sun rising over the river just on the other side of the flood wall. A pair of vultures circled overhead. He squinted with one eye as he spoke. "So we're the flies and what you're offering for this information on your boy here is vinegar, which is nothing. Dig? You need to, uh, motivate us with some kind of bribe. Like smokes or—"

"A chocolate bar," put in another guy, licking his lips, "maybe a Pay-

Day or a Snickers."

"I like nuts," said another, a kid who didn't look old enough to shave. "Nuts and raisins and other stuff. Trail mix. But who are you guys?"

"Of course cash is king," said the first guy, now cupping his palm over his face like a visor. "A ten or a twenty will go far in the loose information department."

"They want a gift card to 7-Eleven," said Cale to Francis.

"We can arrange that…next time. Meanwhile, how about something to go on? A piece of info the size of a postage stamp. Come on, will ya? Please. When's the last time you saw him? Who was he with?"

The first guy, the more flies with honey guy, leveled a critical gaze at them. "I heard my pal ask who are you guys, but I never heard an answer."

"We'll tell you," said Francis, "it's no secret. We've been hired by this kid's father to learn about his associates and activity prior to his death in late August," taking care not to sound accusatory. "He died here, case you didn't know. But I know that you do know because that's got to be big news here and what else you got to do but listen to the news and think on it?"

"More folks dying here than you might think," said purple scarf, thin smile. "We got us a drug problem, imagine that. Ambulances coming and going, taking these stupid sons a bitches to the hospital—"

"Or the freakin' morgue," interjected the kid.

"You name it, we got it," said purple scarf. "Oxy, China girl, vikes, meth, hell dust for starters. Some got scrips from the methadone clinic. But fentanyl, that's the stone killer, the Darth Vader of all this happy shit." He looked to his comrades. "And what do we call fentanyl?"

"The easy way out," said one.

"That's right. You take a street dose of that you're dead before you know it."

"Little Xs in your eyes."

"So the guy in the picture, if he died here it was probably just another OD. Not huge news, not enough to remember him by."

"I see," said Francis, scratching his ear. "Okay, if we did come back with treats to loosen your tongues would there be anything of value? Could you give us any concrete information?"

"Maybe," said purple scarf, "definitely maybe."

"This is gonna be a tough nut to crack," said Cale. "We're batting zero for ten."

"All we can do is keep trying, something will shake out. They can't all be uncooperative."

They came upon a guy under a tree singing "Dream Weaver" off-key and they let him be. "I hate that song," said Francis. Ditto from Cale. A bit later they found a wild man, paranoid eyes, clothes hanging off him like a sad manikin. They showed him the picture, tried to elicit a response. He ignored them, continued his routine, what he'd been doing when they walked up, haranguing thin air.

"I said I was done with you!" he chafed. "No one gets what they want all the time." He had his back to them, speaking to someone not there. Now he whirled on them, shouted, "Why can't you listen?" Francis threw up hands in exasperation.

Cale said, "God bless you and I hope you get some help for that."

* * *

Jacob Vorhof watched them from a distance. Jacob was sitting on a folding chair, the kind you see on the sidelines at soccer games, getting ready to set up the kitchen. He wondered why they were talking to Owney as if he were somebody important in this camp. It was obvious they were trying to get something out of him. The old goat couldn't carry a conversation if you strapped it on his back. But who were these guys? Plainclothes cops? Social workers? Reporters? Would they see him and come over, try to chat him up too? That would answer his questions, but it would also put him on the spot, having to choose between being candid or cagey or somewhere in between. He decided he did not want to play their game whatever it was so he took his chair and coffee cup and went into the shack that would soon become a buzzing hub of activity. There, he would still watch them, but from an open window. Of the pair, the taller one seemed the dominant one, that is, he did the talking while the other one stood around.

Jacob's Winnebago Brave, an ugly baby-shit yellow monster that looked like it could have belonged to a utility company, was parked within sight, maybe fifty yards away. The doors were locked, but the engine was running. There was an orange extension cord running from the vehicle to the shack, providing the necessary power for lighting and a few appliances; the stove propane. He cleared out space on a long folding table, making ready for the caterers. Most weekdays, they made the soup here from scratch, he and a few helpers. Gallons of it, lentil, potato, vegetable beef—garden variety, both literal and figurative, and it was salubrious and decent but nothing special. But on that fourth day, always a Thursday, he had a specialty soup brought in from a local gourmet grocer. His treat, for he liked to see the look on their faces as they tasted something truly delicious. No one guessed it was his treat. They all thought it was the grocer's generosity, and that was perfect. The last thing he wanted was to set himself up as some patron of the homeless, not with his nefarious agenda.

* * *

They left the troubled man to his own madcap delusions and continued on through the camp. The tents, some of them resting on sheets of plywood, tended to be arranged in circular fashion, and fires burned within each of the circles. Folks were drinking either coffee or tea from the Quik Mart five blocks away, soda, or, some, fancying an early morning buzz, 40-ouncers. They were not well-received by these scruffy campers, circumspect and distrustful as a whole. Surly bastards, as Cale would later say. While being told to take a long walk on a short pier by a couple of vagabonds, a deep voice was heard to say, "Hey, I know that guy. He was in the protest downtown, got picked up and put in the slammer like the rest of us."

A huge black man came out of nowhere, walked up to Francis, slugged him on the shoulder. He stood there a foot taller, a grin crossing his face. "I don't know his name," he said to no one in particular, "but this motherfucker's all right."

Francis said, "Hey, Cleo, how's it hangin'?"

With Cleo's blessing, they all looked at the picture of Austin and offered what they could. Yeah, he'd been around here earlier in the year. Quiet kid, kept pretty much to himself. He was a vet, they thought, he wore those fatigues. He was a regular at the soup kitchen and he liked getting his feet washed. Feet washed? Yeah, there's a guy over on the far end of camp washes everyone's feet. It's a spiritual thing. Goes by—can you guess?—Jesus.

No one knew that Austin had been found dead here in the camp.

After fist bumps all around and some discourse on cowardly police tactics in the face of legitimate protest over a very important social justice issue, Cleo led them to Jesus, the oracle and washer of feet. Gone was the fierce jungle animal that fought the police tooth and nail. This Cleo was all talkative and insightful. Francis wondered if he was on something. Turned out that Cleo was named after Amos Cleophilus Brown, an African-American pastor and civil rights activist. "When I was born, he was the president of the San Francisco branch of the N-double A-CP," said Cleo, "and my mama thought that you couldn't get any more important than that. Mama comes from a long line of civil rights champions," he added.

"And she passed the torch on to you," said Francis.

They passed one of the few women in the camp, squatting in the brush just off the path, urinating beneath the folds of her flowing sundress. She smiled at them as she wiped herself. "Well, yeah, pretty much," said Cleo. "I grew up on the speeches and stories of M L King Jr., Malcolm X, and Mahatma Ghandi. Rosa Parks, The Little Rock Nine, The Freedom Riders—those are my heroes. Muhammad Ali too."

He walked with the ease and confidence of a large ungulate, a moose or a rhino. He wasn't wearing multiple layers of clothing like many of the others, a solution to not having to pack a wardrobe, but he had on baggy jeans that were falling to the crack of his ass, and the same black tank top that he'd worn to the demonstration that day.

"We're nearly there," said Cleo to the two following behind.

It became clear to Francis. "And then along comes Anthony Smith to jump start the call to action?"

Cleo stopped and turned. "You ever hear of Bloody Sunday?" They allowed as how they hadn't. "Figures," he said. "Sunday, March 7, 1965. Six-hundred peaceful demonstrators organized to march from Selma to Montgomery to protest the killing of black civil rights activist Jimmie Lee Jackson by a white police officer. Sound Familiar?"

"Except that Anthony Smith was a drug dealer, not a civil rights activist," said Cale.

Cleo stiffened, his lips pursed. "He was my cousin," he told them, "a proud black man *and* a human being and that makes it a fucking travesty to kill him the way they did."

"Okay, sure, we'll go with that," said Francis.

"So, Bloody Sunday in Montgomery. As the protesters approached the Edmund Pettus Bridge, they were blocked by Alabama state troopers and local police sent by Alabama Governor George Wallace—as you know from history, a notorious bigot and strong opponent of desegregation. That guy was the worst. Refusing to stand down, the protesters moved forward and were viciously beaten and teargassed by police. Dozens hospitalized." They were still stopped in the path, taking time out for this history lesson.

"That was fifty-two years ago and the same shit's going on today. I did my part because I had to and fuck the consequences."

Francis said, "You got a court date, huh? You got a lawyer?"

"'Course I do. Oscar Baylor, the same one who represented Reverend Al Sharpton when he was arrested here." Back in 1999, protesters shut down the Interstate in both directions during rush hour, the flashpoint being the lack of minority contractors and construction workers on the repair of I-70 through North St. Louis. Reverend Al flew in from New York to sit with local activists Erik Vickers and James Buford and 300 others who snarled traffic that day.

"Well, that'll be a fun trial," said Francis. "You'll have to let me know the date, I'll be there."

Cleo just looked at them. "You were there, man. You saw it. Beaten, maced, made to get on our knees. We pay them to protect us, we shouldn't have to be protected from them. Cops stomping and chanting, 'Whose streets? Our Streets!' It was like being in some authoritarian regime, like we were living in some fascist state. You know that's right."

Francis wanted to say that every story has two sides but instead, "Yeah, Cleo, that's right. My sentiments exactly."

They started walking. Again, Cleo stopped and turned. He wasn't done. "Y'all know what you'll be doing on December 20?" he asked.

"Same 'ol same 'ol," said Cale.

"What day of the week is that?" wondered Francis.

"You know what I'll be doing?" said Cleo. "I'll be thinking of my cousin Anthony because that's the day he died. I'll be thinking of him playing with his dog, Ganja. I'll be thinking of him buying snoots for everyone at Big Bob's Snoots, he was generous like that. I'll be thinking of him sweet talkin' his girl, Lawanda, bringin' her presents. So in love, he jus' couldn't leave her be."

Francis and Cale looked at one another. "Well, all right then," said Cale.

The flood wall had stopped further back and you could see the river unobstructed, brown water rushing past on its way to Cairo and Memphis and points south. They came to a clearing off to the side of the path. There, a canvas tipi festooned with all sorts of colorful objects was strung together with rope and bungi cords. Out front, vinyl chairs that looked like they'd been swiped from some auditorium were placed around aluminum wash basins. A man wearing a long embroidered robe or caftan fastened at the waist with a necktie was busy carving a long circular hunk of wood that looked like it might have been a telephone pole.

"*As Salam Alaykom,* Jesus," called Cleo with a whispered aside to Francis and Cale. "He's into multiculturalism." The man looked up, gave a sign of greeting. "I bring visitors, perhaps a foot wash or two."

"Welcome," said Jesus. "Let us talk while I finish. This is the last depiction." They stood around watching him carve something on the pole, no telling what it was. Cleo explained that his friends were looking for information on a young man from the camp who would come to have his feet washed.

"His name was Austin Lambert. We have a picture," offered Francis.

"One thing at a time. Do you like my totem pole?"

"Oh yeah," said Francis. "It's a humdinger. I can see you've put a lot of work in it. What's that there?" He pointed to a relief on the pole, looked like a fat lizard with spikes.

"That's the universe made manifest."

"Oh. Yeah, I see it now. So how will you get it in the ground?"

"You guys will help me."

It was nearly impossible not to like this guy with his long brown hair parted in the middle, colorful beaded headband, and a smile positively beatific. Wisdom and dignity seemed to emanate from him. Francis imagined that meeting the Dalai Lama would be something like meeting Jesus of the Homeless.

With a spade and a pick they dug a deep hole for the pole, but they had no cement to secure it, keep it from wobbling, so they packed it with paving bricks that must have come from nearby Laclede's Landing. The bricks all had an imprint that said ALTON BLOCK. When finished, the pole stood quite straight, maybe fourteen-feet in height, a worthy monolith.

"Yeah, all right," said Francis, wiping his palms on his shorts. "It's done, it's fantastic. Now about Austin Lambert." He went to show the picture, but Jesus held him off.

"First, we wash feet," he said with a flourish.

"Uh, can we do that another day? We still have folks to talk to."

Jesus regarded him. "Unless I wash you, you have no part with me." Francis was starting to like this guy a little less. "I will ready the wash basin. You will remove your boots and socks."

Francis looked to Cale, who shook his head vehemently to say no way. "Bunions, man. I've got bunions. Painful. No one's touching my feet."

Francis sat in a folding chair while Jesus gently moved his hands over Francis' feet. The soapy water barely splashed. It was a massage as much as it was a cleansing, and Francis had to admit that it felt nice. They were communing, Francis felt it, and Jesus was going on about the significance of this lowly task, how, as we walk through the world, some of the world's spiritual filth clings to us, and that needs to be washed away. How he is the one to do it because he is as humble as the dust in the road and only a truly humble person can bring about the right effect.

"But if you're bragging about how humble you are, doesn't that sort of negate your humbleness?" asked Cale.

Jesus looked up from what he was doing. He frowned and waved off the comment.

"Just let the man do his thing," said Cleo.

"Will you get in between my toes?" asked Francis.

Jesus began washing between the toes. "We serve one another in lowliness of heart and mind, seeking to build one another up in humility and love. Part of that humble service is to forgive one another. True greatness in heaven or *Jannah* is attained by those with a servant's heart."

"I just hope I can remember all he's saying," said Francis, "seems important."

Jesus toweled him off with a T-shirt that had a picture of a squat smiling comic figure and said BILLIKEN BASKETBALL. He announced he would now address the question of the missing young man. They moved to a picnic table, the four of them, and sat. "Yes, I know him well. Austin was a disciple," he began. "There was a time he came every day to converse and have me wash his feet. He was very self-examining. It was obvious from the many misgivings he spoke of that he had made some bad decisions in his young life, felt that he had let some people close to him down. I tried to get him to see that these recriminations were holding him back from self-actualization. But he was so fragile mentally, he was stuck on feeling sorry for himself. Walked around in a kind of gloom. Like I say, he visited frequently, but then he stopped coming. Around that time, there was an outbreak of crabs here and that caused all sorts of havoc, maybe he got caught up in that." Jesus folded his hands, he was done.

"That's it?" said Francis. "That's all you've got? An outbreak of pubic parasites?"

"You might try the soup kitchen, Austin was there a lot helping out. The guy that runs it, Jake, he might be able to tell you more."

But when they got to the soup kitchen it was closed, everyone gone. Sign on the blackboard: TOMORROW'S SELECTION: OXTAIL SOUP WITHOUT OXTAIL.

They were saying goodbye, Cleo saying how he's glad he ran into them and maybe they'll meet again. Francis said that was probably a sure thing because they weren't done here yet.

"Just curious," said Cale, "where's your tent? How do you like it here?"

Cleo laughed merrily. "No, man, I don't stay here! I've got a place in the Ville. Live with my auntie and uncle. I'm here to try to find my brother, he's disappeared."

— 8 —

ONE OF THE GREAT REGRETS IN FRANCIS' LIFE had nothing to do with his own actions, but with the archdiocese and that was the closing of St. James The Greater Catholic Church as a viable parish. He had seen other parishes in the City forced to shut their doors, the result of the church having to shell out millions of dollars to pay judgments in civil suits involving priests diddling altar boys, but he never thought it would happen to his parish. The feeling he had about the whole thing could be summed up in the lyrics of that Joni Mitchell song: "Don't it always seem to go that you don't know what you've got 'til it's gone…" He had gone to grade school there. First Communion, confirmation, reconciliation, mass every morning before class. The St. Patrick's Day Parade, the Fall Homecoming Festival, the Lenten fish fries, nothing but good memories. And the church itself, the way a church should be. Built of cut stone quarried from nearby Cheltenham, and situated on the highest ground in Dogtown, there was always a sense of awe upon entering. Inside, the altar so incredibly ornate, the stained glass windows casting colors on the pews, and the statues of Jesus, Mary, and various saints seeming to speak to him during mass when he was receptive to daydreaming. Funny how those likenesses in the church distracted him from the liturgy itself, forty-five minutes of monotone phrases and timeworn actions.

Although the school had closed and St. James was no longer officially a parish, there were still masses held during the week. Monday, Wednesday, Friday 7:30 a.m. Francis and Martha tried to make it to one mass per week. Today being Wednesday they sat in the back where they had sat separately when they first met. Their shared belief in the Catholic faith was the cement in their relationship, they both knew it and never took it for granted. Not to say they wore their Catholicism on their sleeves, flaunting it with showy displays of, say, piety—if that were possible—or reciting the Nicene Creed in a resonant voice as if they were in a play. Or closing their eyes tight and scrunching up their face to make it look like they were praying extra hard. None of that, just quiet in their pew, listening to the priest convey the gospel, recite the sermon, walking up to the altar to take communion. At some point, he would put his arm around her waist. He was very happy to be here with her.

"Body of Christ," spoke the Eucharistic minister, a woman of about fifty with missing teeth.

"Amen," said Martha. "Amen," said Francis. They took the host on their tongues, both old school when it came to the rituals. Take it in your hand and pop it in your mouth, that's not how they were taught. They both went for the communion wine as well, a man in a sad pale blue suit two sizes too big for him holding out the chalice. "Blood of Christ," he said. Amen, the response. She took a sip, he wiped the rim with a cloth. He said the same to Francis, then Francis took a sip.

* * *

"Do you actually feel different after communion?" Martha asked him over coffee and pastries at Coffee Cartel, the place on Tamm where they had first spoke after mass twenty-six years ago. Only then it was called The Urban Oasis.

Francis pondered this. "Yeah, I've never told anyone this, but I get a warm runny feeling down around my solar plexus and it slowly spreads throughout my body until it seems I'm glowing. All my senses seem heightened too. Acute power of smell like a hound dog on the trail of a convict. Hearing, I can hear a mouse fart from a block away."

She made a face, shook her head. "Go on. That doesn't happen. It was a serious question, why make light of it?"

"Don't know," he answered. "It just came to me. You? Do you feel different?"

"Yeah, I do, and we'll leave it at that."

They drank their coffee and ate their croissants with cream cheese and preserves.

Finally, he said, "I did think it was coincidental that Fr. Gillis' sermon was about beggars and the homeless when I spent much of the day yesterday in a—"

"Homeless camp. I thought about that too," she said. "It was taken from Matthew and I thought it was powerful. I can recap if you like.

Father said that he can't imagine having to beg to survive. It has to be an absolutely demoralizing thing to do. Begging is admitting that you have nothing to trade for what you need. You're completely at the mercy of the person you're begging from. We pray that we'll never be homeless, but the truth is that we are beggars when it comes to our relationship with God. We have nothing to offer Him, we have nothing of value to trade. All we can do is kneel before Him and beg, and when we do, we're like the true down-and-out indigent and yet we know that Jesus feeds us all we need, even if they seem like crumbs."

"Good recap," Francis said, then leaned into her across the table. "You know what I was thinking as he said all that? I was thinking if I should be ashamed at looking at the homeless in quite another light, looking at them living in squalor and expecting handouts and thinking why don't you just pull yourselves together and get a job?"

She said, "I think it's easy to see it that way, that this welfare attitude is bringing down society. People start living off the charity of all these agencies that want to help it's nearly impossible to get them back in the workforce. They're like, why bother? I can make just as much or more with my hand out."

"It's a sad state of things. A lot of those people I saw yesterday I think have just given up on ever trying to get ahead. They found a place where they can just roll over and play dead. Just exist, you know? Nothing beyond eat, sleep, smoke, drink, fart."

She gazed at him with those enchanting brown eyes that could really hold you. "Yeah, and apparently this has been going on since Jesus was a carpenter, literally. The down and outs, how to deal with them. You think about it, the Bible has a lot to say about the poor, the destitute. It tells us that we are supposed to help them out, not look down on them."

"The Christian thing to do, right?"

"Yeah, it's not easy to show that attitude but it's sort of a cornerstone of the faith, help those less well off than you. Even the bum panhandling in the street."

Francis guffawed. "Like you give money to beggars? I've never seen that."

"I've thought about it, but the light turned green before I could dig into my purse. But that's not the point. The New Testament tells us we should treat the homeless with sympathy and respect, equality too. It says so in Luke, I can show you."

Oh, she was up on her Bible verses. More than anyone he knew, she could quote the scriptures. From Abraham to Zebediah, she could tell you who they were, what they said, what they did. He loved that about her. "It goes 'But when you give a feast, invite the poor, the crippled, the blind, and you will be blessed, because they cannot repay you.' You hear that? You are blessed because they *cannot* repay you."

He threw up his hands in surrender. "Okay, okay, you win. From now on, I'll look at the pathetic, grubby population of Hopeville with a sweeter disposition—and if I'm really nice to them, give them the things they demand, I mean, ask for, then I'm a shoe-in to heaven, right?"

"That's assuming far too much."

"Did I tell you that a guy named Jesus washed my feet?"

They were getting ready to go their separate ways, into the workaday world. She put her hand on his arm, said, "We had a situation at work yesterday during lunch. A man came in and caused a scene, a spurned lover of one of the servers. Young guy, very brash, he wanted to try to convince her that he was the right guy for her, I mean, then and there during the rush. It was ugly, Francis. She's trying to tell him to leave and he's just getting more stubborn, saying they're going to have it out right now. The diners are all looking, wondering what's next. Marco went to deal with it and he did the best he could. He told the server to go in the kitchen and wait there. He ushered the heckler to the door, you know, had him by the arm. What do you call that? Frog-marched him. Told him don't come back, told him firmly—I heard it, the menace in his voice. But I think he will come back because I don't think he cares one tiny bit what happens. He's in that place of eternal gloom where all he can think is that he's got to get his former sweetheart back and some-how doesn't realize there's not a chance of that happening."

Francis made a low chuckle. "Obstinate, likely the least attrac-tive trait in a human being. Tell you what, tell the server—what's her name?"

"Heather."

"Tell Heather to go to the adult abuse office in the Civil Courts building and take out an order of protection on this guy. Do it today, this morning. I'll serve it free of charge. Then, if he does come back the police will deal with it and not Marco." Marco was her younger brother, manager of the restaurant, a bit of a hothead although he had to curb that tendency because Pastori's had been awarded a Michelin Star. They had to keep up appearances.

"That's a good plan, I'll get right on it." She kissed him goodbye and they parted for the day.

— 9 —

FRANCIS LOVED THE EARLY MORNING WITH ALL ITS PROMISE. Fact, that was one of his mottoes, Anything Can Happen, and nothing could be truer. He could have some loose plan that involved serving papers over in Illinois when suddenly there's a phone call that he's got to pick up an emergency TRO—temporary restraining order—and make haste to some hamlet in Franklin County. What happens when you're on call with twenty-some lawyers and each one of them thinks he or she is your priority. Nevertheless, the morning was the best time of day, his mind clear and sharp, motivation high, eager to get into it. He had his coffee, his car radio, his Garmin, the window open, the breeze on his face. Always solo. No one riding herd over him. He was a latter-day bounty hunter, collecting a premium for each paper served. As long as I can drive a car and knock on doors I'll keep it up, what he told people.

This morning he called Cale on his cell and they divvied up the jobs. "Can you get by Myers Solomon to pick up two subpoenas, one going to Mercy South and one to a school somewhere in South County? Yeah, depo subpoenas, easy. Okay, next go to Legal Services on Forest Park. Talk to Rita the receptionist. She should have one or two summonses going not sure where. Call me when you're done. I'll be going up to Troy in Lincoln County, three subpoenas there and a summons in St. Charles on the way back. Yeah, right, we've both got our work cut out for us."

He listened for a minute as Cale recounted some hairy experience with serving a construction worker on the job. The guy took a swing at him. Cale kicked him in the knee and got the hell out of there before his buddies could grab him. "Be careful," said Francis, "be super careful. Just walk away from any trouble, it's not worth engaging these people. Once they're served that's all that matters, you're done. They can curse your back as you're leaving the scene. Well, I don't know, when do *you* want to go back to the homeless camp? It's so uplifting I don't see how we can stay away. It's true, we're not done there. How about tomorrow, around ten-thirty, I'd like to get there when the soup guy is setting up."

* * *

Okay, he got the subpoenas served in Troy, one to a transmission repair shop, one to a hardware store, and one to a residence that he thought would be a place of business. All three papers were concerning a divorce, the lawyer wanting payroll records on the opposing party, the soon-to-be ex, his former places of employment. The last one was directed to a business, Apex Metal Finishing. The lawyer's paralegal had looked on the Secretary of State homepage and gotten not the address of the plant but that of the registered agent, which happened to be a home nestled in some quiet subdivision. Fortunately, the registered agent/owner of the company was still home or he would have had to track him down or come back another day and catch him home. Luck played a big role in this business. Success or failure was largely attributed to timing and luck. You drive sixty miles to knock on a door out in the boonies, not knowing one pertinent thing about the person you hope to serve. You knock for ten minutes because whoever may be in there could be a sound sleeper or on the can or otherwise indisposed. No answer. You're about to leave and the party pulls into the driveway. Served. Or it happened that you left and a minute later the party pulls in. Unserved. Chance. Luck pulling the strings.

The job in St. Charles County was quite interesting, a houseboat on a private marina situated on the backwaters of the Mississippi. Great long sheds housing boat slips, traffic going in and out, amenities such as sandwiches, beer, ice, fuel, engine repair available on site. The slipholders enjoying life, partying in and on their floating boxes, music playing, grills fired up. Francis was amazed that this nautical enclave existed only fifteen miles from the grungy streets of St. Louis. This was his second attempt on Ralph Casey, an over-the-road trucker who had a berth in this marina but apparently was rarely here. The woman in the adjacent slip, all bangles and piercings, gave a crooked smile, said, "You police? What'd he do now? Good luck catching him."

But now he had a phone number, Ralph's cell. He rarely called those people he was trying to serve, tip them off to where they would avoid him if they saw him coming. But this was a divorce and a lot of guys are okay with getting divorce papers. He had called twice already, left messages. He called again now. Ralph answered.

"Yo."

"Hey, Mr. Casey, this is the process server been trying to reach you for a while. I've got your divorce papers and I'm here at the marina now."

Silence. Then something that sounded like gargling. "She finally decided to go through with it, uh?"

"Yup. She got a lawyer and that lawyer hired me to serve you with these papers. How about it? You gonna be around?"

He could hear the sounds of the road rushing past an open window on the semi. Again silence, three-four beats. "I'm in Virginia now, back middle of next week. I've got your number, I'll call when I get there. That work?"

"I guess it will have to. Give me as much advance notice as you can, I cover a lot of territory."

"Okay, all right. So...what happens if you don't get to serve me?"

"Well, I still get paid for trying, but the divorce doesn't go through until you're served."

"Hmm, so I could rack up a hell of a bill by avoiding you? A bill that dear sweet Gladys will have to pay? I might want to go that route, I mean, she certainly deserves it. Life's a bitch and then you marry one, you know?"

Francis cleared his throat. "Nah, you don't want to do that, just take your papers like a man."

Ralph laughed raucously. "Take my papers like a man! That's a good one! I like you. See you next week." Click.

He stopped at the Mississippi Mud Shack on the way out. "I'll have a Dr. Pepper and a marina dog," he told the clerk at the register.

She seemed to be sizing him up. "Special today is catfish nuggets, a dozen for a buck ninety-five."

He made a face. "Yuck."

"You don't like the taste, no problem, they make good bait."

— 10 —

Ed Gannon was in an argument with James McNeary over the alcohol content of the various beers they drank. Ed was saying that most of the standard Anheuser-Busch brews were down in the low four percent range. "Your Busch Light, Michelob Light, Bud Light, Busch—all between four point ten and four point thirty. But here's something you may not believe. Guinness is right there with 'em at four point two."

"You're right," said McNeary, studying his half-downed pint of stout, "I don't believe it. How can I ever believe that when I can drink a dozen Busch and not get as soused as I would drinking five Guinness? Even the taste is heavy, no way it's a lightweight beer in the same class as Busch Light or Bud Light."

"You got a smart phone? Google it, you'll see I'm right."

"No thanks," said McNeary. "I don't want to be proven wrong. I want to go right ahead and keep thinking that my favorite beer has some punch to it."

"Guinness is a stout not a beer."

"There ya go quibbling again."

"I'm quite the quibbler," said Ed Gannon.

Francis walked up with a pint of Busch, white foamy collar, compliments of Tommy. "Some of these microbreweries and their so-called craft beers, some of them have alcohol content approaching that of wine," he offered. "Eight-nine-even ten percent. They have weird names too."

"Yeah," said McNeary, "more and more of these craft breweries opening up."

"And closing just as fast," said Ed Gannon, "some of them anyway. I mean, honestly, how do they hope to stay in business when they're offering some exotic brew you never heard of at a steep price—six-seven bucks a pint—and all it does is give you a headache."

"Let's drink to that," said Francis, and they clinked glasses.

"How's life in the trenches, Francis?' asked McNeary for Francis sometimes had some funny story to tell.

"It's a grind," he said, "but an interesting one. The other day I served a woman who came to the door in bra and panties. I must've woke her up. I'm an early morning guy."

"Hoo boy!" said Ed Gannon. "She invite you in?"

"Those days are done for me," said Francis. "Besides, she couldn't hold a candle to Martha. I was content just to get a look."

"The panties," pursued Gannon. "What color?"

"Hmm, you know, I think they were a teal, maybe turquoise. They had a mermaid on the front."

"Little black pubes poking out the sides?"

"Jesus, Ed. Say, look at that, would ya?" McNeary pointed to the TV at the end of the bar. A newscast was showing a group of blacks walking through a shopping center, shouting and holding signs, people with shopping bags pressed against the walls, frightened looks on their faces. The headline read PROTESTERS INVADE GALLERIA — STOCKLEY UNREST CONTINUES. Francis wondered if Cleo was there among them.

"Jesus Christ, when's it gonna end?" asked Rory Denigan who had wandered over.

"No time soon," replied Ed Gannon. "Plenty of time on their hands for monkey business, they got no jobs to go to."

"Monkey business is right," said Ted Pollack who'd also dropped in. "I'd like to see 'em pull that shit here in Dogtown. Give 'em a good spanking and send 'em cryin' back to their mamas, we would, eh?"

"Fuckin' A right!" several chimed in.

The group was getting worked up over this, saying how people were afraid to go out and how they weren't going to let a bunch of spooks intimidate them, no way, when the newscast moved on to another scene, a press conference on the steps of the Civil Courts. A stout fiery-eyed black man with a Homburg was addressing a sizable crowd, several other topcoats behind him. The sound on the TV was turned off but you could see him gesticulating dramatically, cheeks puffing, vocalizing with passion and verve, getting his point across to be sure. The kind of man you'd want to convince the hangman it wasn't your time yet. His message? The caption at the bottom of the screen read REV. J.B. ROBINSON AND OTHER CIVIC LEADERS CALL FOR SUING THE CITY and the Police Board Over Police Brutality During Stockley Protests. Latest Count: 31 Civilians Injured. A related caption said the Reverent J.B. Robinson was bishop of the Wesleyan AME Church in North St. Louis. AME stood for African Methodist Episcopal with headquarters in Nashville and an aggregate congregation upwards of three million. Their churches were spread all over St. Louis but were mostly in the City.

"How 'bout it, Francis," from Ted Pollack, "you lookin' for a piece of that action? You were there, sure as shit. Any day now, you'll be getting that letter from the law firm, embossed stationery, 'Sign here, brother, join the class action lawsuit, plenty for everyone.'"

Francis made a show of draining his glass, then belched. "That letter would go right into the circular file, don't want any part of it." From the corner of his eye he saw a figure walking his way. He turned to look. A young woman, pretty, with long wavy auburn hair and a healthy complexion. Green eyes, full lips and nice teeth. She wasn't smiling though, there was a seriousness about her. The strap of a purse crossed her chest and lay on a cotton T between sizable breasts. She had one hand behind her back obviously holding something. Looking right at him. An assassin?

"Are you Mr. Lenihan?" she asked.

"The one and only."

"Oh good, Martha told me I'd find you here. I'm Heather…from the restaurant?"

"Oh, sure," he said. "And you have something for me?"

"Right here," and she brought her hand around and handed him the protection order, rolled up.

He took it, unrolled it, glanced at it. "You want a drink? Let's sit and talk for a minute." The respondent's name was Cary Finch and he lived in South City. Francis drilled her with the standard questions: Where does he work, who does he live with, what car does he drive. A description and the times he's most likely to be home. The only thing that surprised him: this Cary Finch was younger than her, barely out of his teens.

"It was just one of those things," she explained. "I met him at a rave and he seemed like such a cool guy. We hung out all night, got nasty in the mosh pit, drank too much, um, took some ecstasy, you know, ended up in his apartment." She shrugged. "I left around noon, thought that was the end of it."

"He's fixated on you."

"That's one way to put it, he's convinced that I'm his soul mate or some such crap. He won't let me be. I'm really hoping you can help."

"He's as good as served," Francis said. "I'll let you know when that happens and once he's served he's supposed to stay away from you until the court date, which I see is October 13. If he shows up to court, he gets a chance to tell the judge his side of the story. Then the judge will make a decision whether the protection order will be in effect. If he doesn't show in court, the protection order automatically goes through."

"This scares me," she admitted, "because I don't know him hardly at all and I don't know what he's capable of."

He looked at her intently. "You've got a good head on your shoulders, you can deal with this. And if he does come around your work or your residence—does he know where you live?"

"I think so."

"If he comes around your work or your home after he's been served, you call the police. You will take a copy of the order and carry it with you and you will show it to the cops when they arrive. Got it?"

"Can I use my pepper spray?"

He gave a wink. "Point blank on the eyeballs if need be."

—II—

THIS TIME THEY CAME BEARING GIFTS, a sack of goodies that needy people might slaver over, treats such as candy bars, peanuts, cigarettes, chewing gum, beef jerky, little bottles of airline booze. It was an overcast day, presently around sixty with rain in the forecast. The soup shack wasn't open yet so they walked along the main thoroughfare, a dirt path with tents on both sides, busted shopping carts, fast food wrappers, a sign that read EASY STREET. There was virtually no pedestrian traffic, there being no attractions in the camp and people not inclined to take a morning stroll merely to invigorate. They found a man and a woman sitting in chairs just outside their tent. It was Cale's idea to try a slightly different approach. Instead of Have you seen this guy? Do you remember him? Now it would be: His brother's looking for him, got a job waiting. But that didn't produce results either.

They may have talked with eight or nine folks, asking about Austin Lambert and also for Charlie Spinner, the former Washington University prof who gave Dr. Lambert information about Austin's demise. One person said that Charlie had moved on to a group home in South City, at least that's what he heard. "No one keeps tabs on no one around here," he announced with finality.

A couple hours before, Francis had gone to the home of Cary Finch and served him personally with the protection order. Finch was a biracial kid with close-cropped black hair, the scruff of a goatee on his chin, a gold stud earring glinting from his left ear, the build of a gym rat and body language that said Try me. He didn't like being served, not at all, and he made noises that this wasn't going to change anything. Francis looked him in the eye and warned that he could be in serious trouble if he violated the order. Finch sneered, said, "Yeah, we'll see about that, won't we?"

Francis walked off muttering something about the foolhardiness of youth.

They doubled back and saw the soup man setting up along with a helper. "Hey," said Francis. The man was carrying a box that rattled with something inside. He set it on a large folding table, turned and looked. He nodded hello, barely. "I see you're busy," Francis said, "just want to talk for a minute. Okay with you?"

"May-may-may-may-maybe later. Not, uh, na-na not now," the voice somewhat nasal and tremulous.

Francis continued as if he hadn't heard that. He brought out the photo, shoved it under his nose. "Look here, we're asking around for this guy, name of Austin. Seems to have disappeared, his family is worried sick about him."

The man looked like he was dressed for safari with khaki cargo pants, fishing vest with lots of pockets and an Aussie bush hat. Average height with curly brown hair and brown eyes. Full mouth that looked like it knew how to pout. Pudgy. He had a mole or blemish high on his cheek that reminded Francis of De Niro, but other than that he was nothing like De Niro. He took the picture and held it out, turning it this way and that, pretending to study it. "Yes, yes, he's been here, buh-buh-buh-buh not lately." He screwed his eyes tight when stuttering like he was concentrating at fixing it.

"Okay," said Cale, "so when's the last time you actually saw him?" They still did not know his name other than Jake, as Jesus had said, but they had spoken earlier and agreed that they wanted to see if this guy knew that Austin had died. Francis asserted that the best way to obtain information is to ask directly, but in this situation where almost everyone is cagey let's leave it open and see what blanks get filled in.

The man said in his halting staccato speech that Austin did come around, he remembered now that he liked the potato and cabbage soup with chives.

Said Francis, "We heard he was your helper, that right?"

The soup man regarded them in silence. Then, "Who-who-who—"

"Is there an owl around here?" It was the helper, an older shabbily dressed man looked like he crawled out of a sewer. He laughed merrily, pointing his finger at the speaker, who seemed mortified. "Oh, come on, Jacob," he said, "that was funny."

Jacob said, "Roland, would you p-p-please get the rest of the provisions from the RV?" For whatever reason he hardly stuttered when he spoke to the help. He looked to Francis and Cale. "I'd li-li-like t-t-t-t to…know who I am talking to."

"We're working for the family," said Cale, "looking into this young man's whereabouts. So again, was he a helper like your pal Roland here?"

"Yes, he would sometimes help out cleaning up around the area af-aft-after the people were through. I duh-duh-duh…don't remember asking him to do this, he just d-d-did it to be nice."

"Were you two friends?"

"No, I wuh-wuh-wouldn't say tha-that." His demeanor growing cautious, getting a little testy now. "I won't g-g-get personally involved with the-the-the-cli-cli-cli—" He stopped. It was too much, the stutter anxiety had seized his larynx. Normally, his stubborn self would complete the sentence no matter how long it took, but these guys were really bugging him.

"That's what they are, clients?"

Jacob shook his head in frustration. "Clients, cuh-cuh-stomers, diners, whatever you like. Uh, excuse me, I have to get this p-p-place ready."

They watched as he put on a white chef hat and went to work at a portable propane stove, pouring ready-made soup into pots to be warmed and served. The helper, Roland, arranging Styrofoam bowls and plastic spoons on a folding table, placing everything just right. Jacob seemed quite content in his element, stirring and fussing with burners, adding this or that seasoning.

"What is it?" wondered Cale. "The soup of the day."

"Ham and bean," said Roland with pride.

"Do we get a bowl?"

"Are you homeless? You wouldn't want to deprive one of the deserving, would you?"

"No, we would not," said Francis. "My friend is joking. So, Jake—you go by Jake or Jacob?—just curious. You're not homeless. Have you been homeless? Why do you do this?"

Jacob looked up from his task. "Uh, m-m-make things a lit-lit-little easier, that's all. Give them something to look forward to. Why not? They've hit buh-buh-bottom, meh-many of them."

"Very altruistic of you," replied Francis. Then to Cale, side of the mouth, "He's a saint. This place is a passion play. We've got Jesus at one end and St. Jacob at the other."

"With all sinners in between," added Cale.

Jacob Vorhof watched them go.

Leaving Jacob they roamed around hoping to rustle up some more helpful intel. Francis had small hopes of running into Cleo again, for he probably had come to some sort of conclusion about his missing brother. Cale was pilfering from the sack of goodies and had made short work of a bag of trail mix and a Snickers. They came upon two men walking along the path, one white and one black, both in their twenties. They were in good spirits because they were about to head out to their day jobs, panhandling on busy city street corners.

"I hope that retard isn't in my spot when I get there," said the white guy to the other. "I'll kick his ass into next week."

"Betcha five bucks I net more'n you," said the black guy.

"No siree, I ain't gonna take that bet. You look so pathetic, like a mongrel dog that's been starved and beaten half to death, you're bound to clean up."

A short silence between them, and then, "Woke up this morning an' my mess kit was gone, some fucking asshole. This place pretty much sucks, don't you think?"

"Yeah," agreed the black guy, "we knew that coming here, right? But the level of suck isn't as bad as those other places—Reverend Larry Rice's joint, the Salvation Army, they got all these fucking rules."

"Ain't no rules here—"

"Except watch your ass."

"And your shit."

They came to a face-off on the path, a pregnant moment, each set of travelers waiting for someone to start something. Francis was about to make his spiel when the white guy, seedy and unshaven, exclaimed, "Hey, I know you," meaning Francis. "You're the guy served me papers for child support, 'member?"

A spark went off in Francis' brain. He snapped his fingers. "Yeah I remember. That was in Arnold, wasn't it? About a year back?"

"Yeah, except it was Imperial, not Arnold. I made you work for your money didn't I? You were sitting in your car out front like a junior G-Man, staking me out. I was watching all the while through the window. It was kinda fun. Then, one day, you parked more out of sight and you finally caught me driving up. I didn't see you until it was too late." He grinned big. "Fair and square, man. I don't hold a grudge." He put out his hand. "James Robb."

Francis nodded. "I remember the name. I left my card on your door, didn't realize it would make the job that much harder."

"Oh yeah, you shouldn't have tipped me off. There was a lot to lose if I got served. And I did lose it, that's how I ended up here."

They got around to showing the picture of Austin. "Yeah, I knew him," confirmed James Robb, "we were buds. Shame he passed, but he was having troubles here."

"How so?"

A grave look came over Robb. "Austin was being bothered by someone here, the guy doesn't live here but he comes here and he glommed on to Austin and wouldn't let him alone, always trying to get him to go somewhere, do things maybe he didn't wanna do. It messed with him to the point where he thought about getting a restraining order. That card you put on my door? I had that in my wallet. I gave it to Austin, said, If you do get a restraining order, call this guy, he's like a tick on a bloodhound or whatever that saying is. He'll serve it for you."

Francis looked at Cale. Cale nodded, said, "Well, there's one mystery solved."

Francis flushing with suspense. "An OP huh? Who's the offender? Is he here? Can you point him out?"

James Robb ran his tongue over his lips. "Yeah, you know the soup kitchen? The guy who runs that, he's the one. That stuttering bastard."

* * *

Jacob Vorhof had watched the two men walk off with relief. They made him nervous with their probing questions about Austin as if he were still around. Did they not know he was late or were they only pretending not to know. Hmm. Austin had served his purpose and took the honorable way out, that's all that need be said about him. But he had a feeling those two weren't done with him, the way they came on, the way they left things. And sure enough, he looked down the path off in the distance and saw them returning.

There was a small line at the open window for soup, four men and a woman holding flimsy bowls. Anticipating sustenance, looking forward to that contented feeling in their bellies. "Roland," he said, "I need you to take over. You're up to that, aren't you? Just remember, only two ladles per person and one roll. I'll be in the vicinity, but I'll be gone for maybe an hour."

"Sure thing, boss. Can I call you if something comes up?"

"Ah, no, let's have radio silence. Whatever it is can wait for an hour."

He was irritated at having been put out, at having to vacate the soup stand to avoid more idiotic questions by those two buffoons. They had no authority over him, he could just say buzz off. But that would seem suspicious, wouldn't it, like why is he not being totally forthcoming? The whole thing was giving him a headache.

He made for the Winnebago and once there looked all around before unlocking the door and entering. He went to his fold-out bed, fluffed up the pillows, stacked them so his head was elevated, and lay down. He reached for his book nearby, opened it at the bookmark, and began to pass the time by reading. At the rate he was going, he would finish this delectable narrative by tomorrow. He was devouring the words, the chapters, and all the while learning things that would come in handy. *The Big Book Of Serial Killers*, the title, by Jack Rosewood. It had just come out. He'd seen it at that hippie bookstore on Euclid and once he read the words on the back cover he had to buy it. "There is little more terrifying than those who hunt, stalk and snatch their prey under the cloak of darkness. These hunters search not for animals, but for the touch, taste, and empowerment of human flesh. They are cannibals, vampires and monsters, and they walk among us."

He shifted a bit to make himself more comfortable. Let them knock, he thought, they can't know for sure I'm in here. I am not budging from this spot.

"Brace yourself, Martha."

She grabbed the headboard, laughed into the pillow. "This good?" she said. "Hope so, because I'm ready to be ravished."

It was 5:30 on a Thursday morning. When it came to making love they were both morning people. It wasn't exactly spontaneous either, not after twenty-four years of marriage. They had both brushed their teeth beforehand. He was over her, in the push-up position, all systems go. She was spread-eagled, breasts flopped over to the sides, dark patch of glistening pubic hair like a welcome mat. He leaned down to kiss her and at the same time eased himself into her. "Well, hello sailor," she said.

They writhed and squirmed and undulated. They knocked things off the nightstand. She moaned and he grunted. This went on for a good fourteen minutes and when it was done they shuddered. She had made coffee beforehand and now they lay in bed drinking it.

"This is nice," she said.

"Good way to start the day."

"Yeah, but it's also nice because I don't have to worry about birth control or getting pregnant. No worries, more satisfaction."

He didn't know what to say, except, "Hmm."

"I mean, that is one good thing, maybe the *only* good thing about turning fifty. Menopause, an end to the curse."

"I think it's so funny you call it that, like you come from a family of Gypsies."

"Close. We Italian women have colorful names for many things. The curse gets the point across far better than period. Period is neutral-sounding, like you're not invested in the thing. Curse is so biased that there's no doubt what you're referring to is nothing but a nuisance."

"Point taken, but it still cracks me up."

"Oh I forgot to tell you. That guy, the *cattivo ragazzo* came by yesterday, but he didn't come in. He only stood outside on the sidewalk staring into the restaurant like some sick pervert. You said you served him."

Francis sat up. "I did, yesterday morning. He's testing the system, daring someone to call him out. He's an idiot. If he read the order he'd know it says he must stay five-hundred feet away from her, Heather, until the court date and once the judge rules it'll likely be the same afterward for up to year. Not just five-hundred feet distance but no phone calls, no letters, no texts, no looking, no following her around, no thinking about her. Just let her be."

"How do we handle this?"

"I don't want it to escalate. I know a cop over in the Second, Lauria. I'll go talk with him. Tell him what's going on, give him a heads up so if it happens again, you call him."

* * *

That morning Francis found himself near South Patrol on Sublette. He parked in the small parking lot and went through the big doors to the service counter with the bulletproof glass. He asked for Officer Ed Lauria. The desk sergeant said that he'd gotten off shift about an hour ago but he still may be here writing up reports. Two minutes later a side door to the lobby opened and Lauria stepped out. His uniform was slightly crumpled and you could see the outline of the Kevlar vest beneath it. He was early-forties, short in stature, maybe five-four, stocky, with expressive hazel eyes, black curly hair and a scar that ran parallel to one eyebrow.

"Hey, Francis, good to see your face. How's everything?" He put out a paw, Francis shook it.

"Hey, Ed. It's been a while, huh? Not since that mess with the disgruntled renter over on Oleatha. Sure glad you came to the rescue on that one."

It had been two years ago, Francis was serving an eviction notice to the occupant of an apartment in a two-story flat on a quiet residential street. A tenant from hell, the guy hadn't paid rent in five months. No response to his knocking and since the paper was POST OR SERVE he went to his car to get duct tape and a folding knife. He had just taped the summons to the occupant's door and was about to photograph it with his phone when said occupant burst out with an eight-inch carving knife, waving it around with a wild gleam in his eye, promising to cut Francis and anyone else who would try to make him leave.

You better believe I'll use this, he swore.

Okay, okay, said Francis, have it your way. I'm out of here, and he began to back up as the irate prick scowled at him while uttering threats of castration. Of course, as soon as Francis was out of sight he called 911 and a pair of officers on duty soon arrived. One of those officers was Ed Lauria. The raving tenant was subdued in no time and taken to the station, but not before Francis had a chance to thank the officers profusely. Since then he had seen Ed Lauria around the neighborhood, at the grocery store, the Columbus Day parade on The Hill. They were friendly, if not friends.

Though Ed Lauria was fifteen years Francis' junior, he was aware of his reputation as an intrepid process server and his involvement in the investigation of the murder of a Jeff Co woman in the early nineties, a case which was never resolved because the prime suspect disappeared without a trace. Aware also of Francis' role in rescuing the murdered woman's daughter who was abducted from Francis' front porch in Dogtown. Francis and his partner pursued them to a horse barn in DeSoto, where they surprised the pair who were torturing her. There was a standoff and then an old-fashioned shoot out and the partner had his foot blown off by a shotgun. That case was never resolved either because the abductor escaped on horseback and was killed the next morning by a hunter who mistook him for a deer.

"Yeah, that one turned out all right, didn't it?" said Lauria. "So what's up now? There a problem?"

Francis related the events surrounding Cary Finch and expressed concern that the situation could blow up.

Lauria frowned mightily. "That's your wife's family's place, right? A very nice place with excellent food. I eat there occasionally, love the Fiorentina with asparagus. I can't have one of my favorite restaurants compromised, worried about some menacing shitbum showing up. No, if he does that again, drops by to intimidate or even decides to enter the place, you call me immediately. I'll give you my cell."

"That's great, Ed, that's what I was hoping for."

"Give him a little guidance, right?" Lauria gave a wink. "Some of these youngsters seem to have lost their compass, yeah?"

Jacob Markheim Vorhof grew up in a toney neighborhood in Town & Country, the only child of parents who doted on him to the point of spoiling him beyond hope. As a youngster he took an interest in painting and sculpting and art in general so his parents set up a little studio for him in the back of the house. They showered him with paint sets, canvases, brushes, modeling clay, and a personalized apron with his name embroidered on the front for just the right effete look. "Isn't he just darling?" his mother would say, "our little arteest." An art student recruited from a nearby university would drop by once a week and give lessons. Anything little Jacob would produce would promptly be framed and put on the wall. He would eventually attend the prestigious Kansas City Art Institute and make his mark as a mediocre student artist.

He attended exclusive private schools and soon the speech impediment became apparent. It began as a stammer and evolved into a stutter that was quite onerous both to young Jacob and his parents. Of course, he began speech therapy and that helped if only due to the assurances from the therapist, a cheerful young woman named Monika Hapsberger, that he was not alone. There were thousands of speech-challenged people, maybe millions, who either overcame the problem or learned to lead happy lives despite it. Elvis Presley, Andrew Lloyd Webber, Carly Simon, Tiger Woods, Britain's King George VI—stutterers! Success stories who refused to let their handicap get the better of them! He needn't be ashamed or embarrassed. His tongue wasn't taking directions from his brain, she told him, maybe there was something haywire in there. They would figure it out.

Having a stutter can be really debilitating, Monika knew, and she was very sympathetic toward her young student, for she herself had been plagued with a pesky sibilant S that took years of practice to overcome. She saw also that he had his days, days when he hardly stuttered at all, days when he had trouble with 'P's, days when he had trouble with 'S's, and most days when he had trouble with 'CH' words like cherry or chicken or Chattanooga and she encouraged him to stay away from them. Instead of chicken he could say pullet and so on.

Monika admired him in that he would not give up in mid-sentence because of hurdles in his speech. No, he would doggedly continue the recitation whatever it was, a simple declarative sentence or a poem by Emily Dickenson, until he got the word out. He was not one to allow his thoughts to be trapped inside. Of course, he was always more fluent when with her. She made him feel at ease. Out in the uncertain world of every day life, with his parents at the supermarket, the mall, the art museum, the zoo, it was a different story. When he became the least anxious about anything, he could be transformed into a babbling nit-wit—at least that's how he thought others perceived him.

She had him singing and it was true, when a stutterer would sing the stutter vanished. She had him singing selections from *Les Miserables*, *West Side Story*. He loved the lyrics from "The Quest," that inspiring ballad heard in the musical *Man Of La Mancha*: "To dream the impossible dream, To fight the unbeatable foe, To bear with unbearable sorrow, To run where the brave dare not go." He imagined himself as the character of that song, surmounting the daunting trials of life or at least trying with unwavering determination.

And that was fun and all, but the non-singing stutter was stubborn and looked as though it was there for the duration. It became clear to him that if he wanted to communicate effectively he was going to have to sing. By now, he was thirteen and he had a hard time imagining expressing himself as if he were in a musical. Asking for the simplest things, talking to friends if he had any, asking a girl out to a movie if he knew a girl to ask, basic everyday discourse sabotaged by a bad connection in his nervous system.

So, he simply resigned himself to the situation and tried his best not to be too self-conscious about it and to not let it destroy his confidence, and that wasn't going to happen because he had a surplus of that. A Vorhof would never think of himself as anything but the best, so his parents said.

Life went on and he was sheltered from the throng of base humanity that lie beyond the iron gates at the foot of their driveway. He liked the kitchen, enjoyed making savory dishes, following recipes in cookbooks verbatim. Of course, he had cute customized aprons for that pastime too. Then he took an interest in insects. He had discovered anthills in the far reaches of his backyard and their industry fascinated him. One day he found a June bug. He tore off a couple of its legs and dropped the hapless creature into the ant metropolis. He watched, enthralled, as they swarmed it, the June bug writhing on its back. What fun! He went looking for more creatures to sacrifice.

There was a girl, once upon a time, a fairy princess named Claudette whom he met at a birthday party for a kid in the neighborhood. He was on the cusp of puberty with hormones raging. She was the most beautiful thing he'd ever seen. And he couldn't believe his luck, for she treated him kindly in spite of his speech defect, never looking away in embarrassment as she heard his uncooperative tongue mangle the syllables. They sat at a table and had cake and ice cream. They laughed at silly things. She was an only child like him. Her father was a plumber, her mother cleaned houses with a team of maids. She wasn't a local, the family lived in Overland, a blue collar suburb. They were related to the family throwing the party. They exchanged addresses and phone numbers.

Over the next month, he called her. They talked for hours, she telling about the meat shoots at the VFW Halls and Rod and Gun Clubs that she went to with her grandfather on Sunday afternoons. He going on about the current exhibit at the art museum. He penned love letters that he agonized over, every word carefully considered. And then he stopped writing, her calls went unanswered. Change of heart. She could have her fried baloney sandwiches, her meat shoots. It was all too obvious: he was entitled, she wasn't. She was low class and always would be.

One day they took a ride into the city. It was just before Christmas and they were going to the Fox Theater to see the *Nutcracker*. As they sat on the exit ramp of Highway 40, waiting to turn on to Grand Avenue, his mother indicated a forlorn figure, a beggar, classic in attire and demeanor. He held a sign that said HOMELESS ANYTHING HELP PLEES! And he was walking along, stopping at each car, fixing the passengers with sad eyes. "How hideous, how horribly hideous!" said his mother, stiffening as the man drew near. "He is asking for handouts. This man who is perfectly able to work and fend for himself."

"How do you know this mother?" asked Jacob, truly curious.

"Look at him," she said, "look at those shifty eyes, the bad posture, the shabby clothes. Has he no self-respect? Does he care that he is ruining our evening with his wretched presence? I should think not. And is he grateful if someone hands him a dollar?—no, he expects it! And if they do not comply with his beggarly wishes, he curses them. Look! He is doing that right now, under his breath. You see his lips moving?"

Jacob looked. It was hard to tell.

His mother, Corinne, went on. "Do you know what I would like? I would like to gather them all up and send them to a remote island, what they used to do with lepers."

"There's an idea," said his father, Lawson, who would not look at the panhandler either.

"But won't more come and take their place?" asked Jacob.

"Not if you're diligent about rounding them up," said mother.

That exchange stayed with Jacob, he ruminated on it for the longest. His mother loathes the mendicants, he should too. It was easy and required no more thought than dropping a live beetle onto an anthill. And it was perfect. Jacob's mother, and by extension Jacob himself, needed a class of people whom they could tear down and despise. As he grew older and the psychosis set in, he held a special place in his black heart for the homeless and those who coddle them.

— 14 —

CALE TWOHEY FELT LIKE SHIT. HIS BRAIN THROBBED WITH PAIN, his tongue felt strange and foreign, and his mouth, like the inside of a slop bucket. Last night at the bar, a birthday party for one of his biker buddies, shouldn't have had those last two rounds of tequila. What'd Randy call it? Ta kill ya. And the plates of chicken wings, pizza, and nachos. What, did he think he had a cast iron gut? Trying to make it to the aspirin in the next room, to the shower with the jets of hot water. Or should he try to barf first? Hangovers weren't his thing. He was such a wus that way.

An hour later, more back on pace, sitting at the round table in his kitchen, coffee and toast, he thought about his assignment. Francis would head to St. Charles County to some marina where he would meet up with a truck driver. This guy was hard to catch up with and there was no telling just when or where they would meet. But Francis had to be in the vicinity when the guy called. So, he wasn't going to be around this morning but he'd like Cale to go to Hopeville and try to scare up the soup guy, press him as to Austin's activities prior to the overdose. What was their relationship? If Austin overdosed, who was his supplier? Maybe the soup guy would shed light, maybe not, but they were near the end of this job and needed to tie up just a few loose ends before he would make his report to Dr. Lambert.

Cale tried another bite of toast, no good. His stomach was unsettled, churning. He looked out on his backyard, saw a blue jay dive-bombing a squirrel.

* * *

Francis drove along the Missouri River north of St. Charles in St. Charles County. It was a beautiful fall morning and he was singing to the radio: "Here's your ticket, pack your bag, transportation is here..." Oh yeah, today is gonna be a good one, he thought, already is. He wheeled the Escort left off State 94 toward the marina. Soon the aquatic avenues came into sight, slips with boats, people in some of those boats. What would it be like to live on a boat, he wondered. You'd have to get used to the motion, the rocking, the sound of wavelets splashing, the funky smells—and he was aware of that from his last visit, river muck mixed with an odor of rotting vegetation, seaweed or whatever. He passed the Mud Shack where catfish nuggets lay in wait, and came to Ralph Casey's slip. The same woman, all bangles and piercings, from the neighboring boat was tending something on a Weber Grill, but no sign of the trucker. He got out, walked the plank to the guy's boat, stood there, taking it all in.

"Not here!" called the woman. He waved thanks and went back down the plank. The man said he was coming in from Kansas City and should be here by 9:30. It was 9:50. A good judge of character, Francis didn't think the guy was playing him. He called the guy's cell, it went straight to voice mail. He spoke his piece, that he was waiting and these divorce papers were begging to be handed over, so hurry up and let me be on my way. Then, he went to his car, popped a Seven-Up, cracked the novel he was currently working on, *Miami Blues* by Charles Willeford, and settled in to read.

* * *

"You know, you're going to get arrested the way those pants fit around your thighs." The queer had watched Cale dismount from his Triumph, remove his helmet, set the kickstand, hitch up his britches, Levis that weren't even tight. Cale regarded the fey young man with his plaid schoolgirl skirt and yellow cotton blouse, combat boots and long brown hair piled high in a bun. He was definitely on the hunt.

Cale said, "I'll bet you're the envy of every cross-dresser here with that get up."

"That's right," he assured, sidling up, "and I wore it just for you."

Cale smiled. "You can stop right now, man, ain't gonna happen."

The man appeared crestfallen. "Oh, why you wanna be that way? I could make you feel *soooo* good."

"Already feel good," Cale told him, "although I've felt better. I think I need the can."

He found a port-a-potty and went in, but it was so nasty he came right back out, a cloud of flies and gnats in his wake. Don't they ever empty these things? It was getting on eleven and he made for the soup kitchen. One way or another he would get something tangible from this fool. Francis said to press him. He would do more than that. He would hold the son of a bitch's feet to the fire.

En route he was intercepted by a film crew, two young women and a guy, no media affiliation, independents trying to get something on YouTube no doubt. They asked to interview him. He corrected their presumption. "No, I'm not a citizen here, uh, a resident. I'm just passing through."

"Sure, we understand," said the woman covered in tattoos, oozing empathy. The guy stuck the Panasonic Mark II video cam in Cale's face while the other woman asked, "Would you say the city-provided services here are adequate? How can they be improved?"

Cale moved the cam off his face, flashed them an irritated look. But he was pondering their question, they could see that. "Empty the shitters with some regularity for starters. Organize games like tug-of-war, three-legged sack races—I don't know." He snapped his fingers, said, "You should talk to this character Jesus," pointing down the path. "Guy has a serious foot fetish—he'll wash your feet and tell you anything you wanna know. Really. He'll give you an earful."

They moved on down the path.

Jacob saw Cale coming and he almost dropped a stockpot of chicken soup. "Fuck a duck!" he muttered. Roland heard this and was confused.

"Duck? Think you're mistaken, sir. I thought today was chicken soup."

"Shut up, you moron!" hissed Jacob. "When he comes, you don't say a word."

Cale got there, all effusive and chummy. "Whatcha got cookin'? You notice I didn't start that with Hey, good lookin'," and he chuckled. "No, seriously, man—Jake, is it?—can we talk for just a few minutes?" Today he wore pleated slacks, a white button down long sleeve poplin shirt, a navy blue Cardigan and penny loafers, no socks. Jacob paid little attention, kept on doing what he was doing, stirring the contents of a large pot. "I'm talking to you," moving a step closer, thinking how he'd like to snap the man's ass with a wet towel. "Give me five minutes, hey? I came way out here just to talk to you."

Jacob looked up from his soup. His expression could be described as flustered. "I-I-I-I already t-t-told you what there is to-to-to-to tell."

"I know that, Jake, and believe me your cooperation is much appreciated, but I'd like to go over it again. Plus, I have a few more questions."

"Na-na-not a good time."

Cale walked around the back of the structure, went inside. He went up to Jacob, put his hand on the man's shoulder, gave a little squeeze. "Well then, make it a good time."

Jacob led him to the Winnebago, no words between them. He unlocked it, they stepped in. There was a small table, they sat there. Cale led off with a compliment. "I've gotta say, the outside is ugly as sin, a real turn-off, but the inside ain't so bad. You got a nice ride here," looking around, "very cozy. Well, it's a ride and a home."

Jacob nodded. He would keep his words to a minimum.

"You live in this or do you have a regular house you call home?" Jacob stared blankly. Cale shrugged nonchalance. "Okay, enough small talk. Let's get to Austin Lambert. I think he was your helper just like that guy out there now is your helper. You knew him a lot better than you're letting on."

Jacob got up and went to mini fridge, got two bottles of water. Came back.

Cale tilted to one side on his chair and farted. "Ahh," he uttered. He fixed Jacob with a look. "Okay, that wasn't a question, it was a statement. Here come the questions. The coroner says he overdosed on fentanyl. Was he a regular user? Where did he get this fentanyl?"

Jacob was busy staring at a point on the ceiling. Cale reached over the table and shook him. "Come on, man, cough up some answers."

Jacob came out of the stupor he was in. "It-it's everywhere in this place."

"Yeah, and where did Austin get it?"

"I-I-I-I..." He couldn't even get it out. He was in stuttering hell.

Cale threw a 'don't bullshit me' glance at Vorhof. "Spit it out, man."

"I don't have a name."

"His father the doctor says that Austin wouldn't have taken a drug like that. Someone slipped it to him, isn't that right?"

Jacob was extremely uncomfortable with this interrogation. This guy was unbearable, so aggressive. He began to tremble. "I d-d-don't know," he said.

"That's okay," said Cale, leaning back, "we've got all morning." He reached into a pocket and took out a Snickers bar, one of those jumbo-sized ones. He opened it and slid the wrapping back, took a healthy bite. He offered it to Jacob, who declined. Cale chewed noisily, every mastication audible. Finally, he swallowed. Then he leaned forward and got right into Jacob's face.

"When we first spoke to you about this, you never mentioned that Austin had died. Why not? Did you think we didn't know? Did you think we'd just go away and say, 'Oh, well, that's that. We tried.'" Jacob looked away. Cale took him by the chin and brought him back. "Oh no, you don't get to look away. I think you're the one who gave him the drug that killed him. Why do I think that? Because you look guilty, that's why. You look like a guy who would do some fucked up thing like that. What do you say to that?"

Jacob shook his head violently. "No, you're wra-wra-wrong."

"I am not wrong," shouted Cale. "I don't know why you did it, but you did it." Suddenly there was a loud gurgling and Cale looked at his belly. "Oh crap," he said. Again, it sounded, this time like a sump pump in a flooded basement. "I need your toilet," he said desperately. Jacob pointed toward the front of the motor coach. "Don't move," he said, "I'll be right back."

Jacob listened as the sounds of Cale's distress echoed beyond the restroom. It sounded ghastly, the badlands of the intestinal tract in upheaval. And he was thankful for the break because now he could do what needed to be done. He went to a small dresser near the fold-out bed. He opened a drawer and took out a container with a child proof cap. He shook out three small blue pills. One side had a "30" and the other side had an "M" with a border etched around it. He went back to the table. He took the half-eaten chocolate bar and with a finger and then a pencil shoved the pills way in there so they were not noticeable. Snickers has peanuts so the little pills, if they crunched, would likely be taken as that and swallowed along with everything else. There was a risk of being found out, but he felt he had no choice. The guy was an ogre and somehow he was on to the truth. Besides, what was one more?

He sat there drinking his bottled water, waiting. Finally, Cale came out, fanning the air before him. "Hoo," he gasped, "that was a real stinkeroo." He smiled thinly, gave a little shrug. "Sorry about your toilet, man, you're gonna need a power wash in there."

"I should ge-ge-get-get back," he said.

"Hey, you know, while I was doing my thing in there I remembered a joke about soup. You'll love it!"

"No no no." Jacob shaking his head violently and waving his open palm in protest.

"Sure, I'll tell it for ya. So, this old geezer's about to turn eighty and his pals decide to get him a hooker. They don't tell him, of course, they want it to be a surprise. That evening as he's having dinner by himself, he hears a knock at the door. He goes to see. Opens the door and there's this gorgeous brunette in a long raincoat. He can't believe it. He just stands there with his mouth open, probably salivating. She says, 'Mr. Walker?' He says yes. She opens the raincoat, she's totally nude, fantastic body made for love. You ready? In this sultry voice, she says, 'I'm here to give you super sex!' He gives this a moment's thought, says, 'I'll take the soup.'"

Jacob didn't even crack a smile, but Cale was cracking up. His own joke.

"Oh, come on now, Jake, that's funny. You have to admit that's funny." He looked at Jacob, shaking his head. "No? It figures you wouldn't have a sense of humor." He picked up the chocolate bar, took a bite. He finished it off, left the empty wrapper on the table. He took a swig of water to wash it down. "Okay then, where were we? Oh yeah, I remember. So, Jake, when did you decide to kill Austin Lambert?"

"I must ge-get back," he said flatly, "and if you try t-t-t-to stop me I'll call the police."

Cale harrumphed. "Growing a pair now, are you? Okay, that's fine, get back to your soup. Find another young man to take under your wing. Befriend him and then take his life. I suspect that's what you do and you know what? My suspicions are often correct."

He got up and stood there over Jacob, looking down on him in great distaste.

Jacob met his ire. "And d-d-d-don't call me Ja-ja-Jake."

Cale gave a scornful laugh and made for the door. Jacob was terribly relieved. He'd worried that Cale would collapse in the Winnebago.

*　*　*

Francis had lost track of the time. *Miami Blues* was a kickass crime novel and he had just got to the part where homicide detective Hoke Moseley was as pissed as he could be, humiliated too, at being attacked in his sleep, beaten with his own sap, his jaw broken, dental devastation. Just as bad, his badge, his .38 police special, *and* his false teeth stolen. But now, in the hospital, he didn't know the assailant was Junior Frenger, a psycho fresh out of San Quentin, whom he'd met earlier and even shared a meal with. Francis was loving every page of this book.

Then his phone chimed. A gruff voice asked if he was still at the marina.

"Sure am," answered Francis.

"Okay, change of plan. Get in your car, get back out on 94, head north about a mile, turn left on Big Mound Way, go about three miles, no, make that four..." He was to meet the trucker in the middle of a cornfield or some such fantasy. Okay, on my way, he told him. Keep your phone open.

Francis got there, at least he was pretty sure it was there he got, for he was supposed to land at the intersection of Big Mound and Mc-Clure, but the street sign said only Big Mound. Whatever other street name had been there was long gone. He did the only thing possible, he waited.

It had been lush green cornfields all around, but the corn had been harvested probably about three weeks ago and now it was only the stubble of corn stalks stretching in every direction toward the horizon. The sky was blue, the ground was tawny. Off in the distance, a massive flock of starlings eating chaff in the rows of corn. They would eat for a while then rise and swirl as one, a billowing black curtain, then settle back down in a new spot for more chaff. He stood beside his car taking it all in. The setting was surreal and it was nostalgic too, because it brought to mind the scene in *North By Northwest* where Cary Grant waits in just such a cornfield when a crop duster comes out of nowhere and nearly scalps him. He kept on imaging an eighteen-wheeler coming over that rise and pulling up to where he stood. And, finally, at last, that did happen. The semi was like some apparition rolling down a black asphalt ribbon, closer and closer this behemoth until he could see the plumes of exhaust.

He had the papers in his hand. He expected the driver to stop and get out and take them. That would be the civilized thing. But the big truck only slowed and Francis saw it wasn't going to stop. The driver had his arm out the window, palm open, fingers ready to clutch. The semi was on him, slow motion. The hand reached out, Francis stood on his tiptoes and passed the sheaf off. The trucker tipped his cap and drove on. There had been no one else around and that was okay by Francis because no one would have believed it.

Part II

THE FUNERAL WAS ON A WEDNESDAY MORNING AT CONCORDIA CEM-ETERY, in the heart of South City. There would be a gathering afterward at Dino's Bungalow, nearby. Cale didn't have a family that anyone knew of so Francis and the bikers, who were essentially Cale's family, passed the hat for a casket and a plot. The procession, led by a 1967 Cadillac Fleetwood, went straight from the morgue to the cemetery. No funeral home involved. At the cemetery, a fellow with a Bobcat waited with two other fellows at an open grave. Shadrach, a burly, hirsute biker whose Fleetwood it was, motioned for Francis and some others to carry the casket to the grave. The bikers all wore their colors and this was the first time that Francis was made aware of their affiliation. Cale had belonged to a chapter of American Legion riders, lovers of serious horsepower between the legs and the open road ahead. Cale had talked of poker runs, riding from one checkpoint to another, usually country bars, collecting playing cards at each one, best hand wins. The proceeds always went to some charitable cause like Fallen Firefighters Survivors.

The bikers were all standing around as cemetery workers, wearing yellow hoodies with the cemetery name, lowered the casket into the grave with heavy-duty nylon straps. A couple were sniffling and wiping away tears, but most bore up stoically. One by one they gave testimony about Cale and what a great guy he was. "He was the kinda guy, you needed a ride to the hardware store or a jump for your dead battery he'd do that for you," said one.

"Damn straight," said another, "shirt off his back kinda guy. We'll miss him."

"I can still remember that time he stopped to help a snake off the road. Big snake too. He didn't want it to get run over."

"That's right," said another, whose name on his denims said Weezer. "How crazy was that? That snake didn't appreciate Cale giving him a hand either because it bit him. Remember?"

"That's a snake for ya," said tall biker, Waldo.

"It just isn't right," sniffed Weezer.

They asked Francis if he wanted to say anything. All eyes were on him. He had to sound forth. "Well, he was a fellow vet and that counts for a lot."

"Right on!" the resounding chorus.

"And he was my partner, not long enough. And I'll tell you he was a good process server, possibly because he himself had been served with numerous lawsuits, so he told me. The man had no fear. He once walked into a bar and served a teamster with an order for child support. It was happy hour, his liquored up teamster pals all around."

"I'm a teamster," said a biker named Rolf.

"Yeah? Then you know what I'm saying. What I do know is he was a quick learner and needed very little supervision, and that took a lot of pressure off me." He cleared his throat. "And now, and now I'll have to find a new partner, if any of you are interested."

There was a pause, Francis went on. "Uh, we were working a case together when he died, looking into the death of a young man from a drug overdose. The drug in question was fentanyl, the same drug the medical examiner says killed Cale." He shook his head in dismay. "You knew our friend. You can't tell me he took a dangerous drug and then climbed on his hog. He wasn't reckless or foolhardy like that. No way. Someone spiked his drink or his food." He looked them over, one to another, nodded slightly in the affirmative. "I'm going to find out who."

A biker named Odin, long sideburns and a leather cap, walked up and gave Francis a bear hug. "We're with you, brother. You find that son of a bitch and you punch his lights out. Then you tell us who it is and we'll pay him a little visit too."

A member with a name patch that read Donkey Dick walked over to the pile of scooped up earth that would soon fill the hole, grabbed a handful and tossed it on the casket. The others, as a group, solemn as a blood oath, did the same. Francis followed suit, taking a handful of rich black dirt, a couple earthworms poking out, and sprinkled it on Cale's new home. "See you down the trail, my friend."

They were standing around the bar at Dino's Bungalow. Long necks clinking, plates of ribs and potato salad on the pool table. Francis was saying how cool it was that Cale served process on a motorcycle, probably the only process server in Missouri to do so. How the memory of him placing those summonses and subpoenas and protection orders in his saddlebags will always make him smile, when his phone rang. It was Martha and she was quite agitated.

What Francis heard was a disjointed version of the situation. "The guy, *la piantagrane*, he returned. Heather. Not good, Francis. Back door, Marco went out, *combattere!*" When she got excited she began speaking Italian.

"*Combattere?*"

"Marco clocked him, Francis, and he fell and came up with a blade. They fought on the back steps, Marco was cut on the face and the villain had a tooth knocked out. Marco had a meat tenderizer."

He was imagining it, on this beautiful fall morning all hell breaking loose at the restaurant, a place known for its civility. "Why didn't you call Lauria? I gave you his cell."

"I was too caught up in the thing to think straight. But I did call him and he arrived with another officer, but by that time he'd left the scene. They said they would find him and bring him in. Oh, God, I'm looking at this bloody tooth laying on the back steps. We can't have this. Will you come and get it?"

He said, "Wrapping up here. I'll be over in a jif."

— 16 —

It was time to talk to Dr. Lambert. The venue and time was set for 5 p.m. at Cafe Napoli, an upscale restaurant in Clayton, the county seat and center of finance. When Francis got there Lambert was at the bar by his dapper self already on his second Sidecar.

"What'll you have?" asked the doctor. Francis wanted a Budweiser. "So prosaic," intoned Lambert. "Save that for dive bar. Han here is in the Bartender Hall of Fame, why don't you let him make you something special?" An Asian man in a gold brocade vest stood behind the bar smiling.

"Okay, fine." He could be agreeable, Francis. A minute later the bartender placed a Gimlet with a twist of lime in front of him.

"Good choice, Han," complimented Lambert. And an aside to Francis, "Sweet yet tangy, indulge yourself."

Lambert held his glass up indicating a toast. They clinked glasses. Francis noted the doctor was quite convivial in this atmosphere, probably totally in his element. "Okay, I'm ready when you are." Francis looked at him blankly. "Your report," he clarified.

Francis recounted the events and discoveries pertinent to the investigation. How his business card had ended up in Austin's pocket, how Austin had been helping at the soup kitchen and yet he was supposedly in fear of the person who ran the enterprise, a fellow by the name of Jacob.

"Could this Jacob have had anything to do with Austin's death?" wondered Lambert.

"Maybe, big maybe," said Francis, hand on his chin. "I will say he is shifty and certainly becomes nervous when asked about Austin. Whether he put Austin up to overdosing or even provided the means for him to overdose will be difficult if not impossible to prove."

"Yes, I see. Nothing concrete, empirical evidence totally lacking. So this is where it ends, with a hunch, however strong?"

Francis took a drink, ran his tongue over his lips. "You know, this is pretty good."

Lambert gave a wink. "We'll make a connoisseur of you yet."

"There is something else. I told you I had a partner. We were working on this together. We went there twice, to the homeless camp Hopeville, and we spent time with the residents, asking around, showing Austin's picture. As I said, we found a few people who remembered your son and they pointed us toward the soup guy, Jacob. Jacob admitted Austin had helped out with the soup thing, but said he stopped coming and didn't know what had happened to him. I thought that was BS and last week I sent my partner, Cale Twohey, to the camp to grill this Jacob. I don't know what transpired because Cale left the camp on his Harley, got about a mile away, drove straight into a brick building and died." Francis paused for a moment of silence. "Cale was a veteran motorcyclist, no reason under heaven he would lose control of his Harley. But there was a reason. The medical examiner said it was an overdose. Fentanyl." He studied Lambert's face for any reaction.

"A coincidence maybe, but could be a pattern," said Lambert. "Maybe this Jacob's MO is to slip lethal drugs into food or drink, surreptitiously, targeting this or that person for whatever sinister purpose. It's an old trick, like in the old movies, you'd hear 'He slipped him a Mickey,' meaning a spiked drink."

"The same theory crossed my mind," said Francis, "but imagining it and proving it are poles apart." They sipped at their drinks. Francis said, "You know, I ran into a man over there whose brother disappeared at Hopeville. He too was trying to find out what happened. I haven't seen him since, but it might be helpful to know what happened to this brother."

Lambert nodded. "You know, sometimes you have step back from the painting." He reached into his back pocket, took out his wallet and handed Francis three Franklins. "Here. You're doing a great job. I'd like you to keep going, find this guy with the missing brother, look into this Jacob, check him out. Background, where he lives, how he supports himself, that sort of thing. When you pull that together, call me and we'll talk again."

Francis realized he didn't know much about Jacob, and he immediately regretted not jotting the plates on the Winnebago. He wondered if Cale had done that. "Okay, sounds good," he told Lambert. "I'll get on it, give you a report in a week or so."

They had another round and made small talk. At length, Lambert said, "Tell me, do you like art?"

"Not too much. I don't get most of it, not the modern stuff anyway."

"That's okay, it's not for everyone. But I found a gallery in the City that I absolutely love. It's run by a woman named Dagmar Petko and she's put me on to some work by an up and coming artist that I'm pretty excited about. He's somewhat mysterious, this man, goes by Rigoletto. One name like Sting."

"Or Tarzan."

"Right, and art these days, as I mentioned in my office, you may recall, is about ideas—"

"—or Zorro."

Lambert looked at him. "Right you are, and as I'm saying, the conceptual work is in high demand, the edgier the better. Subversive even. And this artist has produced the most intriguing pieces. Effigies or dummies made of all sorts of materials, but not at all lifelike in appearance and they are playing out some sort of drama. Really, it's challenging to try to define it or classify it. I've got one on order, sight unseen, by this Rigoletto. Problem is, I don't know where I'll put it."

Francis couldn't even imagine having a problem like that. "Well, I'm sure you'll figure it out." He downed the dregs of his Gimlet. "I'll be on it first thing tomorrow morning, maybe turn up something concrete. Thanks for the drink."

He rose from the barstool. Dr. Lambert shook his hand vigorously and looked him in the eye, imploringly. "You're a man of action, Francis, I know that. I trust you will see this thing through to a satisfactory conclusion." Then, "Oh, Han, yes, I'll have another, thank you."

EARLY THE NEXT MORNING AT BREAKFAST FRANCIS MADE HIS DO LIST. He was running low on his Cafe Du Monde Chickory Coffee. More of that along with English muffins and Bonne Maman Strawberry Preserves. Yes, and get over to Hopeville, look up soup man. Take over where Cale left off. Call Lauria about Finch. Call immigration lawyer for one of Martha's cousins. Clip toenails. Cell phone? Where? Left @ Murphy's? Time for an oil change and tire rotation. Get Cale's things from the morgue. Pick up summons from Gorman Morley law firm. Serve last of four subpoenas from yesterday. Busy day ahead. He probably wouldn't get everything on his list done, but the breakfast items were first and foremost. These were the only indulgences that he had, small indulgences at that, and they were actually a priority in his life. To be deprived of any combination of them might make for a bad day.

He kissed Martha goodbye, wished her a nice day, and went out into his day. It was 8:30 and he would get to the Toyota dealership in West County just as it opened. Then that batch of subpoenas would be done. En route he called Lauria on his cell, which he had actually left in his car and now the charge was low. It had been two days since the dust up at the restaurant and Martha's family was eager to know if Finch had been taken in. Not wanting to be labeled a victim, Marco declined to press charges for the assault with a weapon, but the police brought it before a prosecutor who issued a warrant. As Lauria would explain it, just because someone doesn't want to press charges doesn't mean that the prosecutor won't issue. Their attitude is we represent the people of the State of Missouri and We The People don't put up with that shit! The violation of the civil order of protection is a second chargeable offense.

"Lauria," said Ed Lauria into the phone.

"Ed, it's Francis. How goes it? Yeah, me too. Hey, I'm following up on this Finch character, the one at Pastori's the other day. Any word yet?"

"There's a warrant out on him, I made sure of that, but no such luck, my friend. At least nothing shaking since yesterday evening when I spoke with my counterpart over in the First. They've been to his house a couple times, not there. He may be in the wind. He lives in the First and so the officers from the First are the ones to handle it. I've told them it's priority, but those guys down there are a lot busier than we are. Bigger fish to fry, right? You know that if I had the case, I'd be shaking bushes all over that skanky neighborhood. But he'll turn up, you wait."

Francis said, "His court date on the OP is coming up. It's unlikely he'll show but if he does maybe you could have someone there."

"Aw, that would be perfect, wouldn't it? Ambush the shitbum, take him away in cuffs. But sorry to say, we don't have the manpower for such an exercise. You wait, he'll turn up."

"Okay," said Francis. "I can wait, but I gotta tell you, these hot-blooded Italians are not so good at waiting. My wife's brother, the one who got cut? He's still frothing at the mouth. He's talking about looking for the guy himself, like a vendetta."

"I get it," said Lauria. "You're talking to an Italian and we Italian men are a proud lot to the point of macho. We don't take well to being humiliated. But you tell the brother vigilantism is not the way to go. The police will handle it and he won't be disappointed."

"Done. Yeah, Ed, I've got one more thing, a favor."

"Shoot."

"I'm trying to find a guy. His name is Cleo, black guy, was arrested during the Stockley fiasco that first day at the courthouse downtown. He said he lives in the Ville. Would you please look at the records for those arrests, probably only one Cleo, and get me an address of record?"

"You're not going to do anything to make me wish I hadn't, are you?"

"No, no, it's just that I need his help with something."

Francis went about his day and he got most everything done, but he knew it wouldn't be like this all the time. No, without a helper the jobs would pile up and he'd be swamped and that would make him anxious, having distant jobs in every direction, and being anxious might keep him up at night and that would not be good at all because he loved his sleep, was quite possessive about it. Maybe he should go to the VA pharmacy and look for another Cale.

Then it was 2:45 and he was powerful thirsty for a draft beer, cold and crisp. He made a beeline for Murphy's and found a spot right in front. He passed through the door with the big Michelob sticker on the glass and stopped just inside waiting for his eyes to adjust. He counted five people at the bar, about ten more at tables. Tommy waved to him and called, "One cold fresh schooner of Busch coming up, Francis."

One of the tipplers at the bar was Red Rush, who had been a regular's regular here for decades, but hadn't been seen for some time because he had cirrhosis of the liver and word was he was on his last legs. Everyone knew about Red's condition because Patty McNew, the barmaid, in a bout of gallows humor, had read the diagnosis that Red brought in, asked to have it, and had it framed and put on the wall. The former hale and hearty union thug and object of apprehension for certain drinkers who would get out of line—if Red summoned you, you had to go to Red to get your ass kicked—now appeared gaunt and frail, and nursed his Four Roses bourbon with a hand that trembled. There was a cane propped up under the bar.

"Good to see you, Red." Francis had taken the seat beside him. Red looked at him, smiled. Patted the back of his hand affectionately.

"My namesake," he said with a slight brogue, "or is it the other way around?" Red's given name was Francis.

"Oh, I'm named after you, to be sure."

"Well then, let's drink to that."

They talked of the long ago, seventeen years to be exact, when those yahoos from Jefferson County invaded this establishment and thought they could intimidate the good men and women who drank here. How wrong they were. Their true purpose in coming here was soon gleaned and a melee ensued, however brief, until the trio was ushered into the backroom, where they were visited with corporal punishment by Red and several henchmen.

Francis wasn't there and it was he the interlopers were after because they thought he had something to do with the disappearance of the ringleader's dad, but Francis didn't. Still, he'd heard so much about it, now the stuff of legend, that he felt as though he had been there.

"It didn't end well for those boys, did it?" asked Red, relishing the memory.

"They had bruises on their bruises." Francis stoking the fire.

"I did release them but only to go crying to their mothers."

"And you paddled them good on the way out as a favor to those mothers so they wouldn't have to do it."

Red gave a broad grin, showing several missing teeth. "Sláinte," he said, raising his glass. Francis returned the sentiment.

The ring tone came from Francis' back pocket. Francis answered. "You got a pen?" the voice asked. Of course he had a pen, paper too. "Good, because I got a name and an address you asked for. Ready?" The name, Cleophilus Sumner Yardley. The address, a street in North City. He knew it well. Francis was in the middle of thanking Lauria when the door burst open and four guys came staggering in, calling for beer, play fighting with one another, and laughing their asses off. Suddenly, there was so much commotion that Francis couldn't hear.

"What the hell's going on?" asked Lauria. "Where are you?"

"What?"

"I said what's happening there?"

"Looks like some sort of raucous celebration," said Francis.

"Always the party boy, huh?"

"Thanks for the favor, Ed."

Francis and Red listened as the newcomers told their story and eventually understood why they were so animated. The fallout from the Stockley verdict was still in play and apparently some protesters had decided to block traffic on the Interstate at Grand Avenue near Saint Louis University. These guys, Cormac Morrison and Phil Connor among them, had come upon the scene in Phil's Eldorado.

"There was like a wall of spooks," said a fellow Francis knew as Hutch. "Just standing there in the middle of 40 with signs and fists raised, like daring us to run them down."

"Shouting all sorts of gibberish about justice."

"'No justice No peace' is what they were saying," clarified Morrison.

"So we stopped rather than run them down," said Phil Connor, "although I was tempted, but then there would've been so much paperwork to deal with." He gave a wink and expected a laugh from that, but only his cohorts chuckled. Others in the bar had meandered over to hear the story and now there were six in the audience including Francis and Red.

"You got out of the car, confronted them? What happened?" asked Rory Denigan. "It had to be scary. They might've had guns."

They had ordered boilermakers and before the story could continue the shot glasses that held Jameson were upended on the bar and the beer was slugged down in audible gulps. Tommy was summoned to bring another round.

"Yeah, we got out and we weren't the only ones," said the fourth guy, a stocky balding guy who looked like Paulie, Rocky's friend and future brother-in-law in the movie. "They had traffic stopped all over Highway 40, it's a wonder there wasn't an accident. So it was a classic standoff, right? On one side of the line people are screaming 'Let us through you assholes, we don't care about your beef.'"

"And on the other side," recounted Morrison, "the blacks are saying 'You better deal with it, it's only gonna get worse. This is what happens when white cops kill black men. You think we just gonna roll over and take it?' Something like that."

"And the other side, our side, is saying 'Fuck you!'" added Hutch with a smirk.

"We were so close to them I could smell their stink." said Phil Connor.

"It come to blows?" asked a listener, wringing his hands in anticipation.

"Phil here's on a softball team," said Morrison. "He carries the gear for the team in his trunk."

"Yeah? So?"

"Baseball bats!" they shouted in unison, laughing.

"It came to blows all right," said Paulie, "I got me a base hit, some nigger's woolly head. Felt good, too."

Said Morrison, "We all got our licks in, though one of us didn't come out untouched. Show 'em, Hutch."

Hutch lifted his St. Louis Blues cap and presented a hell of a goose egg on his forehead. "I think it was a sap or somethin'," he said, sheepishly. "Knocked me clean on my ass, I was seein' stars for a while."

"Little bluebirds flying around his head," said Paulie with a chuckle, "but we got over on 'em, didn't we boys?"

"You should be ashamed of yourselves." This pronouncement effectively killed the spirit of the narrative. They all looked to the author of the remark.

"You heard me," asserted Red. "Beating on those people who are so desperate to get their message across that they choose to shut down a busy highway. Why not give them a fookin' break? It's only a few minutes out of your otherwise idle day. You ever been downtrodden for Christ's sake? You should applaud what they're doing. How else can they get their message across? Maybe they have something that needs to be said, that the cops *are* fooking corrupt and will keep on doing their skulduggery as long as no one steps in to challenge them."

They all looked at Red with astonishment, for they thought they knew him, had taken him to be on their side, sharing their sentiments about the protesters. If there was a rebuttal to his remark it was held back at least for now. But he wasn't done. "Jaysus, didn't you take social studies in school, those of you who made it past fifth grade? If you had you'd see that our proud race, the Hibernians, *we* were once upon a time the niggers in this country. You should show solidarity with these shit disturbers, not try to bash their skulls!"

Finally, Cormac Morrison could take it no longer. "Geez, Red, you can be a real killjoy, you know?"

Red grabbed his cane and lunged for Morrison, almost fell off the barstool. Francis steadied him, got him back to seated. Red's face was beet red but was it from the booze or from anger? He looked at them all with distaste. "You don't wanna listen to me," he snarled, "fuck yas." And he went back to his Four Roses.

The guardsmen and their audience adjourned to a spot further down the bar and continued their boasting. Francis and Red drank in silence for a while, Francis wondering if this would be the last time for that.

Tommy came over and Francis asked for another Busch, but Red, who had just come through a bout of coughing and spitting into a handkerchief, waved him off.

Francis turned to the old man and said, "I heard what you said, Red. I heard it." Red simply looked down at his drink on the bar, nodded in acknowledgment.

— 18 —

HE GOT HOME WELL BEFORE DINNER AND MARTHA WASN'T THERE.
Though he loved Martha, he also loved having the house to himself. He
could putter without interruption. He could pig out on leftover lasagna
without being warned that three helpings will ruin his svelte figure. He
could sit on the back porch with a drink and be alone with his thoughts.
And there were problems and challenges on multiple fronts to mull over.
Like finding a capable partner to help with process serving. Finding
someone, and then training him or her. Like what to do about this Jacob
character. A serial killer? First thing tomorrow, get back to the sad, dismal
camp and learn his full name, eyeball the plates on his Winnebago. And
find Cleo, see what happened with his brother. Lastly, bring to a close the
situation with young Cary Finch, restore peace of mind to the restaurant
staff. Where was he? Would he strike again? Considerations, approaches,
and possible solutions to these problems swirled around his mind like a
dust devil. Probe. Study. Be patient. Act rashly if called for. Make assumptions. Don't trust assumptions. Probe some more. Contemplate. It all fell
on him and he could handle it, although sometimes he really did feel like
Atlas holding the world on his shoulders.

Martha walked in with a bag of groceries and set them on the table.
"You in the mood for something special?" she asked. "I'm making pork
ragu over creamy polenta. I saw it on Rachel Ray and it made me want
to try. I've got all the ingredients."

"Well, bless your gourmet heart. I'm sure I'll love it. Let me get you a
glass of wine to help you along."

While he was pouring the wine she gave the news. Cary Finch had
returned, not to Pastori's but to Heather's apartment. "She wasn't
there, thank God. But her neighbor saw a man at her door, knocking
and pounding for quite some time, and she called the police. He fit the
description all right, but he was gone by the time the officers showed.
Oh Francis, what are we going to do?"

Francis knew what *he* had to do and that was to stake out Finch's
residence. Another fricking job, great.

THE NEXT MORNING WAS STEADY RAIN. Francis was basically impervious to the weather, something he got from his father who often said he'd be damned if he'd ever let the weather stop him from doing something he wanted to do, which was basically get to the comfort of the bar and drink. He would look for Cleo first and then get to the homeless camp around eleven to catch Jacob setting up. But what started out as a day of promise soon turned to letdown.

First, on the way to the Ville to look for Cleo he stopped to serve a summons in a rundown neighborhood. It was a four family flat. He got in, knocked at the designated door, the door opened a crack, a skeptical face asked what did he want. He stated his purpose, "a delivery for Antonio Davis." Not a lie because the summons and petition in his hand was a delivery. "Special delivery," he added. Then, "What kinda delivery?" Now there was no good subterfuge. He had to be forthright. "Legal documents, I'm with the court." The eyes scrutinized him. "Just a minute," the man said, and shut the door. Five minutes later he was still waiting, fuming at how he'd been pimped.

Next, he pulled up in front of Cleo's supposed home in the Ville neighborhood, a street named Cote Brilliante. Francis knew a little about The Ville, knew that it was one of the first areas in St. Louis where blacks could own property and that by the early to mid 20th Century it had produced a number of prominent figures in many fields, Chuck Berry, Grace Bumbry, Arthur Ashe, Dick Gregory among them. It was also a designated historic district in the City. He looked in his logbook and read the name once again: Cleophilus Sumner Yardley. The house itself was two-story red brick, well-kept, with daylilies leading up the walk to the expansive front porch with chairs and a swing. It was 9:30. He got out.

A young girl answered the door, pigtails, brown eyes big as silver dollars. Sweatshirt that came to her knees and said ST LOUIS RAMS. He wondered why she wasn't in school. He asked for Cleo. She frowned. "Cleo don't stay here," she said as if he should know that.

"Oh, could you tell me where he does stay? I'd like to talk with him."

"You a police?"

"No, we're friends. We've shared some, uh, experiences together."

She thought about this, then turned, shouted into the house, "Auntie, there's a man here want to talk with Cleo." She pronounced it "Ahn-tee."

A large woman in a loose floral print house dress came out, just to the open door. An African themed scarf covered her head, tied in a bow on top. Francis explained himself. He didn't expect the answer he got. "You say you know him, then you know where to look."

"Well, I do know him," assured Francis, "but maybe not as well as you think. Would you be so kind to tell me where this place is?"

"What you want with him?"

"Just to talk."

"Talk about what?"

"Is he hiding or something?"

She snorted. "My son don't need to hide from nothing or no one. What's on your mind that you need to see him?" She smiled just a little. "I'm the sentinel, you see. I'll decide if you are worthy of his presence."

He wasn't wearing a hat. He wiped the rain out of his eyes. "Oh, I see. Well then, that changes things. Um, well, that demonstration a couple weeks ago, the Stockley verdict, we were, uh, detained together, like rounded up by police and kept in a big room. And I was processed and released, but Cleo he was arrested and charged because he went berserk and hurt some people."

"Yeah, I'm aware of this," she said, dubiously. "It's not his fault, you know. You don't poke the bear with a sharp stick and expect nothing to happen."

"Well put," said Francis. "And then I ran into him about a week ago at the homeless camp and he said he was looking for his brother who'd disappeared. So, I'm here looking to find out if Cleo ever found him."

"What's your affiliation?" she asked. "Why are you at the protest and then the homeless camp? You stalking my son?"

"No, no, not at all. It was total coincidence. I'm a process server who does some investigation on the side and I was hired to look into the death of a young man at that homeless camp."

"Oh, hmm. And you want Cleo to help you in this investigation? How can he help?"

"If I could just talk with him directly."

She shook her head no, but then. "You got a card? I'll see that he gets it. He'll call if he wants."

He gave her his card, thanked her and turned to go. He was halfway down the steps when she said, "Cleo's brother you mentioned? My son? Bayard, his name. He's been found."

"Oh, that's good," said Francis, pleased. "Where was he found?"

"Ask Cleo."

* * *

The rain had turned to drizzle by the time he got to Hopeville. There were eight people standing none-too-patiently in line at the soup stand, which would not open. Not today, probably not anymore. But hoping against hope, they waited. The basic rule of poverty: if there are hand-outs in the offing, you wait. The Winnebago should have been here by now, it wasn't. The soup of the day as written on the chalkboard was illegible, the rain having obliterated the letters. Yet, the soup lovers knew it by heart: today's selection was Beef Barley. Francis stood there listening to them grouse, thinking how one more amenity, one more comfort had been taken from them. The have nots would now have less. But no soup, that was a tough one.

He trudged up the path to see the Jesus, maybe he would know something. Along the way he encountered a group of people dressed for the rain talking to another group in soggy clothing that hung on them drearily. As he neared, the first group stopped their delivery and waited for him. "Hello there," said a man in a tie and a suit beneath his rain jacket. "I'm alderman Vincent Moore. This is my ward, and I was just telling these folks that their time here is limited. The aldermanic board has passed a bill calling for removal of all persons, possessions, and dwellings on this stretch of land. It is a public health hazard and it poses a threat to the larger organized community all around."

Francis nodded that he understood. The others that were already there were saying it was a bunch of shit, and how the City was treating them like dogs.

"You should see the bulldozers in about a week," the alderman went on, "and you'll definitely want to be out by then. I have a list of shelters and services you may try. But make no doubt, you must move on. You have no choice. Sorry to have to tell you this."

"Anywhere but here," put in a fellow standing beside his boss.

"Can we bring our Weber Grills and croquet sets?" asked Francis.

"I don't see why not," said alderman Vincent Moore, "bring your antique oak armoire too. It's a free country!" And he laughed as did the others with him.

Francis found Jesus washing the feet of a woman who seemed to be in ecstasy, eyes closed, murmuring low moans and breathing heavily. She sat in a chair with her feet in the wash basin. She had her dress hiked up, baring stubby unshaven legs. Jesus must have finished with her feet because he had moved up to her thighs and was now applying the soapy washcloth to an area just south of her crotch and beneath her dress.

"Hey, Jesus, how's it going, man?" Jesus stopped, looked to Francis with annoyance. He vaguely remembered this guy from before.

"Please, could you come back later?" he said. The woman opened her eyes and looked to Francis with annoyance as well.

"Sure, okay," answered Francis, agreeably. "Or maybe not come back at all if you could only tell me where can I find the soup man. He's AWOL."

"That I couldn't tell you," said Jesus with a shrug. "I am not my brother's keeper."

"Seems like I heard that line before. You sure? I guess you are. All right then, you may as well go back to your routine. Lots of tootsies to wash, right? And ma'am, don't forget to tip your attendant. Make his day."

Heading back down the path to his car he was perplexed as to how to locate this Jacob. Someone must know his identity. All he needed was a surname or the plates on the Winnebago. The Vichysoisse that was catered on Thursdays, he got that from somewhere. Some restaurant or gourmet grocer. To glean that would be labor intensive. Then it came to him that Cale carried a logbook just as he did. That last day, when Cale came to pester Jacob, try to expose him, maybe he'd written something helpful. He'd gotten Cale's effects from the morgue and from his spare apartment, hadn't yet decided what to do with all of it. He had it in his car including the saddlebags from the Harley.

He got to the Escort, opened the back hatch. Unfastened the clasp on the saddlebags. There was his logbook, a speckled black-white composition notebook, the sort used by schoolkids. Francis had given it to him. The first entry was dated February 12, 2017, a subpoena to Boilermakers Local 27. Date, time, to whom served, and their title. He thumbed to the final entry, close to the last page. September 28, 2017 10:40 a.m. Hopeville, interview with "Jake" surname unknown. Winnebago present MO plates DE8 Y2A embossed dark blue. Subject not in RV. Look elsewhere. Cale was thorough, bless his heart.

* * *

This was a day of not getting any real work done, but rather laying foundations for real work later on. Finding Cleo, ferreting out Jacob whats-his-name. And now some windshield time in South City, hoping to spot Cary Finch. He arrived at one o' clock, the rain having stopped, now overcast with the sun peeping through every so often. He parked a few doors down from Finch's two-family flat, a solid red brick structure, zero adornments, four steps leading to a porch with potted plants and a Welcome sign near the door. Typical dwelling for this part of town. He would give it one hour, more than that a bad mood would begin to fester and he hated bad moods. He just wasn't a stakeout person. If Cale were around this would be his assignment.

He settled in. Very little pedestrian traffic. This was a quiet street, no stores or attractions nearby. He had *National Geographics* to pass the time. Reading wasn't going to cause him to miss anything happening on the near horizon. Even in the middle of the day there were cars and SUVs parked on the street, hardly a free space. Which meant, he thought, people were in their houses doing whatever but not at work.

Was one of those vehicles Finch's? No one had mentioned him having a car. Maybe Heather would know. He went to the back of his logbook, saw the number for Department of Revenue in Jeff City. Dialed it, followed the prompts, was placed in the holding queue. He knew from experience that to call anytime after the office just opened meant a long holding time. And sure enough, a recorded voice said, "You are now number fifty-four in line. Your wait time is approximately forty minutes." He put the phone on speaker and laid it on the dash.

A woman came along and Francis sat up and had his hand on the door handle for it looked like she was going into the Finch house. No such luck. On his cell, the colorless voice broke in: "You are now number forty-two in line. Your wait time is approximately twenty-eight minutes." He checked the charge on his phone: seventeen percent. At 1:40 an Amazon truck pulled up and the driver jumped out, ran up to the porch and left a package. Francis waited a minute and then went to look. Generic box, no telling what was inside. The label was addressed to Omar Goodson 3838 Minnesota Unit 2F. Unit 2F was the second floor apartment, Finch's apartment. Okay, that was something anyway.

It was getting on two o' clock and he was growing antsy. Nothing shaking. He thought he'd have better luck in the morning, maybe 7:30 to 9:00, if he could handle that. The voice on the line told him he was number six in line and his wait time was about nine minutes. He thought he'd stay in place here until the actual person answered. No sense in doing this transaction with the distraction of driving. Some kids rode by on their bikes, a picker emerged from an alley toting a trash bag filled with aluminum cans. Finally, a real person came on the line. Francis told her what he wanted, the address of record of a defendant he was trying to serve. He gave his security access code. He gave only the first name of this person, Jacob. She said that wasn't enough, she needed a last name as well. He said he didn't have a last name but he had the license plate of his RV. She hemmed and hawed, said she really needed a last name. What if she gave him the name of the wrong person, someone who owned the vehicle those plates went to but wasn't the one he was looking for. That would be an egregious case of mistaken identity and it would be her fault.

"Please, please, please," he said, growing desperate. "This guy has done some bad things. I've been chasing him for weeks, he's a slippery one. This is only way I can get to him. And I'm positive, absolutely positive that he owns this vehicle, a shitty-looking Winnebago, and that the plates I just gave will go to him."

"Mmm." She was thinking about it.

"Uh, miss?"

"Yes?"

"My phone's about to die."

"Okay, you win. It's against my better judgment, but since when did that make any difference. For the characters on those plates I have one Jacob Vorhof. 14 Deschutes Circle St. Louis 63131."

"Got it, and thank you from one grateful process server."

— 20 —

Two days later he was leaving the office of the general counsel for Washington University, where he had just served a lawsuit for employment discrimination, when his phone chimed. He glanced at the name on Caller ID, Heavenly Table Food Pantry, and stopped right there in the Quad. "Francis here."

"I heard you were looking for me," said a rich, deep voice.

"If this is Cleo, that's correct. How you been, man?"

"Been all right. A few setbacks, one in particular."

"You went to court, didn't you? That it?"

"Nah, that was nothing. They basically gave me a slap on the wrist, fined me two-fifty."

A Frisbee came flying his way and he had to duck. "Then what's the one setback in particular?"

"Come see me. I'm at this food pantry in the basement of the Saving Grace Bible Church 3860 Maffitt. I'm here every day, but usually gone by noon."

He looked at his watch. "I'll come now," he said. "Be there before you know it."

"You do that, brother. I'm waiting."

The same Frisbee hit him in the leg. He picked it up and fired it back at some student prince. He hadn't thrown one of those for years. It brought back memories.

* * *

The church was a grand edifice of red brick and limestone block on the corner of Maffit and Cora. A cornerstone indicated it was constructed in 1902. Francis guessed that it was probably the domain of other denominations before its current iteration as Bible Church. The crucifix crowning the spire high on the front of the building said it was likely a Roman Catholic Church at one time. A side door was open, he went in, found a stairway.

In a spacious room with no windows there were two women and Cleo at a long table sorting food and putting it into cardboard boxes that had the name of the food pantry on the side. There were beaucoup cans of food, glass jars containing certain food items such as preserves and pasta sauce, and loose fruit like apples and oranges and bananas. They weren't skimping on the benefactions for the boxes were full to almost overflowing.

He stood across the table from Cleo, said, "How long you think this would last in a typical household? Some tasty items in there. I'd go for the canned peaches first." Cleo smiled and nodded hello. He kept on working, Francis watched. Cleo made another box, then announced he was taking a break. Sure thing, Cleo, you a hard worker, the other two called, you take all the break you want.

A door opened to a small courtyard with potted plants, some flowering for the final time this year. No chairs or bench so they stood near some boxwoods. "Smoke?" asked Francis.

"I don't partake of that nasty habit," said Cleo.

"Neither do I," returned Francis. Cleo chuckled. "I was in Hopeville the other day," he began, "heard the strains of Taps."

"Taps, don't know that one. Which artist?"

"The last bugle call at night on a military base, lights out, day is done. The City is shutting the place down, gonna remove everything there, probably take it to the landfill. The people have to move on."

"Doesn't surprise me," said Cleo. "It's an old prophecy. The Bible is filled with stories of displaced people. Those people there at least had a society. Now they'll be scattered into small groups or alone. Fucking sad, is what it is."

"You must relate to their situation, working in a food pantry and all."

"You could say that and you did. My mother taught us to lend a hand to those less well-off than you. And why not? What else we gonna do with our time? Watch TV, shoot hoops, bullshit with other guys on some street corner? Someone once said that time is what we have the least of. I agree. May as well make every minute count."

"Well said. Words of a thinker." A short silence followed, the two looking at each other. Francis then said, "Last time I saw you, you were looking for your brother. Ever find him?"

Cleo looked away then looked back. "A minute ago you mentioned a landfill—coincidental because Bayard's body was found in a landfill out in Bridgeton. It was badly decomposed, they said he'd been there for weeks but his wallet was in his pants pocket. Money, ID, everything still in it—only thing missing, the lion pendant he wore. Autopsy was called inconclusive in terms of cause of death, but I'll tell you it sure as hell wasn't natural. They can't call it a homicide so it's not getting investigated."

Francis taken aback. "Oh geez, I'm sorry, Cleo. I'll bet he was a great guy. So, I mean, nothing to go on? The postmortem revealed nothing at all?"

"They said traces of street drugs including fentanyl, so of course they're going to be leaning toward an overdose. And Bayard did like his drugs, no argument there, but he was careful about what he ingested. And even if he did OD he didn't do it in that landfill. Someone dumped his body there."

A small tear crept down his cheek. "Damn, I get so upset just thinking about it."

Francis gave him a minute with his grief, then, "You know, I came to ask about your brother and to see how you're doing, but now this sad news has me on a different track. They found traces of fentanyl in his body? Well, get this. Since I've seen you, my partner, Cale, died on his motorcycle, crashed into a building. Medical Examiner said he'd overdosed on fentanyl, which I absolutely know is wrong. I mean, Cale wouldn't do fentanyl or any hard drug anymore than he would drink Drano. But guess who he was with just before this accident?"

"Don't know."

"The soup man, Jacob, guy with the Winnebago."

This gave Cleo a jolt. "Damn! Bayard spoke of him, said he was bad news. Said this guy was clinging to him, wanting to get him in that ugly shack on wheels, take him places, always giving him stuff. I told Bayard he's probably gay, said, 'He's hitting on you, man. Stay away from him unless you wanna carry a rainbow flag in the Pride Parade.'"

Francis nodded. "Yeah, well, guess what. He's vacated the camp.

Maybe for good. Left all those soup eaters in the lurch, but I think I've got a line on him."

Cleo's eyebrows arched. "Yeah? What you plan to do?"

"I suppose go see him at his place, rattle him, see what makes him tick. There's something there. It's just too many coincidences. The person I was hired to look into, Austin Lambert, died of an overdose. My partner dead of an overdose. Your brother dead of an overdose, and all of them from the same village where this guy is giving out food."

"You think he put something in the soup?"

"No, otherwise more would be dead. If it is him, he's being more selective. Maybe he courts certain individuals who he thinks are susceptible, uses them toward some purpose as yet unknown, and then does away with them."

"It's him, it's got to be him," said Cleo, getting worked up. "It's like a puzzle coming together. It's got to be that little prick. You can see it in his pug face, the meanness, the alienation towards others."

"All the personality of a slug, not a ray of sunshine peeping out. But look, I'll pursue this, it's what I do. Can I count on you for help as needed?"

His face lit up and his gold tooth glinted. "You bet your ass you can. You call, brother, I'll be there."

— 21 —

He felt he was chasing after specters, sitting in this tin can and waiting for certain persons to come along. Show themselves. First, Cary Finch, at whose door he now stood. And second, Jacob Vorhof, who may or may not have been home when he came calling the other day, but his Winnebago was there and the home interior, when you looked through the windows, looked lived-in. He was squandering time best reserved for practical pursuits. This tedious surveillance was taking him away from his real work.

He'd gotten tired of waiting in the car, watching. After a half-hour he decided to knock, see if Finch or this Omar Goodson might answer. Rap, rap, rap. Sharp, resounding raps. The door just to his right, the first floor apartment, opened and a woman leaned her head out. Didn't say anything, just looked at him, wondering. "Hey," said Francis. Her expression blank. "Nice day, huh? I'm calling on Cary Finch. Seen him around?"

"You lookin' for him, uh? Lots of people lookin' for him," she smirked. "The police lookin' for him. I hope y'all find him and when you do, tell him he owes one month back rent." She shut the door.

Francis returned to his car. What if he did see Finch, what then? Would he talk to him directly, tell him in no uncertain terms to stay clear of Heather and Pastori's. Or else. Or else what? What could he do to enforce such an order? No, better to call Lauria and let the police do their work. Finch's hearing on the protection order was in two days, and though it was virtually certain Finch would be a no show, Francis would be there just in case.

Vorhof was a different matter. No police involved with that one. He longed to confront him about his role at the homeless camp. How many young men did he lure into his sinister orbit? Francis was beginning to see Vorhof as the proverbial wolf in sheep's clothing. He needed to find a tear in the man's fabric, get into his psyche, uncover his methods, the how and why of his purported homicides. He'd done some research online. As for social media, no FaceBook page, no Instagram or Twitter account, but there was mention of him attending the Kansas

City Art Institute. He was quoted in the *Kansas City Star* on the occasion of the Monet opening at the Nelson-Atkins, saying how too much fuss was being made over Monet with his "tiresome palette," and how the genuine talent in art these days could be found in street art where geniuses like Banksy use public spaces as their canvas, addressing social and political issues for all, including the bourgeois, to perceive and ponder. He went on to tell the interviewer how "tired old farts like Monet and Van Gogh, though revered by the masses, weren't even worthy to be held in the same esteem as blazing comets such as Dali, Magritte, Serrano, Judy Chicago, Duchamp and of course myself."

A black Camaro came slowly down the street. Looking for something, thought Francis. It stopped almost abreast of him, windows down, and three men looked and pointed to the place where Finch lived. Francis recognized them as guys from The Hill, friends of Marco's. He'd even been with one or two of them at a party Marco had thrown at the Italian-American Bocce Club. One was named Joe Della Croce. He didn't need to be noticed so he slumped way down in the seat, out of sight. The Camaro kept on going, leaving Francis to wonder what those guys were up to.

* * *

They were seated at a table in the back, he and Martha, having a salad before the main course came out. It was 4:30 and her shift had ended. Another employee, Gina Ancona, had taken her place for the evening. There weren't many diners just now, but by 6:30 the place would be full, a lively, bustling, convivial atmosphere, *the* place to be on The Hill. She was saying how earlier a very nice old gentleman had come in and without any fanfare had handed out fresh-cut red roses to all the female staff. No explanation, she said, other than it was something he'd wanted to do, make people happy.

"He sure did that, all right," she said. "What a nice gesture."

"What if everyone had that attitude?" he asked. "What can I do to make someone happy today?"

"The world would be a better place." They raised their glasses, filled with Chianti. "Cin cin," she said.

"Did he stay to eat? Did he give a name? Did anyone here know him?"

Martha shook her head. "He did not stay to dine, and no one here knew him. His identity is a mystery. When we asked him his name, he simply smiled and answered, '*il fiorista*.' You can guess how that translates."

"The florist."

The main course was brought out by a waiter in a white shirt, black tie, and maroon brocade vest. He waited a moment for them to clear a space and set the plates down carefully in front of them. He had a pepper mill in one hand that looked like an oversized chess piece, the bishop. Martha gave the go ahead. The waiter twisted the top and whole peppercorns were crunched and added to the dish. "*Buon appetito!*" and he was gone.

"Oh, I'll enjoy this meal all right," he said, his nose hovering over the plate to drink in the wonderful aroma. Earlier Martha had explained the dish called *braciole*. A thinly sliced steak stuffed with Italian herbs, two cheeses, prosciutto and breadcrumbs. The beef was slow-cooked in red wine and rich tomato sauce. "The epicure's delight," the quip on the menu where it was listed at thirty-two bucks.

They were only a few bites in when Francis recognized someone he knew from the sheriff department. Ken Braxton, dressed in plainclothes but with a lightweight brown nylon parka, SHERIFF on the back, was talking to Gina. Martha saw him too. Francis chin-pointed in that direction, said, "I know him, he's a serving deputy. This may not be good."

Francis got up, went over, serviette still tucked into his shirt. "Hey, Ken, how's it going?"

"Well, Francis Lenihan. Good to see you. Serving many these days?"

He saw that Ken had a folded summons in the back pocket of his trousers. "Oh, yeah," he answered. "I'm as busy as I want to be."

"That's the way to be. Me, I've more papers than I can possibly serve. I've got to work overtime to keep from drowning in papers ha ha!"

"Like now?" asked Francis. "You here to serve someone?"

"Yeah, as a matter of fact I am." He looked at Francis quizzically.

"You have a connection here?"

"This is my wife's family's place. I married into the restaurant business."

"Oh, I see. Your wife have a male relative named Marco? Brother? Nephew? Father maybe?"

"Marco, yeah, her brother. He's the manager, there at the bar. See? He's waving at me right now." Marco lifted his cocktail in a mock salute, ever the bon vivant, and took a hefty drink.

"No, really." said Francis. "Is it for Marco or the restaurant? Someone suing us?"

"Francis, it's an order of protection. I just got it today. Figured this would be an easy one to knock out."

"Who's the petitioner?"

"I should serve it before I give out details. Come on, you know that."

"Oh Jesus, this is messed up." He motioned for Marco to come over. Marco did, still holding his cocktail. "Marco," said Francis, "we three need to talk outside." The smile melted from Marco's face.

When Marco learned what it was he was livid. When he saw the name of the petitioner he was apoplectic. "That fucking prick attacked *me!*" he spouted. "We've got a restraining order on *him* for Christ's sake!"

"I don't try to justify it, I just serve them," said Braxton with a shrug.

"Listen," said Francis to Braxton. "I'm the one served this guy his OP. He violated that OP, came here after he was served, went to the petitioner's home after he was served. He's got a warrant out on him right now. His hearing was today, he was a no show. How can this happen? How in hell can he get an OP for my brother-in-law?"

Braxton took this in. "He was probably a no show because he was in the adult abuse office filling out an application for an OP."

Said Francis, "I guess they don't check all the so-called victims for outstanding warrants."

"Guess not," said Braxton. "Look, I'm sorry to have to do this, ruin your day and all. It's a part of my job that I don't like."

"Ruin my day!" fumed Marco. "Ha! More like ruin my life. I can't have something like this on my record."

Francis explained that he would have a chance to go before the judge and present his side of the story, and if the judge was reasonable he would see that it was Finch trying to get even. Chances are he would not grant the order and it would not be on his record.

"I've got to go explain myself? Bullshit! This shouldn't have happened in the first place." Marco's ears were red, his eyes bulging out. He was like a volcano about to erupt.

Braxton was itching to leave, but he felt he should at least try to get this poor sap to understand how the system worked. He looked at Marco and explained what Francis already knew, that ninety-eight percent of these applications for protection orders are granted. Why? Because the judges have to cover their asses. What if the person whose application was *not* granted became a victim of the abuser, injured or worse—the abuser who otherwise would have been served and made to keep away from the petitioner? A situation like that, if it became public, would destroy any chance of that judge's reelection. But just because the application was approved and the respondent served, didn't mean that it would go into effect. The judge could decide that the petitioner's allegations were borne of malice and likely fabricated.

"I don't give a rat's ass about some judge's reelection," steamed Marco. "Far as I'm concerned they can all jump off a cliff. This isn't right, goddamnit. You know it and I know it."

"Be that as it may," said the deputy and he handed the papers to Marco who took them in one hand and with the other gave the classic Italian gesture, the opposite of a compliment, a flick of the back of the hand under the chin that says Fuck You six ways from Sunday. "*Va fangoo!*"

Fifteen minutes later Marco came to their table, more composed and with a fresh cocktail. Martha scooched over and he sat beside her. "Isn't this some shit?" he began, looking for sympathy. Oh yeah, they agreed. "Can you believe this? Some lowly, ignorant *coglione* putting me on the spot? Using the courts to screw with me." A flagrant misuse of an otherwise good system, they told him. "Who does he think he is, screw with me like that?" Clearly, he doesn't know what he's getting into, they affirmed. Marco leaned forward so as to cloak his words. "He thinks he'll get even with me. I'll get even with him," he spoke conspiratorially. "I've already got eyes on the little cocksucker."

— 22 —

CARY FINCH DID NOT MAKE ANY MORE APPEARANCES where he was not wanted. Still, the implied threat of him had certain persons feeling uneasy. Heather was noticeably jittery on the job and even dropped a tray of appetizers in the kitchen when the back door flew open and a delivery guy burst in with a hand truck of Idaho potatoes. Martha, at the maitre d' stand, was extra vigilant and Marco kept a loaded .22 Ruger pistol in a drawer in his office. Three days after Marco was served, Francis had a summons for a breach of contract in South City and he found himself in Finch's neighborhood. He thought he'd drive by and see if anything was shaking. He found his previous spot on the street and parked. It was 8:10 on a Friday morning and people were coming out of their homes, heading for work or seeing kids off to school. Francis collected his thoughts as he watched the porch of the house in question. If he saw Finch, he would call Lauria as per the plan. Far as Francis was concerned, the guy was still a loose cannon and in serious need of correction.

He was in position maybe five minutes when the door leading to the upstairs flat opened and a young guy stepped out. He had seen Cary Finch only briefly when he served him and this guy may have been Finch, but it was hard to tell because his left arm was in a cast, he had a dressing over part of his scalp and one eye, and he sported a neck brace. He was taking it slow and had trouble walking straight. Francis intercepted him as he got to the sidewalk.

"Good morning," he said.

"Good morning," came the reply. "Do I know you?"

"I'm Francis, your neighbor. And you are?"

"I'm Omar," he said tentatively. "Why do you ask?"

"Oh, you're not Cary Finch? I'm actually looking for him."

The young man became very alarmed. "Not again," he gasped. "Isn't one beating enough?"

"That what happened, the injuries. You were beaten?"

Omar laughed bitterly. "Are you with them? Those thugs."

"No, no. I'm just looking to talk with Cary."

"That's my roommate," he said, "the one who they meant to hurt. Why do you think I'm Cary? If you're looking for him, you should know what he looks like."

"These thugs, they thought you were your roommate and they beat the crap out of you."

Omar laughed even more bitterly. "Worst case of mistaken identity in the history of mistaken identities. Broke into the apartment, three of them. Broke my arm, my ribs, used my head for batting practice. They weren't fucking around. Brutes, they were brutes, cold and cruel. Kept saying, 'This is what happens when you fuck with Marco.' As if I knew who this fucking Marco was."

"What did your roommate say when he found out?"

Omar blew out some air. "He's the one found me. They did their number on me around noon and Cary came in around four-thirty. I'd been lying there the entire time, a concussion, going in and out of consciousness. Cary took me to the ER."

"Where you headed now?"

"St. Alexius over on Broadway, get this dressing changed."

"Come on, I'll give you a ride."

In the car, Francis leveled with him. "Okay, I lied. I'm not your neighbor. I'm an investigator and I can help Cary so the same thing doesn't happen to him as happened to to you. I want you to do something. I'll give you my number and have Cary call me, tell him it's important."

* * *

Later that day on toward evening his phone rang. Cary Finch on the line. "Hold on a sec," said Francis. With no explanation to Martha who was in the same room, he went out in the back yard.

"Finch? You there?"

"What's up?" he asked. "You have something to tell me?"

"Listen, I'm the guy who served you that order of protection. I'm also related to the Pastori family. You need to listen to what I have to say, it's going to make your life less complicated."

"Go on."

"You saw what they did to Omar. They thought he was you. Right now they don't know they beat up the wrong guy, but if they find out... so, look, I have a plan, more like a scheme because it involves deception. Here's what you do. First, turn yourself in to the police. You have a warrant out for violating the protection order and the assault. You turn yourself in, they'll go easy on you. You take whatever medicine they hand you, deal with it, because that's better than the alternative, getting arrested when you least expect it and having them throw the book at you. Second, the hearing on your protection order against Marco Pastori. Skip that hearing, make yourself scarce on that day like you did on the hearing for the protection order I served on you. If you don't show up at the hearing, the order won't go into effect. That's a good thing because you don't want Marco any more pissed at you than he already is. This will diffuse the situation and maybe save you some broken bones. What do you say?"

"Fine, I'm totally on board with it," he answered. "I'll do it and I'll hope it works. I don't know what made me do those stupid things, cutting that guy at the restaurant. I even scared myself doing that. That's not me, I was acting out of pride and hurt, you know? Getting dumped is hard to take, but that wasn't the right response. Look what happened to Omar. Are you Catholic?"

"Yeah."

"Then you know about confession. Reconciliation they call it now. I didn't actually go to confession, though I meant to and maybe I still will. But I said an Act of Contrition and I gave myself a penance of fifty Hail Marys and ten Our Fathers."

"You may as well have said the rosary."

"Yeah," from Finch. "And you know what? I found a new girl and we're in love or at least like. She's perfect for me so I've forgotten all about—what's her name again?"

"Heather?"

"Yeah, I've forgotten all about her. She no longer exists for me."

"I'm happy for you, I guess. Now don't put off what I'm saying. You're turning yourself in tomorrow. Go to the South Patrol on Sublette, ask for Officer Lauria. Do it first thing and he'll be there. Got that?"

He went back in the house. Martha standing there arms akimbo. She asked what was so secret about that call that he had to take it in the backyard. Here was a dilemma. Should he tell Martha what Marco has done, hoping it won't cause a schism in the family or should he concoct a story and keep the truth to himself for the time being? But he knew the answer even as he considered the ruse. There was no way he could deceive Martha.

He told her all of it, not downplaying the seriousness of Omar's injuries. "He could have been paralyzed or brain injured. He could have been a lifelong invalid and your impetuous brother would be to blame."

"I believe what you say," she bemoaned, "Marco has that nasty streak in him. What appalls me is that he had others do his dirty work. And you know, Francis"—tears welled in her eyes—"it does make me very sad because now he is diminished in my eyes."

— 23 —

THE WINNEBAGO WASN'T THERE. Did this mean he was away or he keeps it someplace else? There was a Toyota Highlander in the driveway, older model, a much more practical everyday getaround ride. Big brass knocker on the front door with the likeness of a wizard. Camera overhead. Between knocks he took time to look around. Nice house, he thought, nice yard too. Who keeps it up? Does he have enough money for a lawn care service? The house was one of those stately Tudor-style mansions, secluded by towering trees and situated on maybe a half-acre in affluent West County suburbia.

Looking around he might have guessed that Jacob had come into a nice inheritance and he'd have been right. He had checked the ownership on the County Assessor's homepage and found VORHOF LAWSON G & CORINNE R H/W. Had to be Jacob's parents, but looking further into the name he learned that both parents had died together during a flash flood in the summer of 1997 when Jacob was seventeen. Jacob had never transferred the title to his name. His parents were on their way to a winery in Augusta when they were caught in a cloudburst, five inches of rain in one hour, according to the news brief he found online. They came to a dip in the road and apparently decided to chance it rather than turn back.

What Francis couldn't know was that upon the news Jacob was stoic, did not shed a tear even at the funeral, although many looked to see. Why? He had the emotional make-up of hamster and he had held a grudge against them for the longest—that pony he'd been promised. Fortunately, for their only child, they had set up a very benevolent trust fund.

There was also a RING doorbell and he tried that, reluctantly, for he hated RING doorbells. They were the bane of process servers, taking away the element of surprise. With that camera pointed at him he may as well have announced himself with a loud sign: I'm here! A recorded voice emanated from the device, fuzzy and crackling. "We're not home right now, but if you'd like to leave a message, we'll get right back to you." Francis ignored that and went back to the brass knocker.

In a well-furnished room that might be called a study, Jacob Vorhof sat at a console, watching this busybody via the closed circuit camera poised over the door. He remembered him from the camp, the name escaped him but he knew that he was the partner of the other busybody who had met an untimely end. It didn't bode well that he was here at his home. In fact, it bothered him greatly that this person had found him. I can't even tell him to leave, he thought, because then he would know that I'm home and he might stick around even longer. Then, the snoop was gone from the picture. A minute passed and there he was, but on a different screen. He was walking around the house!

Jacob cursed under his breath. Now he was peering through the large glass sliding doors that opened to the basement den. Wasn't that against the law, looking in someone's house uninvited? Actually, he was spying on him. Spying, intruding, snooping, what did it matter because Jacob wasn't going to make that call, he would not attract any attention from police. Now the snoop was rapping on the glass door and calling his name: "Jacob Jay-cob Vor-hof!" A thundering voice as if he were shouting orders on a battlefield. Certainly the neighbors would hear. Jacob cursed again but not under his breath.

"Why don't you dump a bucket of scalding water on him, do it from the upper window. That'll make him leave." Jacob whirled toward the voice, saw a shape sitting in a chair. The specter looked much as he did in life although his features were somewhat indistinct around the edges and his immaterial being shimmered with a subtle pale glow. He sat comfortably in the velvet swivel accent chair, leaning back, one leg resting on the bent knee of the other. He was dressed in olive drab T-shirt and military fatigue pants. This was not the first time the specter had made itself known.

"That's not a bad idea," Jacob said. "Buh-buh-boiling oil even better, like in Medieval times. Storm the keh-castle, get scalded with oil. Ouch!"

"Is he here because of me?" the specter wondered.

"I don't know," returned Jacob, haughtily, "and I don't intend to find out. I am not speaking to him or any other interloper who cuh-cuh-comes calling."

"You knew or should have known that taking those lives would catch up to you. You befriended us, brought us here to the comfort of your home—"

"I don't neh-need recriminations from you," he shot back. "Either act nice or guh-go back to the netherworld."

"I don't like it there," said Austin, "it's creepy."

"It's supposed to be, dummy!"

Austin was his favorite. Of the four young men he had lured from the homeless camp to his home and, yes, either killed them or talked them into killing themselves, Austin had endeared himself with his unpretentious take on life. From first he saw him at the picnic table, Styrofoam bowl of tomato soup, drinking it, for they were out of plastic spoons, and getting the soup all down his shirt, he knew he had to have him. Have in the sense of possess. He began a week-long courtship, yes, that was the word. First, he acquainted himself, sat with the young man for hours, the conversations becoming more and more intimate, revealing. He learned that Austin was not like the others. He certainly wasn't destitute, but came from a wealthy family. He was not in Hopeville by necessity, he was here by choice, even desire. He actually wanted to live the vagabond life. Some combination of distressing things in his past, failures perhaps or hopes crushed, causing him anguish. You could see the psychological wounds. The fact that Austin, a person of means, chose to live among the homeless, share their privation, made Jacob want him so bad that it was all he thought about.

And maybe he did come on too strong in the beginning. Looking back, it was clear that he had attached himself to the young man, doting on him the way he himself had been doted on by overly affectionate parents. Seeking him out, showering him with gifts. No wonder he began to back off from Jacob's fervent advances. At one point, when he didn't show up for two days, Jacob went looking for him. He found him in his pup tent that was away from the other tents, a kind of outpost close to the river.

It was afternoon and Austin was asleep or pretending to be. What's going on, Jacob asked in a concerned voice, everything okay? Austin looked at his visitor, sticking his fat head inside the flap, and he rolled over so as not to have to look. Jacob's lavish attention was a factor in his current state. The solicitous voice continued. Feeling down are we? It happens, especially in a place like this. You want to talk about it? Go away, muttered Austin. Jacob took a chance and crept further into the tent. There were opened cans of baked beans, spoons sticking out, and apple cores lying about. Austin's back to him, he placed a palm between the shoulder blades and gently massaged, stubby little fingers giving light strokes, thinking to give solace, something foreign to him, but that only made the situation worse. Austin curled into a fetal position and began to sob. This worried Jacob and he had the sense to tone down his ardor. Can you say what it is? I'm here to listen. What's gotten into you? Finally the sobs subsided and Austin turned back over, facing him. I get this feeling, he said, sheepishly, this feeling of what's the use. What is life but endless doubt, a constant feeling of being inadequate. I mean, why go on living?

Here, Jacob could have launched into a pep talk about how depression skewers the psyche and how the afflicted get strange ideas about ending their own lives or others wanting to end it for them. How it can bring on feelings of hopelessness and despair and those feelings can be surmounted, perhaps, with dedicated long-term therapy and the proper medication. Instead, he told Austin that he could relate and sometimes he felt the same way.

Eventually Austin returned and began helping out at the soup stand. Basic clean up, picking up trash around the picnic tables, taking garbage bags to the Dumpster. Helping Jacob bring the supplies and equipment back to the Winnebago. In the RV they would talk some more and Jacob would bring out the appetizers and drinks. Unlike every other loser in this place, Austin didn't self medicate with alcohol or drugs but he was fond of wine and Jacob plied him with several selections of top shelf until Austin settled on one he liked in particular, a Riesling with a savory finish from a winery in Wuerttemberg, Germany. Jacob would keep plenty of that on hand and drink it with him. They would drink and share stories and laugh and drink some more. Jacob would suggest they leave the camp, go into the City and live it up. There were concerts, steakhouses, a visit to an exclusive spa for massage and pedicure. Again, the largesse, and when Austin would protest Jacob's generosity, Jacob would grandly wave it off and utter some chestnut like You Only Live

Once, Make It Count.

During this time Jacob was carefully testing Austin, his obeisance, willingness to take orders, loyalty—the traits one looked for in a minion. One of the ways he did this was by means of hypotheticals. He'd say, "What if a person was a drain on society? I mean, his existence was like a buh-boil on a neck, ugly and disgusting. Worse, he k-k-kills happiness to everyone in his circle. There is nothing beneficial about him, no redeeming qualities. If you had a chance to, um, do away with this person and no one would know, would you take it?"

Austin, he remembered, replied, "That's kind of drastic. Why not just ignore him, stay away from him. Enough people do that, he'll become a recluse." Jacob said that wouldn't work. The only way to fix the problem is to make the man disappear.

Austin thought for a moment. "Okay, yeah, I could do that, I think, but only if, as you say, no one would know. On the other hand, *I* would know and who needs the guilty conscience?"

"Conscience? What's that?" Jacob cynically. "But thank you f-for your candor."

The day came when Jacob took Austin to his home in West County. They pulled up the drive in the Winnebago and Austin liked what he saw. Jacob switched the ignition off and they sat there as Jacob explained how he had grown up in this house, a happy child, with loving parents. How he kept mostly to himself because of his speech impediment, not feeling comfortable around other children. As a child he had an art studio in the house, and a greenhouse out back where he could grow herbs and flowers. Thirty years later, he was still making art and tending plants.

"Have you ever noticed that people don't seem to have a problem making fun of those who stutter?" he asked. Austin said no, he hadn't noticed it. "It's true," Jacob continued, "someone who wouldn't ever think to mock a blind person, say, or an amputee won't think twice about mocking a stutterer. The most common way they do this is to mi-mi-mi-mimic the stutterer's attempt at pronouncing prah-prah-problematic words. Like I'll be stuck on 'cherry,' trying to say cherry pie, for instance. And they'll say something like 'ch-ch-ch-ch oh, come on,

Jacob. Is it ch-ch-chair or ch-ch-chicken or gee, I wish I could get this word out. Ha ha ha.' Just an example."

Austin said that must be hard to deal with and they were a bunch of ill-bred assholes. Sorry you felt that you had to play by yourself.

Jacob turned to him and said, "Oh, it wasn't so bad. Later, I'll tell you about the anthill." Then, he added, "How would you like to be my guest here for a while?"

Down below on the grounds Francis was thinking about Cale and how he should light a votive candle for him. Get over to St. James and do that, he told himself, the big one, the three dollar candle. The notion of Cale being gone was nothing less than appalling. He was a brother, a fellow vet, an able partner. He was everything this butthole Jacob was not. Cale was genuine, real; Jacob, a poor excuse for a man. Cale, fun to be around; Jacob, a drip, a downer. Cale noble; Jacob ignoble and so on.

Francis rapped again on the glass door at the back of the house, knowing the occupant was probably watching him and would never come out. If I can't rouse him at least I can annoy him, he thought. He often joked that he was paid to be a nuisance and that he was good at it. He called out, "Jacob, hey pal, I wanna have a word with you. Need some help with a soup recipe. Come to the window, will you." Did he really kill Cale and maybe others? Taking someone's life, that's the most precious thing you could take from someone. Their consciousness, their perception of the world through five senses, their myriad decisions made each day, everything that made them tick, all gone because of some malevolent prick acting on a wicked, self-absorbed agenda. A minute later, Francis shouted, "Hey, Jacob, I'm wondering if you know a good RV park."

"He's a persistent one, isn't he?" said the specter.

"He is," agreed Jacob, eyes glued to the monitor, "and not a lot I can do."

"That's right," said Austin, "your customary method of murder, slipping pills into someone's food or drink, won't work here. But I know what would."

Jacob looked over to him, shimmering like a lantern in a fog. "You're just an apparition, but I'll humor you."

"You find someone or some way to let him know that you've taken a long extended vacation. You won't return until next year or maybe not at all."

"Hmm," Jacob mused, "not a bad idea. The Winnebago isn't here and he can't be sure that I'm home. But who—my neighbor, he might relay that news, that is, if I make it worth his while."

"Your visitor, I saw him writing down the plates on your vehicle. You just gonna let that pass? You can do the same, you know. It may come in handy."

"You're right," said Jacob. "Two can play this game." He jiggled a toggle on the console, zoomed in on the Escort. "I know someone who can help."

It was almost a week before Jacob got around to introducing Austin to his fellow house guest. Austin had caught glimpses of the fellow shuffling down a hallway, going from one room to another. Once he heard him run the shower in the bathroom. All that Austin could tell from these fleeting appearances is that this person was a hulking, shambling African-American fellow and that he looked familiar. At breakfast, Austin inquired about him. Who is he? Why so covert?

"He is my guest for the time being," answered Jacob pompously, "another lost soul like yourself, someone in need of understanding. He has a room in the basement and muh-muh-mostly keeps to himself."

"I see," said Austin, spooning his oatmeal, thinking how he didn't think of himself as a lost soul. "What does he do all day?"

"That I don't know," said Jacob, "stare at walls maybe. Twiddle his thumbs. You tell me, what does someone whose brain is as dull as d-d-dishwater do all day. But he is harmless, like a big t-t-t-teddy bear. Would you care to meet him?"

"Okay, if you think it's a good idea. He looks familiar."

"Very astute of you," said Jacob. "He looks familiar b-b-because he comes from the same dunghill as yourself, the homeless camp. Or should I say the hopeless camp?"

Guest was a euphemism for prisoner, for that's what Bayard was, a prisoner in this house, being held against his will, although his will to simply walk out the door was feeble indeed. Jacob had shanghaied him from Hopeville three weeks before, invited him in the Winnebago one afternoon on the pretense they were going to make a run to the liquor store. Instead, he brought him to this place, ushered him inside with a promise of cocktails and weed. By one of those coincidences plausible only in real life, Bayard was Cleo's brother and like Cleo, he was a large man with soulful eyes and a round face framed by cigar-length coils of black nappy hair. He had gynomastia—breasts, quite noticeable—due to an imbalance of hormones. He spoke slowly, deliberately, almost, it seemed, with effort. Many who encountered him came away thinking he was simple. Bayard was just the sort Jacob sought for his dark impulses. He was pathetic to the point of revulsion, needy and trusting. That evening at dinner Jacob gave Bayard his first dose of fentanyl with an oxycodone chaser—a special treat, he called it.

Jacob knocked at the door and without an invitation pushed it open. The big man stood in the middle of the room, barefoot, baggy gym shorts, dirty Lakers jersey with a gold lion pendant dangling from his neck, watching. There was a dark wet stain at the front of the shorts. "Hello there," said Jacob in soothing tones as if he were talking to a mental patient, "we've come to p-p-p-pay you a visit. I want you to meet a friend."

The man's expression remained blank. "I...I had an accident," said Bayard sullenly.

"Yes, you did," replied Jacob. "This is Austin, a disadvantaged person such as yourself." Mouth agape, Bayard nodded hello. "Austin is homeless or uh-uh-unhoused, as they say nowadays, but he is not destitute. One phone call to his parents and he would have all the muh-money and goods he could want."

"Well, I don't know about that," said Austin.

"Austin will be staying with us for the time being," Jacob continued. "You may run into him here or there and please be courteous. Remember your manners."

The big man nodded assent, said meekly, "Yes sir, Mister Jacob."

"Good, and now we'll leave you to whatever it was you were doing before we intruded."

"Uh, Mister Jacob, uh," scrunching up his mouth, "do you think I could get some more of them pills?"

Vorhof beamed. "Of course, of course, I'll have Austin buh-buh-buh-bring you some. They're very relaxing, those pills, eh?"

"They give me dreams," said Bayard.

They started to go and Austin said to Jacob, "You gave my name but you didn't give his." He looked to Bayard, standing there looking slightly bewildered.

"Oh, forgive me," said Jacob. "I'm the one who stresses manners and I've neglected one of the precepts of accepted etiquette, a proper intro-duction. Austin muh-muh-meet Number Three. Number Three meet Austin. There you go."

"Here now, you're causing quite a ruckus. What is it you want?"

The voice kind of sneaked up on Francis, looking through the glass door into the darkened room for the umpteenth time. He turned and saw a walking advertisement for L.L. Bean or Lands' End, looking quite outdoorsy in Doc Martens casuals, khaki slacks with cuffs, and classic navy blue Henley shirt. The fellow sizing him up. Francis explained vaguely that he needed to see Mr. Vorhof.

"Yes, that's obvious," he replied, "and you've been trying for some time, haven't you. I can hear your shouts all the way over to my place."

Francis straightened up to his full five-foot-eleven and a half. "It is kind of important," he said.

"Sure, everything's important to the performer in his scene, for that's what you're doing, aren't you? Putting on a show. Well, you may as well close the curtain, scene's over. Mr. Vorhof is on vacation, out of the country, actually, and he won't return for quite some time."

"Really."

"Yes, really. You may leave now, good bye."

The next morning he was in the law office of Sandy Crowley in Clayton. He sat in a chair in front of Sandy at his cluttered desk as Sandy explained what he had only partly explained on the voice message that Francis heard last evening. Sandy was the amiable principal of Bardgette Crowley & Bitttner, attorneys and counselors at law and litigators of a raft of seminal civil rights cases in St. Louis. Sandy handed him the lawsuits carefully drafted by himself over the past few days. Francis looked them over. The venue was the Eighth Circuit, United States District Court – Eastern Missouri. The plaintiff was one Debra Scarlet Bell et al, the defendants were The City of St. Louis and the St. Louis Board of Police Commissioners. Two separate defendants, two lawsuits. The complaint, eight pages in length, detailed multiple violations of the plaintiff's civil rights.

"Go get 'em, tiger," said Sandy with a smile.

Francis was crestfallen. "Geez, Sandy, I'm afraid I can't do this. You're suing the City and the police for rounding up the protesters by unethical means, policing tactics known as trap and detain or kettling. Police surround the protesters to corral them and then decide what to do with them."

"Sure, that describes it. It's a controversial tactic and it's been outlawed in certain civilized countries. I've got statements from law enforcement experts saying how this particular use of force can cause tensions to rise. And I have testimony from local activists how this kettling is a glaring example of police violence, if not brutality, towards otherwise peaceful demonstrators."

Francis saw that the attorney was quite excited about his lawsuit.

"That's fine, Sandy, you've done your homework, but unfortunately I still can't serve these summonses."

"And why not?"

Francis took a breath. "Because I was in that group that got rounded up, one of the fish in the kettle, thought you knew that. I was coming out of the Civil Courts that day and got caught up in it. I was detained with the rest of them and finally let go with a warning. So I'm not a disinterested party here and therefore unsuited to serve process related to your lawsuit."

Sandy stared at him. "But I had you appointed."

"Damn, I'm sorry."

Sandy recovered and waved it off. "It's all right," he told Francis, "I can amend the appointment. It'll probably take all of one day. Who do you think I should get?"

"Try Mitch Romo or Joachin Silva, they're always game."

"I was thinking Brillstein."

"Oh geez, Sandy, please, someone else." Adrian Brillstein was a smarmy fool whose practice consisted of posting eviction notices on the doors and windows of apartments occupied by deadbeat renters. He was the sole process server for a large apartment rental company with myriad units all over St. Louis, many of them in seedy neighborhoods.

"Okay, all right, I trust your judgment. I'll call Romo." Sandy tapped the butt end of a pencil against his chin. "You know, Francis, this is just the tip of the iceberg. This Debra Bell is a real firebrand, works with that activist minister, J.B. Robinson, and she has friends who were in that crowd, who were manhandled same as her. She's putting out the word, and this will turn into a class action suit. Something you may want to join down the road."

Francis wagged his head. "No, man, it's not for me. Frankly, I don't relate to those protesters and I don't want to officially be a part of their cause."

Sandy raised his eyebrows, a bit surprised. "Suit yourself, but just know there's some sweet honey in that pot."

Later that day he gave Cleo a call. Cleo answered on the sixth ring. "Talk to me," the salutation. "It's Francis, can you hear me?" There was a wall of sound on the other end. Horns maybe. Piano. Percussion.

"I can hear you, what's up?" Smooth baritone voice, could be a radio personality.

"What is that noise?" he shouted.

"I'm in a band, thought I told you. We're practicing."

"Oh, that's cool."

"You don't have to shout," hollered Cleo. "I'm the one who should be shouting."

"Yeah, all right. You said to call if I needed help. And I do. I want to mess with the soup man. Actually, I want you to mess with him."

"That right?"

"I figure you got a posse. How many can you round up? A dozen or so?"

"Nobody says posse anymore. It's crew. How many in my crew? That what you wanna know?"

"Come on, Cleo," someone yelled. "You can gab later. We got this number to rehearse."

"To perfection," emphasized Cleo. Then, to Francis, "Look, man, I'll call you this evening. We'll discuss this. I want to hear more. Okay?"

"Sure, I'll be around. But one more thing."

"Make it quick."

"What sort of band is it and what's your job?" He saw Cleo smiling at the other end.

"It's R and B straight up and I'm the singer."

— 25 —

THE DAYS WENT BY AT 14 DESCHUTES CIRCLE. The three inhabitants moving around the house on their own, Bayard and Austin exploring various rooms and cabinets, testing the furniture, watching TV, but not venturing outside. Not allowed, the doors were locked anyway. No phone calls either, their cell phones confiscated. Jacob hovering furtively, always near. Like some patient predator, Jacob had his eye on both, noting their every move, pondering his own moves. He was through with the sorry bloke in the basement, merely taking up space now, his fate sealed, days numbered. It was Austin he was now grooming. And he did this through a series of poignant conversations that he would initiate over drinks or meals they had together. Bayard did not dine with them, his meager meals brought to him by either Jacob or Austin.

On one occasion, Jacob put forth his theory on the inherent frailty of men, particularly those who had given up on life and accepted the abject conditions of destitution. Their lot, as evidenced by much of the population of Hopeville, amounted to a blight on society. In theory, their lives were worthless. They may as well be dead.

"Do you agree?" he asked.

"Hmm," said Austin, giving thought. "I kind of thought that everyone had some redeeming quality. Even if it's only an occasional kind act."

Jacob gave that unhappy little smile. "Even Ted Bundy? John Wayne Gacy? Hitler? Okay, say this reprobate helps an old lady across the street, it happens once a year and it happens only because he's heading the same way as the old lady. It's no inconven-ven-ven-ience for him to help her. Okay, take that one beh-benevolent act and compare it to the mountain, the Mount Everest of shortcomings mah-mah-manifested by this individual all the other days of the year. Think of that one kind act as a single grain of sand on a beach. It's engulfed by dunes of sand that are the man's foibles, his miserable existence."

"Huh, I guess I missed all that at Hopeville," said Austin. "Some of them were really nice, very willing to share what they had. It wasn't like some depressing place, like a concentration camp or something. It's just a bunch of people down on their luck."

Jacob reminded him of that day when he found him in his tent so depressed he was thinking of ending it all.

Jacob had a classical music station piped throughout the house. Ravel's "Bolero" playing just now, an uplifting counterpoint to the dour conversation, but Austin knew it only as the theme from the movie 10. "That feeling is there from time to time," he admitted, "and when it comes there's no making it go away with happy thoughts. It's like a dark cloud descending, a feeling of hopelessness, and all you can do is ride it out…or succumb to it. But it's not bothering me now, not too much anyway."

Jacob could see he had his work cut out for him with this one.

Another day, over a light breakfast, had Jacob reading an article in the *Post* about unknown persons who, in the early hours of morning, had stole into the encampment on the river and tossed lit firecrackers into tents and shelters. He read aloud for Austin's benefit how the residents were very rattled and upset, telling the reporter who came along several hours later that the unprovoked attack amounted to a hate crime and demanded arrests be made. The reporter asked, fairly, which class of people was the hate directed against. After all, the residents here were male and female, young and elderly, multi-racial, and multi-ethnic. The resident, who gave the name Kenyatta Jones, was a thoughtful person, and told the reporter that homeless people are a legitimate class all by themselves and are no strangers to being hated.

Why do you think that is? asked the reporter. Kenyatta said he wasn't sure but that it might have something to do with respectable citizens looking down at us, seeing how we live and thinking 'There But For The Grace of God, Go I.' Kenyatta went on to say how it's true that some folks, seeing us living here out in the open, that might make a person feel grateful that this is not their lot. But I think it triggers a deep resentment toward the freewheeling life. It used to be hippies, and in some parts of the world it's Gypsies, but we all share a common plight. The sight of us causes fear and even hatred, we represent a hole in the fence that's there to keep nasty things out. I think that's what it is, said Kenyatta Jones.

"Wow," remarked Jacob, putting the paper down, "this guy really nailed it, don't you think? The sight of the homeless 'triggers a deep resentment.' I couldn't have p-p-put it better."

"Throwing firecrackers into tents where people are sleeping, that's pretty rude," said Austin.

"Rude? More like a terrorist attack! Can you imagine?" Jacob began laughing and snorting and he couldn't stop. A sharp contrast to his otherwise glum demeanor. "God, I wish I'd thought of that," and he laughed some more. Finally, he calmed down. "But don't you see? This rude action, scaring the crap out of sleeping bums, it's just a symptom of the rancor felt toward vay-vagrants or t-t-transients, however you classify them, and it's not going away. Live anywhere they want, b-b-b-beg for a living, go to the bathroom out in the open. Yuck. Oh, you can say, But we need policies to help them out, get them back on their feet in productive society. Well, here's some news. They don't want to get back on their feet, they've guh-guh-gotten used to sitting on their asses."

"I don't get you," Austin admitted. "You helped out there, you gave us nourishment, good soup five days a week, and yet you're really down on the homeless. Do they threaten you in some way?"

"Other way around, my friend. I am the threat to them." He chuckled to himself and said, "Here, try this marmalade on your t-t-toast. It's exquisite."

* * *

On the rare occasions he left, he would never be gone long. When home, he would check on them periodically, finding them lounging on sofas, watching TV, looking at his paintings framed and mounted on walls, scratching their heads. He couldn't expect them to understand intelligent art, abstract or conceptual. Once, they were seen playing CLUE. They had found the old board game in a closet somewhere. That they were becoming friends posed a problem in Jacob's mind, for it meant that Austin would be more resistant to persuasion. It wasn't practical to keep them separate, though. He would have to lock them in their rooms. But the concern was really of no matter. Number Three had been here for almost a month and his time was up. When Jacob looked at this lump of humanity, legs draped over the end of the sofa, staring up at the ceiling, he saw a corpse.

Though Austin was showing few signs of being indoctrinated, Jacob felt he must press on. One evening, after dinner, Jacob called Austin back to the table. An album on the table, Jacob opened it, told him to take a look. The pictures were something special, he said. The album held four photos per page, and there were only seven pages filled. Austin sat and took a look. The pictures were of two men, one young and one older. They were both scruffy-looking and by their expressions weren't too happy about being photographed. Each man had his own page, at least in the beginning of the album, but toward the end they were in the same frame. There were no captions. The color pictures were made with a Polaroid camera.

"Okay," said Austin after a minute, "who are these guys and why are you showing me?"

Jacob stood behind him with a hand on his shoulder. "Number One and Number Two," he told him, "for-for-for-former guests here."

"No names? Just One and Two?"

"They had names at one time," he explained, "but once they get here those nuh-nuh-names are forgotten. Tell me your impression of them." To Austin this was creepy, Jacob was creepy, and this whole fucked up situation was creepy beyond comprehension, and it didn't help that Jacob was playing Gregorian chants in the background. Why on earth was he still here?

"You've taken pictures of us with that same camera. Does that mean we're going to end up in your weird picture album?"

Jacob's lips curled into a smile. "He will. You, I'm not so sure."

"So tell me about these guys." Austin closed the album. He'd seen all he wanted.

"They were panhandlers, beggars. I st-st-st-stop-stopped to hand them money, came back later, talked them into getting into the Winnebago. First the one, then the other, but it was the same day. I was feeling particularly adventurous that day. I buh-buh-brought them here, asked them to stay for a few days. Nice meals, hot shower, beer, wine, whatever they wanted. They had nuh-nuh-no qualms about snapping up that offer."

Austin saw the scenario, all too familiar, the man's penchant for making damaged people his playthings. "And when they wanted to leave, they couldn't, right?"

"It's amazing how drugs can take away one's drive and replace it with lethargy. Before long they were as docile as sheep. Of course, they're not much fun in that narcotic state. I decided to dispatch them sooner than later."

Austin pushed Jacob's hand from his shoulder. He stood up, stared at him with incredulity. "Just like that, huh? Boom, you took their lives. Why? What did they ever do to you?"

"They took up space on the planet. They were merely human bags of garbage, think of them that way. And what do you do with bags of garbage? Into the Dumpster."

Austin realized that Jacob, by confiding in him, admitting he'd murdered two men, maybe even more, meant that he was dangerous to him. He could go to the police, but that would never happen because Jacob controlled him. Rather than take a risk, Jacob would kill him. Suddenly the image of a fly trapped in a spider's web popped in his mind.

Austin gulped. "That's really cold, I've gotta say. Just kill someone because you don't like their lifestyle. You should get some help for these impulses."

"It's not whatever, not anything goes," he admonished, throwing his hands up. "There are criteria." The more he talked, the less he stuttered.

Austin decided to back off from the critical remarks. Instead he would choose his words carefully. This guy was a full-blown psycho and he didn't want to provoke him. "Criteria, sure, there's got to be some parameters. You have your reasons, justifications, and I'm sure they make sense to you."

"These two were easy," said Jacob, "didn't fight, just resigned themselves."

"Not much of a will to live, huh?"

"I would say not. One of them, Number Two, admitted he had nothing to live for." Austin swallowed hard. He had already volunteered that sentiment to this psycho, just looking for a reason to kill again.

"So, uh, what did you do with them? Their bodies, I mean."

Jacob massaged his chin in thought. "You really want to know?" Austin nodded almost imperceptibly. "I tried two different methods, wuh-wuh-wondering which would be more successful. One I wrapped in a cheap plastic tarp and placed him in a Dumpster—like the bag of garbage he was—in a filthy alley in the City. He was never discovered. I imagine he was picked up on trash day and made his way through the river of trash to a landfill where he was gruh-gruh-gruh-gruh—"

"—grumbling?"

"—ground under by one of those massive compactors. The other one was discovered. I took him down to Hopeville late one n-n-night and propped him up against a tree, made it look like he'd just fallen asleep or passed out. Next morning they realized he was a goner and an ambulance came and took him to the muh-muh-morgue. There had been a rash of homeless d-deaths from overdose in the City, and no one suspected a clever s-s-s-serial killer such as myself. He was just another overdose."

They were both silent for a spell. Austin sat back down at the table and had his hands folded, fingers intertwined, pondering the troubling exchange just now. Things were definitely not looking up. He was having serious difficulty thinking of himself as either pawn or victim, the two roles open to him, it seemed. When he walked in that Winnebago and let Jacob drive off, he had allowed himself to become a part of this horror story. He had only himself to blame.

Not only that but he had blown his only chance of escape because he wasn't thinking straight. He should have bolted, put some serious distance between himself and Jacob, instead of making that phone call. It was a week ago, Jacob had gotten this idea to look for another vagrant to snatch. He got Austin to join him, trolling in this dangerous game. They took the Winnebago to North Grand known for certain transient motels where people would do almost anything to get a fix. On the sidewalk out front of the Guest Host Motel, drug-addicted zombies lay propped up against the building, too wasted to stand, staring blankly at the passing traffic. The RV stopped at the curb. Jacob told Austin to get out and bring one of them over, tell him free drugs, whatever. Austin got out. Jacob saw him hunkering down talking to the guy, pointing to the RV, the guy nodding vaguely. Then Austin was gone.

Austin had suddenly decided to make a break for it. He ducked in to the litter-strewn courtyard of the motel, more derelicts milling about, eyeing him opportunistically. He saw the office and went in, imagining Jacob on his heels. The middle-aged Indian man behind the scratched plastic partition gave him a serious once-over. Austin asked to use the phone. The owner said no. Austin reached for his wallet. He had seven dollars. He held it out: Please, one quick phone call, my life depends on it. It was a cordless, the man passed it through the opening in the partition. Austin dialed, thank God his father answered. He asked about Whiskers then realized he had to be quick. He told his father where he was and to please please please come and get him like right now. As Dr. Lambert was saying Hold tight, son, I'll be there, Jacob burst in and grabbed him by the arm. Game over, he fumed.

Jacob sat opposite sipping from something deep red in a glass, eyes on Austin. At one point he had plans for the young man, plans that would likely take some persuasion. He had never considered an accomplice. Bundy, Dahmer, Ridgeway aka The Green River Killer, Rader aka the BTK Killer, even Jack The Ripper—all solo practitioners. Working alone had suited him just fine but he was not set in his ways, he could train an underling to do his bidding. It would be a novel experiment, an exercise in tutelage, but after the Guest Host Motel fiasco he couldn't trust him and those hopes were spoiled. Now the would-be accomplice would take a detour down the dark tunnel of oblivion.

He said, "I imagine you're wondering what next."

"Yeah," answered Austin, "and whatever it is, it probably won't be good. Can I just go back to the camp?"

"No, I have plans for you here. Would you care for a glass of claret?"

"No, thank you."

Jacob cleared his throat to make way for a crucial pronouncement. "Our friend in the basement, his time has come. Tonight will be his last. I'd like you to assist me."

Austin gulped. "No, thank you."

"I understand your reluctance. He's a fellow human, you may think, he's got every right to live. Life is sacred, we have no call to take it. That sort of rubbish."

"He's homeless, but he's also mentally ill."

"Who cares?"

"He's not bothering anyone."

"On the contrary, he's bothering me and that's all that matters."

When pressed, Jacob had the compelling personality of a Rasputin or a Mephisto, for he eventually got Austin to accompany him to Bayard's room. They found the big man awake, lying on his bed, mouth open, staring at nothing. When they entered, he rose and greeted them. It was heartbreaking for Austin to see him, so trusting, so childlike, without an inkling of what was about to happen.

"We buh-buh-brought you a drink," said Jacob. "Apple juice, which I know you like."

"That's very nice of you," said the gullible fellow.

He handed the glass to Austin, indicated that he pass it to Bayard. Austin shook his head.

"Do it!" he hissed.

"I won't, I *can't*," he replied.

"You *will* do it and that's an order."

"You heard me, there's no way."

"You wait," Jacob seethed, "you wait and see." He took the glass back and handed it to Bayard, who was puzzled by the remarks. "Here you go," said Jacob, quite the congenial host, "bottoms up."

Austin about-faced and left the room. Bayard drank the fatal potion, apple juice, crisp and refreshing, and laced with six tabs of fentanyl, crushed with mortar and pestle and ground into a powder, enough to kill an elephant.

— 26 —

JACOB HAD TO GET HIS DRUGS FROM SOMEWHERE and he thought he had found a reliable supplier in Kiki Fontana. He had met Kiki while she was making a delivery in the early days of Hopeville. He watched her park, a blue Toyota Camry with a cracked windshield and dented fender. She got out and began walking up the path that led to the settlement, oversize purse, more like a satchel, slung over her shoulders and behind her back. He pegged her as mid-to-late twenties, about five-nine, medium build with hair past her shoulders streaked some shade of magenta. She was dressed for February with a long sleeve polyester dress and cowl, a pair of knee-high Western boots that women wear to feel empowered, so he'd heard, and a faded yellow monogrammed baseball cap. When the weather warmed and he would see her again in lighter attire, like a halter top, he would see the platypus tattoo on her bicep. She strode with a purpose in his direction for his soup stand was on the path. He was intrigued by her and realized he was actually going to initiate a conversation with a stranger. Then she was upon him and though he was somewhat intimidated by her, by almost all women in fact, he said hello.

"Hello yourself," she said jovially. Stopping, "What do we have going here?"

"It's uh-uh-uh soup, a soup kitchen. See?" He pointed to the chalk-board which read TODAY CREAM OF CELERY ENJOY! "Would you-you like s-s-s-some? I mean, when it's red-red-red—"

"I know what you mean," she said, putting him at ease. She said she never had that soup before and was it hard to make?

"Yes," he said, "it t-took me-me-me all morning. You have to get it just right."

Sure, she'd have some on her way back.

"You're visiting," he said, "I've never seen you before."

"That's right, visiting, and I'll be off now. But later, alligator," and she gave him a wink.

Twenty minutes later she was back and the soup still wasn't ready so they talked while he and a helper stirred the stockpots and got the place ship-shape and he learned that she attended Forest Park Community College and worked evenings as an Uber driver. She had a side business making certain deliveries.

"Like the one you jus-just made now? What is it you deliver?"

"Oh, things that people want to make them feel good." Again, the wink.

"My soup does that," he offered, "but you're not in the food indus-dus-dus...trade."

She smiled, gave a scampish shake of the head.

"Leh-leh-let me guess, it has to do with contraband."

"Contraband? What're you, some DEA agent?"

"Okay," he said, "then it's either weed or pharmaceuticals."

"Bingo!" she said.

* * *

Cleo and four friends parked the Escalade in a strip mall about six blocks from Jacob. This was their idea, to walk over to Jacob's. It made sense, five black guys in lily white suburbia, here for the express purpose of causing trouble, there was a chance their ride would be impounded if they brought it to the scene. Francis had provided the address, asked Cleo to pay Jacob a visit, mess with him in a way that Francis could not. Cleo was up for it, especially if this jerkoff had anything to do with Bayard's death. They both agreed, though, that any trouble caused, any commotion raised, would stop just short of getting hauled off to jail. They all accepted that the police would inevitably be called.

It was late on a Tuesday, the air warm, the sun concluding its arc on another day. The crew walked abreast through the parking lot and those shopkeepers who saw them hastily drew their blinds and locked their doors. The Stockley verdict unrest was still ongoing in parts of the City and these guys were probably protesters even if they weren't chanting slogans or carrying signs that compared the St. Louis police to Nazis. Already the lights on the police dispatcher switchboard were starting to light up.

The parking lot emptied onto a busy thoroughfare, no sidewalk, and they had to walk single file on the grassy median. Drivers slowed down to take a look, gawking at the incongruous sight of Negroes in their midst. The five walked on, ignoring the hard glances. In fifteen minutes or less, they took the turn onto Deschutes Circle and soon found themselves on Jacob's driveway. They stood at the front door and began calling his name, playful at first, egging him on with a lilting hello: *Jay-cob, oh Jay-cob, come out, come out, wherever you are.* This quickly turned rude with all manner of insults tossed out like confetti. Their prearranged script called for them to act as though he was their dealer and he was holding out on them. And they were clamorous in this chicanery. "Where's my product, you weasel," Cleo called. "You can keep the heroin," another bellowed, "we just want our crack cocaine. You hear? Give us our cocaine!"

Jacob stood in a darkened room on the second floor, pressed against the wall near the window, peering quite cautiously at the scene below. Strong feelings welled up, mostly fear and anger, each fighting for dominance. First, that private investigator causing embarrassment and now these people. Who were they, acting all angry, shouting about drugs?

"You really put your foot in it this time, didn't you?"

He jumped with a start, turned toward the sound. The specter was back. "This is no good," he said, pointing down there. "What have I done to deserve this?"

"That must be the biggest rhetorical question on record," said the specter mordantly. "What *haven't* you done to deserve this?"

He ignored that jibe and went on with his grousing. "Someone put them up to this, five b-b-b-black guys at my door, yelling, putting up a ruse that I have their drugs. What bullshit this is."

"Someone is on to you is what it is," said Austin. "You can't kill four men and not expect to face consequences."

"Five! It's five men. You're forgetting about that biker." The number was important to Jacob, the minimum, he felt, for classifications as a proper serial killer.

"You're right, sorry. I forgot about the biker. But really it should be six. You promised to kill yourself. We had a pact, a solemn pact. You do me and then yourself. You chickened out."

Jacob made an utterance that may have been a giggle. "I've never been any good at suicide," he explained.

"The police will be here any time and you'll have some explaining to do."

"I'll pretend I'm not here," he said. "It's worked before."

The same neighbor as before came out, walking up to the interlopers without trepidation. His name was Dick Thomas and he sold insurance policies. "Here now," he told them, "this isn't the ghetto, this is a quiet neighborhood." They got a kick out of this, the fool thinking they live in the ghetto. But their plan was not to menace or physically harm anyone, rather to cast suspicion on the homeowner, this Jacob.

"We're sorry if we interrupted your TV show," said Cleo, "but the sad fact is that this man, the one you may know as Jacob, is a notorious drug dealer and is holding out on us. How much does he owe, Rico?"

Rico piped right up, "Seven thousand four-hundred and some change."

"And we're here to collect," said Cleo, gold teeth catching the final rays in the setting sun.

"And this is your idea of discreet," Dick Thomas said, "trumpeting your sordid business all over creation?"

"He's right," agreed one called Lonnie, black leather jacket open, showing braided gold chains, "we are being loud."

"We'll try to tone it down," from Rico.

"Good thing we didn't bring the bullhorn," from yet another, a balding imp named Choco.

"Is there a toilet around here?" asked Lonnie.

"But we are broadcasting in a sense," said Cleo, thinking to reason with the man. "We have to make ourselves known. We tried the door-bell, no answer. And those walls look pretty thick, he may not hear us otherwise. Wait!" snapping his fingers. "Do you have Jacob's number? Will you call him for us?"

"Yes, I have his number," snapped Dick Thomas, "and no, I won't call him for you."

"Please."

The man gritted his teeth and seemed beside himself. He said, "I highly suggest that you take your sleazy business elsewhere, and you should move along immediately unless you want to deal with—"

At that moment two squad cars pulled in the driveway, no flashing lights but creeping along. Four cops got out, hands at their sides near their firearms like gunslingers of yore. As they walked over, the neighbor separated himself from the others.

"Is there a problem here?" one cop asked seriously although it was a stupid question.

Dick Thomas spoke out. "Yes, officer, these men are trespassing and causing a major disturbance. I live next door and I watch over this place."

"That right?" said another cop. "What're you fellas doing here? Where's your car?"

Cleo stepped up, speaking with ease and confidence. "That's easy, officer. We're here at the invitation of the homeowner, Mister Jacob. He asked that we join him for dinner but when we get here there's no one to answer the door. We're calling his name because we're concerned about him. He's not been well lately."

"That's not the story they gave me!" cried Dick Thomas.

"We'll get to you in a minute," said the cop. Then, turning to Cleo and crew. "Let's see some ID."

At that moment a blue Toyota Camry pulled in the drive. The car went in about thirty yards then came to a screeching halt. Two cops advanced on the car, which began a Y-turn in an attempt to leave.

"Hold it right there," said one to the startled young woman behind the wheel.

"Get out of the car," said the second.

"Oh shit!" uttered Jacob, watching from the window. "Shit! Shit! Shit! What's she doing here? She wasn't supposed to come until tomorrow."

"The best laid plans of mice and men," said Austin, a smirk on his diaphanous lips.

"Oh, shut up, you damn fool." There were eleven people down below and none of them welcome. Five black guys looking to annoy him, four uniformed cops looking for the reason the black guys were here, one meddling neighbor thinking to sound the alarm, and Kiki, his witless dealer who just got snared like a rabbit in a garden.

He watched with growing alarm as the cops shined flashlights into the Camry.

As the one cop questioned Kiki—"I was just turning around, officer"—the other saw a weapon on the floor in the back, sticking halfway out from under the seat. It was a machete that Kiki carried just in case one of her customers got crazy. This was probable cause for a search. Kiki stood there on edge as the two cops rummaged around in her car. Jacob, with a bird's eye view of the situation, on edge as well, not knowing whether she would bring him into it. As the cops checked their identification, the brothers watched the search with interest as did Dick Thomas. Who was this woman who suddenly rolled up on this hubbub?

Then the cop doing the search brought out a green plastic fishing tackle box. He placed it on the hood of the car and snapped it open. All the trays inside, small, medium, and large filled with all kinds of pharmaceuticals—pink pills, blue pills, white pills, round pills, oblong pills, ones with lines, other with numbers, mostly opioids. "I'm in sales," she told them, trying to sound convincing despite the quaver in her voice, "I work for Pfizer." A half hour later, Cleo and crew were heading back to their car, Dick Thomas had gone back to his jigsaw puzzle, and Kiki Fontana sat glumly in a squad car, handcuffed, pensive, waiting for her own car to be impounded and she brought to the station to be booked on suspicion of unlawful distribution of controlled substances.

Part III

Francis sat at the morning table enjoying leftover Spaghetti Bolognese for breakfast, loving the taste and savoring every bite. Boy, she could make a wonderful sauce! He looked at her in her robe across the table and told her so. She smiled and said it was in the genes like a fledgling knows how to fly. This is the perfect way to start a busy day he said and spooled up another mouthful. He was making his Do List as he did each morning. He did it to remind himself what was to be done that day, of course, but also because it felt good to check off the items as they were accomplished. Papers 2B served in 63017, 63112, 63135, 63118. Library: return audio book, get new one. Another Don Winslow? Pick up subpoenas Wallace McKinney. Haircut? Urzi's Mkt — dinner tonight need wine, cilantro, garlic cloves, peppers, pesto. Call Cleo what happened? Where's my phone? Murphy's? Call.

Even at the early hour, Murphy's doors were unlocked. Alphonse Rourke was busy sprucing the place up, sweeping, mopping, emptying ashtrays, getting ready for the half-dozen sots who would shuffle in around ten, the start of a new day in the old-school bar.

"Yeah, you left it here again, right on the bar. Must've been hidden by all those longnecks, huh?" Alphonse was a short, wiry fellow in his fifties whose disposition tended toward philosophical.

"You'd think I'd check my pockets before I leave," said Francis. "Something that essential."

"Yeah, you'd think, but somehow a dozen or so drinks seems to fog the memory. People leave all sorts of shit behind. In the morning, cleaning up? I find jewelry, watches, playing cards, glasses." He was counting off the items on his fingers. "Money sometimes, jackknives, all sorts of notes scribbled on paper, oh, and dentures. How can someone forget their dentures? Go around gumming their food all day long, geez!"

Francis chuckled, the delivery was perfect Dogtown, what he loved about this place. Alphonse handed him his phone. Dead. He'd have to charge it in the car. Alphonse held out his hand like he wanted a gratuity. Francis took out his wallet and handed him a five, but he withdrew his hand at the last second.

"Go on! I was jus' kidding. I don't need no tip, you're my pal and you sing here. Tell you what, next time we're both here you can sing a song like you do and say, 'This one's for old Alphonse, workin' behind the scenes to keep this place running.' How's that?"

"I'd be happy to do that and I'll make it soon. Thanks, man."

Alphonse may have blushed, but his complexion was so ruddy it would be hard to tell. "Aw, go on with your bad self, get the hell out of here, seize the fucking day!"

Francis did just that, went out into the big wide world to seize the fucking day. He knocked out two depo subpoenas, one to a doctor's office in a medical building and another to an engineering firm. Easy, too bad they weren't all like that. Then he picked up three more subpoenas from a law office in Clayton, but these were going to people and not businesses. No intel, not even are they home in the day or do they work. That would really help, and of course because it's a subpoena only that person may be served, not like a summons where you can do substitute service, sometimes called copy service on a member of the family over the age of fifteen.

He had a show cause order to serve out in Ballwin, one of the ninety municipalities that make up St. Louis County. This one had special instructions. The respondent, Steve Goodman, lives in Denver but he's in town for his brother's wedding. The petitioner informed her lawyer there's only a three-day window to get him served, and then he returns to Denver. It's these down and dirty assignments where Specials come in handy; the sheriff deputy isn't going to fulfill special requests from petitioners.

He knocked at the door of a ranch house on a sylvan street in placid suburbia. A grizzled, pot-bellied bear of a man opened it. As Francis asked for Steve and kind of hinted around at his purpose here—his official court-issued ID on a lanyard giving him away—the man got a bemused look on his face.

"He's here all right," said the man, who identified himself as Steve's dad, "and he's in fine shape after a night of boozing at one of them strip clubs on the Eastside. Got in just hours ago, bachelor party, you know?"

"Well, uh, can you get him to come to the door?"

The man found this funny as well. "Probably not, but you're welcome to go in his room and serve him with them papers you got, right? I won't stand in your way. I know he's not paying child support and fact is, it kinda pisses me off. So, I say let the chips fall where they may."

Francis made his way to Steve's room on his own, the dad going as far as the hallway, pointing the way and then making himself scarce. The door was open and Steve lay sprawled on a mattress, sheets bunched up around him. Francis called his name. Nothing. Called his name louder. "Steve, hey Steve, wake up." Steve gave a plaintive moan and switched position slightly. Another moan issued from Steve's cracked lips and dry mouth, a sign that Francis knew all too well, the wretched state of a five-star hangover. This name calling wasn't going to work. Francis shook him gently. "Hey, man, wake up for just a minute. I've got something for you."

Steve's eyes blinked, his mouth twitched, he looked around for his bearings. He saw Francis standing there, a total stranger in his bedroom. "What is it?" he managed. Francis handed him the show cause order with motion for contempt. Steve took the sheaf, rolled over toward the light coming from a window, tried to make out the words. Then, he understood. "Arrgghh!" he spluttered as if he'd stepped in dogshit. With utter contempt he tossed the papers across the room and went back to his pillow. On the way out, the man of the house standing near the door. "Well?" he said.

Francis snickering, "Done, thanks." The mirth was contagious and the old man smiled wide at the thought of Steve ambushed in his own bed.

"I don't know if this'll get him to dust off that checkbook to pay the bills for my granddaughter who we rarely see, but at least you put the fear of the law in him. Have a good day now, you hear?"

Francis crying with laughter as he went to his car, gasping for air. Ha ha hee hee heh heh. You can't catch someone off guard any more than that ha ha. The look on his face. Like something out of a sitcom. A mile away at a red light, still laughing, he can't stop, the woman in the car next to him looking and laughing because he's laughing.

* * *

Later on the phone with Cleo, listening to what happened. The police came, didn't take long, probably thought they had a riot, took our names, told us to leave, he said. Knocked at his door for the longest, shouting his name too, but he never came out. And while this is happening, a woman drove up, pretty sure they found drugs in her car. They took her away. His dealer? Maybe. I got her plates, said Cleo, if you wanna run them, find out who she is. Good, said Francis, you're already thinking like a detective.

He's already acting the fugitive, Cleo went on, in his big house and watching everything outside, won't come out. Scared of everything. But how we gonna pin anything on him? No evidence no proof of anything criminal and there's never going to be any.

Francis concurred. "Yeah, that is the fly in the ointment, but, you know, if we, um…"

"What? You got a plan?"

"Okay, so we can't prove any past crimes like kidnapping or murder, but maybe we can stick him for a crime he's about to commit."

"Yeah?"

"Yeah, we know he dabbles in drugs, street drugs or legit pharmaceutical, not sure, but he uses them as weapons on his victims. So what if we plant a large stash of drugs on his person, in his RV or his car or even in his house. Then we call in a tip and get him busted."

"I'm surprised to hear you say that. Mister Law and Order breaking the law. We get caught doing that and we go to jail." Actually, Francis was surprised to have suggested it. It was not like him to flirt with such risk. But Cleo put a damper on the idea. "It's not serious enough. Convicted he'll get a couple years, maybe just probation."

"It's what we have," countered Francis, "at least it's something."

"Where we gonna get these drugs?"

"You must have connections."

"Oh, me being a black guy living in the so-called ghetto, every type of vice at my disposal. I have access to all sorts of killer drugs, that it?"

"Well, yeah, maybe. I sure don't."

"Dream on, white boy. When you gonna come hear the band, hear me sing?"

"Whenever you invite me."

"We playing a week from this Saturday at the Harlem Tap Room on Martin Luther King, four to seven. Midnight Velvet."

"What's Midnight Velvet?"

"Name of the band, fool."

— 28 —

THE IDEA CAME TO FRANCIS IN THE PREDAWN HOURS. He lay there in the pitch dark of their room, listening to Martha lightly snoring, thinking how rich life is and how he'll really miss it once he's dead. The next thing that popped up: Wouldn't it be fun to bring a gang of homeless out to see Jacob, kind of like a reunion, they can party and catch up. It was a great idea because it would piss off Jacob to no end. He would get it going this morning.

Later that morning he went to Hopeville, walked around, passing out 3 x 5 cards with a personal hand-written invitation. PARTY WITH THE SOUP MAN! THIS SATURDAY NOON TO 4. FOOD DRINKS GAMES PRIZES FUN! SHUTTLE WILL BE ON WHARF STREET 11:30 READY TO TAKE YOU. DON'T MISS THIS ONE. He hoped there wouldn't be too many. Despite the warning from the alderman no one had moved out yet. He'd rented a Ford Transit Passenger van for the occasion, a twelve-seater. On the day of there was a sizable crowd and he had to turn away eleven people. There was talk of overpowering him and stealing the van for a joy ride, but he whisked the chosen into the large vehicle before the others could get organized.

It was a beautiful day and spirits were high. Of course there was always someone to grumble. Why that soup man wanna give us a party? He don't seem like no party boy. It ain't like he's missing us, right? But we miss that soup, don't we?

Yeah, we sure do. Why he stop comin' 'round?

You didn't suck his dick the way he like.

Oh, fuck you, man!

Just be happy with what you got.

Oh, an' what is it we got? We hobos, tramps, bums. We ain't got shit.

Francis looked good behind the wheel with Redhead brand khaki shorts, Wigwam wool socks, ecco hiking boots, white long sleeve cotton shirt with a green shamrock on the front and MURPHY'S MISFITS on the back, from the softball team a decade ago. Long brown hair falling over Wayfarer shades. They had come to the on ramp at the entrance to

I-44. A red light with a queue behind it.

"Hey, looky there!" A female panhandler stood with a big sign, letters writ in crayons of various colors. 2 UGLY 2 BE A PROSTITUTE. She carried a small basket for donations.

"That's Rhonda from the camp," said a loudmouth named Stinky. "Hey, Rhonda!" he called from an open window. Rhonda waved happily. "You ain't too ugly for that. How's about ten bucks for a BJ?"

"You ain't got ten bucks," she shot back.

"I kin borrow it!"

She gave him a skeptical look. "Okay, but wash it first."

Francis pulled into the driveway of Maison de Vorhof just after noon. Now looking at it in a different light, Francis saw the place had a forlorn look like a moldering old mansion. Neglect, definitely—weeds in the yard and tools out in the open collecting rust. The perimeter of the property was enclosed with a picket fence, the once white slats turned to dingy gray, the gate off its hinges. The passengers climbed out, stretching and yawning. They began to mill around and soon realized that they'd been had for there were no preparations for a party in sight.

"This ain't right," said one.

"You sure you got the right day?" asked another of Francis.

Francis, too, was bewildered. "Well, yeah, he said Saturday and this is Saturday. He's probably inside getting ready, let's knock." They knocked at the big brass knocker on the door. They rang the bell. They called out his name.

Upstairs, Jacob looked down on the scene below, growing more incensed by the minute. How could they? This wasn't happening. Their very presence on his property an affront to all that is decent—no, this wouldn't do. He wished he had a pack of vicious dogs to sic on them. He saw Francis, obviously the ringleader, damn his ass. At last, he couldn't stand it anymore. He opened the window, stuck his florid face out. "Hear me you misbegotten p-p-p-pack of animals," he yelled. "Get your slimy grubby selves off my property! Nuh-now! You are trespassing. Go back to your tents. T-t-t-tents? Hah! More like pigsties.

Disgusting, the wuh-wuh-way you live."

They stood there mouths agape at the unexpected diatribe. A few of them responded. "Aw, c'mon, man. Why you wanna be this way?"

"You cuh-cuh-come to my home uninvited, you s-s-soi-soil my my otherwise happy existence with your filth. How do you expect me to react? I will tell you once muh-muh-muh...leave, depart, go away. Is that clear enough for your addled syph-syph-syphil-syphilit-litic brains? Now good-good-good-good-GOODBYE!" and he slammed shut the window.

The crowd below continued looking at the shut window. "Well, I guess that about does it for the party," said Francis. "Tell you what, though, Uncle Francis will treat you all to some Dairy Queen. I saw one on the way in, so hop aboard the bus."

"How 'bout Taco Bell, they got that Cheesy Double Beef Burrito. I can taste it now"

"No, man, Big Mac. We go to McDonald's.

"Just get on the bus," urged Francis.

Jacob half-expected to hear some snide comment from dead Austin, but the specter was nowhere around. Just as well, he didn't need any advice on anger management from someone who couldn't even move a body without a bother.

Bayard Yardley aka Number Three was a big man and Jacob couldn't move him alone. He needed help and Austin was the only choice. But seeing as how he'd walked out of the room rather than be a witness to murder, it was going to take some coaxing. Jacob found him in the kitchen standing at the counter with a glass of milk. He made the boy a sandwich and for a half hour they talked about anything but the body in the basement. At length Jacob started in about how the man needed a decent disposal and it was their obligation to see that he got one. Austin said he wanted nothing to do with that. Jacob nodded as if he understood and proceeded to make him a bowl of Campbell's tomato soup to go with the ham sandwich. Jacob continued his blandishments saying that Austin would be greatly rewarded if he would help him with this task. Austin wondered what sort of reward. It's a surprise, said Jacob, you'll have to wait and see. Austin held to his position about moving poor Number Three's body, but now it was more reluctance than flat-out no. More time passed, Jacob changed the subject. Then Jacob asked him again, would he please help move this body to a safe place. Austin wavered. Jacob waited. The answer he wanted was not coming so he told Austin that if he didn't help he would lock him in the room with that rotting corpse and throw away the damn key. They could both go to the devil.

When Austin dropped his end of the body for the third time, Jacob really bitched him out.

"What's wrong with you? You're bigger and brawnier than me and you c-c-can't even hold on to him? Concentrate, will you?"

"It just doesn't feel right," he complained. "He's so loose, he's flopping around, it's like holding on to a bag of sand."

"Look, there's the car, think you can make it that far?"

Under the stars, they were walking like penguins, baby steps, a waddling gait under the weight. Jacob walking backwards because he had the legs, and he faced Austin who had his hands in the man's armpits. Bayard's head lolling this way and that, his tongue hanging out, flecks foam around the lips. Suddenly, the dead man released a belch, turning the air fetid. "I really think I'm gonna be sick," said Austin.

They found a construction site in Bridgeton, far from Jacob's home, and parked beside one of those big roll-off Dumpsters for debris and scrap. This one was half full which was perfect as the body would be covered before they came to collect the container and take it to wherever it gets emptied. Upon arrival they'd shrouded the body in a bed sheet and bound it with duct tape. With great effort and lots of grunting they hoisted it up over the rim. Jacob gave Austin a foot up so he could climb in move things around. With Jacob hissing orders at him, he cloaked the body with various discarded materials—plasterboard, sections of plywood, rebar. Then he clambered out and jumped to the ground.

"Well done," said Jacob, patting him on the shoulder. "Now I've got something to show you."

* * *

In the City along South Broadway there's a place where the Mississippi bends and for a distance of about ten blocks south of that bend a series of limestone bluffs arise in tiers above the riverbank and railroad tracks. Years before, these bluffs were crowned with beautiful homes that might be called mansions. Many of these homes have since disappeared or have been adapted for other uses. One of these homes belonged to Jacob's great uncle, Lucius Vorhof, an engineer who, among other noted accomplishments, had assisted James Eads in the construction of the renowned Eads Bridge, a Post-Civil War structure still in use today. Long ago, sometime in the seventies, the Vorhof mansion had been condemned by the building inspector for dereliction and eventually torn down. But the property itself had remained in the family and on this property was a carriage house that had been spared during the demolition. That carriage house was perfect for an art studio.

Jacob's Highlander motored up the incline of streets leading to the top of the bluff. The street was a cul-de-sac and Jacob took it to the very end and parked on the driveway leading to the carriage house. He and Austin got out. The only lights were street lamps far behind them. They walked toward a looming structure in the darkness. Once there, Jacob led him to the back near the precipice and pointed downward to the shimmering river. Lights shone from factories and a power plant off in the distance. Some eighty feet below, a pedestrian walkway was illuminated. A sizable tow churned north up the river, the deck of the towboat lit up like a carnival midway. You could even read the name on the side: the *Kathleen Probst*.

Austin looked at his watch, a Fossil Chronograph with brown leather straps, that his father had given him. He pressed the little button on the side to light the face. It was 2:20 a.m.

The carriage house dated to 1885, a two-story brick edifice with copper downspouts and handsome cornices. Jacob opened the large oak door with a skeleton key. He flipped on the lights.

They could have been in a museum, the interior inviting appreciation if not wonder with its lavish Victorian furnishings.

"Wow," said Austin. "This place is awesome, like stepping into a time machine."

"Yeah," he answered, "I try to k-k-k-keep it just as my uncle had it. But I've added one thing."

First he went to a fridge and got out a couple bottles of water, handing Austin one. They drank in the kitchenette and Jacob wistfully expounded on how special this place was to him, how he didn't need to go to "the lake," as St. Louisans fondly referred to their favorite getaway, Lake Of The Ozarks, because he could come here, a welcome outpost, a refuge against oppressive humanity. And Jacob went on about how this place was ideal for self-discovery and that's what he'd been doing over the years, reading books on criminal psychology and fictional accounts of murder such as Poe's "Cask Of Amontillado." Now there's a sick happy ending, would you agree? Oh, you haven't read it? Hmm.

Oh, and he loved listening to Broadway musicals on the stereo. "*Man of La Mancha* is my favorite," he raved. "Do you know the song 'The Quest'? It's just one of the most inspiring songs of all time, the message being never give up on your dreams no matter how difficult they may seem. I can sing it without stuttering. I may do that later."

Austin was quite leery at this change of demeanor, the man almost bordering on affable.

As long as he was being candid he also admitted to dabbling in drugs. He had tried marijuana and cocaine, and though the experience was educational it wasn't necessarily pleasant. He didn't like not being in control of his thoughts, didn't like having a dry mouth or stumbling into the furniture. But one pastime he did do here that was thoroughly pleasing was to make art. He was an artist, after all, and every serious artist needs a studio.

"Would you like to see it? Follow me." They went down some steps to a room in the back. Jacob hit a switch and the room was suddenly flooded with light, revealing manifold paintings on the walls and leaning up against the walls, sculptures on pedestals and trays, and in one corner a sort of scarecrow in progress. The towering figure stood upright on rods fastened to a flat plywood box on the floor. The skeleton was a form made of woven wire mesh and stuffed with material such as T shirts and crumpled newspaper, to create a human shape and to fill out features such as musculature and, here, what looked like a pot belly. In places, fabric had been applied over the wire mesh and on the upper torso, gory wounds, some with loose stitches and some with "pus" painted on the fabric. It had no clothes yet, only combat boots and an Olga Luxury Lift Full Figure underwire bra. Nearby on the floor, laid out neatly, a pair of lederhosen, a plaid skirt, a distressed leather jacket with chains, and a kimono as if Jacob was a fashion maven deciding what the creature should wear. A plain block of wood made up the head. There was no face and maybe there would not be one, giving it a nebulous, confounding presence. The arms had yet to be attached. The effigy was not comical in any way. To Austin, it was like something out of a bad dream, so patently demented it raised hairs on the back of his neck.

"What do you think?" asked the artist coyly.

"It's really out there," answered Austin. "What does it mean?"

"It doesn't have to mean anything," he snapped. "It's art for art's sake. *Ars gratia artis*, as they say on the movie screen. This is the first of several I hope, and I'm trying to get a show in the West End."

He thought about telling him how at KCAI he had this brilliant idea for a senior art project and how it garnered much attention at the gala opening in this amazing space in downtown KC and how he'd taken second place in the show, losing only to some dilettante who created sculptures made of air. But then why bother? He was a future victim, not a confidante.

"My dad would like this. He collects art, the weirder the better it seems." Austin got a little closer to it, examined a crusty brown splotch on the fabric of one leg. "Is that what I think it is?"

"If you think it's dried blood it is. Adds to the surreal effect, don't you think?"

"Yeah, I guess. Does it have a name?"

Jacob sighed. "Why does everything need a name? Would you feel more comfortable with it if it was named? Go ahead, come up with a name."

"But it's not my creation."

"Give it a name," he said quite seriously.

"Uh, okay. Mmm...how about Hungry Joe?" Hungry Joe was a doomed yet perverted character from his favorite novel, *Catch 22* by Joseph Heller.

"Hungry Joe? That's st-st-stupid and it won't do. I think we'll c-c-c-c-call it Phantasm Number One." From his pocket he took a piece of jewelry. It was a plated gold lion head pendant on a braided sterling silver chain with two bright green emerald stones for eyes. Austin recognized it as belonging to Number Three.

Jacob held it out in the palm of his hand, said, "The lion is a symbol of strength, courage, pride, virility, and authority. How peculiar that nuh-nuh-none of these qualities were evident in the previous owner of this piece." He smiled slyly. "It's a nice s-s-s-souvenir and we can thank Number Three for it. I think this should go right here." He draped the necklace over the shoulders of the figure then stepped back to take a look.

Austin was puzzled if not astounded that Jacob was not taking precautions. Come on, using objects from his victims in his art? Practically asking to be found out. But here was the thing about Jacob Vorhof: He had led such a protected existence and had been made to believe he is a most precious thing, that he could not conceive of getting caught— impossible!—or the consequences that would follow. This belief, of course, was borne of monumental arrogance, but Jacob was thoroughly entrenched in his sense of privilege and entitlement and no thoughts of covering his tracks were ever entertained.

If he had any sense at all he would ask of his precious self: Jacob, old bean, you are vile enough to take the lives of a string of men, but are you smart enough to get away with it?

Francis was in the middle of "The Minstrel Boy" when Martha walked in. Although this gave him a bit of a start, Martha dropping in, he didn't miss a word. Five minutes prior, he'd been enlisted to sing. "Sure thing," he told Cormac Morrison. "Why not?"

John Sullivan called out for everyone to shut their traps. "Francis here's gonna sing for us." Francis stood, took another hit of the stout that Cormac had bought. Guinness was the exact right thing for singing an Irish ballad, giving his voice a rich and vibrant tenor, lending the performance a certain verve and imparting a significance to every word in the old song. When he had their attention, he announced that this song was for Alphonse Rourke, the good fellow who keeps this place shipshape, and that got applause which made the janitor beam proudly.

He sang it the way he was taught, so long ago in the kitchen with his mother and father and brother. "The Minstrel Boy" was a timeworn ballad about a young man who is a minstrel and a warrior. He is slain on the field of battle, probably with the hated English, and just before he dies, rather than allow the enemy to take his beloved harp, he "tore its chords asunder."

A short song and a sad one and that's why it was a big hit here. It took only a few minutes of their time and it struck a powerful chord among the maudlin and sentimental regulars, leaving half the audience crying in their beer.

He was wrapping up when Martha walked in, belting out the song with passion and fervor.

"...and said no chains shall sully thee,
thou soul of love and bray-ay-ay-vry!
Thy songs were made for the pure and free,
they shall never sound in slavery!"

Done, he took a modest bow and held his pint up high. Hoots and hollers, heavy applause.

"Thank you for the clap," he said, and they groaned and guffawed and there were calls for another round. He walked over to Martha who was talking to Tommy the barkeep. She stood there looking comfortable as if she were used to holding up the bar.

"Hey, there," he said, "you're looking good, one fine woman. Don't think I've seen you here before. Buy you a drink?"

She looked him up and down with disfavor. "Buzz off, Jocko. My drink's already taken care of."

"Oh, I see, playing hard to get?"

"With you, I should say so. What? You think you're God's gift to women or something?"

"I'm hoping."

Tommy set the glass down before her, a bottom shelf Merlot purchased by the case at the supermarket. She thanked him, said, "It's on him, Tommy," jabbing Francis in the ribs.

"Of course," said Tommy, "it's only right."

"So what's up? What brings you here—not that you shouldn't be here, but something's amiss, yeah?"

She took a sip of her drink, made a face. "Ugh. I didn't ask for paint thinner. You have a visitor outside."

"Yeah, who?"

"The stalker, Finch. He walked in the restaurant and lucky I was the first one he saw. He asked for you, said it was important. I told him to go to the corner out of sight and wait. I only had ten minutes left on my shift and so here we are. He is delivered. And it's a damn good thing Marco didn't see him."

Francis went out, blinking his eyes in the sun. Over there, leaning on a beat-to-hell Mercury Montego stood the uneasy figure of Cary Finch. They conferred and it turned out that Finch needed his help. There's been men around, on his street, watching. Definitely thugs. He was worried that Marco had sent them, and they wanted to do him like they did his roommate. He's been avoiding them, going in and out of the back door and through the alleys, but how long will it be before they post someone out back, snatch him and fuck him up good.

"Doesn't make sense," he said. "That means they've learned that they beat up the wrong guy and how would they learn that?"

"I don't know," said Finch, "but I'm scared. I didn't go to that hearing like you said and I even told the people at the Adult Abuse Office that I didn't want to pursue the restraining order. They said too late, he's already been served. And I turned myself in, like you said, got a court date coming up, but it's gonna be alright 'cause all that craziness is in the rear-view. But now—now I got a new girlfriend, I'm looking for a job, I'm trying to turn my life around. I don't have time to be scared shitless."

"You're putting me the spot here," declared Francis. "Marco's my brother-in-law, but we're not what you'd call tight. I might be able to talk with him, get some answers, see if he really does have tentacles in your neighborhood or if it's just your imagination." He knew it was not Finch's imagination. He looked Finch in the eyes, the windows of his soul. "But see, I'll have to find the right time to do that so just be patient and lay low."

"Oh, I'm laying low all right."

"Give me your number and I'll call you when I learn something."

"Thanks, man, thanks so much. Listen, bro, if there's anything I can do you for…"

Finch drove off in his beater, plumes of blue-gray exhaust in the street. As Francis headed back to the bar, Martha was coming out. She didn't need to say a word, the look on her face was enough.

"He's scared, he's feeling eyes on him," he explained. "He thinks they realized they hurt the wrong guy and now they're going to nab him."

"*They* being?"

"You know who, a certain family member who's been embarrassed in public and can't let it go."

Her usual blithe expression took a sudden downcast. "Oh, Jesus, Francis, what're we going to do?"

"One of us should talk to him."

"He's always been so vengeful. When we were kids there was a playground we'd go to, not in our neighborhood but blocks away. The kids there were from a different school. And one day this kid was taunting Marco, calling him dago and wop. He was an older kid, a big kid, looked like a grade school bully, the buzz cut, the round red face. The next day Marco went back—I wasn't there but I heard about it—and he waited until the kid was by himself and then he took a hammer to his bike, just obliterated it. The kid was crying, 'Why'd you do that?' And Marco saying, 'What's my name? What'd you call me?'"

"Muhammad Ali," said Francis.

"What do you mean?"

"In the ring, 1965, his famous bout with Sonny Liston. He fought him before but as Cassius Clay, and beat him soundly. But in the meantime he'd come under the wing of Malcolm X and joined the Nation of Islam which meant he had to have a Muslim name. But Liston, proud bruiser that he was, wouldn't acknowledge that name. A lot of people wouldn't. That fight lasted less than a round with an Ali knock out. In the famous picture, you see Ali standing over Liston sprawled on the mat, down for the count, and Ali's taunting him to get up, supposedly saying, 'What's my name?'"

This anecdote produced a dubious look on Martha. "Yeah, well, it's sort of similar, but the point is, in case you've forgotten, Marco gets it in his head that he's been dissed he's got to do something about it."

"Thing is," Francis went on, "This kid's turning a new leaf. He's over Heather, he's sorry he hurt Marco, he tried to cancel the order of protection against Marco, he just wants to get on with his life. We should try to help him, you know?"

Martha looked at him with a knowing smile, the corner of one side of her mouth turned up. "That is so like you to stick up for some wayward person who's in it over his head. Tell you what, *I'll* talk to Marco and I'll do it soon."

The next day Francis was mounting the steps of a tenement on the near Northside, his knees giving him trouble, working his way to Unit 18D to serve a summons, when his cell phone chimed. "They're here now," said Cary Finch without any preamble or greeting. "There's two in front and one in the back."

"Describe the cars," said Francis.

"Only one car with the two guys in it and that's an old Chevy Camaro, black with white racing stripe. The guy in the alley, he's on foot and he keeps looking up here."

"Hold on," said Francis, "let me call you back."

"Hey, big man, what're you doing?" he said to Cleo. "I've got a situation. Can you get a posse—crew—over to South City like now?" Cleo said he could round up two or three, maybe. Francis gave him the address. "I'll be there a little before you," Francis told him, "and if the situation still stands I'll put you to work, okay? I really appreciate this."

"It's all right, brother."

* * *

The Escalade pulled up abreast of Francis' Escort, one pointed north, the other south, Cleo driving, windows rolled down. It was 2:30 in the afternoon and a nice day. "Is it on?" asked Cleo.

"Black Camaro across the street, three cars down. Two guys, bad actors, looking to stir up some shit with a young man in that apartment across the street, 'preciate it if you could talk to them. I can't join you, sorry, those guys are goons for my brother-in-law."

"It's all right, brother," came the reply. A car came up from behind, waiting for the Escalade to move. The driver had sense enough not to lean on the horn.

"There's a parking spot just up ahead," said Francis, "I'll be right here."

In the black Camaro, Joe Della Croce behind the wheel said to Mike Tocco, shotgun, "What the fuck, they having a conference in the street? Is that Francis Lenihan talkin' to those niggers? We gonna have a problem here?"

The answer came sooner than later as three black guys strode up and positioned themselves beside the open windows. "How's it going?" said Cleo at the driver's door, hunkering down to get a look. "We seem to be lost. Would you mind telling us how to get to the zoo?"

"Oh, sure," said Mike Tocco, "are they missing you in the monkey house?" Both men laughed at this.

"That's funny," said Cleo, showing some teeth, the gold prominent. "You're a funny guy, I take it. Good thing for you we can take a joke. But the question is can you take a joke."

"How do you mean?" asked Joe Della Croce, showing poise.

"Well, see," explained Cleo calmly, patiently, "our friend in that apartment," he nodded toward a red brick two-family, "he says you're making him nervous. This concerns not only our friend but me and my associates."

"Who gives a fuck," said Joe Della Croce, adding, "why don't you go back to where you came from and leave us the fuck alone?"

"Guess you didn't understand," said Cleo with a shrug, "some people are kinda dense. What I meant to say is my associates and I are sometimes known as gangstas. We, uh, we don't always play nice." And he reached in the open window and grabbed Joe Della Croce's ear and twisted it hard.

"*Yoww!!*" screamed Joe Della Croce.

"You can't—" Mike Tocco was in the middle of saying when the man outside reached in his open window and grabbed him by the throat. He throttled him until his face turned a shade of red and then he let go but not before he backhanded him.

The three of them watched as the Camaro left the scene and turned at the first intersection, presumably to pick up their pal in the alley.

Francis called Finch who'd been watching out the window. "Okay, come out now," he said.

Finch came out, shorts and sandals, Pink Floyd Dark Side Of The Moon T-shirt. Introductions all around. "This is Cleo," said Francis, "and you know me."

"This big gorilla is Moondog," said Cleo, nudging a massive, completely shaved Buddha-like figure. "Moondog eats nails for breakfast," addressing both Francis and Finch. Moondog's face lit up. "And this character is Payback alias Hoodat. He might even have more nicknames, you should ask him."

"You a colorful person you got to have colorful names," Payback alias

Hoodat and possibly other descriptive monikers explained, fingering the gold chains around his neck.

Finch said to Cleo, "I saw everything. You handled it perfect, those guys bolted and I'm thinking they won't be back."

"It's all right, little brother, all in a day's work."

It was obvious that Finch was in awe of Cleo, hero worship the way he fixated on him. "No, I want to give you something. Be right back." And he was, huffing with exertion from running up and down the stairs. "Here," he said, handing it over.

Cleo turned the gift over and over in his big hand. It was a Kershaw 3-inch pocketknife with clip. It looked like it had just come out of the box. He went to open it but couldn't. Finch took it back, somewhat cautiously. "It's got the SpeedSafe opening," he said and showed Cleo how.

"Oh, that's good," said Cleo, "making it safe to open so you don't cut yourself. I like it. Maybe now I'll take up whittling." Finch glowed with admiration.

"Where's my present?" asked Francis.

Later that same day, as Martha was getting off, Marco came to the maitre d' stand and said, "I think Francis shouldn't come in for a while. Maybe not for a long while."

She looked at him confusedly, brow furrowed. "Why not, Marco?"

"Because I found out he's working against me."

She frowned mightily. "Oh, Marco, that's not good. I hate to hear that. But listen, we need to talk anyway. Please join me at a table in five minutes just as soon as Gina arrives."

— 30 —

WHEN FRANCIS GOT AROUND TO CALLING CLEO HE FOUND HIM AT
THE FOOD PANTRY. "Yo, just a minute," he answered not knowing who
it was. Cleo must have set the phone down because he could hear all the
trash talk in the background. What you say? He gone take you to the Fox
Theater and you leavin' early to get your nails done? Girl, you better hit the
beauty parlor too. You can't take no night on the town for granted.

"Hey, Cleo, you busy?"

"Like a beaver. What's up, big brother?" He liked being called big
brother by Cleo, and the feeling of fellowship was mutual.

"I'm about to fill you in on a couple items of interest. I ran the plates
on that Camry. They go to an Audrey Fontana, age thirty-one, lives in
South City. Except for a speeding ticket a few years ago, clean driving
record. Then I ran her on mocasenet. She's pretty busy in that arena.
Been sued about six times, mostly to collect back rent. But there was a
bust back in 2011. *State v. Audrey Fontana* possession of cocaine with
intent to distribute. Her attorney got her off on a technicality related to
the search."

"So she's his dealer. What now? Supply gone, he gonna go through
the shakes, start losing his mind? Maybe now's the time to make a
move."

"Yeah," said Francis, "if only we knew what that move was. All I can
think of is what we talked about earlier, plant some drugs on him, get
him busted."

"Yeah, I thought about that and, uh, just a moment—Louise, I'm
gonna step outside and take this call."

Francis heard, "You go right ahead, honey."

Then he was back on. "Yeah, I gave that some thought and it's not a
horrible idea. Could get some crack and meth for sure and maybe some
H." A pause. "And I know where there's a gun that was used in a liquor
store store robbery where the man was gutshot—but I had nothin' to
do with that," he added quickly.

"Of course not," said Francis. "And it's good that you can pull together these, uh, items for our project. But I was thinking, um, tips on crimes and criminals, there's probably more to it than they go storming in his house in the middle of night and lead him out in cuffs. I mean, it's just a tip, right? They probably have to have something more than a tip from some anonymous person."

"Yeah, you're right. We need to look into it."

"I know a cop. I'll talk to him, theoretically, about how it's handled. This is big, this is criminal, what we're up to, kind of scary, you know?"

"Yeah, I know," said Cleo, "but we're doing the right thing."

"But what if we're wrong and he's not the fiend we think he is?"

"We're not wrong," replied Cleo.

"Okay then," said Francis. "Moving on, after you were out to his place I brought a gang of homeless out there to annoy him and, boy, did it work. And while he was screaming out the window at everybody I put a tracker on his vehicle."

"What's that gonna do?" Cleo wondered.

"It'll show us where he goes, how long he stays, if he uses the Highlander and not the Winnebago. It may provide good info or it may not. I thought it might help so I did it."

"That's good, brother, good you're thinking of all the angles. We're gonna nail this sucker, you'll see."

* * *

Francis ran into Officer Lauria the next day at the QuikTrip on Hampton. Lauria was in uniform, paying the cashier for a soda and a lotto ticket. Francis stopped him on the way out.

"You ever know anyone who's won in that crapshoot?"

"This?" said Lauria, looking at the blush-colored ticket with writing and numbers all over. "Yeah, matter of fact, I have. Woman at the station won four grand in the Mega Millions, and my neighbor almost won the jackpot in this very game. He was one number off."

"I won a free ticket on a scratch-off," said Francis, deadpan.

"Well, good for you!"

"Hey, listen, I have a scenario I'd like to run by you. Theoretical, of course. You got a minute?"

"Sure, go ahead."

"Okay, well, say someone is aware that someone else is dealing drugs and is in possession of a weapon used in a crime. And say this person wants to turn this other person in, like get him arrested, and he phones in a tip, anonymous, conveying this information. What happens next?"

Lauria nodded and gave it a moment's thought. "A tip, huh? We would take it seriously and we would probably put some surveillance on the location in question. Is it a house or a commercial building?"

"A house."

"Well, that makes it harder as you know from your own work. You do surveillance from time to time, I'm sure, and it's difficult not to be made on a quiet residential street. Who's this person sitting in his car out front of my house for an hour now? But never mind that, we'd keep eyes on the house looking for persons going in and coming out. Because we're busy and short-handed, we'd probably have to do this on our spare time. But if we saw someone coming out and we're able to pull them over for some infraction, say broken taillight or moving violation—that's probable cause—and if they had drugs in their car we'd arrest them and hopefully get them to trade up, turn on the dealer for certain considerations."

Francis pondered for a moment. "So even with a solid tip it's still a matter of luck. You've got to be there when something's going down."

"Yeah, there's laws that keep us from going all cowboy. But we can put some real pressure on the person who was stopped, like 'Give us something we can use or we'll sic the DA on you then you're looking at some serious time.' Of course anyone who watches *Law and Order* will know we don't have any say in the sentencing, but the scared perp doesn't know that. And if he does give us a name or names, dates, and what was transacted, then we apply for a warrant which lets us go in for a look."

Francis could see that his plan suddenly got more complicated, but already wheels were turning as to the thorny problem of finding a patsy willing to be pulled over with drugs in the car. He said to Lauria, "Well, all right then, that's what I wanted to know. You filled me in, thanks Ed."

"When you gonna phone this tip in? There's a special number for that. You don't call nine-one-one."

"Oh, it's not me," he was quick to say. "I'm just asking for a friend."

Lauria gave him a wink. "Sure you are, and I'm gonna win this jack-pot."

— 31 —

JACOB BREEZED THROUGH THE GLASS DOOR OF THE DAGMAR PETKO GALLERY just before noon on a Monday in late August, days after he'd killed Austin Lambert and left him by the river in the homeless camp. Typically, art galleries are closed on Monday but Jacob had come by invitation and Dagmar herself was eagerly awaiting his arrival. Jacob had been here before, having attended several fabulous openings of artists he knew of but had never met, openings on the first Friday of the month, from fall to spring each year. Openings with unlimited complimentary wine, platters of cheese and grapes and veggies. Wall to wall people taking in art all around them, forming circles around the artist du jour, pressing him or her with banal questions such as "Where do you get your inspiration?" Or gushing praise over the work which made him sick to overhear. And now he was here not as a nobody, not a suck up or a sycophant, but as an artist to be courted.

Dagmar was seated at a long Montserat desk with keyboard, monitor, books, papers, a leafy green plant, and a cup of coffee. She pushed a swivel chair back and rose to face the visitor. "Mr. Rigoletto?" she said in a cultured voice. "Welcome, welcome!" As he approached she held out her hand for a shake. He held back.

"It's jus-just Rigoletto," he told her, a bit flustered. "No mi-mi-mi-mister."

Trouble getting his words out? Perfect, she thought, dealing daily with adversity, probably his entire life and the humiliation that must come with such a condition. That could play into the tortured artist image.

"Certainly," she said. "What would you like to drink? Coffee, soda, Pellegrino, or a cocktail if it's not too early. I make a wicked Bloody Mary." Slight accent, he noted. European?

"The Pellegrino, thank you."

"Good choice. Here, take a seat and we can talk." She brought the Italian carbonated water in its green glass bottle, set it on a tray beside him. Nice touch, he thought. Everything about her was classy, from the selection of drinks to the Donna Karan satin blazer and wide leg pants to the location of the gallery, on a 19th century tree-lined street in the posh West End. "I admire your work," she began, taking her chair at the desk across from him, "thanks for sending the photos. I know you probably sent pictures of your work to several galleries and, if so, that's a bit gauche, but in the end I'm the one you hooked and I must say, I am enthused over the thought of discovering such talent as yours. So, go ahead, Rigoletto, tell me about yourself and your work—I mean beyond the curriculum vitae." She leaned back and prepared to listen.

He told her about growing up in West County, an only child with artistic interests and how his parents encouraged him, giving him a studio in the house and hiring an art teacher to guide him. How his stutter had alienated him from most other kids and how he preferred to be by himself anyway. In fact, he told her, you may notice that I'm stuttering less as I go on talking and that's because I feel comfortable with you.

"Why thank you," she said. "The feeling is mutual." He took her in objectively. Mid-forties, trim, good color, stylish in attire and coiffure, her long brunette Dutch braid falling to the side, revealing a pair of gold-plated pearl earrings. Yes, she was charming, cultured, and glib, everything an art dealer should be, he thought.

He went on about getting accepted at the Kansas City Art Institute and how it turned his world around. There, he was around other highly creative minds, both teachers and students, and everyone fed upon one another. The school was big on conceptual art, promoting innovative visual approaches, daring and contemporary art styles. Serrano, Edward Kienholz, Christo, Erwin Wurm, Sarah Lucas to name a few—they were held up. Ideas were floated constantly, the studios humming with activity late into the night. For the senior show, seventeen of twenty-seven projects were in the avant-garde column. One woman made a lot of textile art, he recalled. She knitted a sweater with pornographic stills embroidered into it. Another student made this giant pill-shaped metal contraption. It lowered down from the ceiling on a pulley system and it was made for two people to stick their heads inside. There was little space and when that happened their noses actually touched. They had to stare at each other and decide for themselves how long they wanted to be inside "the hat" and what they wanted to do with their encounter.

Dagmar Petko, listening raptly, smiled at the thought of this. "My kind of art," she remarked. "And your own entry in the senior show, what was that?"

He took a sip of Pellegrino, rinsed his mouth, and swallowed. "Sure, let me tell you first that I am n-n-not a messy person, I abhor filth and clutter. Yet I felt that I should explore this condition, this sickness, how and maybe why we create it."

"Grunge," she said distastefully, "I hate it too."

"Grunge, squalor, depravity. The way I see it, as society attempts to put on a face of cleanliness we move everything that does not fit that notion to the outskirts. We have spuh-spuh-spaces devoted entirely to dispose of our created dirt and in these spaces abjection thrives. In our homes where we feel the most comfortable, we let dirt collect—it's our own duh-duh-dirt, after all. But if a visitor would happen to encounter it they might be concerned for the well being of the inhabitant. As we let people into our lives and our homes, we try to make it look like our homes are spotless and clean. We sweep, pour bleach down the drains, wipe windows clean, and put all of our belongings back to their designated places. I said I abhor filth and I also abhor those who cultivate filth, who wallow in their own g-g-grime and muck. So…I was interested in the person who may not have anyone to impress or perhaps they no longer care what is thought of them, the kind of person who has muh-muh-muh-made a space so homey it is truly disgusting."

Dagmar clapped her hands lightly in approval. "Oh, this is rich! And how did you express these ideas?"

He answered, "I created a most disturbing diorama, a bathroom that no decent person would think to use. The sink was discolored with toothpaste and hair dye and what-have-you. The dingy tile floor stuh-struh-strewn with dirty clothing. The bathtub half-filled with b-b-brown-gray water and a ring of gunk that would never be scrubbed away. Crusty soiled towels hanging from hooks or bars. The toilet overflowing with shit and piss, I mean the real thing! I even had some fake ruh-rubber roaches placed here and there."

"I can see it," she said. "The essence of revulsion."

He nodded. "Squalid to say the least. And it was extremely difficult for me to create this in the studio, having to be so intimate with these base materials. I wore rubber gloves and a hazmat suit. I took frequent breaks to get my stomach to calm down. The duh-duh-day before the show, I and a hired man loaded it up carefully in a rental truck. The installation took all day and when we finished the hired man wanted double pay, said the abomination of the thing would never leave him. He claimed he was psychologically scarred by *Becoming Room*, the title of my piece, and I needed to compensate him for that. Can you imagine?" Dagmar raised her brows and gave a light chuckle.

"But here's the worst of it," he said. "Another student, a rank amateur by my account, had come up with a sculpture made of air. That's right, air. In other words, nothing. Well, there was a tank, an old rusty thing with paint flaking off, and he claimed this was an endless tank of oxygen and of course it was still just a tank that belonged in the junk pile. He called it *Fresh Air* and would explain to anyone who would listen that it was, quote, The Idea Of Art. It took first prize, my piece took second. So aggravating! So unfair, my piece having so much more thought put into it, and labor intensive. His piece of crap requiring no labor at all."

"It's a tough break," she said sympathetically as if the injustice had happened to her, "but it didn't stop you from making more art, did it?"

"No, certainly not," he replied. "When the show was over I dismantled tha-tha-that installation, pitched it in the Dumpster, and went back to the s-s-studio."

"That's the spirit. But you weren't Rigoletto back then, were you? You had a regular name. Mind telling me what it was?"

Jacob pursed his lips and looked at her in a way that suggested he was having some inner turmoil. He wasn't Rigoletto to the mailman or to utility companies who sent bills or to his neighbors or the denizens of Hopeville who waited in line for his soup. He just thought it would be cool to have a name that people would remember and wonder about. Originally it was to be Demosthenes after the famed Greek orator who as a child stuttered terribly and overcame the condition by going to the beach, putting pebbles in his mouth and shouting words above the sound of the waves, but Jacob felt the name was too long and would be constantly mispronounced. "I chose that name because I *don't* want my identity known. I wanted to start anew with a mysterious persona and as a serious artist I'm growing into that notion. You understand."

"Well, yes, I do understand, we all have our idiosyncrasies, but unless Rigoletto is your actual name I can't very well write a check to that name." He could see now that he was going to get a show—hooray! The looming question: would it be solo or as part of a group show?

"You can tell me," she continued, "I'll still call you Rigoletto."

"It's Jacob, Jacob Vorhof," he said in a whisper.

"Ah, sounds German," she said approvingly. "I'm Hungarian by nationality, our ancestors were neighbors in the Old World."

"Yeah, that's cool."

"So, as for the new work, these tormented-looking life-size figures that entice me so, you do plan to make more? How many could you have ready in the next two months?"

"Um, I have one now, maybe two more. They take time and thought."

"A wraith trapped in a charnel house, that's what came to mind when I saw the picture. Yes, three would be perfect," she said. "And I'll need an artist statement from you, the sooner the better." She smiled munificently upon him. "Yes, I'm giving you a show and again you're in luck as to the timing. You probably know that a gallery such as mine is booked at least two years in advance, but there's been a cancellation. I'm doing a three person show in November and one of the artists, Gayle Johnson, has come down with a bad case of mono, poor thing. She's homebound, drained of all energy."

"Oh, fantastic—not her with mono, but moving me up like that."

"What sort of price tag are you thinking?"

He sat up, placed his hands on his thighs, leaned forward. "Mm, I hadn't thought about it much."

"I'm thinking in the range of twenty thousand or so."

"Wow, could that actually happen?"

"You're in luck again," she said, "because the collectors who may be drawn to your work are wealthy and think nothing of spending that much, especially if I promote you as The Next Big Thing. And there is one collector in particular who is practically guaranteed to purchase one of your pieces."

Jacob leaned back in his chair with a Cheshire cat grin. This is it, he thought, I've made the big leagues, the world will know my name.

— 32 —

FRANCIS IN THE MIDDLE OF A LEFT TURN INTO A BUSY INTERSECTION IN WEST COUNTY, one of those bustling intersections where you can't actually see where you're going until you get there, when his phone rang. The phone was in his front pants pocket and he was struggling to get it out while managing the turn and looking both ahead and behind for other vehicles to avoid. He got the phone out but couldn't answer for several seconds, not until he leveled off onto the straightaway.

He looked at the number and the message next to it. SPAM RISK. "Hello," he said cheerfully.

"Is this Francis Lenihan?" Francis affirmed. "I hope I didn't catch you at a bad time," by way of introduction. "This is Tom Nanzig, I'm a reporter with the *Business Journal* and I'd like to talk to you about the class action lawsuit building as we speak against the City stemming from the mass arrests of protesters downtown back in September. So far more than a dozen people arrested in a police kettle, as it's called, are suing the City, police officers and their supervisors, alleging they were roughed up, pepper sprayed, illegally detained. I understand you were among that group."

"Yeah, I was but I wasn't protesting. I was just hanging out and got caught up in it."

"Perfect," said Nanzig. "I'd love to hear your story and I'd like to know if you've been approached by the law firm mounting this class action to join in. May we talk now?"

"I'm driving, but I'll pull over and we can talk for a bit." He went into a strip mall and found a parking spot away from other cars, Nanzig waiting on the line.

"Yeah, okay, now's good," said Francis. "You say more than a dozen in this lawsuit. No, I haven't been contacted to join and I probably wouldn't." Was it Sandy Crowley's firm? Probably. No need to say he works for them.

"Oh," said Nanzig, "why not?"

Francis could see him at the other end, jotting notes on paper or maybe typing his comments on a desktop computer. "I guess because I'm basically a law and order type. I think what the police did, this kettling thing, was not unreasonable. Those protesters were really out of control, something had to be done."

"Yeah, I'm sure that's true for some of them," said Nanzig, "but this kettling method rounds up the unruly *and* the innocent bystanders and pedestrians alike, people who just happen to wander into the demonstration, persons such as yourself. There were ninety-four people arrested that day and many more detained. I imagine that once word of this class action gets out there'll be many more plaintiffs."

"Sure," agreed Francis, "sue the City, easiest thing in the world. Sign your name, sit back and let the big law firm do all the work. Two-three years down the road collect your settlement, go out and party like there's no tomorrow. And don't forget to thank the police for trying to do their job."

"I understand your sentiments, I do. May I quote you for my article?"

"Go ahead, but if get any blowback I'll say you misquoted me."

"Oh, well, that would be a lie wouldn't it?"

"There's lies and then there's white lies. And while you're at it, you can quote me on this as well, that St. Louis has the finest police force in the nation."

"I'm sure many would disagree. I must say it's refreshing to talk to someone who's not captivated by the chance of possible big money from this thing."

"Someone once said 'Be happy with what you've got,' and I decided to make that my motto.

"One last thing, Mr. Lenihan, what is your occupation?"

"Special Process Server every living day."

After the conversation ended and before getting back on the road, Francis looked in the mirror and saw someone who was less than right, whose once-high ideals were slowly ebbing away.

"You are so two-faced," he told himself. "Coming off all high and mighty with that reporter. 'I'm too good for that money.' Yeah, right. 'I'm on the side of law and order.' Yeah right, and before long you're off to find some patsy who will help you commit a crime. Oh, you hypocrite."

Part IV

"I probably never told you this," said Francis, "but I'm glad you don't shave down there."

"Honey, that is so romantic of you. I practically swoon when I hear you say that."

They were lying in bed on a Sunday morning, having just made love for the second time this week. She had turned over to get something off the nightstand and he was stroking the small of her back, a light back-and-forth touch, soothing. "I mean it," he went on, "I used to think all women had to shave away their body hair, it was unfeminine not to. But then I was stationed in Germany for two years and I saw the women there and found that I like the natural look."

"Saw the women as in their birthday suits?" She turned back over to face him.

"I don't want to get in trouble here and this was way before we met, but, yeah a couple without any clothes—just friends, mind you, but mostly I'm talking about legs and armpits. They don't shave those and it looks all right. You get used to it and eventually you like it."

"Some of these women who go in for the bikini waxes or who shave down there, as you say, so they're bald as a baby's butt, they look so prepubescent, you know? It may be a kind of perversion."

"Yeah, glad we're of one mind on this. Plus, think of all money you're saving on razor blades and shaving cream."

"Sometimes you get an infected hair follicle from shaving and that's no good. So," she concluded, "I continue to be unshaven, full bush in all its splendor, and it makes my husband happy. It's the least I can do as a devoted wife."

"I have a joke about the bush," he said. "A short one."

She snuggled up closer. "Okay, let's hear it."

"A woman goes into a doctor's office complaining of a bed-wetting problem. The doctor tells her to remove all her clothes, go over to that full-length mirror, stand on her head facing the mirror and spread her legs. She's very skeptical about this, but she does it with some difficulty.

The doctor comes over and puts his chin on the woman's crotch. He looks in the mirror and says, 'Hmmm.' The woman says, 'But doctor, what does this have to do with my bed-wetting problem?' The doctor says, 'Nothing, I just wanted to see what I'd look like with a beard.'"

A little later over breakfast he said, "I've got a new friend. His name is Cleo. He's in a band and I went to hear them yesterday. They played in the afternoon at the Harlem Tap Room on Martin Luther King. It was great, I really enjoyed it, maybe we go together some time."

She gave him one of those looks that said I'm looking out for your welfare even if you're not. "You be careful in that part of town. Did you go alone?"

"Yeah, it was fun and the people in that bar? Just as nice as could be—well, it did help that I bought a round. But you should've heard Cleo, big black guy with this deep resonant voice perfect for singing the blues. His new song 'Down And Out In The River City' is a hit. They play it now on MAJIC 103 point 7."

"That's nice, maybe ask them to play at my niece's wedding, if they're still around next year."

"If it pays, they'll probably jump at it. That song? Goes like this.
> 'Why, baby, why? Why you wanna do me this way?
> Say you will when you won't Say you can when you don't
> I give you my all Just to take the fall
> Come on back, 'cause I'm down
> down and out in the River City.' "

His not so sonorous voice filled the kitchen and then got caught up in the ceiling fan. "There's more to it, of course," he told her.

"I think I'd rather hear Cleo do it," she said.

The topic of Marco and his prohibition had to come up, but it was not made into a big deal. Martha had spoken to him and he'd dug in his heels, said, No, not now, I'll tell you when.

Francis had to serve a sentence.

"Fine," said Francis, "I'll stay away for a month or so, let him cool down, nurse his pride, and I'll go back when you ask me to or when I get a hankering for some of that good risotto with fennel and Parmesan."

"Now you can say you've been expelled from the best restaurant in St. Louis," she said.

"Given the boot, and it took a lifetime to get that done."

"What will you do for an encore?"

* * *

Francis' day got underway with a drive to the suburbs in West County where he had divorce papers for two women at addresses about five miles apart. Sunday mornings usually found occupants at home, just getting up or getting ready to go to church or head for a workout. Sure enough, the first attempt successful, the middle-aged woman in her nightie taking the summons and petition for dissolution with trepidation as if it were smeared with goop. "That damn fool," she muttered, "I told him *I* was going to file. I wanted this on *my* terms. But no, he had to jump the gun, always thinking of himself first."

Next stop a well-kept home on a quiet street in Ballwin, bikes on the porch, a portable soccer goal in the yard. He knocked, she came, he explained. "Oh, thank you," she offered. "Well, maybe I shouldn't say thank you for changing my life the way this is going to, but I knew it was coming and I suppose it's for the best."

He put her at mid-to-late thirties. "I guess it could be a good thing," he said, solicitously. "At least you knew it was coming, some people don't. They're blindsided, they freak out, and that always makes me feel terrible." He didn't know why he was telling her this, except he sensed that she was having a moment of vulnerability and she was uncommonly pretty in her cut-offs and Scotch plaid flannel shirt, auburn hair accenting hazel eyes. Fact, he was right then wondering something in particular and not for the first time, and that was Why on earth would someone choose to divorce someone such as this, seemingly so nice to be around and so attractive she could stop traffic? The answer, he supposed, might be found in a saying he'd once heard, that even the prettiest girl in town was a pain in the ass to someone. But that was just a saying and it didn't very well answer his question.

He offered some platitudes in parting. "Well, I'm sure you'll land on your feet. One day at a time, so the scholars say." She liked hearing this, he could tell, words of encouragement.

"Would you care for some coffee?" she asked as he turned to go.

"Uh, no, sorry. I've got a high colonic scheduled for nine."

"Okay," she smiled, "maybe another time. You know where I live."

* * *

Hopeville was down for the count. He got there a little after eleven, the settlement dormant compared to the last time he was here. Where there had been tents, there were none or few. Where there had been people standing around fifty-five gallon drums warming themselves by a fire, there were only ashes of a fire that had been. The place forlorn, he guessed, because the inhabitants had finally moved on in anticipation of the bulldozers heralded by Alderman Vincent Moore.

It was a beautiful day, though, and he walked the path and he smelled the river and he kept his eyes open for someone, his unnamed patsy, to show themselves. This was a delicate matter. How would he phrase it, the proposal? The promise of money was always a great opener. How would you like to make five hundred bucks by driving a car with a small amount of contraband? You're not selling it or delivering it, you're just going to get stopped by the police and searched. You'll get booked, charged, and then released until the hearing at which time you'll plead not guilty and a lawyer will handle your case. Everything will be paid for, you'll actually make money on the deal. How's that sound?

He was well along the path when he heard a hullabaloo, someone yelling at someone or something. It sounded like a string of curses and obscenities, a loud litany of denunciations against—what? When this person came into view, Francis saw a ragtag tramp with a bulging backpack and clothes practically falling off him. A fierce-looking white guy in his fifties, Francis guessed, raging and ambulating in herky-jerky fashion. Francis supposed he was mad at the world in general. Even as he approached, the man was spouting off volubly. "Fuggers bastards shit piss jackoffs fuggin' jackoffs shit—try me goddamnit, try me you pricks you'll see, goddamnit all to hell." Francis stood in his way, palms out as a suggestion to stop.

"Hells bells!" said the man irritably. "Who the fuck are you?"

"I could be your deliverance," said Francis, "if you'd calm down a minute so we can talk."

"Talk? Is that all you people think of? What the hell's there to talk about that hasn't been talked to death already?"

Francis's gaze lowered to the man's filthy trousers. "Your barn door's open and the cows are getting out," he informed.

The tramp looked, snickered. "Just giving it some air," he said, and he placed his dingus back in the barn.

Francis knew with every fiber of his being that enlisting this guy in his scheme was a bad idea. For one thing, conspiring to use him as a pawn made him as bad as Jacob Vorhof. "How would you like to make some money just being you?" And with the man standing there, fidgeting and shuffling in the gravel, Francis explained the job. We drive to a certain location. I get out, you knock at the door, whether he answers or not doesn't matter. You get back in the car, you drive off. You'll be stopped by a cop in a patrol car or maybe unmarked car. The car will be searched, they'll find a small quantity of weed. You say it's not yours, they don't care. They take you to the station, book you, and you spend the night there.

"So how's that sound? Two hundred bucks, easy money."

The man scratched himself and wiped his nose on his sleeve, said, "Arrghh."

"I'll take that as a yes," said Francis. "Do you have a record?"

"Who doesn't?" snapped the tramp.

"I'll need a way to contact you when the thing is about to happen. You live here? Got a cell phone? What's your name?"

"Pudden Tane," he answered, "ask me again, go ahead, ask me again."

"You have a license don't you? Any ID at all?"

"The fuck I need a license for, I ain't never drive no car."

He found another possible candidate on the way back out, a doubtful fellow with sunken eyes and cheeks who Francis suspected had been taken advantage of throughout his young life. This man was reluctantly open to the idea but balked at the fee. "Three hundred for getting arrested? Come on, man! That's got to be worth three thousand, and I'll need half of that up front."

Francis decided to look elsewhere for his patsy. Nearly to his car he passed the soup stand and conjured the image of Jacob Vorhof ladling steaming soup from a huge steaming pot into Styrofoam bowls, white apron around his waist and a checkered chef's hat on his head. All this is for you, he thought, I'm compromising my principles, risking jail time, all in the hopes of bringing you down, you sniveling son of a bitch.

He saw the chalkboard used for listing the soup du jour. Someone had written BLACK BEARS MATTER.

"Hey, Cleo, did you hear that the animal rights group PETA has come up with their own version of the slogan Black Lives Matter?"

"Is this a joke?" Cleo asked at the other end of the line.

"Maybe," said Francis.

"Okay, lay it on me."

"It's Black Bears Matter." He waited for a reaction. "Well?"

"It's not that funny," said Cleo. "So what's up, big brother?"

"As per our plan, sketchy as it may be, I'm trying to find someone who will drive away from Vorhof's house with a stash of weed or other goodies, get pulled over, searched and arrested so the police can get a warrant. It's not easy," he added. "Do you know anybody?"

"Not off hand," from Cleo, "but let me think on it."

"It's not easy to find someone who'll do it—did I say that?—but I can't think of any other way. We've got to give the police a reason to search his place. How else are we gonna get him put away?"

"You'll find someone," said Cleo, "you're one resourceful mother."

* * *

Luck was kinder at Murphy's Bar. Francis walked in, Tommy got his Busch poured and sat it before him on the bar. Sunday afternoon, not a full house. Francis had taken a stool beside Mickey Queenan, the retired schoolteacher who drank Bailey's Irish Cream and coffee. As a fellow regular, he'd been in the presence of Mickey quite often but he couldn't remember the two of them ever having any sort of meaningful conversation. Mickey said hey and Francis returned with the same. The moments passed, both men attending to their libation.

"Did you hear about Pollock?" said Mickey at last.

"What about him?" asked Francis.

"He got a DUI driving home the other night. Spent the night in jail."

"City or County?" Francis wondered, already sure of the answer. It was almost impossible to get a DUI in the City, the cops were so busy with much more serious crime. You'd have to be driving down a one way street the wrong way, blasting your horn and waving a fifth of Jack Daniels out the window to get pulled over.

"County, it was near his house. He lives out in Sunset Hills."

"It pays to live near where you drink, I've always said that," said Francis.

"Amen to that," added Mickey and held out his personalized mug for a toast.

"How was your day?" he asked of Francis. "Out serving those warrants, it must get pretty hairy at times."

Francis felt obligated to correct him and did so gently. "I'm what's called a Special and we don't serve warrants, the Sheriff Deputy does that. We serve summonses, subpoenas, court orders, and believe me, that's enough to keep you busy. But today I served two summons early and then I went on a nearly impossible mission to try to find someone to commit some skulduggery."

"Oh, I love that word. As a teacher I tried to use it in class whenever possible. 'There is much skulduggery going on around here.' So did you find this person?"

"No," said Francis, "I did not and it's understandable because only a fool would take the job."

Mickey clasped his stubbly chin and wagged his head a few times as if he were privy to some important info. "Hmm. You know, I have a nephew who is a complete fool. Twenty-seven, lives in his mother's basement, last job he had was years ago and that was washing cars. No girlfriend, no car, no spending money, although he certainly has enough to buy tattoos, and virtually no ambition. He's one of those gamers, spends his waking hours with eyes glued to a monitor, the headphones, the joystick—what do they call it, controller—like something out of Star Trek. He's not Jimmy anymore but some fierce avatar dispatching wizards and demons left and right. I'm thinking he may be your fool. You want to tell me the proposition?"

Francis told him the situation, leaving out certain lurid details such as the target in this scenario likely being a serial killer. "And this person would be arrested for drugs?"

"Yeah, just some pot, maybe just enough for a misdemeanor. He's basically a tool. I'll take care of his legal fees or fine if there is one."

"He's perfect for the job," said Mickey with a grin, "he can put it on his resume under Really Stupid Things I've Done. Let me call him right now, see if he'll pry his fingers from the joystick and get his lazy butt over here."

— 34 —

WITH TWO MONTHS TO COME UP WITH TWO MORE EFFIGIES Jacob was going to have to work hard. That is, he was going to have to scramble to find the materials. The physical appearance, what the viewers saw, would take care of itself and it would be enigmatic if not discomforting, but the materials, they need not be in short supply, he only had to use his brain, think outside the box, as it were. If the first effigy was composed of muslin, polyester fiberfill, wire mesh, straw, plastic bags, paint, clothes, and some human tissue courtesy of Number One who went to the landfill—then the two in the making could be similarly manufactured except for the human components. He was out of those, he would have to kill someone else to extract those parts. He wasn't going to the homeless camp anymore so that supply was gone. Maybe entice a panhandler to get in the Winnebago? Pretty risky, he thought. He'd been lucky in the past, but what if the guy overpowered him? Yet, for his effigies to have that ghoulish look he would need organic parts of a living thing. What about the animal world? Dogs are easy to come by and dogs have fur and teeth and ears and tongues, long ones. A mutt from the pound, why not? That would do the trick.

He had settled into the carriage house sometime in mid-October, just after that ugly business with the Hopevillians. The Winnebago now in storage, the other place closed up. It was much better here, his mind more at ease, no bands of needy bums or unruly darkies to come calling, as in West County.

He busied himself with the making of effigies. He went to Home Depot and bought pliable sheets of metal that could be cut to reinforce the extremities. He already had the basic tools—saws, hammer, nails, tin snips, pliers, sawhorses—but he bought two-by-fours and plywood to construct pedestals for his figures. There were trips to the military surplus store and to JOANN Fabric and Crafts, an artist's candy shop with a cornucopia of frivolous items for adorning his figures. He visited Goodwill and Salvation Army for second-hand clothing to dress them, his own clothes being too nice. He went to Johnnie Brock's Dungeon, a warehouse chockablock with costumes and accessories for every festive occasion. There he found a section of theatrical makeup offering realistic open bloody wounds. He had to think about this; some gore was fine, but he didn't want to get all crazy with it. He stopped at Walgreen's for bandages and gauze and surgical tape because one of the figures had been run down in the street. He went down to the Mississippi and walked along the shore, or as close as he could get, collecting flotsam and sundry litter. He dredged up sections of stout rope, beer cans, bottles, child's toys, sodden and covered in guck. When he had most of what he needed, he piled everything on the floor of his studio and went to work.

He loved nothing more than being totally engrossed in his art. The hours went by like minutes, meals were skipped. He had his Snapple and Cheez-Its to see him through the day. He had a radio tuned to a classical station. Mahler and Beethoven and Satie and Ravel were his companions. At one point the announcer said she would play selections from Verdi's opera, Rigoletto, and Jacob hummed right along, happy as a spoiled egotistical murdering psychopath could be.

The effigies began to take shape. The one he'd already made stood off to the side, a hulking seven-foot figure wearing a plaid skirt fastened with a 12 gauge leather belt with longhorn buckle, a camo shooting vest with shotgun shells in the holders—he decided against the Olga Luxury Lift underwire bra—and combat boots, standing watch like a sentinel. The head was a plain wooden block, curiously chipped and gouged by unknown implements. He chose to leave the face blank. No eyes to see, no ears to hear, no mouth to utter, no expression by which to judge. Its surface was made of strips of cloth, yarn, papier-mâché, and the torn canvases of paintings that he had once attempted and abandoned. He'd kept the scraps in a box and pulling them out for re-purposing was quite an emotional thing tantamount to reliving the different stages of his art as it evolved over the years. Found objects from the river shore and elsewhere along with Number One's teeth and slices of his scalp were attached in various ways to the torso. Paints were drizzled and splashed over the entire figure, open wounds were stitched with fishing line. The figure stood more or less at attention on his pedestal, paint brushes in one hand and a curved blade sickle in the other. Jacob saw him, this Frankenstein's Monster, as his masterpiece and he worried to some degree that he could do no better.

The two in progress, being built from the ground up, he began to have paternal feelings about, and though he resisted at first, he grudgingly gave them names. Wilbur and Orville. Kind of dumb, he thought, he didn't give two shits about the Wright Brothers or the history of aviation, but those were the names that popped in his head. These he gave faces to. Wilbur was the bigger of the two, a twisted bogey with crabbed disposition who appeared to be looking askance at Orville, mouth in a grimace, eyes made of marbles, glaring. But the mouth needed something, teeth. Orville, the hit and run victim, was slightly bent at the waist and listing to one side. There was a gaping hole in his side, linear, like a cavity on a dead tree. His compact frame warrior-like in stance, one arm reaching out, gnarled hand about to pluck something from thin air. That was pure inspiration, that arm extended, giving the character an air of mystery. What was he reaching for or was he trying to hold something back? The papier-mache head with pained expression sighted down the reaching arm and fixed on some point in the distance, a wall perhaps or whatever would be in the background at the gallery. But the head needed something, hair or fur. An old fashioned string mop wouldn't do.

* * *

It was no longer called the dog pound. Like almost everything these days, the facility had to have a more dignified name. The shelter, located on Gasconade Street in South City, not far from Jacob's second home, was now called The Center For Animal Rescue and Enrichment, and it housed strays and problematic pets brought in by animal control officers and concerned citizens. Jacob entered through large glass doors and immediately was confronted with a strong scent of disinfectant as if the place had been so thoroughly gone over with Mr. Clean and other industrial cleansers that no germ would dare enter the building. He stopped at the desk and a young woman with a bright smile directed him down a hallway to the kennels. Even before he reached the kennel door he was met by a deafening cacophony of barking and howling which put him on edge. He didn't like dogs to begin with, and these animals were highly agitated. There were people in the walkway, kennels on both sides, and they were stopping to consider certain canines to bring home and become part of the family. How nice, Jacob thought bitterly, they want to make some animal's life better, give it love and attention, be its buddy. If they only knew what I'm thinking.

Over the din he heard a woman say to her companion, a man with a skeptical look, "Oh, look, Paul, isn't he just so cute?"

The man, Paul, said back, "He's awfully big. I thought you wanted a lap dog."

"I might change my mind for him," replied the woman. "Look at those eyes, he's practically begging to come home with us."

"I don't know," sighed Paul, "let's look at some others." And they moved on.

Jacob looked at what they had been looking at, a large animal, definitely a mutt, brown with a white patch over half its goofy-looking face. Big paws, floppy ears, long brown fur, mouth open showing rows of sharp white teeth. A sign on the cage said BISQUICK.

Jacob hunched down and gave it a good look. "Hey, Bisquick, you want to come home with me? I've got a nice surprise for you, what do you say?" The dog, rhythmically panting with its long pink tongue hanging out, looked at him quizzically, and seemed to nod. "Well, okay then, let's do it," said Jacob.

At the desk, once he told them he'd made his choice, he had to fill out a pet adoption agreement. The form, which had been partly filled out by some employee, described Bisquick as a four-year-old Shepherd-Pit Bull Terrier mix, male, fixed, friendly. This form asked him to agree with several things, among them that it would be his pet and he would not sell it to some other person, dealer, auction, and so on for any reason. No problem there, he thought. And he agreed to care for his new pet in a humane and responsible way and to provide it with clean and adequate shelter, food, water and veterinary care. He had no qualms in checking that off for he was a pathological liar at heart. He paid a fee of $80 which included the neutering that had already been done.

When this business was done, they presented him with a red nylon leash and led him back to the kennel where they brought out the dog and out the door they went. No one had a wisp of a clue that Bisquick was going to meet his demise.

Back at the house on the bluffs, Jacob paid close attention to the dog, exploring every area, sniffing the furniture, looking out windows. He'd forgotten to ask if the animal was house-trained and now he was watching to see if he'd lift his leg or worse, make a deposit. If you have to pee, just scratch on the door, he told it. He got a throw rug and held it up for the dog to see. This can be your bed, your blankie. Sit on it, lie on it, make it your own. For now, anyway. I'll put it here. The dog approached and looked it over. He looked at Jacob with that goofy expression as if to say, Okay, Bud, what else you got? Jacob went down the steps to his studio where his figures awaited completion. The dog followed. Jacob turned the radio on, got his tools and materials arranged, and began to work. The dog jumped up on a small couch and watched.

Even with his back turned, he could feel the dog scrutinizing him. It put him off-kilter. "I got you off death row, got you a reprieve, but I'm not going to get attached to you," he told it firmly. "No squeaky toys for you. I'm not even going to give you a name. I mean, other than Bisquick, which is such a stupid name. Who would name a dog that?" The dog's ears perked up slightly. "No, the sooner I do you in, the better."

He continued at his labor. He got a step ladder and ascended over the figures, wide brush and several small open cans of paint in hand. He began dripping paints over the figures, conjuring an obsessed Jackson Pollack. He had a wooden paint stirrer in his pocket and that worked even better than the brush. After a bit, it looked good and he pondered just how much color to give them, where to stop, because he didn't want them to look like some harlequin character in an Elizabethan comedy. But then he had a thought, one of those sudden inspirations that come to true artists, and that thought was blood. He would finish by dripping blood on the figures. It would be messy, sure, and as it dried the crimson color would turn to brown, but it would look pretty cool. And people would wonder. He turned his gaze to the dog and smiled.

He got the dog's dinner ready. He hadn't bought any dog food so he went with what was in the fridge, Marie Callender's Cheesy Chicken & Bacon Pot Pie. He put two in the oven, one for himself, and followed the baking instructions. He waited. When they were finished he put them on the counter to cool. He went to a drawer and got a pill bottle. He opened the child-proof cap and took out four tabs of fentanyl. When the pies cooled he put one of them on a plate, turning the tin upside-down, and, with a fork, scraping every last morsel onto the plate. He added the tabs and stirred them into the meal, which smelled so tantalizing, something a dog would love, he thought. Right then he was also thinking about how convenient it was to have these potent little pills, pain relievers prescribed for post-surgical patients but just as easy, in the right hands, a lethal dose to unsuspecting man or animal alike. But he was nearly out of them now and it was anyone's guess when he would need some next. He made a note to get more.

The dog had been watching him, watching his every move in fact. Jacob had never seen such a curious animal. He set the plate on the kitchen floor. "Here you go," he said. "Chow time." He stood back. Bisquick approached cautiously. He sniffed it circumspectly like a picky eater. He didn't go for it, he backed off instead. Jacob didn't think of this outcome, he thought all dogs would eat whatever was put in front of them and do it with gusto.

"What's going on?" he asked it. "I made this for you, it's good stuff. I eat it myself. Come on, chow down, okay?" The dog didn't like the whiny voice he was hearing, he also smelled something that alarmed him. The smell of malevolence. It was a foregone decision in his uncomplicated canine mind that he wasn't going to touch the food on that plate.

A minute passed with Jacob growing more impatient, exhorting the dog to eat, at first coaxing in what he thought was a friendly tone and when that didn't work becoming shrill and demanding and finally cursing the dog. "If you won't eat then I'll make you eat!" he told it viciously. He bent down and took Bisquick by the scruff of the neck and began to drag him across the tile floor toward the food. Bisquick resisted, splaying his paws on the slippery floor, but Jacob had a good grip. He got the dog right up to the plate and was forcing his nose down in it when Bisquick, quick as a piston stroke, bit him on the wrist of the hand that held him, and he wasn't letting go. Jacob screamed bloody murder. He jerked his hand to get away, but the dog held fast. Jacob pounding Bisquick's skull with his free hand all the while screaming "Oh, my god! Oh, my god!" The dog was freaked out too but he had no other way of defending himself. Finally, after what seemed like a minute, Bisquick released the hand of this bad man. He skulked out of the kitchen, knowing he'd done something wrong, and he made for the studio, the only place he knew, to await the coming of the bad man.

Jacob moved his wrist, he *tried* to move his wrist, but it was swelling fast and changing color. It looked terrible, puncture wounds where the dog's canines had pierced the skin oozing blood. He was torn between tending to his injuries and killing the dog here and now. He chose the latter. He went to his studio, saw the dog cowering in a corner. He grabbed a hammer from a bench and came at him, teeth bared. The dog had never known a fight or flight response to any situation; there was only flight. He hurried out of the room back toward the kitchen, Jacob close behind. "I'll get you!" he called. "You're a dead dog. Dead!"

Once in the kitchen the dog jumped up on the counter. There was a window at the sink. The window was open but there was a screen. Bisquick, desperate, clawed and bit at the screen until it tore, leaving a gap large enough to fit through. He was nearly through the opening when he felt his tail being pulled. He'd never had his tail pulled and if a dog could feel humiliation he felt it. It was a sickening feeling and all his brain could manage was a sense of the bad man trying to bring him back, get at him. And he was mostly outside, but now dangling by his tail with the ground close enough that he could touch it with his front paws. He twisted and torqued his 45-pound frame as if his life depended on it, and with huge relief felt the grip on his tail released.

Jacob stood at the kitchen counter with his meager supply of first aid items contained in a plastic case the size of a cigar box with a red cross on the front, the one he'd bought years ago for ten bucks at Walgreen's. Even the large Band-aid wouldn't cover the wound entirely, he had to use two, and the so-called antibacterial ointment was runny. First, he'd washed the wound with soap and water, that much he knew to do, and now he was dressing it gingerly, whimpering, making small ouch noises.

"Serves you right."

Jacob wheeled at the sound of the voice behind him, already know-ing who it was. This he didn't need. "How do you get around?" he asked. "It's almost fifteen miles from West County to here. Do you fly? Do you just think yourself from one place to another? Is there no escape from you?"

"Serves you right," repeated the specter, "you were going to kill that dog like you killed me. He fought back, I wish I had."

Jacob's brow furrowed, he scoffed. "You said you wanted to die. You were such a fuck up, your words, nothing to live for, that it was buh-buh-best to end it all. You were on board with it, I merely assisted you and never even a th-thank you."

Light from the specter flashed momentarily. "Oh, you want a thank you? How funny. How about a screw you because I loved life, loved be-ing alive, and you made me feel like it was—"

"Can it, will you? I'm trying to play nurse here and I need to concen-trate."

"I hope it gets infected and you lose your arm," said the specter.

* * *

They had talked it over the night before, over Cognac. A suicide pact. They would drink the fentanyl-laced Snapple and wait for the end together. They would do it in some less trafficked area of Hopeville so they would be found within a day and taken to the terminal stop of all lethal overdoses, the City Morgue. Autopsies would show the presence of opioids. They made a promise that they would do it and not even think of backing out. They toasted to eternity.

It was a Sunday morning in August, dawn having just broken. They parked the Winnebago on the side of the Union Electric Light & Power behemoth. They got out, looked around, the Arch looming about 200 yards distant, one leg catching the early light. They walked the path toward a spot they agreed on, a sidetrack that led to a small clearing that overlooked the river. The glow of the Lumiere Casino could be seen. The camp was quiet except for someone's battery operated radio set to a talk station. Here and there, the smoking embers from campfires the evening before. They walked in silence, each with their own aching thoughts. At length they got to the clearing, found a tree and sat beside it in the ankle-high grass wet with dew. The eastern horizon was ablaze with the rosy hue of just past sunrise and the rushing river reflected that color.

"A new day," observed Austin. "Our last."

"Does it make you sad?" asked Jacob.

"Sure it does," he answered, "thinking about how differently things might've turned out. I might have made something of myself...if only I had more drive and didn't get swallowed up in this dark cloud that comes along. It's like I'm trapped in a bad dream and don't know when it's going to end."

Self-pity suits you, thought Jacob. You want it to end, you want the grave. "All that's going to be over," he said, philosophically, "everlasting sleep, no more troubles—depression gone."

"Tell me again it's the sensible thing to do," he said.

"Sensible? Probably. The right thing? Yes without a doubt. Indubitably. Would you like me to go first?" He patted him on the arm. "Okay, I'll go first."

They watched a towboat with more than twenty tows push upriver. They could see men on deck. "They've got their problems, I'll bet," said Austin, "but they're not thinking of suicide."

"How do you know?" He had the Kiwi-Strawberry Snapple in hand. He took off the cap and held it out with both hands like a priest with a chalice. "Hmm, this is my opportunity for last words," he said. "What are my last words?"

Austin shook his head in wonder. "How can you be so flippant about this? It's the end of our lives."

"I don't know, it's just my nature. So my last words, um, You can learn a lot about life from an anthill." And he took a big swig from the bottle, licked his lips and, theatrically, "Ahh." He reached into his nylon day pack and brought out a bottle of Mango Madness. He unscrewed the cap and passed it to Austin. "Your turn."

Austin took it with trepidation. He turned the container slowly and appeared to read the contents and other nomenclature on the label. "Any time now," said Jacob.

"Do you feel anything yet?"

Jacob looked to his companion, smiling contently, "Yes, a feeling of euphoria, a tingling of the extremities, I would say. Anticipating what comes next. Go ahead, drink, catch up to me."

"I don't know, I may be changing my mind." That didn't go over well.

"Oh no, you don't," insisted Jacob. "We have a pact, you cannot back down."

"I only had sex with two girls," his voice cracking with a sob.

"Sex is overrated," said Jacob offhandedly.

"Still…"

Jacob looked him square in the eye. "Drink up or would you like me to slit your throat?"

"I could get up and walk away now," he said by way of rebuttal, "leave you here to cash in by yourself." He studied the Snapple container with its bright label and picture of a ripe mango with a single green leaf. He held it out in one hand and brought it to his lips, "But what the hell." He took a lusty draft and drained half at a single gulp.

"You tricked me, you bastard!" said the specter. "Your drink wasn't poisoned, just mine. That was the dirtiest trick on record, how could you sink so low, be so underhanded?"

"I told you, I've never been any good at suicide."

"Cute, very cute. I thought we were friends."

Jacob refused to look at the specter, but replied, "I liked you well enough, certainly more than those other wastrels and I didn't stutter as much around you. But when it came down to it, you're still a no account bum."

"I was somebody! What does it matter that I didn't have money in my pocket?"

"Hand me the iodine, will you? Oh, I forgot, you have no substance. Tough break."

"The most precious thing we have, life and you robbed me of it.

You'll pay. You can't see it coming, but I can. You'll pay dearly."

Jacob scoffed at this remark. "The last thing I need or want is to be stuck in a house with a pissed off ghost. So, goodbye." He took a peek, still there. "*Sayonara, arrivederci, auf wiedersehen, adios.*" He shut his eyes and waited for the thing to go away.

Back at the clearing overlooking the river, the sun rising, Austin was zooming through space, one foot on the earth, his head in the cosmos, dodging asteroids and meteorites, colors flashing all around like a fireworks spectacular at night.

"Like wow," said to no one though Jacob was beside him, watching intently. "I feel like I'm up in the clouds." He was on his back now, looking to the sky. Jacob leaned over to better look. Pinpoint pupils, he saw. Mouth wide open, staggered breaths.

"Am I dead yet?"

"Just about," said Jacob. "What do you see?"

"A white light," he whispered, "like a star and I'm in—I'm in space traveling very fast toward it." Silence, his eyes scrunched tight. "I don't want to go into the light," speech now an effort, "but yet I do...doesn't matter 'cause I can't stop."

— 35 —

FRANCIS HAD GONE TO BEST BUY FOR THE TRACKING DEVICE he put on Jacob's Highlander. The device itself came with a strong magnet which allowed placement on the undercarriage of the vehicle. That he did on the day he was there with the homeless folks, pretending like he dropped something, then quickly crawled beneath the car with a flashlight and put it in a little nook near the rear axle where it wouldn't be dislodged from hitting a bump or whatever. That was step one. Step two was easy enough, downloading an app provided by the Japanese manufacturer onto his smart phone. Martha, who was better with apps than he, did the set up which took all of five minutes. Like magic, the image of a street map appeared on the screen—the map could be enlarged so even certain cross streets were readable. There was an icon representing a vehicle, and this icon was contained in a circle and was stationary. When you hear this beep, she said, reading the directions, that means the car is on the move and you should see the little circle moving along through the streets and roads. You'll see where it goes. What beep? he asked. What's it sound like? She played it for him as a test. Oh, okay, I'll try to pay attention, he said, it's just that I'll probably think it's a text coming in and ignore it. Well, you'll have be alert, she said, if you want this to work for you. Look, there's even a phone number you can call for support, isn't that nice?

He had filled her in about Vorhof, his suspicions, the man's diabolical nature, the frustration over not being able to pin anything on him. It didn't sound like the man was a mastermind, she told him this Vorhof would trip up sooner or later and everything would come crashing down. Nice thought, he said, wish it were so but I need results now. She knew it was important to him, even to the point of obsession, that he find a way to bring him down.

He'd had the device for almost two weeks now and he was getting used to it. Luckily, Vorhof drove the Highlander exclusively, the Winnebago likely in storage somewhere. And it was soon after the surprise visit with the homeless faction, when the device was planted, that Francis realized Vorhof had moved his base. The tracker showed him in the City, deep South Side, stationary for long periods. Through the wonder of satellite technology, Francis sniffed him out and located his where-abouts, a charming little house on Bluff Drive. That was a surprise.

He couldn't know Vorhof's destination just by looking at the screen, the moving circle with a thin blue line behind it moving as well. And though the screen showed certain busy streets, he would have to drive to the location where the SUV had stopped and see what it was. This day, a perfect autumn day in late October, he heard the beep and pulled over to see where the soup man was headed. By the time he got the map to the screen his quarry was already well underway, heading north on I-55 toward downtown. He sat in his idling car watching Vorhof's progress. He'd merged on to I-44 West and exited at Grand. Taking Grand to Lindell, the College Church at Saint Louis University, he turned left and went the six blocks west to Euclid Avenue and turned right. Now in the Central West End, the SUV came to rest on McPherson near Euclid. Francis was only a mile away.

He parked within sight of the Highlander. He did not know what business Vorhof had here, but he would wait to find out. He took a *National Geographic* from the back seat and began doing a crossword puzzle on the last page. The clues were enough to stump a Jeopardy contestant. Twenty-three across: Pinky without a prosthesis? Twenty-six down: Persian for "king." Come on, he thought, there's got to be one that I know. Thirty-four down: Unwelcome home happenings. Hmm, electrocution while changing a fuse? Choking on a big piece of steak? Slip in the shower, crack your skull? The phone rang, the number on the screen unfamiliar. He answered. "Francis here."

"Hi, it's Cary Finch," said the caller. "Got a minute?" Francis said he did. "I wanted to tell you those assholes who want to break my legs haven't been around and I'm thinking it's you that made that happen. I just want to thank you for stepping up, that was really decent of you."

"Hey, it's all right," he assured. "It's nothing that Batman or Captain America wouldn't have done."

"Yeah, ha ha. So I noticed the X in your name on the card you gave me. Is that for Xavier?"

"Sure is," he replied.

"That's my middle name too. How cool is that?"

"A good name," said Francis. "It's definitely stood the test of time."

"There's a famous saint by that name, Saint Francis Xavier."

"Know him well."

"So, Mr. Lenihan—"

"Francis."

"Yeah, Mr. Francis, do you happen to know of any work available. I could really use some funds, if you know what I mean. Almost any kind of work, even janitorial."

"Not off hand," said Francis, "but let me—" He saw Vorhof coming out a door, shuffling along the sidewalk, one hand wrapped in a bandage. "Gotta go," he said, "we'll talk later."

Vorhof heading to his SUV when he was approached by a rough-looking man on crutches. Francis saw there was only a pantleg where a foot would be. He saw the man giving Vorhof a story, his hand out in supplication. He watched as Vorhof shoved the man, causing him to fall backward, his crutches clattering on the pavement. Vorhof walked off shaking his head. He got to his vehicle and drove off.

Francis crossed the street, helped the beggar to his feet, or foot. He asked if he was okay. The man shook himself off, said he was and that some people are just assholes. He asked for a dollar to buy a 40-ouncer.

Francis went into the art gallery that Vorhof had left. Spacious it was with no one in sight but lots of bizarre art on the walls. He would check it out while waiting for someone to appear. There were scribble-scrabble paintings that didn't make any sense, there were collages of a highly personal nature, sculpture on pedestals that could have been door-stoppers.

"Can I answer any questions?" said a voice behind him.

Francis pivoted, saw a fellow in his twenties, bald, round black-rimmed glasses, neatly trimmed beard and goatee. "Oh, no, thanks. Just looking."

"Well, actually, we're not really open just now but go ahead, look away." He smiled. Francis said all right, he'd look some more. A minute later, the assistant came over and stood beside him, a large confusing painting presenting itself. "That's a Helen Frankenthaler, during her

Fauvist period. Quite colorful, you see?"

"I'll take two," said Francis, grinning.

"Yes, quite so. But all these are coming down soon to make way for the new show."

"Oh?"

"Next Friday," the assistant confided, "gala opening, a three-person show, visually stunning, even disturbing. One of the artists was just here, came to see the exhibition space, to imagine how his pieces would blend in. Rigoletto, have you heard of him? No? Not surprised, he's an up-and-comer. Dagmar is selling him."

"One name, huh? Like Picasso. I'd like to see his work, and he'll be here in person?"

"Most certainly," said the assistant.

* * *

Late that afternoon he gave Cleo a ring. "The thing is on," he told him through a wall of sound. "Can we meet soon?" he shouted.

"You don't have to shout," said Cleo. "I can hear you. What did you say?"

"I said it's time for that thing we talked about. With the soup man, you know. Do you have the items?"

There were horns and guitar in the background, drumming too. He heard, "Come on, man, this ain't no time to gab with your baby mama. Get back in the mix now."

"Call you back in a bit," said Cleo.

"Where are you?" he shouted, "I'll come to you." Cleo gave an address.

Rehearsal was in another room in the basement of the church that housed the food pantry. Francis followed the sounds through a minor labyrinth and came upon six guys making music. They were tight, Francis saw, blending beautifully. Base guitar, lead guitar, keyboard, sax, drums, and Cleo with no instrument, singing in that soulful voice.

"I wanna stop, silly little games you and me play, and I'm feeling right

on, if you feel the same way, baby…"

Francis found a folding chair and listened some more. *"I'd love to make you wet in between your thighs 'cause I love when it comes inside you, mmm, I get so excited when I'm around you, oh baby, oh, ah, oh, baby…"* Like he was having an orgasm. But Francis was disappointed, that was the last song and now they were packing up.

Cleo came over. "Thanks for coming, brother. What'd you think?"

"Great, loved it," gushed Francis. "Love to hear more. That song, it sounds familiar, R-rated. I had a lump in my shorts. I guess you won't be doing that one at church socials."

Cleo laughed. "D'Angelo 'How Does It Feel.'"

"I was just going to say that."

"His tribute to Prince. It's one of our favorites. So what's up?" Cleo said so long to his band mates and they adjourned outside on the same concrete patio with potted plants and flowers.

"We talked about setting the guy up, remember?" He spoke in hushed tones. "It's time. Do you have the items we discussed?"

Cleo put a hand to his bearded chin, rubbed it thoughtfully. "As I remember, your plan was sorta complicated with several moving parts. Let me see if I have it right. You were going to find someone to get stopped leaving the house, the cops would search the car and find drugs, which would open the door to a search warrant for the soup man's crib, and there they would find all sorts of incriminating shit, which we planted, and which would result in that fool's arrest. That about right?"

"Yeah, I'd say so. And you're right, there are some iffy situations where luck comes into play, mainly the driver getting stopped. I actually found someone who's willing to get stopped and searched and found with drugs—a small amount, but still. What's tricky is making that happen while the house is under surveillance. I'll have to know the cop is watching and get the driver there pronto. I'll have to surveil the surveillant."

"It's so complicated, it'll be a wonder if it goes off. How about we just off him, bullet to the brain."

Francis stared at Cleo. "Really? You'd do that?"

"Me? Hell, no. We hire someone."

"No way," said Francis, astounded. "I'm already putting my career at risk, I'm not going to put my freedom at risk, spend my life in prison or get executed over the soup man. And neither are you."

"I was kidding," said Cleo, "I think. So when do you need these 'items'?"

"I need a small amount now," he said, "to plant in the car that gets pulled over, and just after that a larger amount of drugs and that handgun you told me about, the one used in a robbery, to plant in his house awaiting the search warrant."

"Who's gonna plant the stuff in his house? That's breaking an' entering, burglary prob'ly, although you aren't taking anything you're leaving something."

"I thought you might do it."

"Uh, no, big brother, you thought wrong."

"Okay then, I'll do it. Know why? Because we've *got* to get this guy out of circulation."

"Agreed," said Cleo, "so how 'bout I get you some crack? Baggie filled with rocks, ready for sale on the street. That's plentiful enough, I can get you that by tomorrow."

"Okay, just call and I'll meet you. After that, I'll phone in the tip. We got to get this thing underway before I lose my nerve."

"I hear you, big brother, and welcome to the exciting world of lawbreaking."

PART V

IF THIS WAS SATURDAY AFTERNOON IT MUST BE CONFESSION AT ST. JAMES. Francis entered the old church, walked down the nave to the confessionals near the front and off to the side. He saw there were half a dozen ahead of him. He saw also that the priest wasn't Fr. Gillis but, according to the name plate slid into the holder, it was the newest clergy, one not long out of the seminary, Fr. Duerer, and he was glad about that because the elder priest had been somewhat snippy in the past. He waited his turn and finally went in. He knelt in the dim little cubicle facing the screen. "Bless me father for I have sinned. It has been two months since my last confession." Fr. Duerer did not know Francis and he asked a few questions beforehand. Single or married? Regular churchgoer or infrequent? Did he tithe or did he believe that others would carry the weight? The priest had an assuring tone that pleased Francis and made him want to confide.

Francis launched into his confession with a list of venial sins. There were no mortals that he could think of and he wondered if the priest believed he was such a goody-goody that his worst sin was thinking prurient thoughts about a woman that he had served and didn't even know. Then he remembered that he had shoved a potato into a guy's tailpipe, some mook in Dogtown who had flipped him off for driving too slow and taking too long to go when the light went green. It was a deliberate act, he told the priest, I had to go to the market and buy a nice-sized spud.

"Potato in the tailpipe, what does that do?" asked Fr. Duerer behind the screen.

"His car won't start and he won't know why."

"Hmm," mused the priest. "I'd call that a prank, not a sin."

"Oh, thanks Father. I've got to come to confession more often."

"Are we done now?" he asked.

Francis cleared his throat. "Well, there is one more thing. It's not a sin because I haven't done it yet but I will be doing it pretty soon, probably within the week. It's kind of a big one."

"Okay, but if you know you're going to commit a sinful act wouldn't now be the time to reconsider?"

"You would think so, wouldn't you? But please understand, this thing, I've *got to do it*. It's for a good cause. I can't back out even though there's danger to myself."

"And to your soul," said the priest, a tinge of rebuke in his voice. "You should do everything in your power to avoid the occasion of sin, not to court it. What is the nature of this deed that you're so intent on keeping to yourself? I assume it's a felony."

"Um, well, I decided that I would only say that I'm about to commit a sin and, yes, a crime. I can't give you any details because you might try to talk me out of it."

"I certainly would, that's my job in case you didn't know."

"Okay, how about this? After the whole mess is over, if I'm not in prison, I'll come back and confess this one. You can slap a thousand Our Fathers on me."

"You would have to rob a bank to get that sort of penance," he chuckled through the screen. Then he asked if Francis was sorry for his sins and Francis the penitent said he was. Fr. Duerer then said the Prayer of Absolution to which Francis responded "Amen." For penance he was tasked with ten Hail Marys and ten Our Fathers.

By way of parting the priest said, "Give thanks to the Lord, for he is good." He waited for the response.

"Um, help me out here," said Francis.

"His mercy…"

"More, please."

"His mercy endures forever. There, I've finished it for you. Now go in peace."

Francis thanked him and left the confessional. Fr. Duerer waited a half minute then he exited, stepped out to the aisle and stood there, hands on hips, watching as Francis walked off. He wanted to know who this character was.

* * *

Francis didn't waste any time calling in the tip. It was short and to the point.

"Nine-one-one, what is your emergency?" the dispatcher sounding somewhat bored.

"Oh, it's not an emergency," he said. "I just want you to know that my neighbor is selling drugs, people coming and going at all hours of the day and night. Expensive cars with tinted windows blasting ghetto music."

"Where is this taking place, sir?"

"Fifty-five oh-six Bluff Drive. Please do something. I heard them say things."

"What things, sir?"

"I distinctly heard 'smack' and 'angel dust' and 'ganja.' Not that I know what these things actually are, but they sound illegal."

"We'll look into it," she informed. "What is your name, sir?"

"Gotta go," he said, "thanks for your help."

He called in the tip even before getting the drugs from Cleo because he knew it may be two or three days or longer before they start surveillance. But now he had the ball rolling. Next was to meet with Mickey's nephew, the slacker Jimmy who had already missed the initial meet up a few days ago because he suddenly had to go to a comic book store and sit in on a *Dungeons & Dragons*. This time they were meeting at a skateboard park in the City and he'd better be there.

There was no mistaking Jimmy standing there in his baggy cargo shorts, WE ARE NOT YOUR KIND Slipknot T-shirt, baseball cap on backwards, and two-inch platform leather boots with lots of buckles and pointed metal studs. Lean and rangy and heavily tattooed, he looked like the "after" picture of a public service poster warning of the ravages of drug abuse.

Francis walked up and stood before him. "Hey there, Jimmy."

Jimmy smiled revealing some less-than-attractive dentition and gave him a fist bump. "Dude, I was hoping you'd show because my uncle says you're the man and you've got a job for me and that's all I need to hear."

There was a bench beneath a tree and they sat while Jimmy vaped and Francis explained the mission. "You need to be ready at all times," he told him, "on call. That means your phone is with you, you can't let it out of your sight and it must be charged. You also need to be near the car, ready to roll. Got that?" Mickey had been nice enough to supply a car, a 1965 Chrysler Newport that used to belong to his dear deceased mother. He'd kept running all these years.

"Oh yeah, no prob."

"I'm thinking it'll be in the next week. I'll call and say get over here now. You get in the car and rush over to the location. I'm going to take you there after we're done here so you'll know where it is."

Just then a beaming long hair sauntered over, skateboard in hand. "Hey Jimmy, you see that nosegrind I just did?"

"Sure did, bro. Sick, really sick."

"Where's your board, bro?"

"I'll be along later, bro."

Francis watched the kid walk off. He wore his baseball cap backwards too. "Tell me," said Francis. "Why is that a thing, the ball cap worn backwards? I mean, isn't the point of the bill to keep the sun out of your eyes. How's it gonna do that in the back of your head?"

Jimmy gave an indifferent shrug. "It makes a statement, doesn't matter how practical it is."

"What statement is that?"

"Hell if I know…you got any weed?"

On the way, Francis had the radio tuned to talk format but Jimmy pleaded for Z107. Francis said go for it. They broke into a song by Eminem and when that was over the DJ announced a contest. "Win a trip to our iHeartRadio Music Festival and a thousand buckaroos!"

"These contests are for real," Jimmy remarked, "Last year I won tickets for Nicki Minaj. Killer show at The Pageant. You've gotta keep calling and calling, can't let that busy signal throw you off. Speed dial helps."

Once in deep South City they turned off South Broadway on to the incline that was Bluff Drive. They drove past the house, nestled back off the street. Vorhof's SUV wasn't there. He saw the front door and he could barely make out a side door with a little awning. Encouraging. That was another thing. How was he going to artfully break into this man's castle? He didn't know how to pick a lock and he worried that breaking a window might rouse the neighbors, although there were only two other homes in the vicinity. Maybe Vorhof was a fresh air freak and would leave a window open for him. There had been an idea about this, but he couldn't remember what it was.

"Okay, that's it," said Francis, "one with the dormers and green shutters, an old carriage house." Jimmy nodded. He parked down the street and laid it out, how it would transpire. "When I see the patrol car, probably unmarked, I'll call you. You get here as fast as you can. Probably take you twenty minutes if you're ready to roll and you will be. Once here, all you do is go to the door, you pretend to knock, and you just stand there like you're talking to him, the weasel who lives here. Then go to your car, the tote bag, which I'm going to give you, in plain sight for anyone to see, and you leave. The cop is far enough away, he can't know that you didn't encounter Vorhof but he will see you with this tote and he will be suspicious."

"Yeah, okay, I get it," said Jimmy. "Then, like you said, he stops me because the car has a broken headlight."

"Broken taillight too," added Francis.

"How should I act? Worried? Nervous? No biggie? Should I give him attitude?"

"Oh yeah, give him attitude he's sure to search the car. Cops hate attitude."

"Never been arrested but there's always a first time, right?" The kid didn't seem too worried.

"You'll be fine. You've seen *Law & Order.* You go to the station, they book you, make you see a judge, then release you until your hearing. It's a process. This, that, this, just keep your cool. But in this case, before they release you, they're going to put you in a room with one or two detectives and those detectives are going to ask you where you got the crack, why did you go to that house, who there supplied you."

"Yeah, what do you call that? There's a name."

"Interrogation. They are interrogating you, it can get tense. They're looking for the bigger fish and after holding back, after they threaten to throw the book at you, you're going to give them a name. Just say Jacob or even Jake, you don't know his last name. You met him at a club and he's been your supplier for a couple years now."

"I'm digging myself into a hole," Jimmy dubious. "You said I wouldn't do any jail time."

"A small batch of cocaine, no, not a day. Plus, you're giving them what they want, the supplier. Plus, we'll have a lawyer ready for you. Don't you worry."

"When do I get paid?"

"Half down before the bust, and the rest after."

"A thousand bucks, hmm. That might not be enough for my mental anguish. How about two?"

"Probably not," he said. "I'd have to sell my daughter to come up with another grand."

Jimmy was silent for a bit, then, "No, I ain't never seen *Law & Order*, but I have seen reruns of *Spenser: For Hire*. Is it anything like that?"

"No, not at all. Spenser's a private eye in Boston, these are overworked cops in St. Louis. But now I'm thinking something else." Looking at the house, stroking his chin thoughtfully. "Problem is if you're not ready to roll and it takes you too long to get here, the cop may have given up by then and our whole plan is shot. So, the alternative is I have you come along when I go to see if the cops are watching. We ride together in the Newport. If we see the cop watching the house, I'll get out and you'll do your thing. I'll have to catch a bus back to my car. What d'ya think?"

Jimmy nodded agreement. "I'm down with that, sure thing. You're the boss, I trust your judgment."

I wish I did, thought Francis.

* * *

Later that day he and Martha sat at their kitchen table with plates of savory food and glasses of Merlot between them. Martha had brought home from the restaurant a container of traditional tortellini stuffed with prosciutto and cheese. At the restaurant it had been served with a side of broth; here at home it was served with Alfredo sauce. It had been the special this day. They loved good food and this was right up there on their list. They made cursory talk about people they knew, upcoming events, and how their day went.

"Let me tell you what happened today," said Francis. "This afternoon, just a short time ago, I had two depo subpoenas for a plant in South County, one for the CEO and one for the company itself, Alpha Manufacturing. So I go into the lobby, state my business to the receptionist. She says just a minute and disappears down a hallway. Comes back five minutes later and says, 'Someone will be with you.' She goes back to work and I'm left waiting. And waiting and waiting. I'm looking at things on the walls, testimonies about the excellence of this company, I'm pacing. I ask the receptionist what's going on, I'm waiting fifteen minutes now. She repeats the same line, someone's coming."

"The old waiting game, test their patience, show them they don't have time for peons like you."

"Right on, dear." He took a sip of Merlot.

"So finally this guy in slacks and sports shirt comes out and you can tell he's irritated or else suffering from indigestion. I have the subpoenas spread on the counter. Politely or at least professionally, I explain. The CEO's retired, he snaps. And the company has changed its name, from Alpha Manufacturing to something else—Omega Gadgets, I don't know. So your subpoena is no good, he says. I say, the subpoena for the CEO, I'll take that back with me. The one for the company, come on, on the way in I passed at least three signs that said Alpha Manufacturing. The subpoena is for Alpha Manufacturing under any iteration it may have. Doesn't matter, says the guy, who I learn is the top dog there now that the CEO is gone, get the name right. You'll take this one back too."

"I know the rest," said Martha with humor, "but go ahead."

"The guy was in my face, Martha, determined to prevail and it was a classic battle of wills. Me deciding I'm going to serve this paper and him saying no way. I told him point blank I'm leaving this paper. I had his name so that wasn't a problem. I began to walk out and he's making threats. He caught up with me at the door, he had the subpoena in his hand. In a surprising move, this guy, this honcho who oversees a big company, crumpled the subpoena and stuffed it down the back of my shirt."

"Go on!"

Francis chuckling at the memory, "So I reach behind me and pull out the subpoena. I drop it on the floor, I tell him it's served. He picks the paper up and tries to stuff it down my shirt again—unbelievable. I push him away and he comes at me trying to grab my shirt, but he grabs the ribbon of my scapula and he pulls it and it breaks. I don't think he knew it was a scapula, but now it's hanging loose down the front of my shirt. I keep on walking and he stays put, shouting feeble threats."

"Wow," she said. "He actually assaulted you. You could have called nine one-one."

"I don't have time for that. But look," he reached in his front pocket and brought out the scapula, the one with Our Lady Of Mt. Carmel. He laid it on the table. The soft brown fabric ribbon evidencing tiny loose threads where it had been torn away. "Exhibit Number One. I can truthfully say I've been persecuted on religious grounds. What d'you think? Am I on the road to sainthood?"

She nodded gleefully. "Oh, I should say so. Saint Francis, they'll probably name schools and churches after you—oh, sorry, I think we've already got one of those."

They had a laugh, tucked into their tortellini some more, made satisfying sounds, and she said, intriguingly, "Well, let me tell you about my day."

She had been dispatched to Schnuck's on The Hill to buy some broccoli and onions, the chef running short. She was in the checkout line, reading the latest *People* magazine when she felt a tap on her shoulder. "It was Sandy Crowley," she said. "Behind me, shopping cart filled with provisions for some party they're having at the law firm. I'm friends with his wife, Harriet, you know. Anyway, we made small talk in the line and he said for me to wait when I'm through because he had something important to tell me. So I waited for him and what do you think he wanted to discuss?"

"Um, the uptick in jaywalking citations in St. Louis?"

"No, silly. This is serious. He wanted to talk about the class action suit he's mounting for people who were rounded up that day of the demonstrations downtown. He said he's already signed on twenty-three people. He said that you qualified as a defendant. You were in that kettle, is what he said."

"Yes, I had the indignity of being a fish in that kettle," giving a little snort. "I'd like to forget about it."

"No, no, you can't forget about it. That's the whole point. According to Sandy, the police were out of line in the way they handled things. That tactic has been decried by civil rights groups and activists all over. This class action is going forward and it's going to mean big money for those involved." She raised her eyebrows a couple times like Groucho Marx.

He wagged his head back and forth. "I don't know, looking to get paid for that, it doesn't sit well with me. I made a stupid mistake is all, I waited too long to leave."

"Okay, fine, blame yourself, but if the police did something wrong you may as well benefit from it. How will you feel when some of those who were there, people you may know and like, get their settlement checks—ten thousand, twenty thousand, who knows? You won't feel left out, like, well, maybe I should have jumped on board when I had the chance?"

He looked at his tortellini covered in Alfredo sauce and was thinking some lightly sauteed baby bella mushrooms would really be nice. "In truth? I'd probably be envious for a minute and then get on with my life," he told her.

"I know what it is," she said. "You don't want to be associated with that unruly mob down at the courthouse that day."

She knew that he knew she was right and she dared him with that certain look of hers to say otherwise. "Um, you would be right, but that isn't the only thing."

Martha sighed heavily. "Francis, we could really use that money, please don't pass this up. The roof in the garage is falling down. The toilet upstairs has no water pressure, it never flushes all the way. I've been plunging, when are you going to start plunging?" She could see he was surprised at the reproach, mild as it was. "I'm sorry," she added quickly. Then, leaning forward to stress the importance of what she was about to say, "*And* there's our well-earned vacation, two weeks in Northern Italy, hiking, restaurants—*spettacolare cibo, primo vino*"—kissing her fingertips—"you and I together in love. That may not happen, Francis, without an infusion of cash."

He hated the way she made sense while putting the pressure on. He thought, she really needs my assent. What harm would it do to agree? Was he really willing to disappoint her? He could make her happy with just a simple...

He met her expectant gaze, those expressive brown eyes the color of almond. "Oh, I don't know, maybe—"

"*Buono!*" she exclaimed. "I'll tell Sandy you'll be there tomorrow to get signed up. Thank you, thank you, thank you!" She gave his hand a squeeze.

"You're welcome," he said. "Please pass the Parmesan."

— 37 —

JACOB SAT ALONE AT A TABLE NEAR THE DOOR WAITING FOR HIS CA-
PRESE SALAD and Stromboli, the special of the day. He sipped at the ice
water the waiter had brought and contemplated a glass of wine, maybe
Chianti. He'd heard of Chianti going with various Italian dishes, but he
had never tried it. He had his phone out and seemed engrossed in reading
the screen, emails perhaps or some news feed. But he was really studying
the woman at the maitre d' stand. Earlier he'd seen her emerge from the
modest home in Dogtown and get in her car and drive off. He followed,
flush with excitement at such clandestine activity, like a real private eye.
He'd been watching the house because that's where his contact had said the
owner of the Ford Escort, Francis X. Lenihan, lived.

The contact was Earl Roerig and he was a friend of the family, had
worked with Jacob's father at the brokerage. At his parents' funeral Earl
had put his arm around Jacob, offered heartfelt condolence, and said
emphatically if ever there was anything he needed to just call. Jacob had
called him maybe three times over the years and Earl had come through
each time, whether it was a recommendation to the Old Warson Country Club or season tickets with private club level seats to the Opera
Theater of St. Louis. Earl also managed Jacob's trust fund. When he
called to ask about getting a name and address connected to a license
plate, Earl didn't balk. Nor, to Jacob's relief, did he ask the reason for
the request. Give me two days, the answer.

Now he had that bastard in the palm of his hand. Come to his
house and create a scene, attempt to unload a batch of filthy vagrants
on him. What cheek! Who does he think he is? He won't be so brash
when he learns what happens next.

So it stood to reason that the pretty olive-complected woman at the
maitre d' stand was his wife. Such a nice smile too. Too bad for her.

His food came and he did order the Chianti. This was a first class
restaurant he noted. It was going on two and the main dining room
was full, servers hustling from table to kitchen and back to table. There
was another dining area behind this one. He continued watching the
woman, waiting for a chance. He was taking his time, being patient. If it

didn't happen today he could always come back, try again. She seemed so poised and genuine standing there at her post, greeting people as they entered, saying goodbye to people as they left. Then he saw her talking to another woman, younger, obviously an employee. His table was closest to the maitre d' and he rose, pretending to check for something in his trouser pockets. He moved a few steps closer, straining to hear the conversation, something about going to Eovaldi's to get a log of Genoa salami. They both walked off leaving the stand unattended. He saw his chance. He walked toward the stand on his way to the restroom. No one paying any attention to him, just another lonely guy eating by himself. As he passed the stand he deftly dropped four tabs of fentanyl into the iced tea that he'd seen the wife drinking from. They were the last of his supply.

When he returned from the restroom he was surprised to see the younger woman at the maitre d' stand. Plump, cheerful, vivacious, he hated her on sight. The other one, the wife, must have run the errand. He didn't know how far Eovaldi's was, maybe she'd return before long and his wicked plan could still proceed. Then he saw the woman, the replacement, lift the glass of iced tea and down the hatch. She wasn't supposed to do that. It was somebody else's drink, didn't she have any manners?

Flustered, he waved to the waiter and asked for the check.

* * *

"Oh, it was just the worst," said Martha, "and I wasn't even there to help her."

"But she's going to be okay?" asked Francis.

"The doctors say yes, probably, but it's going to take time. Her brain is in a fog, cognitive impairment. That takes time to clear." Returning from Eovaldi's Deli, she saw the big red EMS rig parked in front of the restaurant, paramedics bringing out Gina strapped to a gurney. She was half-conscious, eyes rolled back, a nasal canula feeding her oxygen. Marco, visibly shaken, informed that she'd suddenly collapsed and fell onto a table of diners. Martha followed the ambulance to Barnes-Jewish ER.

"I don't understand," she said, plaintively. "Can you help me understand why Gina, who I've known since she was a teenager, and who is nothing less than perfectly healthy, would suddenly pass out in the restaurant? I was gone, like, twenty minutes."

"I don't know," said Francis. "It doesn't make sense."

"The paramedics asked me to look through her purse for any medications she may have been taking. I did, there were none."

"They're thinking an overdose of some kind?"

"Maybe, I don't know either. Oh, Francis, what's going on? I tried to call you, it went straight to voice mail."

"Oh, yeah. My phone died. I forgot to charge it last night and it crapped out around mid-morning. I couldn't charge it in the car because I couldn't find that plug, the one that goes with the cord. Sorry."

If Francis' phone had been charged he might have heard the beep from the Tracker app and seen that Vorhof had been at his house and later at the restaurant.

"She's got to come through this all right," Martha, hot tears running down her cheeks. "There's no way she can have permanent damage."

"She's a great kid," said Francis reassuringly, "she'll be okay."

TWO DAYS HAD PASSED SINCE HE CALLED IN THE TIP and now it was time to put the ball in play. On the first day, he drove by Vorhof's house once in the morning and three times in the afternoon, seeing the Highlander in the drive but no sign of a stakeout. The next day the same and he wondered if the tip had been taken seriously. More likely the cops were so busy dealing with the plethora of shootings, robberies, burglaries, assaults, and car thefts plaguing this city that they hadn't had time to get to it. Patience, he kept reminding himself, patience. Of course, he had his regular work and that could take him into adjoining counties, far from South City. This thing was really putting him out.

While he was there within sight of the home he pondered the eventual break-in. He saw the front door had little windows around it. Theoretically, he could break one of those and reach in to turn the lock. If he did that, though, Vorhof would see that he'd been breached and start searching to see what had been stolen and he would find the planted drugs and pistol and what-have-you before the detectives did. He might even call the cops to report a break-in, but probably not. If only he knew how to pick a lock. Then he remembered the idea he had for breaking into Vorhof's place. He knew a locksmith, Paul Krauss, knew him from Murphy's and he seemed like a guy who was not entirely on the up-and-up, which was good. He would approach Paul and ask if he would teach him how to pick a lock. Nothing illegal, he would assure him, not thinking to burglarize anybody, just thought it would be a fun thing to learn.

The locksmith shop was on Manchester out in Brentwood. Walk in and there are racks of keys everywhere, key rings and key holders galore, some with novelty features like familiar cartoon characters or miniature cars or a lucky rabbit foot. Locks too. Door handles and door knobs with lock and key. Electronic lock sets with a panel of tiny numbered buttons to press. Paul Krauss was at the cluttered counter, a thin pick in hand, working on a lock that looked like something from the Middle Ages. A hand-lettered sign on the wall behind him: I WORK AS A LOCKSMITH. A JOB THAT REALLY OPENS DOORS FOR ME.

He saw Francis and ceased his toil. "Hey, there," he said, effusively, removing his magnifying spectacles and placing them on the counter. "Great to see you. Outside of the bar, I mean. What brings you in, you need a key? A lock changed? I'm your man. Thanks for thinking of me." Paul was a massive man with a fat round face, red cheeks, mirthful blue eyes, long sideburns, and a well-oiled pompadour, black in color. Francis put him at forty-six.

"Ah, good to see you too," he started. "I came because, well, it's sort of weird, but I've always wanted to know how to pick a lock. Not that I'd do that to steal or rob, unh-uh, but because it's an art and I've seen it done in the movies and I just thought it would be something good to add to my skill set."

Paul just stared at him, a smile creeping across his face. "You want to learn how to pick a lock, become the next Alfred C. Hobbs, huh?"

"Yeah, sure, why not? Who's Alfred C. Hobbs?"

Paul explained that Alfred was an American locksmith who, in 1851, crossed the Atlantic to put a state-of-the art security lock called the Detector to shame. An English locksmith, Jeremiah Chubb, bragged that it was impregnable, but old Alfred called it merely a plaything. It was on display at the Great Exhibition in London, and Alfred, before a crowd of astonished onlookers, went at it and had it open in twenty-five minutes.

"Good story, American ingenuity at work. But I just want the basics, the crash course, if you're willing."

Paul scratched an itch on his ear. He got serious now. "There is no crash course, pal. You got ten years, twenty? It's such a specialized skill, that's how long it takes to become a good lock picker. It's one percent theory and ninety-nine percent practice. Even I, who has taken the time to learn can only pick the most basic of locks. And that's just manual locks. Electronic locks, forget it."

Francis found himself looking at Paul's hands and fingers. He presumed that locksmiths would have slender nimble fingers like a concert pianist, but Paul's gnarled digits were more like a stonemason's. He said, "I was really hoping…"

"It's all right, pal. I couldn't do what you do either. Know why it takes so long?" Francis said he didn't. "Because so much of it is *feel*. You have to *feel* your way through those pins, back to front, pushing each pin up just enough for it to catch, keeping the tension exactly right." He paused. "I can see you have no idea what I'm talking about. And you don't know until you actually start if it's standard pins or mushroom pins or even serrated pins. There's no manual for lock picking of the criminal sort, you learn as you go and the reward is hearing that cylinder click."

Another bump in the road, thought Francis. This isn't going to happen.

"Here, I'll show you my set," said Paul. Reaching under the counter, he produced a leather case and opened it to an array of slender metal picks each in its own little holster. "I got this from Al Baxter, my predecessor here," he said with a flourish of hand. "Criminal implements, and he taught me how to use them. Patiently taught me. Picking locks requires finesse, time, and patience—what he would say. Al got them from his predecessor whose name I don't even know."

"Wow, they're beautiful! May I borrow them?"

Paul was quite taken aback. "No, you *cannot* borrow them. How about a Betty Boop key ring instead, it's on me."

— 39 —

ON THE FOURTH DAY AFTER HE CALLED IN THE TIP, Francis had a feeling, an intuition that Vorhof's place would be watched. He called up the app on his phone and the tracker map appeared on the screen showing that the Highlander was there at the house. It was getting on two o' clock. He called Jimmy, told him to get the Newport out on the street, he was coming by in ten minutes. Jimmy enthused, said, "Hot damn, we gonna do it, uh? Let me comb my hair for the mug shot."

En route Francis' phone rang. He couldn't find the damn thing for three rings and then he saw it on the passenger seat under some papers. He knew he'd seen that number before, but couldn't place it.

"Hello."

"Francis, this is Doctor Lambert," the voice confident, somewhat superior. "I called to see if there's any update on our little project."

"Well yeah, there is," said Francis. "As I told you, we're never going to find proof that he's been murdering homeless people *and* my partner and he's never going to confess to that. But I think we've got him where we want him." Should he tell Lambert about the plan afoot? What if his phone was bugged, but why would his phone be bugged? It wouldn't, but he would have to choose his words carefully. "We've found a way to, uh, get him in trouble, maybe even get him some prison time. I can't go into details right now, but I do need to ask you for something that will facilitate this plan and that is a loan—or better, a contribution of funds that will pay for a lawyer."

The other end of the phone was silent for about five seconds. "Not a problem, my boy. If you say you need it, I'm there. I know human character and I know you wouldn't do anything to try to scam me. How much are we talking?"

"Three thousand and if there's any left it will be promptly refunded."

"Come by the office tomorrow and I'll have a check ready. Make it out to you?"

"No, leave the 'Pay To The Order Of' blank. I'm not quite sure yet. Thanks so much, doc. It couldn't go to a better cause. I'll keep you posted on the outcome. So, how's it going with you?"

"Oh, pretty well. The practice is coming right along. I'm planning a trip to Cape Breton Island next month, a whale watching tour, something that Austin would have loved. I still miss him so. Oh, and I got a call from that art director. The artist I mentioned, the one whose piece I had bought in advance, is having a show Friday in the Central West End. I'm excited to meet him in person."

Francis was stunned. What were the chances? "What's the name of the place?" he asked, masking his surprise.

"The Dagmar Petko Gallery on McPherson. She's some sort of major player in the art world. Why don't you stop by, it's from six to eight. Complimentary refreshments."

"Maybe I will, yeah, I'm in need of some cultural exposure."

* * *

Jacob was struggling with the artist statement, sheets of crumpled paper representing various starts on the floor around him. He wasn't good at explaining his art, he felt that he shouldn't have to explain. What they saw is what they took away, the work speaks for itself. Did Warhol or Pollock have to make artist statements? Yet Dagmar wanted something from him and she wanted it yesterday. Oh sure, coming right up. What is my artist statement? What are these bizarre figures, what do they mean? He could say they symbolize the frailty of man. Dejection? Despair? Lost opportunity? The path not taken? Oh bother, philosophical musings weren't one of his strong points. What was that phrase from high school lit class, one of the established categories for plot device? Man's inhumanity to man. Maybe that's it, he thought. The figures are about human cruelty, barbarity, lack of pity and compassion toward others, something he certainly felt, essentially a person's tendency to see and treat other people as less than human. But after considerable thought he scotched that idea, too close to the bone. He wasn't going to reveal his innermost feelings for the world to see.

He went online and looked at other artist statements. They were all so sweeping in thought, so general. He was in a tizzy. He ransacked his brain thinking of who might help. He thought of calling one of his fellow students or teachers from the art institute, but he'd lost touch with them all even though a few of them had made effort to include him in gatherings held in St. Louis and Kansas City. Finally, he settled on one name: Kiki. She was fairly sophisticated, urbane—well, not really but she seemed to always have answers for things. He phoned and she answered.

"Hey, how are you? Everything going okay?" playing the concerned friend.

"Yeah, it's going. What's up?" She had that snide way of talking.

"I've got to write something about my work for a show I'm having, a paragraph or so and I just can't seem to produce anything. Would you mind coming by to help?"

"I don't know jack about your work, how would I be able to help?"

"I think you're good with words. The pieces are already at the gallery because the show's tomorrow, but I've got photos. You could look at the pictures and come up with something. Please."

"The last time I came by I got busted and I'm still in Dutch for that. Got a hearing on the twenty-eighth, hoping to get probation."

"Hope you do. But a bust, no, that won't happen," he assured. "And I'm at a different location, South City."

"I don't know."

"Bring some tabs with you, okay?"

* * *

Francis and Jimmy drove slowly past the turn onto Bluff Drive, Jimmy at the wheel. In the distance, they caught a glimpse of a gray Ford Taurus parked down the block maybe fifty yards from Vorhof's place. Up the grade further, the Highlander parked in plain view. Could be, said Jimmy. Only one way to find out, answered Francis. They did a U-turn and came back, nosing the Newport into the dead end street.

"Just take it slow," said Francis, "you can even stop. Make like we're looking for an address."

Mopering along they passed the Taurus and without making any sign of gawking they saw a man in a sport shirt sitting behind the wheel, window open. Though they made no show of looking directly at him, pretending to look at house numbers, he definitely eyeballed them.

"If it looks like a cop in an uncool car, it must be a cop," said Jimmy. "What now, bro?"

The street widened into a turnaround at its terminus. "Just turn around there," said Francis, "and drive away slowly, not a care in the world."

As they passed him on the way out it looked as though he was writing something. "Taking down our plates," said Francis. "We've succeeded in raising his suspicion."

They got back out on South Broadway and turned into a driveway. "This is it," said Francis. "I'll get out and you go back, this time go up the driveway and park. You can leave the engine running. You get out and do what?"

Jimmy sighed. "I go to the door and pretend to knock. The guy inside, he doesn't hear me but I pretend to talk to him. I take the baggie of coke out of the tote, reach out as if I'm accepting it, and place it back in the tote. The cop is watching, he's thinking it's a drug deal." Two days before, Francis had gotten a baggie filled with crack cocaine. The off-white rocks were tidily grouped into sets of three or four and tightly wrapped in cellophane tied off. It was the first time in his checkered life he'd ever scored hard drugs and it made him sick. To be caught with that cache was to be branded a pariah among his pals and professional associates and he knew plenty of lawyers, cops, and judges. Such a risk to bring down this treacherous conceited clown. He'd kept it in a compartment of his process serving satchel and it made him nervous as hell but he felt he had to keep it close by, that satchel always with him either in hand or in the car.

"Right, then what?"

"I walk back to the car carrying the tote, making sure the cop sees it. Then I drive off and expect to get stopped. Those flashing lights to make my day."

"Good. I'm counting on you. Where's your tote?"

He reached down near the space under the seat. "Right here," and he pulled out a small fabric bag with straps and St Louis County

LIBRARY written on one side. He opened it to show the baggie within.

"All right then, let's do it." Francis got out and Jimmy drove off.

Jimmy got to the street, was waiting to turn left, traffic this time of day a bit heavy. The last oncoming car had its turn signal on for a right turn. It turned in front of him. A blue Camry, woman driver. She eyed him momentarily through the open window, gave the slightest of smiles. Hell yeah, I'd do her, Jimmy thought as he followed her in. He was close behind as she went along, going slow, maybe looking for a particular house. He saw the rear plate hanging down like a screw had fallen off and not only that, the sticker saying February 2017, nine months expired. The Camry went past the Taurus and drove straight into the driveway where he was going. Alarms going off in his head, he pulled over to watch.

The officer's name was Randall Kitchen. He was thirty-eight years old and had been on the force for eleven years, a real straight arrow, having made detective two years before. Most of his family was law enforcement—cops, sheriff deputies, correctional officers, bailiffs—and he was quite dedicated in the pursuit of catching bad guys. Or gals. He watched like a hawk this driver pull into the drive of the target residence, get out of her vehicle, approach the front door and appear to knock or ring the doorbell. He noted her attire, jeans and sneakers, black hoodie with something written on the front, a ball cap atop a head sprouting long brown hair, a bulky purse slung over her shoulder. He looked at his watch: 2:43. He couldn't quite make out the plate, hanging precariously, a citation right there, and that was unfortunate because he could run the plate on his laptop, find out who she was in real time as he's observing her. Detective Kitchen had a good feeling about this visitor who looked like a druggie come to call.

Inside, Jacob was in his studio in the back of the house with the radio on. Putting some finishing touches on a large abstract painting that looked like a crimson cyclone in a dust storm, he didn't hear the knocking or the doorbell. The radio played a rousing rendition of Rossini's "William Tell Overture" and Jacob was imagining himself as conductor, gesticulating to a rapt and adoring orchestra, baton in hand.

Meanwhile, Kiki continued to knock and ring, growing more irritated by the moment. This asshole, she thought, asks me to drop by and then doesn't even answer. His car's here so he's here. Maybe taking a shit. She called him, but his phone was out of hearing range in the kitchen. She looked around, kind of a nice place, she thought. He's doing well to have two homes. She didn't know he was a trust fund kid, didn't know what he did for a livelihood except he didn't have to work. Hell with it, she decided, I'll come back later or maybe tomorrow and I'll charge him extra for the inconvenience, the shit.

Detective Kitchen watched as she got in her Jap car and started to back out. From that distance he couldn't tell if she'd made contact with anyone in the house. The suspect might have come to the door, drugs and cash quickly changing hands and off she goes. He looked at his watch: 2:57. He radioed in that he was about to stop a vehicle for a non-moving violation and possible possession of drugs. He reached for the Responder Mini Lightbar, "cherry" in the vernacular, on the floor, half-covered in candy bar wrappers and crumpled bags of chips, and slapped it on the roof, strong magnets holding it in place. She got nearly to the mouth of the street, to the turn onto South Broadway, when she saw the flashing lights behind her. "Oh, no, not again!"

Jacob had come up from the studio to see if Kiki had yet to come by. He went to the front door, opened it, saw what was happening down the street. Wasn't that her Toyota? "Oh, no, not again!"

Meantime Francis had walked from where he'd been left and came to Bluff Drive. He was just another pedestrian strolling along. What a surprise to see the undercover cop ordering some woman out of her car. He looked down the street and saw the Newport parked. He continued walking not wanting to be observed. When out of sight he called Jimmy.

"What happened?" he asked.

"This chick got in front of me," he said, exasperated. "Went to the guy's house, stood there at the door, knocking, ringing, I guess, for a pretty long while. I don't think he came out. Then she left and got stopped as you probably saw."

"You didn't even get to the driveway?"

"No, un unh, I saw that and I parked at the curb. Don't need company. Do I still get paid?"

"Okay, listen, I'm a block south on Broadway at a bus stop. I want you to come pick me up. Pull out slowly, turn around, and as you pass the cop and the woman you get her plate. Don't stop to write it down, memorize it, you hear?"

"I don't know about that. Can't I just stay here until they go away? I don't want to make the wrong mistake."

"Jimmy? Do as I tell you," said Francis.

Francis said no, they can't go back to his car and to Jimmy's pad where he had a game of *Grand Theft Auto* going with some gamer in Taiwan. Not yet, they had to see what would happen with the woman. One look at the plate characters Jimmy had written down and Francis knew it was the same woman who pulled up on the police presence that time when Cleo and crew came calling. They stayed in the neighborhood, driving past the scene about every five minutes, wondering which way it would go. On one pass they saw her stamping her foot like an enraged bull and it appeared she was desperately trying to explain something. Then, they drove by and saw a white Chevy Tahoe, EVIDENCE TECH written on the side. The woman was standing off to the side on the sidewalk as her car was searched. They couldn't stop to watch, but they went around the block, made another pass, this time slowly. It looked like some personal items were laid out on the back of her car, a purse, a backpack, and a cop was going through them. "That's a good sign," said Francis. "Maybe she is dirty."

They stuck around longer, taking a chance that they'd rouse suspicion if the police paid attention to passing traffic and began to wonder why these two suspicious characters kept driving by. But they had to know the outcome, at least Francis did. Finally, and to great happiness, they saw that she'd been placed in handcuffs and was about to be driven off, to the station presumably, her car to be impounded. They slowed to let the Ford Taurus by, the woman in the back, her head down.

"What is it you want to know? I'll tell you everything," she said.

"Not so fast," said the detective, the burly one in the crumpled sport jacket. "We have to break you first, then you can tell us everything."

They were in an interrogation room at South Patrol. Kiki had already been booked, the fear of prison put into her. She spent three hours in a holding cell before this other detective, hard-bitten, looked like Steve Buscemi, spoke to her through the bars, asked if she was ready to talk.

"Talk, sing, yodel, whatever you like," she said. "Let's do it."

In the room one bare industrial table and three metal chairs. A tape recorder on the table not activated. A pack of Marlboros and an ashtray also on the table. The smokes were for her if she wanted. She smoked American Spirit—Gold, the tobacco organic, mellow, but she wasn't going to make a fuss. At the onset of the questioning, she lit a Marlboro and coughed like hell.

"Based on a tip, our man was staking out that house," the burly detective began. His name was Skypeck or something like that, she didn't get it clearly. "And here you come in your hoopty, all happy and shit, you're gonna get a fresh supply of drugs."

Huh? They thought that she was getting drugs from Jacob. What a break, she thought.

"Detective Kitchen saw you at the door, accepting delivery from the occupant of that house, one Jacob Vorhof. Do you deny that?"

"No, sir, I don't. I didn't know I was being watched," she added. "It's like you can't get away with anything these days."

The other detective chuckled at this. His name was Beganovic, a Bosnian. St. Louis had the greatest population of Bosnians outside of Bosnia. But his mirth was short-lived. "Do you have any idea the damage that opioids are inflicting on the metro area?" The question like a blade in her side. "The amount of pain and suffering these drugs are causing?" She looked at him somewhat dumbfounded, wasn't sure how to reply.

Beganovic's patience was not long. "Well, *do you?*"

"I know that some people take too much and they get sick or die."

"You got that right," said Skypeck. "Every day the morgue makes room for more, young people, many of them, it's a fucking epidemic."

"Even the surgeon general says so," said Beganovic.

"You like stats?" asked Skypeck, standing over her now. "Listen up, sweetcakes, here's some stats for you. Last year, 2016, set a record for the number of drug overdose deaths in the St. Louis region—256 lives snuffed out in the fatal quest for the ultimate high—cocaine, methamphetamine, you betcha, but most of them opioid-related and most impacting younger St. Louisans. Statewide, with 908 deaths in 2016, Missouri ranked nineteen in the nation for opioid overdose deaths." Skypeck was standing over her so he could look down her top and better see her cleavage.

If Kiki Fontana knew these stats they either made no impact on her or she didn't care. "Wow," she said, "I had no idea it's such a serious problem. Are you ready for me to talk now?"

"We'll get to that," said Skypeck. "Ricky Pfeffer," he said intriguingly. He let that hang.

"Huh?"

"Ricky Pfeffer was my next door neighbor, nice kid, used to mow my lawn, used to help me work on my car. He was like a son to me. Then one day...what do you think?"

"I don't know," she said, although she did.

"His mom gets a call, he's dead of an overdose. Fentanyl. He was twenty-six, had his whole life ahead of him. Fucking shame, wouldn't you say?"

"Uh, yeah, for sure." She lit another smoke.

"And you are part of the problem, maybe a big part," put in Beganovic. "Your friend, Vorhof, your dealer, it's people like him playing the Grim Reaper."

"He may as well have held a gun to poor Ricky's head and pulled the trigger," said Skypeck.

"He's not my friend," she said.

"He is when you need a fix, isn't that right?" Skypeck.

"He ever mention to you where he gets his supply?" Beganovic switched on the tape recorder.

"Um, something about a rogue chemist in St. Charles County." There actually was a rogue chemist in St. Louis County, not St. Charles County, where she got her supply, a guy she'd once picked up from the airport and taken home. She really was an Uber driver. Between this enterprising chemist and the shady characters in the parking lots of nightclubs who moved loads of Chinese fentanyl pouring over the borders, she was flush with street drugs. And now it was coming to an end, maybe.

"Am I officially talking now?" she asked.

"You bet your ass you are, sweetcakes," said Skypeck.

— 41 —

Now that the warrant was virtually assured Francis called Cleo. "I need to get with you," he said, "it's time."

He heard the big man's voice in reply. "Time you say? Time is at a premium but not for you, big brother. This evening around six, come to the Taproom."

"You know what I need?"

"Yeah, I remember the conversation. I'll have it, just be there."

After he'd dropped off Jimmy and convinced him he should be happy with the five-hundred he'd already gotten, that crazy woman his unwitting proxy, he went home. He took a Bud longneck from the fridge and sat at the table waiting for Martha to get home. This was it, the plan had unfolded pretty well with unexpected good luck in an otherwise very tense situation. Now was the crucible of him becoming a common burglar for a common good. He was very uneasy about the task ahead and he wondered how many beers he should drink to fend off the willies and yet keep him sharp enough to do the B & E flawlessly. He was on his third Bud when Martha walked in.

"Hey, babe." She acknowledged, smiled a weary smile. "Have a seat, join me. Beer or wine? I'll get it."

"Beer sounds right," she said, taking a chair. "What a day."

He popped the cap and poured the contents into a pretty beer glass that said Peroni Nastro Azzurro. "What a day, why?" he asked. "Marco pop a gasket?"

She took a long quaff of beer, wiped the foam from her lips. "Hits the spot," she said, "thanks. No, Marco didn't blow a gasket. He's been copacetic lately, at least he's tending to business in his managerial way although we did have a spat in the kitchen between the prep cook and the sous-chef and he had to step in. No, what a day refers to a bevy of red hat ladies who swooped in without warning and took up all the tables. It was a heck of a job seating them all and then the real fun began with them asking for this and that and then changing their minds and changing it back again. As a society, they're supposed to be about fun and friendship, but these women acted as though they're royalty. The servers were all complaining and they were stingy tippers. Please don't ever ask me to wear a red hat." She took another long swallow and looked at the glass. "I wonder what Peroni would think if they saw me drinking A-B from their stylish beer glass."

"Probably mark you for a vendetta. What's the word on Gina?"

"She's back home recuperating, happy to be *compos mentos*. That was an extremely scary situation for her. The doctor told her it was an opioid overdose and we both know she didn't take any opioids either on the job or off. So where did they come from?"

Francis met her look of disbelief. "Some malicious person slipped it to her, food or drink. Has to be it."

"So distressing to hear that," she shuddered. "You may be right, but I just can't imagine one of our people doing that. It would change the whole way I think of the restaurant."

"Someone from the outside maybe."

"Oh, Francis, this is so hard to take. What if it happens again?"

"I don't know, babe, we'll catch this person whoever it is."

"Let's hope so. I like mystery novels but this is real life, too close to home."

"What're you doing tomorrow?"

"After work? Nothing, why?"

"How would like to attend an opening in the West End at a gallery? It's near McPherson and Euclid, we could have drinks after."

"Yeah, okay, it'll be something new. Maybe I'll run into some friends. I used to know people who went to those things with the wine and cheese and the art on the walls that you don't know what to say about. Hmm, is it 'nice' or is it 'interesting' or just plain confusing. When did you become an art appreciator?"

"You know how people are following so and so on Twitter?" he ventured. "Well, I'm following this character, Rigoletto, and his work is on display." Though he had told her about Vorhof, he forgot to mention that Rigoletto was he.

* * *

Francis said to Cleo, "Do me a favor." They were outside the entrance to the Harlem Taproom, leaning on Cleo's Escalade, the vivid pink and rose hues of sunset off to the west.

"What's that?"

"Tell me you want me to plant these felonious goods in Vorhof's house. You want me to get in and get out without being seen."

Cleo studied him, a slight frown. "Why do that?"

"So I can say I did as I was told."

"Look," said Cleo, putting his hand Francis' shoulder, "just keep your head about you. Don't do anything that'll get you caught 'cause it isn't worth it. What's the good of him being in prison if you are too?"

"I can't think of a good comeback to that," said Francis with a shudder, "just give me the stuff and I'll go. No sense in putting it off because the suspense is killing me right now." They each had a drink, a plastic cup of beer that they'd brought from the bar. Francis held his out for a toast. Cleo met him, said, "To Bayard and to Austin and Cale and any others this bastard may have done in, may he rot in hell." If the cups had been glass they would have clinked.

Cleo popped the trunk of his ride and handed Francis a gym bag. "It's all in here," he said. "Enough street drugs to put him away, plus that handgun I told you about, plus a few other things. It's best you don't examine it, just plant it. You got gloves I hope."

"Oh man, I forgot."

"No worries, I've got some. Prints, shit, may as well leave your business card."

The door to the bar opened and some folks came out, laughing and carrying on. They waited for them to go on. "Okay, this is it," said Francis.

Cleo went to embrace him. Francis, a bit shy at the affection, didn't give back one-hundred percent. "Bring it in," said Cleo, assuringly. The bear hug lasted ten seconds, his breath on Francis' ear.

"You'll be fine, now get on with your bad self."

"I'm already gone," said Francis.

"You call me when you get done so I quit worrying about your ass," Cleo called after him.

Just past twilight, Francis drove into the street. He realized he probably should have waited until later, but he'd checked the tracking device and saw that Vorhof's vehicle was somewhere in Midtown. Maybe he'd gone to a show at The Fox. Whatever. No neighbors outside, good. One working street light in the middle of the block, good. He cut the lights and drove right up Vorhof's driveway, stopping as far back as possible. The engine still running, he was thinking. He did a Y-turn so he was facing the street, ready to roll when the job was done. He could see lights on in the house. He could see a back door that he'd missed before. He put on the gloves Cleo had given. He checked his pocket for the compact but powerful flashlight. He grabbed a hammer and a towel he intended to use to break a window on the door or near the door. He grabbed the gym bag. He rubbed his lucky rabbit's foot and made the sign of the cross for good measure.

He could smell the river down below, a reminder that he was on the bluffs. He went straight for the back door, expecting it to be locked. Just try it, hoping against hope. Oh! Open. All that worrying. This was the best break he could ever hope for, and it gave him a surge of confidence. He went in, closing the door softly behind him, now a true burglar. Okay, where to stash this stuff?

He was in a studio, that was obvious with paints and brushes and partly finished canvases on easels. There was a chest, like a footlocker he'd had in boot camp. With gloved hands he opened it and saw art supplies. Lights on in the rest of the house, but dim in here, only a small lamp on a bookshelf shone. He held the flashlight in his mouth and opened the gym bag. There was a pouch of soft fabric with a zipper like something his grandfather would put pipe tobacco in. He opened it, saw vials of powder and small white rocks. There was also a baggie with needles, syringes, a sturdy spoon, and beige powder. He'd never seen one, but he knew the name: shooting kit. He put the pouch beneath the first layer of art supplies.

He decided to plant all of it in this room, which seemed to be a likely place for the police to search quite thoroughly, the place where Vorhof probably spent the most time. He looked around. There, a cabinet. The handgun, a Glock .45 caliber semiautomatic, was wrapped in an oilcloth. He put that on the middle shelf of the cabinet, also containing art supplies and whatnot, and shoved it to the back. Next was a manila envelope 9 x 12 with clasp that sealed the contents inside, something flat. He didn't know what was in there nor did he want to know. He put that in the cabinet as well, covering most of it with sundry supplies but leaving one corner sticking out, inviting scrutiny.

He looked to his watch, nine minutes gone. He was done. His heart no longer racing, he stepped back to take a quick look before leaving, telling himself to be sure not to leave anything behind. He bumped into something. He turned to see an easel falling along with a painting, the whole thing unfolding in slo-mo. He caught the easel before it hit the floor, but the painting slipped away, tumbling several feet across the carpet, landing on its painted side. His heart went back to palpitating. He set the easel aright, picked up the painting. He beheld squiggles and swoops and swirls, red and black with splashes of yellow and purple, but mostly red. It looked like chaos on canvas, visual gibberish, and he couldn't believe someone would actually buy it. But it had been on an easel so it must be art—to Vorhof, anyway. Confusion and panic enveloped him. He turned it one way and then the other. It didn't make any sense. There was no way to know its original orientation, and yet he had to put it back. If he got it wrong, he supposed Vorhof would know but there was nothing to be done.

Francis was so pumped he knew he couldn't just go home and watch TV. He called Martha to say he'd be late and please don't wait up. He then called Cleo.

"Where are you?" he asked.

"At the bar like I was," he answered. "Did it go all right?"

"I'll be right there."

"Did it go all right?" Cleo repeated.

"I'll be right there."

He walked in the Harlem Taproom a little after ten and was ensnared by the sounds of Doc Terry and the Pirates, a revered St. Louis blues band formed by Doc himself in the seventies. Francis had seen the band only once before at the Broadway Oyster Bar and he loved their style of electric blues. Doc himself, now in his seventies, was harping away on a Hohner with a white girl, Patti Thomas, belting out "Things Can't Stay The Same." They were on stage at the rear of the bar. Drums, guitar, and bass rounded out the ensemble.

He spotted Cleo at a table with three others, laughing, talking loud. He walked over, Cleo gave him a soul shake. They made room. Cleo motioned a server over. "Get my brother an ice cold Miller, please." he told her. She went off.

"Oh Jesus," said Francis. "Why'd you do that? I can't drink that sludge. Busch, man. Or Budweiser, get with it."

"Look around you," said Cleo. Francis looked around, they were all drinking Miller High Life. "So don't keep me in suspense. How'd it go?"

Francis nodded in the affirmative. "It's done. Went off smooth except I knocked over a painting and didn't know which way was which. I might've put it back wrong."

"Can't worry about that," said Cleo. "Now we sit and wait for the cops to storm in and find that shit. How long you think it'll be?"

The server brought his Miller, set it down in front of him. He made a face at it, said to the woman, "Uh, can I have a Bud longneck with a glass, please. For a chaser, you know." He looked around the entire bar for the first time, saw that he and Patti Thomas were the only whites here, yet he felt totally at ease.

"It won't be long," he informed. "That girl in the Camry who got popped leaving Vorhof's? She was making a delivery. They've got her dead to rights, she'll give him up, guaranteed."

Cleo wore a grin when he said, "I'm looking forward to the trial, that is if he doesn't just plead guilty and be done with it."

"He's got money, he'll get a good lawyer. We'll see." The other guys at the table were talking among themselves, pointing at something or someone, men gossiping just the same as women. The band took a break and a stooped and graying old man hobbled from table to table holding a bucket that said TIPS FOR THE BAND. He came to their table, Francis dropped a ten.

"He's having a show tomorrow. I'm going with my wife. You should come too. It could get interesting."

"A show?" said Cleo. "Who?"

"Vorhof, he's an artist, people buy his work, I guess."

"What? He's an artist, since when?" Cleo shook his head in dismay. "He runs a soup kitchen, he fucking murders people *and* he's a successful artist. Fuck me."

"I know, it's hard to take, but the noose is tightening." He told Cleo the place and time of the opening. Cleo said maybe, he didn't know if he could stomach seeing the guy being the center of attention.

They sat there not talking for a while and then a thought came to Francis. "Hey," he said, "did anyone call you about a class action lawsuit against the City because of the way the cops handled the demonstration?"

Cleo's ears pricked up. "I heard about it and wanted to get in on it, but didn't know how."

"Oh, well I've got what you need. My wife wants me to do it, she talked to the lawyer in charge of it. It's going to happen. It'll be tied up in the courts for a while, the City not just going to roll over, but when it's done there could be a nice chunk of change." Listen to me, thought Francis, I'm talking like some put-upon activist with a major ax to grind.

"I'll get right on it," said Cleo. "I know some others who'll want to get in on it too. Might be the only good thing that comes of that sitch." He shook his head despondently. "The cop still free as a bird, never brought to justice. My brothers and sisters beaten and maced, no redress."

"Until now, maybe," put in Francis.

"That's right, big brother, let's hope so."

* * *

The next morning Jacob shuffled into his studio in his robe with a cup of coffee. He had a hell of a hangover, unusual for him because he was not a drinker. But last evening was a wonderful occasion with Dagmar taking him and the other two artists out for dinner at an exclusive sushi bar in Midtown. What a time it was! Rolls, nigiri, sashimi prepared right in front of you and served with explanation so you knew what you were eating. Dagmar said they had taken food to an art form and she was right. And refreshment, first, sake, served with ceremony which he found laughable because he thought it tasted rather nasty. But that was followed by after-dinner cocktails which made up for the rice wine disappointment. Lots of cocktails and, wow that Dagmar really can drink. The night wore on and the conversation scintillating, he liked to think he hardly stuttered at all. They must have run the gamut of the art world in terms of topics, opinions flowing freely, some of them pithy, some vapid, but what the hell. He loved that he was among peers, one of the established cognoscenti, and he savored every moment of the experience. And now he was paying for it with this damnable headache and shaky feeling, but if that was the price then so be it.

And that soiree was so well-deserved after that fiasco with Kiki, God what a mess!

He looked around, saw the painting he'd been working on the day before, not yet finished. He lifted it from its easel. Is this painting upside down or is this the way I made it? He turned it 180 degrees, looked at it the other way. It looks good either way, he mused. Of course no one would know any better because it was an abstract piece, his feelings at the time transferred to canvas and he was feeling somewhat frisky when he'd started this. He remembered now that the piece with its vigorous brushstrokes, squiggles and swirls, and commanding red palette had brought to mind the title of a book by the young, decadent French poet Arthur Rimbaud, *A Season In Hell*. But now, when he held it so, it looked like a cauldron of blood, thick and bubbly. He placed the painting back on the easel and gave it no more thought.

His head ached terribly and he wasn't knowledgeable about hangover cures. All he could think of was coffee and aspirin. He'd go to his laptop and Google something up, maybe he'd have to go to the pharmacy, but it would have to be something effective because today, in just eight hours, he had a show to attend—not merely attend, but preside over.

—42—

DR. LAMBERT WAS ONE OF THE FIRST THROUGH THE DOOR of the Dagmar Petko Gallery. Decked out in pleated khaki slacks, thin blue pinstripes on an ivory shirt with a peach silk ascot, classic Brooks Brothers hopsack sport coat, Rockport wingtips, he looked every bit the discriminating connoisseur of fine art. His first stop was the drink station, not a bar per se but a folding table with a nice cloth. Bottles of wine whose labels he approved stood at attention. More were being chilled in bowls of ice. He asked for the Pinot Noir and was duly served. The server, an aspiring artist herself, watched him go and noted his aspect, decidedly aristocratic, certainly someone of breeding and wealth. Someone, she thought, I shall keep in mind for future encounters.

He passed up the table with *hors d'oeuvres* and went straight to the exhibit space. Low strains of smooth jazz—Lee Ritenour?—coming from speakers followed him. There, in a corner and extending out onto the floor, three shapes beckoned. He stopped and beheld the trio, bathed in soft glow from track lighting above, enthralled. They seemed to be speaking to him, not in words but a sort of telepathy and this telepathy said, "I am human, I am flawed, I have seen the depths of despair and wallowed in misery, yet I am standing here before you unbowed, unbroken." Well, something to that effect. The doctor recognized the one figure from a photo that Dagmar Petko had sent to spark his interest. The work of an artist "who will be very important someday," her words. There was a two-foot white picket fence around these figures to keep the louts from getting too near and touching the works. Lambert got up to the little fence and studied the one figure. Enigmatic yet powerful, nothing playful about it, conjuring a sense of dread. Yes, that was it, dread. He shuddered.

The wall label is a card that gives information and sometimes context to what the piece is about. The labels for these pieces were not on the wall but on the floor at their feet. Lambert bent down to read. "Transgressor 2017 Height: Seven feet. Canvas, paint, muslin, wood, wire, polyester fiberfill, plastic bags, lath, animal parts, found objects. There was a red dot on the card which meant it had been sold. To him. It wasn't the piece he thought he'd bought from the picture. It was Wilbur, one of the two effigies that Vorhof had constructed after he'd landed the exhibit. Dr. Lambert liked this one just as well.

He sipped at his Pinot and looked at the figure again. He noticed a partial set of teeth protruding from the torso. He saw a gaping cavity on one side, like an open wound, the edges around it torn and ragged. One arm had a hand and one arm did not. The arm with a hand sported a Fossil Chronograph and it was actually ticking. Incredible, the doctor thought, it's the same watch I gave Austin when he went into the service.

The gallery was filling up and the crowd was truly disparate. There were the obvious Yuppies out for a good time on a Friday evening, this stop one of several in the area. There were the fashion mongers, male and female, tuned into the latest nuance of style, preening like peacocks. Streetwalkers from Taylor and Delmar, six blocks over, who'd heard about the lavish event and stopped in for some free drinks and snacks and to possibly solicit. Academic types with button-down collars and bowties, expounding to anyone who'd listen on the works at hand, their plausible meanings, their narrative, if any, how this or that piece was derivative of some other piece, their overall significance.

And then there was Francis and Martha, not necessarily Philistines—after all, they attended Broadway musicals at the outdoor theater, the MUNY, in Forest Park—but certainly not well schooled in the marvel that is modern art. They walked in to a swirl of activity, fashion and stylish coiffures and animated chatter all together under one roof. They made for the wine table, took their fill, and continued to the appetizers at another table.

"I'll bet Cohn's Deli catered this," said Martha, "the bacon-wrapped water chestnuts, it's got their signature."

"Let's walk around, take a look," from Francis, mouth full of red seedless grapes.

"When you spot the mysterious Rigoletto, please point him out," she said. "I want to bask in his presence before the paparazzi arrive."

They saw firsthand paintings and sculptures by the other two artists who were on the program with Vorhof, and they saw pieces that were on display for the long term, big names, the toast of the New York and Chicago art scenes. Finally they got to the alcove where Vorhof's three effigies were on display, commanding the space around them. They stood there mute taking it in. Finally, Martha said, "I don't know quite what to say."

"It's, uh, really out there," spoke Francis, thinking so this is what he's been doing in his spare time when he's not plotting some murder.

"Is that a hairpiece or someone's actual hair?" asked Martha. "Whatever it is, it needs a shampoo. It lacks body."

"So what do you think?" came a voice from behind. They turned and the dapper speaker greeted them most amiably.

"Martha, this is Dr. Lambert. Doctor, my lovely wife, Martha."

They shook hands warmly and Lambert looked upon the figures with pride. "So, tell me, what do you think?" he repeated.

"I think they'd make a nice family living off somewhere in the wilderness and keeping to themselves," offered Martha deadpan.

Lambert laughed heartily. "Quite right," he said. "Except that one of them will be coming home with me. That one," he pointed, "I've bought it. I really like it, it speaks to me, only problem is I don't know where to put it."

"Yeah," said Francis, "you have to decide if you want others to see it and possibly judge you by it or whether it's for your eyes only."

"Very insightful of you," said Lambert. "Of course, I realize it's not for everyone. I can't put it in my office, the patients would definitely wonder. I could put it in my apartment but I'd have to move furniture around, probably have to get rid of something. You can't crowd these figures. I do have a summer retreat at the Lake, I suppose it could go there."

"There you go," said Martha. "Put him at the window, keep the burglars away."

"I'm waiting to meet the artist," said Lambert, checking his watch, "but like all true artists he's fashionably late. Oh, I almost forgot. Francis you'll appreciate this. Look at the arm of that one, look at his wrist and you'll see a watch. It's a Fossil Chronograph, the same watch I bought for Austin when he went into the Marines. Isn't that a remarkable coincidence?"

The realization struck him. Of course he hasn't figured it out yet, he doesn't know that Rigoletto and Jacob Vorhof are the same person. "What are the chances?" Francis said.

There was a commotion in the distance, a bevy of gallerists forming a circle around someone and the bevy was coming this way. Francis saw Vorhof in the middle of it all, decked out in what he likely thought was uber cool attire, a hipster nod to the common man, but made him look like a used car salesman. He was walking and smiling and holding forth as he made his way to the tortured figures he had spawned.

"That must be him," Dr. Lambert said, shooting his cuffs. "Get ready."

* * *

Some six hours earlier, after Jacob had left for the day, running last minute errands before the opening, a platoon of detectives and crime techs and a drug-sniffing German Shepherd entered the home on Bluff Drive. They had a warrant signed by a judge that very morning. There was no answer from within and no vehicle present so they correctly assumed the occupant, one Jacob Vorhof, Caucasian, age thirty-seven, was away. They called for the "Donker" and one of the detectives, Teri "Lautrec" Aubuchon, went to the squad car to get it from the trunk. The Donker was a forcible entry tool designed to defeat heavy fortified doors and concrete block walls. The police enjoyed using it, it made them feel special. Just as they were about to destroy the front door there was a shout from the back of the house. The door was unlocked.

They found everything Francis had planted, found it without looking very hard. It was almost as if the items wanted to be found. Detectives and crime techs nodded triumphantly to one another, another indictable bust. Now they just had to find the occupant. The other detective, Saul "Caveman" Pickman, held a large manila envelope. He'd already seen the what was in there but he peeked once again. He looked to his partner about to light a smoke. Detective Teri Aubuchon got her nickname Lautrec because off duty she wore loose fitting T shirts with no bra. Too Loose Lautrec. Now her chest was encased in a tight-fitting bullet-proof vest, as was his.

"You don't want to know what's in here," he said.

"Let me see," said Aubuchon.

"It'll bring you to tears," he warned.

"I'm a big girl, I think I can handle it." He handed the envelope over but at the last second withdrew it. She continued to hold her hand out, waiting for him to stop shitting around. He passed the envelope. She opened the flap and pulled out the contents. "Oh geez!" she muttered.

* * *

As Rigoletto drew near his own installation there was a hush. Onlookers could see that a personage was in their midst. That was Vorhof's perception. Dr. Lambert stepped forward to greet him, holding his hand out for a shake.

"Finally, at last," he gushed, "I get to meet the renowned artist. Sir, my name is Elliot Lambert, Doctor Lambert. I am an ardent admirer of your work and in fact I have already purchased one of these amazing figures or effigies as you call them in your artist statement. It will stand beside other sterling pieces in my collection, the work of cutting edge artists such as yourself."

Suck up, thought Francis, standing within earshot. This is killing me. He squeezed Martha's hand. "We've got to move on," he told her *sotto voce*. He did not want Vorhof to recognize him.

"Why?" she whispered back. "It's just getting interesting."

"Tell you later," he said furtively.

"I've seen him before," said Martha. "He was in the restaurant, just recently."

"What! When was that?"

"It was, um, it was last week. The day that Gina took ill. What a coincidence."

Two detectives entered the gallery, sticking out among the art crowd like muskrats in a goldfish pond. The reason they were here had to do with a glossy color announcement found affixed to the refrigerator in the home on Bluff Drive: Power Of Three, it read. Join Us For a

DYNAMIC SHOWCASE OF ART, COLLABORATION AND CREATIVITY. And it gave the names of the three exhibitors and the date of the show which was this very day. "We're in luck," Aubuchon had said. It made sense that Vorhof was one of the artists on the card, the one with the obviously made up name. And there was a busy art studio in the back of the place.

They looked for someone who might be in charge. Finding no such person they circulated. "God, would you look at this stuff," said Pickman, distastefully. "A frickin' four-year-old could do some of this crap."

"Yeah, but that child didn't do it," said Aubuchon out of the side of her mouth, "an adult with too much time on their hands did it and now they're taking it to the bank."

"You're more cynical than I am," said Pickman. "I think I see our guy, over there in the back, a crowd around some statues."

They strode toward the gathered, unsure as to which one was Vorhof. "Maybe him," said Pickman. They stopped before a tall young man with a lavender Mohawk and garish tattoos all over his exposed neck and shoulders. He had enough facial piercings to fill a tackle box. He was their idea of what an artist looked like.

"Mr. Vorhof?" said Aubuchon expectantly.

"Me?"

"Yes, you."

"Vorhof, what is that, a cocktail or something?"

"Just answer the question—" from Pickman. He almost added asshole to the end of that sentence. Pickman got the moniker Caveman because he was short-tempered and abrupt and prone to physical violence.

The fellow clucked his tongue. "No, man, I'm Rooster, boyfriend to one of the artists—but not that squirrelly dude over there," he quickly added. "Everybody knows me."

Francis and Martha off in the wings, Francis keenly attuned to what was unfolding. The detectives, though in plainclothes, had handcuffs in sight. With Pickman, hanging from his leather belt; with Aubuchon, sticking out of the side pocket of her pantsuit. Gradually, the crowd was becoming aware of their presence, that something was about to go down and there was this intense, if not morbid curiosity over who they were after. Francis wanted to walk over and stand behind Vorhof and proclaim with pointed finger, "Here he is, the drug-dealing sicko serial killer, right here. Take a look!"

Aubuchon said to Pickman, "Hey, remember the name on the announcement was Rigoletto. We figured that was Vorhof."

Pickman took the announcement from his back pocket. "Yeah, you're right. Forget Vorhof." He tapped a young woman on the shoulder. "'Scuse me, miss, could you please point out this Rigoletto character?"

The woman had a pierced tongue which made her lisp. Her name was Sandra and she had been a docent at the Pulitzer in Midtown, but with this self-imposed speech impediment she had to quit. "Thath him, I thuppose," she said, "in the thupid thuit."

Vorhof now stood before his installation, giving an impromptu address to several rapt admirers. His speech was halting and peppered with stutters but he continued unfazed. "There is nothing c-c-comical about these figures," he went on, "they reh-reh-represent the darkest impulses of man. They are the boogeyman under the bed, the killer who lies in wait, the—"

"That one over there," interrupted a woman in a T that said MAKE ART NOT WAR, "what's he supposed to be doing?"

Vorhof turned and saw something he could not believe, something that sent a shock wave through his entire body. There were four figures within the little picket fence. Vorhof moved in for a better look. The figure wore a colorful dashiki and a Kangol bucket hat. It looked like he'd been tapped in a game of freeze tag, for he posed like a statue with his arms out in supplication, his fixed gaze somewhere off in the distance. Vorhof stepped over the white pickets and came up on this counterfeit.

Vorhof gulped and backed off a step. He thought he recognized this guy from Hopeville.

"See here, you cannot—" The statue came alive and grabbed him by the throat. The statue towered over Vorhof and looked down on him with daggers in his brown eyes. He pressed the flaccid flesh around the man's neck, he squeezed hard. Vorhof's eyes began to bulge. The statue grasped Vorhof's neck with his other hand and lifted him off the floor by his head, arms flailing, legs kicking. All around people watched, what was this? Some stunt?

Cleo said nothing for a full ten seconds, easily holding Vorhof out before him, face turning purple, thoughts of a horrible death percolating through his brain. Cleo studied his squirming victim, relishing the man's distress. Finally, he said, "Rigoletto, huh?" He got right in Vorhof's face. "Sounds like a pussy name to me."

Just then Aubuchon and Pickman came up. They flanked Cleo and Vorhof, still aloft and choking to death. "Jacob Vorhof?" she asked formally. When he failed to answer, Aubuchon pointedly commanded Cleo to release him. Cleo acknowledged this with the trace of a smile, looked to Vorhof on the verge of passing out, said, "You're goin' down, fool," and dropped him to the floor in a heap.

Vorhof gasping for air, they gave him a long minute then repeated the question. "Are you Jacob Vorhof?" Alarms and bells went off in his head. Whatever this was he would have none of it. "Ah, no," he answered.

"Oh, that's him," boomed Cleo, sneering in Vorhof's direction. "Jacob Vorhof, the soup man, the drug pusher, the killer of trusting young men. Hold out your hands, asswipe, let them put the cuffs on you."

"Let's see some ID," said Pickman.

He was still shaken from the throttling that Cleo had delivered. "No, na-na-na not here," a mortified look on his face. "I will na-na-na-not be confronted by you," scrunching his eyes with effort to communicate, "I don't even nuh-nuh know who you are."

"Oops, our bad," said Aubuchon, flashing her badge. Pickman did the same. "Now that we're acquainted," she said, "let's see some ID from you." Vorhof looked around, saw that everyone was watching. Talk about being on the spot.

"No no," shaking his head vehemently, "you cah-cah, you cannot di-di-di do this. You must leave nuh-nuh—must leave now." But his forceful words had no effect, they weren't leaving. Instead, they were ruining his evening. He felt like he was in a play, the hapless victim of circumstance.

They were closing in on him, grabbing him by the biceps.

All he could do was to repeat the exhortation. "You must leave nuh now. This is not happening," and he stamped his foot for effect.

"Jacob Vorhof, you are under arrest for distribution of controlled substances and violation of the US obscenity law." Keeping it vague.

When he heard this something tripped in his brain and he went crazy. He started pushing them away, acting like a six-year-old in a tantrum. This reaction was not new to Aubuchon and Pickman, old hats at subduing suspects in denial. Pickman went to put him in a full nelson so Aubuchon could get the cuffs on, but Vorhof was quick to stiff-arm the detective, open palm on his stubbly chin. Pickman, surprised, moved his jaw around, and then he delivered two swift solid punches to the solar plexus. Vorhof went down hard and fast, making croaking sounds and gasping for air a second time.

Dagmar Petko came rushing up and knelt beside her artist. "You poor dear," petting him flamboyantly like he was a precious lapdog, "what have they done to you?" She turned to the detectives. "What have you done to him and why? Brutes! You are not welcome here. You must stop this now and leave my gallery. I'll call the police." Pickman chuckled.

Vorhof rolled over and spit up something brown and soupy. A string of snot depended from his nose. He was prostrate and beaten in front of his fans and it caused even greater mortification, if that was possible. The detectives went to pick him up. Dagmar Petko tried to intervene and they shoved her aside with a warning to steer clear or she'd go to jail with him. They picked him up unceremoniously, slapped the cuffs on him; it was the custom. They led him out past a column of open-mouthed attendees clucking disapproval at seeing one of their own so greatly reduced.

Dr. Lambert saw Francis and Martha and he went over. "Well," he said, bemused, "that was quite the show. High drama at the old art gallery." They agreed, you don't see that every day.

"Do you really think he's a criminal, this Rigoletto?"

"Probably," said Francis, "he just has a guilty look about him. Oh, by the way," he said, reaching for his wallet, "here's your check back. Not needed, but thanks anyway."

"Thank you, sir. You know," continuing where he'd left off, "there's a rich history of criminality in the art world. Jimmy Boyle. Mark 'Chopper' Read to name two. Killers who turned to art and became sought after, collectible. I read about it in *Apollo*. Look at Stéphane Mandelbaum, whose work you saw in my office. He was not only an extremely talented artist but an art thief as well."

"Yeah, stranger things have happened," said Martha tactfully.

"So, that begs the question," said Lambert. "I now own one of his pieces. Do you think this will make my piece more valuable?"

— 43 —

FRANCIS HAD BEEN MEANING TO CALL LAURIA TO SEE WHAT HE KNEW about the arrest at the gallery, but he encountered him, again by chance, at the Quik Trip on Hampton, Sunday mid-morning. The cop was gassing up for a family excursion on The Great River Road above Alton. Do the fish markets, Pere Marquette State Park, hit a winery, ride the ferries. Francis saw that he was in a good mood and he was happy for him.

After brief small talk, Francis put it out. "Hey Ed, I was at a gallery in the West End Friday evening and there was quite a ruckus. Two detectives came in and arrested one of the artists who was showing his work. He fought them and they had to subdue him with everyone watching. Finally, they led him away in handcuffs. You know anything about that?"

"A little," answered Lauria, placing the pump nozzle back in its holder. "I'm friends with one of those detectives, Teri Aubuchon, saw her yesterday, Deke Williams' retirement party at Syberg's, and she said it was like a scene from *Law & Order*, the original one, not the Special Victims Unit. They'd found evidence at the guy's home in South City, they found some card that said where he'd be that evening, they went there, found him among the crowd. Like you say, it was his show and he wasn't about to go quietly. He took a poke at Pickman and Pickman gave him a dose of humility."

"I saw that," said Francis, "it was inspiring. Bim bam boom, the guy went down like a sack of potatoes. He's one of those artists goes by just one name, Rigoletto, something like that."

"It could be Pavarotti for all I know. But I do know that he was good for a veritable cornucopia of street drugs and opioids, the stuff just laying around his house almost in plain sight, and there was a hand-gun that's now being checked in forensics. And all that would be bad enough on its own, but it was the child porn that really sealed his fate."

Within minutes of parting with Lauria, Francis had Cleo on the phone. "You had me carrying child porn? What the hell were you think-ing? What if I'd been picked up? My life would turn to shit and all you would do is say 'Sorry.'"

"Oh, I thought we'd throw that in for good measure," Cleo nonchalantly. "We found it in a Dumpster in the alley behind the police station, thought it might come in handy someday, and what do you know? It did. I think it belonged to some dirty old man who used it to get off, I mean some of the pages were stuck together." He heard Cleo chuckling on the other end.

"Well, damn it all to hell," not sounding as indignant as he wanted to. "You could have at least told me."

"And then you would have pitched it. The way it stands, it'll add years to his sentence. That's what we want, right?"

"If he has a sentence," Francis, glumly. "Some five-hundred dollar an hour lawyer might get the charges thrown out."

"Nah, ain't gonna happen and if it does we'll think of something else, something more drastic than setting him up."

Francis had an idea of what 'more drastic' meant and he definitely wasn't willing to go there. "So what else is going on?"

"What're you doing this afternoon?"

"Did I tell you I've taken up quilting? Friendship, sharing ideas, the art of sewing. We have a meet up this afternoon at the VFW Hall. You should come, but bring a thimble, you don't want to prick your finger."

"Nice try, big brother, but how 'bout instead you come to Fairgrounds Park. We're having a fundraiser for some folks, victims of that police brutality that we saw downtown that day, a day of shame for this city I used to love. The band plays at three."

"Yeah, all right, y'all gonna have some chitlins and collard greens or should I bring my own?"

"You need some work on your sense of humor, big brother. No, we uns ain't gonna have no chitlins, but we will have succulent baby back ribs and wings, so tasty it'll ruin chain chicken places for you. I'll see you there, huh?"

"I told you about that class action, did you make a move yet?"

"I owe you a solid for that an' I'm working on it. I'll call that lawyer this week."

"You do that, mention my name, it'll put you at the back of the line.

Hey, one last thing. That food pantry where you work? Do they need more people? I know someone who needs work."

AUGUST 2018

"Yes, TOUCH ME THERE, IT'S ALL RIGHT," she breathed into his ear.
They were in their pensione in the utterly charming town of Rovereto in
Trentino. They had just returned from a two-hour bicycle ride through
the Northern Italian countryside, drinking in the scenery of this charming
town situated between picturesque hills and vineyards, friendly pedestrians waving hello along the way. They got to their room overlooking the
river Leno and they both felt aroused, Italy can do that to one. It was hot
and the room had no air conditioning, only fans, so he removed her shirt
and brassiere. She shook her full breasts at him and said how it was good
to unbind them, sometimes they needed to be at large. She then removed
his Trout Fishing In America T-shirt and they embraced bare chested and
still sweating from the ride.

His hand moved from the small of her back to front of her black
linen shorts. There was only a drawstring keeping them up. A deft tug
and they came loose, fell to the carpet. No underwear, panties or briefs,
to contend with. He placed his hand on her cupcake, she spread her
legs slightly, said, "Yes, touch me there, it's all right."

He touched her there, all right, exploring, massaging, she getting wet
and moaning softly. She tugged at his shorts and down they came, his
erect penis springing forth like a jack in the box. He'd brought some
Viagra just in case, but it would stay in the packet for now. Her nude,
glistening body was all he needed. He guided her over to the bed and
they plopped down. More foreplay, fingers, tongue, eyes open, eyes
closed. She scratched him lightly on the chest with her nails, bit his
ear lobe. He was thinking of William Hurt and Kathleen Turner, that
steamy scene in *Body Heat*. She was conjuring the sexy food scene with
Kim Basinger and Mickey Rourke in *Nine ½ Weeks* as she guided him
in while arching her back. They made love slowly and passionately and
despite all the activity outside the window, the vendors hawking, the
children playing, they were blithely suspended in a world populated by
two.

They finished and lay there spent, entwined, taking in the spice of
the moment, and she said, wistfully, "I wish I could still get pregnant,

this would be such a nice place to conceive."

When in Rovereto one can feel the different identities of the city, its medieval heart around Rovereto castle, the agrarian aspect with open air markets on the piazza selling fresh produce and fish, and the more contemporary side hosting the Modern Art Museum. Martha's grandfather, Eligio, had grown up here, a stonemason before coming to the States. None of the family had ever visited the town that he spoke so fondly of, she was the first. Before they left St. Louis, her father had given her a thousand dollars with two requests: Once you switch to local currency, give half of this to the Catholic church there, Chiesa Arcipretale di San Marco, built to honor the patron of Venice. You tell the priest there the gift is in memory of Eligio Pastori. The other half, he said, just enjoy yourselves.

The second request is an easy one as well, her father went on. I want you to visit the Bell of the Fallen when it rings at nine o' clock each evening. Your grandfather talked about this bell, how it was cast with bronze taken from the cannons of all nations who fought in the First World War, and as you know, Eligio was in that one. That's where he got the injury that made him blind in one eye.

By the fifth day they were starting to feel Italian, getting in tune with the rhythms of the old city, rising at a decent hour, not too early, not too late, making love, watching some local TV, finding their way to a sidewalk cafe and if weather permitted, sitting to a continental breakfast while watching the town come to life. Surrounded by mountains and nature, they spent their days walking or cycling, throwing stones into the river, visiting shops and kiosks, sampling local fare in quaint restaurants—*zuppa di datteri*, a shellfish soup, their favorite. If they really wanted to treat themselves, there were several Michelin-starred restaurants scattered around. It was a gourmand's dream. By the seventh day Francis was ready to go back home.

"I like it here," he explained to her over breakfast that morning, her expression one of disbelief. "I mean I *love* it here, look how tan and fit we are, and drinking in this wonderful culture, and the food—oh man! But I've gotta say I am a bit worried about my practice."

She eyed him, brows furrowed. "Sandy said the money will come, we're good to go." A month earlier Sandy Crowley told them a decision had been reached in the class action, a deal was worked out with the City of St. Louis, a payout was coming but it would take months for the reams of paper to be processed by umpteen lawyers. He said they may as well take their dream vacation now, end of summer while the weather was nice, because the money was as good as in their account. Martha bought the tickets with her savings, Francis notified his two dozen lawyers that he'd be away for two weeks and if they needed something served they should call Joachin Silva, a capable process server and fellow graduate of the sheriff's class. Joachin mostly catered to the Hispanic community in South City, and he didn't have near the load of work that Francis had.

"I know the money's as good as there," he said, "but I worry that they won't call Joachin or that Joachin may screw up a case. I'm the best, most of them know it, but if they can't reach me or become unhappy with Joachin they call someone else and maybe they stick with that person."

Martha scoffed at this. "If they're that disloyal, screw them." She softened her demeanor a little. "But I get it, if even a few regular clients drop you because you're unavailable that could be thousands of dollars gone."

"Besides," he said, "I'm done with my book." Francis had brought Larry McMurtry's *Lonesome Dove* along, a novel he'd been meaning to read, all 960 pages of it. Also bugging him but he would never admit it to her, he was missing his daily ration of Busch beer. You can take the man out of the neighborhood, but not the other way around.

She reached out, took his hand. "Still, I think you're stressing over nothing."

"I can't help it," he said, exasperated. "It's keeping me up, didn't you notice me tossing and turning last night?"

"I thought maybe it was indigestion." She looked at him with lips pursed, some sort of sign, she kept mum for long seconds. Finally, "Okay fine." No bitterness attached.

"Okay fine what?" wondered Francis.

Martha took a gnocchi dumpling from her plate, dipped it in a small bowl of extra virgin olive oil and popped it in her mouth. Francis sat there impatiently, waiting for her to finish. Her mastication, deliberate and slow, seemed to go on and on. Playing with me, he thought. At last she swallowed and spoke. "It means okay, fine, let's go back. It's been fun, but I think I've had enough too."

* * *

The Boeing 737 touched down at Lambert International at 2:43 p.m. on a Tuesday. They had departed Rome that morning and, flying "against" the time zones, an eleven-hour flight with an hour and a half layover in Newark had got them home in time for dinner. But they did not go home first. They got their car from The Parking Spot close to the airport and drove straight to the restaurant. Francis knew that Martha felt as at home in Pastori's as she did in their own home so this was no surprise and he felt quite comfortable there too, whether dining at a table or sitting at the bar, a drink before him, watching sports on TV. The thing was, Marco had not officially lifted his prohibition on Francis' presence there. Francis imagined and Martha confirmed it that Marco was still stewing over Francis having "worked against him" in protecting Finch. The few times Francis had gone there to see Martha he'd kept out of sight of Marco who was usually in the kitchen or the back office. But not today.

They walked in and all the staff on the floor came rushing up with Welcome Back! and What A Nice Surprise! They proceeded to the bar and got their drinks from Gianni, a Jameson rocks for him and a Negroni for her, the better to reminisce on the world they had left behind. This was not a busy time. Between three and five, diners were scarce, and the servers and bus persons, Gina Ancona among them, had been at the bar watching a competitive cooking show on TV. They turned the sound down so they could listen as Martha regaled them with the sights and sounds of Rovereto in Trentino.

"The most romantic place, and a river runs through it—the River Leno as in Jay—with cliffs or, I suppose, buttresses of stone walls supporting housing on both sides. Homes set into the cliffs, atop one another, imagine! And the food, so fresh and delicious—swordfish, tuna, the sea is not that far. The salads," she went on, "were fantastic, all local produce including cilantro and spinach and radishes, the dressings just perfect. And the ways they use Risotto, I brought some recipes back with me."

"How about the pizza?" a young fresh face asked. "How do you rate them?"

"Oh, we had their pizza," she replied eagerly, "and believe me it is nothing like ours. The crust is different, thin and crispy, made with a very fine flour and cooked *il forno* at 800 degrees or higher, the result being the poor thin crust looks burnt. If we served something like that here it'd be sent back! Oh, the sauce is different *and* the toppings. Their toppings are so different that most Americans would probably be disappointed." Francis sat next to her as she went on, enjoying her enthusiasm. "Where our pizza has a variety of toppings, their toppings are minimal. No such thing as deluxe or meat lovers special. In the Italian *cucina* less is more." She took a breath. "Pizza may have started there but we Americans have brought it to a higher—"

"Hey look who's back!" Marco pushed through the gathered and gave Martha a big hug. He stood back a step, put both hands on her shoulders. "What's the story, sister? You're back early, everything all right?" He wouldn't look at Francis. "Gianni, I'll take a Maker's Mark, rocks, please." He looked florid and puffy like he'd had a surplus of rich food at his table. For the last couple decades.

She said with good cheer, "Well, Marco, the truth is I missed you so much that I just had to get back to the same old grind, this beloved place we call our own." She raised her glass in a toast. He didn't have his yet so he saluted her. She took a drink. "Good to see you, brother."

"Back at you, and who's this character you dragged in with you?" He gave a momentary glance to Francis who was looking at Martha like Here We Go.

"We're not going to do this, are we?" she said.

"Well, something needs to be said. What's that saying about the hippopotamus in the room?" He cleared his throat, pivoted slightly to face his brother-in-law. "Francis, I see you're here in spite of my telling Martha you're not welcome because you helped that shitbird."

"Here in the flesh, Marco."

"And you know why I gave that order."

"Because you're the general of this company and orders come natural to you."

"Always the smart ass. I gave that order because you put those moolies on my guys. Why'd you do that? You spending your quality time with them, your bosom buddies from that shitstorm downtown? You were on the news with them, you stay in touch with them. You call them to put a wrench in my plans?" Francis saw he was balling his fists. The servers were looking on. He had to be cool and he knew it.

"Marco," he said evenly, "those guys intended to send that kid to the ER. I just couldn't let that happen. He's sorry for what happened, he wants to apologize. He even went to confession over it. So—"

"Enough! Okay then, I need to say this." An apology, Francis thought, about time. Marco took a slug of his bourbon on ice. "I will rescind—is that the right word? I will take back the ruling if you'll apologize. Sincerely. After all, as they say, blood is thicker than water and you're family. I don't want this coming between us."

Francis gave a little chuckle. "Oh, you want *me* to apologize? Fortunately I know how to swallow my pride, so here goes." Palms out in appeasement, "I apologize sincerely and profusely for any upset I may have caused you and I hope to never do it again, but there may come a time when it can't be helped."

"That's not a proper apology," Marco glowered.

Martha inserted herself in the dialogue. "Marco, listen, there's something important."

"What's that?"

"In the town where we stayed, where *nonno* grew up, Wolfgang Amadeus Mozart gave his first concert in Italy in the church there. Isn't that interesting?"

"Sure it is, Italians always being known for something or other." He went back to Francis, one last grumble. "You see that sign there? Over the bar." Francis looked and saw the sign, red letters printed on white background on a smooth wooden board: *Sii Gentile O Vattene.* He knew the translation: Be Nice Or Leave. "I put that there eighteen years ago. You know what it means so follow it, brother, follow it to the letter."

* * *

Two weeks later a call came from the law firm of Bardgette Crowley & Bittner. It was Sandy Crowley himself. "Francis," he said, brightly, "the ship is in, the funds secured, the course is served, now come and get it. In short, there's a check waiting for you at my office."

In the ensuing investigation, it had come out that the kettling tactic served as an excuse to harm the protesters caught within the cordon. Subpoenaed phone records showed that certain officers had exchanged texts prior to the action, damning messages such as "Let's whoop some ass," and "Wait 'til dark, it's gonna be a lot of fun beating hell out of these shitheads." Such disclosure causing the cadre at the City Counselor's office to throw up their hands in resignation.

The line at Sandy's office was out the door and into the hallway. Francis recognized several from the demonstration, the rising up against the verdict that set this whole thing in motion. The mood was jubilant with lots of back-slapping and happy chatter about how civil unrest pays and what they were going to do with their money. Some had flasks and were taking sips, passing them around. Said one, I'm gonna buy me the best car on the lot, one with mag wheels and the megawatt subwoofers. You can bet you'll hear me comin'. Said the other, I'm gonna get my mama that washer dryer at Crutchfield's and a years' supply of Colt 45. She loves her Colt. Another said she was gonna buy space on a billboard, put up a sign, her smiling face with the caption Y'all Think You Can Keep Us Down? Think Again!

The Reverend J.B. Robinson was there too, sitting in a chair in the hallway, smiling and talking glibly, assuring everyone that their gallant cause had prevailed and how the police would think twice from now on if they tried to muzzle them. The clergyman hadn't been there in the melee that day, hadn't been caught in the kettle, but no matter, he would collect his portion of the settlement when these people came to his services and the solid brass collection plate was passed around.

Everyone was spending their settlement check before it was even cashed and there would be plenty of pissing and moaning later when they learned they couldn't get immediate access to the funds. The check, large as it was, couldn't simply be cashed at a bank or the local payday loan or the liquor store and the bearer walks away with a wheelbarrow of greenbacks. No, federal regulations enacted after 9-11 said that large sums of money, if deposited in a bank—the most trusted venue—had to be held by the bank for so many working days until that check cleared and the funds made available.

About every five minutes someone would come out the door into the waiting crowd and they would be holding a slip of paper aloft like it was a ticket to Easy Street. The slip of paper of course was a check written on the law firm's account at Bank Of America and the bearer, giddy and effusive, would show it around, even letting people hold it, saying, "Look see, look what you got coming." Francis had found Cleo and they stood together in the hallway watching this antic scene. They were last in line, feeling charged, when one wizened fellow with a long beard and an ornate carved walking stick came out the door, shouting, "Hallelujah motherfuckers!" As he passed, Cleo tugged at his ratty sweater, "Say, brother, you mind if I see your check."

The man held it out for Cleo to see. His hand was shaking. Cleo took his hand and brought it closer. Cleo whistled respectfully, said it was a nice chunk of change. Francis leaned in and saw the figure: 58,312 dollars and zero cents. Whoa.

"I read the City had to shell out four-point-nine million," said Francis. "That divided by what? How many in this class action?"

"I don't know, big brother, enough to short a fuse in the City Treasurer's office. And it's a happy day for those who signed on."

Francis considered this. "Have you stopped to think about the services that are probably gonna be curtailed or even cut because of this lawsuit? Bus routes, trash pick up, animal control, all sorts of services cut short so we can blow this money? Cops and firefighters and paramedics not hired because of a shortfall in the budget. You think of that?"

The big man wore sandals with baggy shorts down to his knees, a Black Uhuru T and his Kangol bucket. He lifted the brim of his hat, the better to fix Francis with that look. "No, man, I don't think about shit like that. If anything I think about me and my brothers and sisters getting our asses beaten by the police and them with a gleam in their eye, no holding back, no mercy, no understanding of why we were there, to proclaim for our departed brother Anthony, murdered by one of those cops you're feeling sorry for."

"Oh," said Francis, dubious, "if you put it that way."

"What other way is there to put it?"

"Oh come on, Cleo, you can't condemn all cops because of the actions of a few the same as we whites can't judge your race by the actions of a few lawless opportunistic criminals—well, maybe more than a few, but you get the idea. Look, if it weren't for the cops Vorhof would still be preying on homeless people, still getting away with it. But they shut him down, didn't they? With our help, of course."

They were aware that Jacob Vorhof was convicted in a three-day trial back in April and is now incarcerated in Bonne Terre prison, a 2,684-bed facility set aside for adult males with substance abuse problems or who are mentally defective or morally corrupt. What they didn't know is that he is the sweetheart of the cell block, because he has such a pretty mouth. When not giving blowjobs or taking a beating, he visits the dispensary to have his virus load checked because he turned HIV-positive after that gang rape his first week there. He reads dog-eared back issues of *Art In America* and dreams of the comeback he'll someday have. He also dabbles in art right there in the prison, does some painting with materials he's allowed to have, brushes and paints and sketch pads, but no pencils or pens because they're pointy and he might hurt someone or himself. He's friends with another inmate, in for killing a slew of pet dogs in his neighborhood, who also stutters and together they have long halting conversations about nothing in particular.

There are days he feels mortality closing in. There are days he wishes he'd drank the spiked Snapple with Austin on that riverbank.

During their last visit, his shyster attorney Boris Liebman said he's working on another appeal based on evidence planting and if they prevail Jacob will be released forthwith, but if not he'll have to serve the entire twelve years.

Francis didn't have the heart to tell Dr. Lambert that Vorhof and

Rigoletto, the artist he so admired, were one and the same. Rest easy, he told Lambert, Vorhof is behind bars and he isn't getting out any time soon. Let the man enjoy his art.

They were getting closer to the office door, closer to the payout. They could see a suit in there sitting at a desk, someone standing before him. The suit writing in a ledger and tearing off a check, handing it over. Cleo spoke, "Well, brother, this is it, the end of a long road with more than a few potholes. What're you gonna do with your bounty?"

"There's this water flosser I've been wanting, it's cordless."

"Yeah, you buy that and then you buy the entire inventory, one for each day of the year. Me, I'm gonna get some new instruments for the band. Hey, you remember you asked me to put that kid to work at the food pantry? So that that didn't work out, the kid says he don't wanna work in no pantry."

"Ah, too bad," said Francis, "I really thought."

"It's all right, it worked out fine. He now manages the band."

"What!"

"Yeah, our manager, Kenrick, got bit by a brown recluse spider and he was laid up for a couple weeks, he's still not good. So we're working at the pantry and I mention this to Cary and he says 'I'm your man,' says he's got experience, says he handled a grunge band, Coffin For Two, and how he's got connections in the music scene and besides, the thought of putting cans of food in cardboard boxes day after day is driving him crazy. And I've got to say, Francis, this kid's got talent, he gets us in clubs and places where otherwise we wouldn't be. We're very happy with him."

"So glad to hear that."

"And this the same kid your brother-in-law sicced those goons on."

"Yeah."

"He'll be pissed if he finds you helped him. Why'd you help him?"

Francis mulled this over for a second. "I don't know," he said, "maybe I like trouble and risk in my life." He punched Cleo on the bicep, cordially. "And because I'm contrary," he added.

* * *

Francis walked into Murphy's just as Rory Denigan was about to throw a punch at Cormac Morrison. Both were sitting at the bar and Rory had the front of Cormac's shirt bunched in his fist. Cormac was pushing to get away, slapping at Rory on his stool and knocking over drinks, a cardinal sin in this bar. "You take that back," barked Rory.

"It's true I tell ya," insisted Cormac.

Tommy saw the ruckus and rushed over. "What is it now?" he said. "Do I have to be a babysitter too?"

"This joker says that Peter O' Toole was a fag."

"I said he was light in the loafers," corrected Cormac.

"Same thing," said Rory, "now take it the fuck back." He tightened his grip on Cormac's shirt. Tommy weighed in. "With those sleepy blue eyes and full lips that look like they want to be kissed, I can see where Cormac gets his idea. The man is very handsome, but not in a manly way. Now stop your silly bickering or there's the door. How's about another round? On the house."

Francis took a seat next to Ed Gannon who was two stools down from Rory and Cormac. Tommy placed a pint of Busch before him. Francis lifted the glass, toasted himself in the mirror, and poured the beer down his throat.

"Celebrating something, are we?" said Ed.

"Nah, not really," said Francis.

"Oh, come on," said Ed. "Fess up." This caught Rory and Cormac's attention. They keened to hear more.

"Of course there's always things to celebrate," said Francis, diplomatically. "A new job, the birth of a child, your candidate won the election." He toasted himself again.

"Or the gift of a buttload of cash from the City of St. Louis, as if they can afford it," said Cormac down the bar.

"That's what he's celebrating," added, Rory, "the settlement from that clusterfuck a year ago, the one where they rounded up all the shit disturbers, Francis among them. Then the lawyers got together and said how can we make money off'n this, how can we exploit the City and make ourselves rich?"

"Is that what you're celebrating?" asked Ed Gannon, frowning.

"You know, earlier today, I served a Bosnian, a Mexican, and a Vietnamese. Know what I call that?"

"What Francis, what do you call it?" said Ed Gannon.

"Celebrating diversity," said Francis.

"Don't change the subject," said Cormac. "We saw the newsclip about the settlement, how the City was on the hook for four-point-nine million and that money was going to a law firm who would pay out to a bunch of loafers in the lawsuit."

"And the law firm would take its share of the plunder," added Rory. "But we know you're one of them, you and all those freeloading niggers who don't give a damn that the City's going broke as long as they get their cut."

"Is that true?" asked Ed.

"Sure it's true," said Cormac. "He's one of them, probably got his check today, look at that smirk on his mug. That's taxpayer's money, man, your fucking windfall is coming out of my pocket. What do you have to say for yourself?"

In twenty-three years of coming to this bar he had never been the target of abuse, had never been seriously confronted or made to feel small—not like this. It was really bothering him. He felt cornered. What *did* he have to say for himself?

He stood up. He took the check from his wallet, unfolded it, held it up for all to see. Once they all saw the figure, handwritten in bold cursive, he said, "Nice work if you can get it."

Acknowledgments

Thanks to Charlie Stella, novelist, and to Tom Karsten, attorney, for their critical reads and suggestions of the work in progress.

Thanks to Bob Ray, Market Master, Soulard Market, for his insight and first-hand account of the civil unrest, downtown St. Louis, arising from the Stockley verdict, September, 2017. Thanks to Brian Millikan, former cop and attorney, who represented St. Louis Metropolitan Police Department officers accused of wrongdoing in the Stockley verdict uprising, and who offered his take on the events.

Thanks to Pablo Weiss, friend, for his heartfelt essay on race relations, titled "We can talk amongst us white guys—right? A critique on race relations in St. Louis from the 1990s into the second decade of the 21st century," which was used, in part, in the bar scene in Murphy's.

Thanks to my daughter, Margaret, for *Becoming Room*, her piece in the senior art exhibition while attending Webster University and which was described by Jacob Vorhof to Dagmar Petko as his entry in the senior show at Kansas City Art Institute.

Thanks to Jared Minnick, surveyor-artist for the idea of Vorhof's seminal work, "Transgressor"

Brief passages were taken from the following musical compositions:

"The Minstrel Boy" composition / lyrics Thomas Moore 1779-1852

"The Impossible Dream (The Quest)" 1965, composed by Mitch Leigh, lyrics Joe Darion.

"Down And Out In The River City" 2017 Cleophilus S. Yardley

Jacob Vorhof reads *The Big Book Of Serial Killers* by Jack Rosewood for inspiration and ideas.

NOTE: St. Louis does have a neighborhood, Dogtown, and in that Irish-American enclave there is a parish and Roman Catholic church, St. James The Greater, but those parishioners and clergy depicted in this work are wholly imagined.

Murphy's Bar is a composite of at least four Irish bars in St. Louis where the author is a regular and made to feel at home.

FOOL FOR LIFE

LUCKY BASTARD

Wm. Stage gets paid to be a nuisance, and he is good at it. A process server in St. Louis, bearing bad news to strangers—no wonder people shun him. Apart from this peculiar work, he has his own secret mission: To find his unknown biological family and have cocktails with them. His neurotic mother aids in the search, hoping to bolster her theory that the child she and her husband adopted has indeed become a sociopath. Meanwhile, Stage desperately seeks a woman with a "friendly womb." Why is he trying to reproduce like some rutting animal? It takes a series of painful and awakening life-lessons for him to find out.

Troubles abound yet Stage takes it all in stride, stumbling through life like a hod carrier at a tea party. Whether trying to weasel out of a shoplifting charge, chasing after troublesome factory workers, or being held prisoner at Lambert International Airport, he manages to land buttered-side up. But where will it take him?

"Stage weaves a journey filled with hilarious situations, tightly written with sharp one-liners."
　　　　— Jim Orso, *The St. Louis Beacon*

"... a poignant and illuminating work that walks a fine balance between side-splitting humour and philosophical seriousness."
　　　　— John Gillis, *The Inverness [Nova Scotia] Oran*

"Pour another round, Fool For Life is a twisted testament to Baby Boomer sensibility, at once poignant and ridiculously funny."
　　　　— Peter Took, *Modern Drunkard*

"[Stage's] take on the adotion-reunion story is both fresh and candid, told with verve and wit."
　　　　— Menachem Gelder, *The Jewish Standard*

Memoir / Comedic / ISBN: 978-0-96291247-4

CREATURES ON DISPLAY

SEX AND CONSEQUENCES IN THE WILD AND CRAZY 80S.

It's 1981, and epidemiologist Shaun Malloy is overworked and under-appreciated. Running syphilis and gonorrhea day in and day out, he and his colleagues in the St. Louis STD clinic are not prepared when a fatal wasting disease appears and seems to hone in with laser focus on the city's gay community.

As they strive to understand this new threat, matters are only made worse by Trey Vonderhaar, who runs a lucrative private men's club that caters to the appetites of a privileged class. Despite warnings from health officials, Vonderhaar is intent upon furthering his enterprise without regard to the dangers his luxury sex hotel presents. Perhaps too dedicated to his job, Malloy is just as intent on putting Vonderhaar out of business, and, along with a remarkable cast of characters, including best friend and bondsman Teri Kincaid, isn't above resorting to extreme measures to do it.

"Creatures On Display is not for the faint of heart; it is quick-moving, irreverent, often explicit in the situations and attitudes it describes. But it also displays the author's ability to combine history and memory, bold acts and flawed heroes, the devilish and the noble."

— Aarik Danielsen, *Columbia* [MO] *Tribune*

" ... a gritty mystery set in the seedy underside of St. Louis."

— Don Marsh, "St. Louis On The Air,"
St. Louis Public Radio 90.7 FM

"Stage's novels excel at capturing the grit and weirdness of life on the streets of St. Louis ...[Creatures] envisions a fascinating historical moment as the tab came due for the Dionysian revels of the 60s and 70s ... a fun time-travel back to St. Louis in its more feral days."

— Stef Russell, *St. Louis Magazine*

Fiction / Literature / ISBN 978-0-69234807-9

Not Waving Drowning [Stories]

How Did It Come to This?

A panhandler has a plum situation in the city, until she takes in a stray dog. A process server is caught relieving himself in an alley, a seemingly mundane event that sets off a cascade of ever-worsening misfortunes. During their getaway, two bank robbers make a wrong turn and accidentally end up in St. Louis' Hibernian Parade—a serious problem since Black Irish are not welcome. These are some of the hapless characters in *Not Waving, Drowning*, Wm. Stage's new work containing eight short stories, all set in the St. Louis area.

"The confidence of this writing is an important feature of the book. Stage has developed a prose style that is quite his own, and really can carry a story convincingly..."

— Chris King, *St. Louis Magazine*

Well-crafted Tales, Dark and Comic. In this collection of short stories, Wm. Stage captures people on the flip side of normalcy with strange and sometimes tragic turns and twists but with a grim sense of humor lurking in the shadows. Highly recommended.

— Meandog, *Amazon Reviews*

"Stage's stories are about real people who face up to life like the rest of us ... no bullshit, no pretense, just the guts of what makes life work for the fringe players in this old river town."

— Steve Means, *St. Louis Journalism Review*

Fiction / Literature / ISBN 978-096291249-8

No Big Thing

White Trash to Pick Up Trash

1992 Rural Missouri — A grain elevator operator with ties to the KKK and an idealistic lawyer fight to overturn the state highway department's decision to disallow a roadside sign. The battle won, the man enlists his grandson, an army vet, to do the clean-up and, as he finds out, litter patrol on the outskirts of St. Louis is an even more dangerous mission than the ones he faced in Iraq. *No Big Thing* is a thoughtful, comedic take on the obvious and not-so-obvious forms of discrimination and a reflection of the crazy times we live in.

"This vividly imagined historical novel is a compelling, eye-opening, and important read."

— The 2017 *Booklife* Prize for Fiction

"Stage's light style and smooth writing present an interesting story, raising issues that Americans have debated since the infancy of our nation. Great fiction does more than tell an interesting story, it provokes thought beyond the book's pages."

— *Illinois Times*

"Stage's narrative touches on the country's widening racial gap and suggests that millions of Americans might be quietly seething white supremacists—"honorary Klansmen." It's a startling and timely premise to a well-written story—one that includes Old South traditions and dirt road romance, with a healthy dose of beer joint camaraderie."

— *Blue Ink Review* [Starred Review]

"The novel initiates conversations about discrimination and displays how attitudes can change over time."

— *Missouri Life*

"Stage's story successfully raises many thought-provoking questions about hidden racism and free speech ... and includes plenty of humor and interesting local lore throughout ..."

— *Webster-Kirkwood Times*

Fiction / Historical / ISBN 978-0-692-87027-3

ST. FRANCIS OF DOGTOWN

A RANDOM ENCOUNTER TURNED DEADLY

1989 ST. LOUIS — A woman is brutally murdered in a quiet rural subdivision. The killer is just leaving as Francis X. Lenihan pulls up. Francis has come to serve papers, but there's no one home just as the "caretaker" had told him. Francis leaves his card in the door, and two days later, in St. Louis, homicide detectives are at his door. Francis helps the police all he can, but they need more. If only he could sort through his beer-soaked memory and recall the vanity plate on that muscle car he saw. Meanwhile, he has reluctantly taken the assignment placed on him by Rose, the formidable young woman who has tracked him down to his favorite bar: Find this son of a bitch and bring him to justice.

" … wonderfully fresh, smart, artfully constructed, and one hell of a read"

— Ken Bruen, author, the Jack Taylor novels

"Stage's prose style is clear and direct and it serves his characters well. He shows a particularly sure hand with the smart-alecky banter his characters dish on one another, be it … the tough talk of the criminal heavies, and the equally tough talk of the proud Irish regulars at the local bars."

— The 2019 *BookLife* Prize For Fiction

" … a story that delights and depresses, that lifts many a stein and drops many a curse, that feels Irish-American in its cold beer and hot tempers. Author Wm. Stage has given us a tale to talk about."

— Harry Levins, *St. Louis Post-Dispatch*

"Trying to do his job, one man finds himself the focus of the police and the bad guys after he stumbles into a caper gone very bad. The city of St. Louis and a memorable cast of characters sets the stage for a tale of murder, mischief, and mayhem in this page-turning and entertaining story."

— *Seattle Book Review*

Fiction / Literature / ISBN 978-0-578-52462-7

A Friend of King Neptune

Why Did I Ever Listen to You?

1991 St. Louis — Leo Kraszewski aka Dingus has come to visit his army pal, Francis Lenihan, now a busy process server. It's been 19 years but Dingus is still the same—impulsive, foolish, quick with a wisecrack, uncouth yet worldly. Dingus leads Francis to Southern Illinois, the town of Bunting, where spoils from World War II—the Speer Collection—may lie hidden in a private museum. The story has legs as Dingus is given a task by Anselm, the museum's conniving curator to retrieve a stolen historical artifact. Dingus does Anselm's bidding, at a dear price. Meanwhile, a Haitian witch doctor, a teenager—a budding Nancy Drew—and Francis himself join Dingus in the search for Speer's cache with fickle Fate orchestrating their every move.

"Stage is top of the game in both dialogue and humor ... a joy to read. Fun stuff, start to finish."

— Charlie Stella, author *Cheapskates, Shakedown*

"The action is often accompanied by moments of levity and heart. Author Wm. Stage has written a fine book with a quirky pair that will win over the reader almost instantly."

— Philip Zozzaro *Seattle Book Review* (5 star review)

"Wm. Stage's writing is witty, with clever dialogue and quirky characters that keep the reader engaged from start to finish. If you're looking for a lighthearted and humorous adventure, look no further than this gem."

— Rahul Gaur, *BestSellers World*

"The banter varies from the comical to the downright ludicrous, but through it all one aspect remains constant: the uncanny ability of this talented author to create an interesting story out of even the most mundane of episodes."

— Essien Asian, *Reader's Favorite* (5 star review)

Winner Indie Author Project 2023 Literary Award – Adult Fiction

Fiction / Literature / ISBN 979-8-218-14464-7